# MURDER
# BY
# PROXY

## A Donae' Detective Thriller

### ELLEN M. FOSS

Library of Congress cataloging – in – publishing – data
Foss, Ellen M., 2020 – Murder by Proxy
2020906010

ISBN
978 – 1 – 7348904 – 0 – 2

First published in 2020 in the United States

# ACKNOWLEDGEMENTS

I want to thank my loving husband, Art Foss,
for his years of listening to my Characters, Plots and Story Lines.

Thank you, Patricia Loughrin,
for your no-nonsense approach to editing.

Thank you to all my friends for your support and encouragement.
You know who you are.

*I dedicate this to my Grandson Ryan Scott Wagner.*
*Love you forever. Happy 21st Birthday*

# CHAPTER 1

D onae' started to push the door open, then stopped to vainly appreciate the significance of his shiny new plaque. The adornment had only been added recently and he thought it looked quite attractive on the wide rosewood door. Smugly, he smiled as he realized for the first time how much he liked the gold brilliance of the italicized letters. He was proud of the way it boasted his name almost majestically, **"Lawrence Donae', Private Investigator."** Although, in truth it should read, **"Lawrence Donae', Cold-Case Investigator,"** for over ninety percent of the cases he dealt with were from police cold files, cases that had been shelved and forgotten. Donae' again assessed the symbol; bravado was unlike him and he pondered if he should have the emblem removed. Yet, it was a gift from a previous client, so he felt obligated to display the plaque openly. Though, silly as it seemed, it made him feel uncomfortable. He had always valued his privacy and never thought it necessary to display a declaration of who or what he was. He at this time realized the plaque was in need of a good polishing and he lifted his arm to use the sleeve of his jacket, then decided against it. Instead, he made a mental note to remind Silvia, his secretary, of its need.

Once inside and before he could relay the request, he was met by an unexpected, "Ouch! Oh, dammit anyway!"

"Well, a jolly good morning to you, too, Miss Perez. Is everything okay?"

Grumpily, Silvia grumbled, "Good morning, Mr. Donae'."

"That, my sweet lady, is much more pleasant."

Silvia smiled humbly but said nothing more. She was muted by her ill disposition and continued to staple the stack of papers piled high on her desk.

Donae' threw his brief-case on the credenza near the coffee pot while he continued, "Silvia, I hope you took a minute or two out of your busy schedule last night to at least have caught a glimpse of that splendid sunset? I genuinely believe it was one of the most beautiful I've ever seen."

"Sorry . . . sir, but no, I didn't. To put it bluntly, I didn't get a chance to catch a glimpse of anything last night, unless you count the inside of a manila folder and a damn file draw. OOPS, damn, there I go again. Sorry about the foul language, Mr. Donae'." Silvia pointed angrily and pouted, "But, that damn staple gun just got me again."

"Oh, my, can I get you anything? Are you bleeding? Tell me what to do, and what should I get for it."

Laughing at his overreaction Silvia spouted, "Nothing, Sir. Just relax I think I'll live, and we have plenty of time before it turns gangrene."

Silvia searched her desk drawer, eventually coming up with a tiny band-aid and began to tear open the wrapper with her teeth. Donae' hurried around to where she sat and caught a glimpse of a newspaper on his desk. It was folded, but he noticed she had circled the headline which read, "*MURDER*." The rest he could not see. At this same time, Silvia captured his attention again when she said, "Ooh."

He immediately commanded as he snatched the bandaid from Silvia's hand, "I can do that. Let me see." Donae' ripped open the wrapper then asked tenderly, "I see blood. Does it hurt?" Silvia shook her head and he went on, "I must be working you too hard lately. You appear a bit on the tired side. And if you can excuse me for saying, you seem somewhat out of sorts. I hope I've not over-burdened you. I imagine with me being out of town and all . . . well, as they say, things do tend to fall in your lap, don't they?"

"Yes, of course they do, Mr. Donae'. That's what I'm here for and as for working me too hard, you always do. But I think I'll survive." Grinning she added, "Besides, that's why you pay me so well."

Hesitating momentarily, Silvia began to evaluate her last task. Then decided it, along with her next duty, would have to wait. Smiling warmly, she declared, "Okay, I tell you what. Give me five minutes and I'll get you a cup of tea. Then I'll fill you in on what I've been up to since you've been out of town. Boy, I tell you, this week and a half . . . well it's been one hel . . . well, never mind. I'll get the tea."

"Silvia, no, you sit, I'll get the tea."

"But, sir."

"SIT Silvia," ordered Donae'.

Once handed her cup of tea, Silvia quickly took several sips of the honey-sweetened liquid before she realized it was hotter than she usually liked. Donae' watched her reaction and started to apologize as he seated himself across the desk from her, but Silvia waved her hand and began to blow softly into the cup while she decided where to start with her report.

Donae' waited. Then from the corner of his eye he noticed the newspaper again. He had not noticed before that it looked old and was tattered at the corners. The headline that had caught his attention earlier now lay open where he could see it more easily and he picked the paper up and started to read.

**"Socialite and four-year-old daughter . . . Murdered . . ."**

At this time Silvia became satisfied with her tea and began to efficiently fill Donae' in. After the first couple of nonessential tidbits she stopped suddenly and sipped her tea once again, then lifted her head slightly to one side. Her hair fell over most of her face but she just pushed it back so he could see her face, and she smiled her sweetest smiled and whispered, "I missed you, Mr. Donae'." Then without a moment's hesitation or waiting for a reply she went directly back to stating the business at hand.

Silvia's report took close to a half-an-hour, and never once did she mention the old newspaper article. When she paused momentarily to swallow her last mouthful of tea, Donae' reached for the paper and started to inquire why it was on his desk.

But first she said, "Whew, you sure made that tea hot. You know Mr. Donae', things have been so hectic around here these past few days that this is the first cup I've had since you left town. By the way, I hear your family business went well."

He laid the paper back on the pile and answered, "It did indeed and as sorry as I am that I had to leave you with all the days' drudgeries, I have to admit that I truly enjoyed the holiday."

Silvia looked at the empty teacup and concluded, "That was good."

Setting the cup aside she answered, "I really didn't mind, Mr. Donae'. It gave me time to catch up on some old files and besides, I got to play sleuth." At that moment, in her own style of proficiency Silvia went directly back to her prior report.

Donae' had always liked that she was good at changing a subject in mid-sentence. In all the time, he had known her he had never known her to miss a beat. She always went right back to where she had ended the discussion minutes before.

"Let's see . . . client-wise, Gerimee called. That was two days before yesterday. And he had several concerns about a friend of his. He asked me if I would check on some old police records that related to her case. He seemed anxious, as if it were extremely important, so I immediately did as he requested." Grinning proudly, she volunteered, "And, of course, as I did so I also took it upon myself to create a new file. Filling it with all the usual informational data you request on any new case."

When Gerimee's name was mentioned, Donae' had sat forward in his seat and began to listen more attentively than he had in the earlier part of Silvia's dialogue. Now he shifted back against his seat and questioningly raised an eyebrow as he repeated, clearly doubtful, "Gerimee has a case? What kind of action are you talking about Silvia? I have no knowledge of any pending case with Gerimee."

Silvia opened her mouth to speak and Donae' cut her short. He continued before she could answer any of his arguments. "This time, Miss Perez, I'm afraid you might have jumped the gun and created a lot of unnecessary work for yourself. Particularly, since I have no knowledge of any matter with Gerimee. Nor do I know of anything that could possibly be connected with him that would need my expertise."

Silvia sat forward in her seat and exhaled a challenging, "Well, I'm sure . . . ."

"No, Miss Perez, certainly not. Not at this time or any time, will I ever take on a family matter. Why, Silvia, I can't even imagine Gerimee with a problem that I would take on as a case."

Silvia never so much as blinked an eye as she continued with, "That's very true. I, too, was surprised and as for your reluctance, that is also something I anticipated and informed your brother in-law of such. Along with the fact that you've been presented with several new cases, which you are in the midst of reviewing. Therefore, you may not easily be convinced to participate in his case without further persuasion."

Donae' crossed his arms and asked earnestly, "So, Miss Perez, you feel quite in control, do you?"

Smiling confidently Silvia added. "Gerimee and Sharon will be having a dinner party around seven-thirty this evening. I told him that you could be there around six-thirty for cocktails.

That way you and Gerimee will have time to discuss the case before dinner. Oh, by the way, they also invited Patricia Woodts. She will be arriving at seven-fifteen."

Donae' sat there not uttering another word. He was trying to think quickly enough to save face, but in the end, he simply smiled and said, "Sooo . . . you say, Patricia will be there around seven-ish?" Lightly, he tapped his finger to his lips and mused, *I haven't seen Patricia in over a month. I've really missed her.* His mind immediately drifted as he thought about his attraction to Patricia Woodts. She had accompanied his sister in-law, Shelia, on a visit to her hometown in London to see her parents. And on the same day that she was due to return home from her three-week excursion, he had already left for northern California on family business. Before this trip he had not realized how much he had grown accustomed to seeing her. He had always been self-governing, and at first it was hard for him to admit he needed another human. Yet, he had to face it, he missed Patricia terribly. Eventually he accepted the unmistakable truth and now no longer denied his feelings. Once he had acknowledged this fact, he began to realize that he was not at all uncomfortable with the new sentiment; as a matter of fact, he kind of liked it.

Suddenly Silvia sprang up and out of her chair, knocking her notepad to the floor. Without stopping to pick the pad up, she made a dash to answer the jangling ring of her telephone. Her quick movements disrupted Donae and his image of the lovely Miss Woodts as she shouted louder than necessary, "I'll be right back; then I'll go over the rest of my report." This at once terminated all contemplation of his new fondness for Patricia.

Donae' shoved his chair back and walked over to pick up her notebook. Before he laid it on her chair, he peeked at its contents to see if there was any mention of the newspaper article. Nothing was there.

Still interested, he swooped the newspaper off the front of his desk and hurried back to his seat so he could read the article, except this brought about as little satisfaction as Silvia's notes had. The news article said no more than a socialite had been murdered in her sleep and police had no leads. The newspaper was dated October Twelfth, Nineteen-sixty. Why would Silvia be reading a three-year-old newspaper? Which cold case could it pertain to? Certainly not Gerimee's.

Donae' set the paper aside and waited for Silvia to finish her conversation. He half-listened to what she said, but soon his mind shifted in and out of the conversation. His thoughts were still on the newspaper article but soon they moved to why Gerimee needed to speak with him. *What is this with Gerimee and a possible case?* He couldn't begin to guess what that was all about, *But, if I accept the dinner invitation, I will find out soon enough. Not to mention, how delightful it would be to see my baby sister Sharon, plus the strikingly beautiful, Patricia.*

Suddenly the prospect of Sharon and one of her so-called small get-togethers dawned on Donae' and he yelped, "Ooh, no! Silvia! Silvia, did Gerimee say that it would only be Patricia and I for dinner? He did, right? Gerimee . . . he didn't hint at a party, did he? You know how Sharon is, Silvia; she does not know the meaning of small."

Silvia walked briskly back into his office, her hands on her hips, laughing at him as she answered, "Don't worry, you're safe, Mr. Donae'. I believe Gerimee said it would only be you four. Oh, on second thought, maybe not. He did mention that another couple might be there, but he wasn't sure if they would make it. It all depended on the gentleman. I guess for the past several years he's had bad health and there are good days and bad days. So, he and his wife will only be attending if he's feeling up to par. I don't know if you know them or not. It's Gerimee's Art Gallery Director and his wife, Mr. and Mrs. Addison Hobart. Let's see, I think Gerimee said her name is . . . is . . . ah . . . wait, one second. What was it? Oh, yes, Carol. That's it, Carol Hobart."

Donae' had never met the Hobarts, but he had heard Gerimee speak of Mr. Hobart many times. Despite this, as soon as he heard the name it instantly rang a bell for something other than merely hearing it before. Nonetheless, he couldn't recall why. Finally, he concluded that it must simply be that he had heard Gerimee talk of them so often over the years. He mused, *maybe my sub-conscious picked up on the familiarity*. Again, there did seem to be something other than mere acquaintance lurking in the back of his mind. He just couldn't put his finger on it.

Suddenly he was jolted back to the present when Silvia began to speak. Donae' looked up slightly embarrassed by his rudeness. "I am sorry. What did you say, Silvia?"

"I said, since you're not listening to me anyway, I have several errands to run before lunch. Do you want me to pick anything up from the deli?"

His mind already back on other matters, Donae' absentmindedly shook his head and mumbled, "I do not think so."

Silvia grabbed her purse and headed for the door. Just before she closed it behind her, she shouted, "And, don't forget to call your grand-mother. She already called twice this morning. She seemed very eager to hear about your business deal and trip. I think she really missed you, Mr. Donae'." Just before the door slammed shut, she added, "Oh, and don't forget to look at those case-files. I laid them on your desk last . . . well shoot, I can't remember when."

Silvia had been gone a good twenty minutes, yet Donae' was still staring at the three folders. They had been lying open on his desk for the past few weeks. He grabbed the first, then put it aside and picked up the second. He tried several times to read each one. But, for some reason he had a hard time concentrating. His thoughts kept returning to Gerimee and his undetermined plight. *What could be so urgent that Gerimee would want to see me right away?* He couldn't imagine what Silvia was working on for him. "Damn," he muttered, "Why did I not simply order her to tell me?"

Sighing, he again began to read the first file. He needed to decide which case he would investigate next. For some reason, he was having a difficult time choosing between the three somber causes. He was well aware that these families had been waiting for resolution long enough, so why was he not out and about finding answers? He would have to decide soon, for each of these actions had its own merit of urgency. His mind drifted back to Gerimee and at once he made the decision that he would wait. He would make his choice after he heard what his brother in-law had to say. For, in truth, if Gerimee and Sharon needed his investigative abilities, he would help.

Donae' decided to leave the office early. He was locking the door when Silvia returned from her errands. "Don't lock it Mr. Donae', I'm back. Are you going to a late lunch?"

"No, Silvia, I am leaving, and I do not expect to be back today. I could use the extra time to go home and change clothes before dinner. It is imperative that I look my very best this evening. I am sure if I do not, Sharon will most definitely chastise me. You know as well as I that to Sharon it is important that I present myself as a regal and polished gentleman at all times." He laughed and added,

"just in case she is up to her old match making tricks again." Silvia joined his laughter, for she was aware of Sharon and her antics.

# CHAPTER 2

When Donae' arrived at Sharon and Gerimee's estate, he saw that the Hobarts were as early as he was. It was no more than ten minutes after six.

The butler, Sergio, immediately answered the door after the first ring. "Good evening, Mr. Donae'. Mr. Gerimee is in his study; he is expecting you, although he asked if I would show you to the sitting room. Mr. Gerimee will be joining you directly. At the moment he is still meeting with Mr. Hobart."

"You need not bother, Sergio, I believe by now I am able to find the sitting room on my own." Donae' grinned at Sergio. He was full of cheerfulness this evening and always enjoyed a good tease, "And, I dare say my friend, without too much difficulty."

Donae' turned on his heels and headed for the parlor and immediately poured himself a glass of white wine to sip while he waited for his host. He then noticed that Gerimee's latest work stood in the center of the room. There the painting could easily pick up light from all four corners of the chamber. Again, he thought for more times than he could count, "What an amazing artist."

Donae' strolled over to study the piece. After several minutes he decided, *I have never seen anyone who could catch a sunset in a garden setting like Gerimee. His light and colorings are magnificently luminous.* He stepped back and silently admired the new piece.

Soon his mind moved back in time and his memories filled his heart with warmth and as always, he missed his beloved mother. They had spent so many pleasant hours together. Many, he recalled, were sitting in her garden gazing into the evening sky. *Yes,* he reminisced, *together we appreciated the glory of the universe.*

Those cherished moments between Donae' and his mother were always referred to as their night-time serenity. He surmised dismally, *I believe I will miss you until the end of time, Mother, and will forever hold dear those precious moments we shared.*

Donae' returned to the scene in front of him and continued to marvel at the canvas. He studied the transcendence of the garden below the sunset. The bushes of intense reds and rich white geraniums almost looked dimensional, which only added to the exquisite blush of the iris that seemed to glow to perfection. He stepped back, then noted the depths of color in the smallest buds, these were wildflowers that were strewn throughout the garden. Nearby he noticed that the blooms on the daisy bush stood up charmingly begging to be acknowledged. All of this to accompany the beauty of the most vibrant and colorful of sunsets he had ever seen. *Yes indeed, Gerimee you are remarkably gifted.*

Within minutes of Donae's arrival, Gerimee walked through the parlor-entrance and greeted him with a warm and friendly hello "My dear friend, I am so happy that you could make it tonight. I'm also glad to see you helped yourself to some wine." Then he immediately moved to present the gentleman beside him, "By the way, let me introduce you to Mr. Addison Hobart.

He owns the gallery in New York, where I show my work." His arm moved to envelop the older gentleman. Then Gerimee continued, "Addison, this is my brother in-law, Lawrence Donae'."

"It is very nice to finally meet you, Mr. Hobart. You are a lucky man to work with such an accomplished artist and please, call me Lawrence."

Addison grabbed Donae's hand and with a warm handshake he patted him on the back while he agreed, "Indeed, he is gifted. And it is very nice to finally make your acquaintance, Lawrence. Gerimee speaks of you so often that I feel that I've known you for years. Also, if you could do me the same courtesy by calling me Addison, I would greatly appreciate it."

Addison freed Donae's hand, then moved to the window and peeked out as he proceeded, "My lovely wife, Carol will be in to join us shortly. Or maybe I should be a little more precise and say in about a half-hour or so. She and Sharon are ambling in the garden. and since they rarely get to see each other, I'm sure they have a lot of catching up to do."

Gerimee moved to the bar and poured a brandy. When he handed it to Addison he asked, "Do you want to sit for a while before dinner?"

Addison shook his head and answered, "I'm fine, Gerimee, no more mothering, please."

Donae' noticed that Addison Hobart did look a little wan, although youthfully handsome for a stout gentleman of what, Donae' guessed to be around sixty-five. He also noted in his hasty evaluation that Addison appeared to be a man who felt the confidence of his success, a man well-aware and comfortable with the knowledge that he himself was the reason he was where he is today. Still, there was something, something that was hard not to notice, a gloom. A touch of sadness that one could not ignore. It showed deep within the narrows of his full bushy brows and shadowed the darkness of his jaded chestnut eyes.

Gerimee's voice filtered through Donae's assessment. "Hey, Lawrence, did you see that the wine you poured came from our newly procured Napa Valley Vineyard? I really must tell you; Grandmother was so excited when you called and confirmed that we had finally purchased the HollyHock Vineyards, that I . . . . Well, I thought she was going to dance down the hallways," he laughed.

Gerimee turned to face Addison and explained, "Grandmother enjoys their wines, greatly. But since she rarely drinks anything stronger than tea, we were mystified why she wanted to own a winery. So, dear Sharon had begun teasing her that she was going to start checking her cup at four o'clock teas." He laughed again and turned back to Donae'. "But, from the stats Grandmother has recited I've come to the conclusion it's the profits she's mostly excited about, an excellent investment, Lawrence, excellent."

"Thank you, Gerimee. We all know how much Grandmother loves a profit, as do we all."

"I agree, and as Grandmother said, you always make the best decisions when it comes to the family's resources."

Donae' poured himself another wine, then faced both men and raised his glass in a toast, "Thank you Grandmother for your vote of confidence."

To Gerimee, he said, "I assure you I would hate to let the family down and while we're on the subject of the vineyards, let me tell you, this trip was a hell of a lot more agreeable ... weather-wise and otherwise, than the one to Wyoming when we purchased the cattle ranch. I'm quite sure both of you can imagine what an escapade that was for a city boy like me. Whom, if I may remind you, was born and raised in New York and in the lap of agreeableness. And who, by the way, always thought horses only came to one one-way, saddled and ready for ride. I also had no idea that they could smell so, so ..."

Both Gerimee and Addison burst into laughter. The stench was self-explained by the expression that instantly covered Donae's face while he recalled the pungent odor he had to endure on his adventurous trip to the ranch in Wyoming.

Excitedly, Donae's eyes lit up and a smile spread across his face as he promptly changed the subject. "Oh, Gerimee, you and Sharon must visit this one area ... it's near central California. It was the rarest picture of beauty. The sea simply pounded along the rocky Pacific coastline, and ... and ...." Donae' stuttered at the loss of words, "well ... well, all I can say is its beauty was almost intimidating."

Gerimee teased, "Lawrence, for you to not find the words to describe it I would have to say it must be so."

Good-naturedly, Donae' smiled, then went on, "I found it inadvertently while driving to Los Angeles. I must admit I did go, let's say, a round-about way, but it's near San Luis Obispo and runs miles up the coast. The area, Gerimee, is inspiringly beautiful and magically peaceful. I also think you would be interested in a quaint little village I found a short distance pass Hearst Castle; it is called Cambria. And I believe this village housed every variety of artists you could think of. I am absolutely positive you and Sharon would appreciate the area."

Gerimee nodded but was distracted before he could respond. All three men turned in anticipation of the voices and Sharon's laughter ringing throughout the halls. Casually, she and Carol entered the room. Sharon's arm was draped comfortably around the shoulders of the attractive petite woman, who, Donae' immediately guessed was Carol Hobart and a most exquisite match for Addison. Without waiting for an introduction, Donae' smiled his most charming greeting and said, "You must be the lovely Carol Hobart?" Donae' took the delicately slender hand she offered into his and bowed slightly, then kissed it lightly. Yet, when he looked up to face her pleasant beauty, he was startled. Because there, beneath her powdery blue eyes, he detected the same haunting sadness he had earlier beheld in her husband's troubled eyes.

"I am, I am indeed, and I can confidently guess you must be Sharon's charming brother, Lawrence Donae'. Sharon talks of you often." Carol quickly glanced over her shoulder in Sharon's direction and confirmed, "Yes, Sharon, I agree with you he is as charming as he is handsome."

Donae' winked at Sharon, then said, "Thank you, Mrs. Hobart, but please do not let my sister's influence taint your judgment. I do love her dearly, but I should confess she does tend to exaggerate."

"Oh, you are most definitely charming, Lawrence, and I shall call you Lawrence. That is, if you do not mind, and you will call me, Carol."

"You, my darling lady, have a deal," declared Donae'.

Immediately Donae' turned towards Sharon and braced his stance so he could receive his sister's vigorous, warm welcome. He was not in the least bit disappointed, for suddenly she threw her arms around his neck and squeezed rigorously. "Oh, Lawrence, I have truly missed you. I am soooo glad you're home. Will you come and stay with us for a few days? You will, won't you? Please . . . , I really want us to spend some time together. You seem to be away so often lately."

Everyone in the room could easily see the open and honest warmth Sharon felt towards her brother. Donae', as well, beamed with affection as he agreed, "That sounds wonderful, little sister. I would be delighted to spend some time with you. But . . . , sadly it will have to wait for a few weeks or at least until after I catch up on all my neglected affairs." As soon as the words were spoken, Donae' heard Sergio inform Patricia where everyone was. Right away, Donae's smile grew and he freely said, "Ah, and there I believe comes the most delectable commitment for which I speak of ignoring as of late."

Sharon giggled at her brother's confession. Her pleasure was evident and obvious to see as it spread across her delicate face. Her expressive, blueish-green eyes sparkled with mischief. And a hint of gratification escaped her sweet lips.

Her marvelous big brother had finally found a love and she was thrilled that she had something to do with it. For, thankfully, Donae' had met Patricia at one of her glorious parties.

Donae' witnessed Sharon's happiness and instantly made a mental note, that whatever Gerimee had summoned him for had little to do with Sharon, since she was pleasingly in her normal, cheerful frame of mind.

It was obvious to all Patricia was as happy to see Donae' as he was to see her, and in view of everyone they shyly said their hellos, then promptly fell silent as they gazed longingly into one another's eyes.

Gerimee, along with Sharon, realized the two wanted to be alone but for now that was not to be. Quickly, Gerimee introduced Patricia to everyone, then announced, "I hope everyone's hungry because Consortia has prepared a wonderful meal, which will be served in just a few minutes." He faced Sharon, then asked, "My dear, if you do not mind, Addison, Lawrence and I will have a short meeting after dessert."

Donae' saw the flustered look on Gerimee's face, when he threw Addison a quick glance. And he asked himself, *Do the Hobarts have something to do with Gerimee's enigma?*

Without hesitation, Sharon nodded and looked over to include the other ladies, who also nodded their approval, at which point she excitedly professed, "Oh, that'll be perfect, Gerimee. That way, we'll have time to catch up on all our girl talk."

Gerimee kissed Sharon lightly on her forehead as he teasingly replied, "Let's see, gentlemen. My wife's girl-talk . . . usually consists of government affairs." He slightly arched an eyebrow and added, "And I do mean affairs."

Sharon threw Gerimee the evil-eye, and he jumped back and crossed his arms in front of him to ward off any wicked malice. Laughingly, he continued, "Along with the social aspects of our First Lady which, if I may add, includes the world's most famous and exorbitant clothing industries. One can only deduce that this, in a sense, is Jackie's own *affaire d'amour*. Thereupon, I would guess the conversation could vary and may even involve such tidbits as local gossip and upcoming social events. Finally, but no less important, the conversation will then settle on a more serious topic, woman's rights, not only stateside, but abroad as well." Thoughtfully, he rubbed his chin as if he were calculating, then quipped, "Sooo . . . I would say gentlemen, taking all that into consideration, I think we will have more than ample time to complete our business discussion. Would you not agree, Sharon, my dear?"

Sharon gave Gerimee a little shove as she giggled. Both were obviously trying desperately to hold back their laughter, as well was everyone else in the room. And on that note Gerimee ended his jest with favor, "So you see, my sweet lasses, you are in for a unique and special treat, for Sharon is the most entertaining woman I have ever met. She truly knows the art of story-telling and is a mesmerizing *allegorist*."

Donae', as well as the others, could easily see throughout his banter the genuine pleasure Gerimee felt for his wife. It not only showed on his face but also filtered through his rich, articulate voice. Although, no one was surprised by this, for it was well known that Gerimee was proud of his warm and gracious, yet loquacious wife. Even so, he forever loved to tease her.

The group laughingly agreed with Gerimee's observations while they made their way to the center of the room where Gerimee's new painting still effectively stood. Trying hard to be unassuming, Patricia and Donae' hung back, hoping for a few moments alone.

Sheepishly, Patricia grinned then asked, "So how are you, Mr. Private Investigator? I'm happy to see that you were able to be here this evening. Sharon wasn't entirely sure if you could make it. But then I had a feeling you would."

With Patricia's comment new confidence emerged and Donae' murmured under his breath, "My dear, I would not miss any occasion where there is an inkling of a chance on seeing you."

Patricia coyly smiled back at him and in the same flirtatious manner unwaveringly replied, "And that is exactly what I was counting on, Mr. Donae." She laughed and gaily said, "Oh, Lawrence, I have missed you much more than I can comfortably say." Just then the dinner bell rang and quickly she added, "Well, as they say in the movies, saved by the bell."

Donae' stepped closer to her side as he took pleasure from the sweet scent of her satiny brown hair and murmured quietly in her ear, "If I were you, Miss Woodts, I would not count on that, for I am not easily distracted. Furthermore, I'm extremely tenacious, if not diligent, and will expect to continue this conversion further, later this evening. Until then, I shall stay as close by as it is permissibly proper."

Patricia's smile said all that he had hoped it would, as they walked slowly from the parlor to join the others in the dining room.

# CHAPTER 3

Almost immediately after dessert was served the men excused themselves. Still mystified, Donae' silently followed Addison and his brother in-law to Gerimee's studio. He was told to make himself comfortable at the small conference table in the center of the spacious room. Donae' had always loved the feel of this chamber. It housed an infinite number of bay windows that touched from ceiling to floor, along with the most impressive skylight. There was a large platform about eight feet away from the center of the window, where Gerimee did most of his painting. Donae' had heard Gerimee say that this was a room that forced you to face your innermost-self, and he agreed. He could easily understand why and how someone with Gerimee's talent would conceivably reap its unrestrained benefits.

Gerimee moved across the room to where Addison sat and handed him a glass of port. At the same time, he asked, "Lawrence, how about you? Can I get you something besides that god-awful tea you're always drinking?"

"No, thank you, my friend. If you don't mind, I'll just continue to enjoy the Earl Grey."

Satisfied that both men had what they wanted to drink, Gerimee moved on to what seemed to be an attempt to keep himself busy. He sat several files in the center of the table, then hurried back to the bar and poured himself a snifter of brandy. This entire time Donae' watched and appraised the transparent nervous mask that covered the structure of his brother in-law's strong face. A face that usually only portrayed his good-looking noble traits obviously displayed anxiety. By this time Donae' could not help but ask himself. *Why is Gerimee so apprehensive? This is unlike him. He is one of the most straightforward men I know and yet this evening that is in no way apparent.*

As far back as Donae' had known Gerimee, he typified nothing less than a man in control, which, of course, in Donae's mind was one reason he always thought Gerimee was so perfect for Sharon. Sharon was completely the opposite; self-discipline was not even in her vocabulary.

Donae' pushed back against the seat and felt the soft comfort of the armchair; it was well over-stuffed and pleasant. He stretched his legs out in front and waited for Gerimee to join Addison at the table. Meanwhile, Donae' contemplated Gerimee's tall, lean body as he watched it move from one side of the room to the other.

Gerimee seemed morose as he grabbed pencils and papers along the way. To Donae' it was obvious that Gerimee was stalling. *Why is he trying to avoid what is ahead?* This awareness further bewildered the investigative side of Donae'.

Finally, he saw his brother-in-law seat himself across the table from Addison, and after a minute or so Gerimee looked up and faced him then nervously professed, "I'm sorry, Lawrence. I guess I must appear abhorrently fearful, but, but . . . ." He played with the file in front of him. Then without looking up he stammered, "Bu . . . but, I didn't realize this was going to be as hard as it is. I suppose I should begin, but I really don't know where I should, or should I say *we* should, start. However, there is something we need to get straight before we do get started."

Again, he fidgeted before he began to speak. "Lawrence, I must ask that anything we discuss here tonight, stays in this room and between us three solely. And, I stress, without exception."

Donae' didn't like what his brother-in-law was asking. Suddenly he felt uncomfortable and shifted in his seat. Gerimee read Donae's expression then added, "At least for the time being, Lawrence."

Donae' immediately stood up and walked around the table, his eyes fastened on Gerimee's face. When he stood in front of him, he wrapped his arms across his chest and asked, "Let's see, if I understand this. You, Gerimee, are asking me to keep this from Sharon? Something, I'm sure you know as well as I, that is near impossible. And something I am uncomfortable doing. Furthermore, you have been acting strange since before we left the dinner table, which is beginning to truly concern me. This whole array is not like you. Are you in trouble, Gerimee? God, I hope this is not about another woman."

Donae' instantly relaxed when he saw the laughter glint in Gerimee's eyes. "No, Lawrence, there could never be another woman. And I am most definitely not in trouble. Not in the sense that you're referring to."

"Well, I will admit, Gerimee, you did give me a start; you had my heart missing a beat or two for a minute. But now that we have that prospect cleared up, you positively have my word nothing leaves the confines of this room."

At that time, Addison stood up and coughed lightly into his handkerchief. His stanch manner gave the appearance of a speaker, readying himself to address his audience. His voice sounded dire, but nonetheless intense, as he began to speak. Apparently, he too, felt uncomfortable with what was about to be said.

"Thank you, Lawrence. It is only for the safety of all our families that I have even asked for such secrecy. Furthermore, I would rather not bring Carol into this until it is completely necessary. She has had enough to contend with these past few years."

Addison began to move nervously and play with the papers on the desk in front of him. He cleared his throat then coughed nervously once more before he looked up and hurriedly moved on. "In front of each of us we have a copy of the police report from September, Twenty-ninth, Nineteen-sixty. These folders are filled with all the facts and photographs that the New York Police Department accumulated from that night, along with the notes on the follow-up investigation."

He wiped his forehead awkwardly with his hankie and Donae' noticed his other hand that held a sheet from the folder shook, and when Addison began to speak again his voice cracked several times. "Tha . . . that night Law . . . rence, was the night our daugh . . . ter, Jennifer Hobart Peterson was brutally murdered. Along with her four-year old daught . . . ." He hemmed then choked back a cry. "Our beautiful granddaughter, Patty Jean Peterson."

Donae's mind swiftly moved back to the old newspaper he had seen on his desk. Now he realized that the article was part of Gerimee's case folder.

Addison watched as Donae' sat there for a full minute without movement, not even to release the breath that he had sucked deep into his lungs just before Addison delivered his last words. It was obvious to both him and Gerimee that Donae' was surprised and shaken by the announcement. He appeared to be completely caught off-guard.

Donae' tried frantically to decipher what he thought he had just heard. Slowly, he let the air from his lungs and glanced over to where Gerimee sat.

He noticed that he was balanced on the edge of his chair and Donae' was astonished by the amount of pain in his eyes. Finally, Gerimee glanced up and his and Donae's eyes locked for several minutes. No one in the room spoke and all scrutinized the other's expression. Without a doubt, Gerimee's look was much more than Donae' had expected to see. It was one of entanglement and once again, this puzzled him. Donae's educated guess; there was more to Gerimee and this case than a mere friendship between him and his art dealer. At this time, he remembered where he had heard the Hobart name. Sharon had told him about Jennifer and Patty Jean's murder several years ago. At the time she was too broken up over it to go into many details, but he could see that she felt close enough that she mourned their deaths deeply.

Addison remained silent and gave Donae' a few minutes to get his thoughts back on track, then moved on with his summarized account in a tone that carried little or no emotion, Donae' later described to Silvia, as deadpan. It was obvious that a part of him also died that night, along with his daughter, Jennifer, and granddaughter, Patty Jean.

"Our son in-law was called out of town earlier that same day on an unexpected business trip. So, that night Jennifer and our granddaughter were alone in their upstairs bedrooms which were located on the third floor. That night there were two servants in the house, but they were on the first floor and didn't hear or see anything. The police believe some-one broke in about midnight." Addison stopped and turned away from Gerimee and Donae', and when he completed his sentence, it was in a broken whimper.

"A-n-d ... they, th-ey bru-tally ... stabbed both of them ... to dea ... death."

Gerimee and Donae' felt helpless. They watched in silence as Addi-son's shoulders heaved up and down. After a while, Addison cried out in powerless frustration as he once again pictured the brutal act. Minutes ticked by, and the only sound in the room was that of the pendulum movement on the grandfather clock as it oscillated back and forth, along with an occasional hiccup or breath being drawn in when Addison gasped for air. Eventually, weakened, Addison turned to face them and slowly added in an unstable tone, "The police .... the police said they killed Patty Jean first, then her mother. Afterward, they went around Jennifer's room and took all her jewelry, plus anything else they saw of value. The bastard took everything he could find even her wedding ring." Just then Addison again choked on his pain.

After several minutes, he pushed onward, "The police said that Jen-nifer must have forgotten to set the alarm and whoever broke in knew how to silence their victims instantly, therefore not alerting the staff."

Donae' shivered for he could almost feel this man's torment. Addi-son's unsuccessful attempt to control his anguish had grown with each added account of that night's horror. And understandably, it soon be-came impossible for him to deny its release.

Soon after Addison had begun his narrative his anguish had become visible and Donae' recognized it as the pain he had seen earlier in his eyes. Now, though, he thought he saw something more; there was a new vehe-mence of anger, which also became impossible to hide. Finally, his wrath heightened to the point of eruption and Addison screamed in a harried and uncontrolled voice. "Lawrence, I know who killed Jennifer and

Patty Jean. But the police won't listen. I truly believe with all my heart my son in-law killed my daughter and our granddaughter that horrid night. Maybe not with his own two hands. But I'm sure he paid someone to do the job. I am as sure of this, as I am of me standing here before you."

Donae', stunned by the accusation, didn't know how to reply. It was easy to fathom that this man would feel the tremendous magnitude of pain he so obviously felt. Most any tragedy of this infinite gravity would have any person looking for just about anyone to blame. But, to accuse his own son in-law, without concrete evidence?

Donae' looked over at Gerimee, and Gerimee stood and walked over to stand in front of him. At first, he said nothing but held his head stead-fast as his eyes sharply glared into Donae's. It was as if Gerimee was attempting to penetrate and overcome Donae's misgivings, to force his own heart-felt feelings into Donae's mind for validation. Shortly, Gerimee openly declared his agreement with Addison's resolution. "Lawrence, I know it's hard to believe but I, too, know this is the truth. I feel this, deeper than I ever felt anything before, I know he did it . . . I know Brian killed Jen."

By now Donae' was exasperated with Gerimee and Addison. He paced around the room in an attempt to burn off some of his frustration, finally he stopped in front of the open bar and poured a stiff brandy. After he gulped down the single swallow, he poured another.

Gerimee and Addison watched as they waited for confrontation. They could see Donae' was disturbed by their allegations. Yet, when Donae' turned to face them, they were not ready for the height of his anger. They had hoped he would at least support them; instead he reprimanded them. "All right, this debacle has got to stop right here, right now. Both of you are letting your imaginations get the best of you."

"Lawrence, we are right about this, I swear to you," interjected Gerimee.

"Then there's something you are not telling me, Gerimee. And another thing, I want to know what in damn's hell you have to do with this mess. You must be involved in this someway other than what you have told me thus far. What I want from you is the complete story, so knock off the tentative assumptions and tell me the facts. And as for you Addison, I know damn well that the police would have checked your son in-law first thing. So, dammit, both of you sit down and tell me the complete story. Because so far all you have done is beat around the bush. Dammit, I want facts."

"Listen, Lawrence," Gerimee began.

Donae' turned and yelled, "No! NO! You two listen! Starting right now I want facts only, or so help me I'm out of here! Do you hear me? Do you both understand? NOW, DAMMIT, SIT DOWN AND TALK TO ME!"

Gerimee immediately jumped in, "Lawrence, you have to hear us out; everything we're telling you is the truth and we need your help."

Addison blurted out to support Gerimee's appeal. "Yes, and you are correct in assuming that the police suspected Brian, Lawrence. Of course, they did. They checked him out first thing. But since it was confirmed that he was out of the town they dropped him as a suspect."

"Okay, Addison, Gerimee, so what do you think that tells you? Would you not agree that if they had found something, anything at all that was suspicious, they would not have dropped him as a suspect? Dammit, Addison, they would have leaned on him until he cracked and then they would have busted him."

"Yes, that's probably true," returned Gerimee. "However, you don't know Brian and most of the time, at face value anyway, Brian appears innocent. He's Mr. Perfect and this time is no different. But listen to this; Brian took a million-dollar life insurance policy out on Jen and . . . . also, on Patty Jean. And when the insurance company finally paid Brian off, about a year ago, he suddenly took a quarter of a million dollars out of the bank and that money mysteriously disappeared."

"Whoa, wait one damn minute. How would you two know what he took out of the bank? And how would you know how he spent it? Maybe he bought himself a yacht or something. Besides, why at this late date are you initiating an inquest?"

Gerimee said under his breath, "Brian . . . he's getting married again."

Addison added rapidly, "That's the first reason. You see, we want to stop him before he does this again. And, to answer your prior question, my niece, Maeve, works at the bank where Brian keeps all the insurance money. The day he came in for the quarter-million-dollar withdrawal, she thought he was acting strange. Lawrence, I want you to know Maeve is entirely ethical and wasn't prying or anything. She was merely concerned since Brian had been through so much with the murders of Jennifer and Patty Jean. Well, she was worried so she called me to let me know that he might need me. She said she hoped she wasn't over-reacting, inasmuch as she realized it was natural for someone to feel strange when first using the insurance money from a loved one's death, although, she thought Brian's peculiar behavior was more intense than usual and that is what worried her."

Gerimee, who now stood at the window turned so he could see them when he added, "This is where it gets ruinous, Lawrence. Maeve mentioned to Addison that she was sure Brian's nervousness was simply him not being familiar with a quarter of a million-dollar withdrawal. But still she would feel better if Addison could check to make sure he was okay."

"So how does that incriminate him, Gerimee?"

"Lawrence, Brian took a quarter of a million dollars out of the bank and it vanished."

"Gerimee, Addison, none of what you said thus far points to Brian's guilt," challenged Donae'. "And Maeve was probably right, Brian was just nervous about so much cash."

"Please, Lawrence, wait," begged Addison. "Lawrence, there's more. Later that day when I went over to check on Brian, he wasn't distressed at all. As a matter of fact, he was in a great frame of mind; he was even cheerful. He said he was flying to Chicago on some business. Then planning to meet a friend in a nearby city called St. Charles."

"Okay, I still don't see the connection."

"Lawrence," Gerimee asked, "Can't you please listen with an open mind? Just let Addison finish his account before you pass judgment."

Hurriedly Addison continued with his story, before Donae' could further interject. "Lawrence, this whole trip came as a surprise. In all the time I've known Brian, he had never mentioned anyone in Chicago, and as for business in Chicago, his region doesn't even service that territory."

Donae' started to speak and Addison cut him off as he rapidly continued, "Coupled with that, after I made a comment about that very fact Brian became incensed and quickly changed the subject. The rest of our visit was strained. Lawrence, Brian was not only angry, but he became extremely cold and distant. At first, I chalked it up to what my niece had told me earlier. I then decided maybe I should try to support him, and I approached the subject of the settlement. I asked him if he had any thoughts on what to do with the insurance money. He didn't answer but stared right through me as if I wasn't even in the room. Consequently, I asked him if he'd acquired anything new lately. I guess my question was a little too blunt because he immediately became more agitated.

Then I thought maybe he believed my first question was about an earlier conversation we had, had when Carol and I asked him if we could match the insurance funds and start a College Scholarship program, in Jennifer's and Patty Jean's names. We hoped that would help keep their memories alive."

Addison could see the cynicism across Donae's face, and hastened, "Lawrence, Brian doesn't need the money, Jennifer left him well cared for. He inherited all kinds of money from my daughter. Over a million and half-dollars, plus the house we gave them for a wedding gift. It alone is worth at least three million dollars. Plus, Brian earns an extraordinary living, That's the reason we were hoping he'd put the insurance money to good use.

Anyway, that day he turned livid and screamed that he didn't want to discuss it. He said he hadn't even begun to think about the money or what to do with it, then added, I haven't touched a damn single cent of that dreadful blood-money and I don't intend to any time soon. So, if you don't mind, I'd appreciate if you and Carol would drop the damn subject. Then he reminded me he had packing to do and asked me to leave."

"Excuse me, Addison, let me see if I can get this straight. I want to make sure I didn't misunderstand. Are you trying to tell me that at this point and with this so-called evidence you two came contiguously to the conclusion that Brian paid someone to kill your daughter and grandchild? Have you forgotten that they were also his wife and daughter? Are you accusing him of savagely killing them for the insurance money? A mere two million dollars?"

Gerimee moved to the table where Addison sat with the police files clutched close to his chest. Donae' noticed Gerimee's jaw was set and he appeared to be ready for a fight.

But Donae' was past the point of game-playing and he, too, stepped forward. His voice was stern when he spoke, "Gerimee, I know you pretty damn well and it is not like you to jump to conclusions. You usually give a person the benefit of the doubt. And I would think that with something as serious as this you would do the same here. Moreover, I can also tell by your reactions tonight, that you are in some way involved, other than as merely a friend. To put it candidly, I sense a stronger tie then simply a friendship with this girl's father and mother. And this, I fear, has tainted your perception."

"You are wrong Lawrence, for I am seeing this with my eyes open and clear for the first time since it happened."

"Then, Gerimee, I want the whole truth, or like I said earlier I am out of here. I know you are not being forthright with me, and if you are asking me to involve myself in a homicide case, I need to know it all."

"Okay, okay, Lawrence, but let's not do this tonight; we've been in here and ignoring the ladies long enough. So why don't we set an appointment for tomorrow morning at your office. And Addison, if you want to join us, I wouldn't mind. I think it might even be helpful for me if you were there."

Addison's look was full of distress as he nodded his head in agreement. At the same time, he added, "I'll be there. I want you to know I'll do whatever it takes to find the killer or killers of Jennifer and Patty Jean. So, please, Lawrence, Gerimee, keep me involved throughout the investigation. I'll be available anytime you need me. I mean what I say. I want to help anyway I can, not just financially, but any way."

"Addison, to be honest with you I doubt there will be an investigation," announced Donae'. Gerimee walked over and put his arm around the stooped shoulders of the old man. Anyone could see he truly respected and loved Addison Hobart.

"Addison, believe me, we'll make this happen. He's not going to get away with it. Brian's been out there enjoying life on borrowed time. If Lawrence can't help and the police continue to refuse us help, then my friend, there are always you and I," promised Gerimee.

Donae' interjected with a shout, "Dammit, Gerimee! We cannot have you walking around making idle threats. Dammit, what are you thinking anyway?"

"Well, my friend, that's where you are wrong. Because, for one thing, I can and will do whatever it takes to take care of my own. And secondly my threat is in no way idle. I am fully aware of what I say."

Gerimee patted Addison on the back to reassure him and began to speak further with deeper conviction. "Lawrence, Addison and I will repay Brian in kind . . . if that's the only way Jen's and Patty Jean's deaths can receive reparation. If you won't help us do it in the legal sense, then we will choose our own path and help ourselves."

Again, Gerimee turned his attention back to Addison as he authoritatively terminated the conference. "So, let's not go into this any further tonight. I say we agree to meet tomorrow, about ten in the morning." He turned back to face Donae' and concluded, "And at that time, Lawrence, I promise you will understand where Addison and I are coming from and how we have arrived at these conclusions."

When Gerimee had turned to face his brother in-law. Donae' could see his jaws were still set, except the anger was now replaced with determination, and his eyes registered sympathy and concern for Addison.

Gerimee scratched his head, then rubbed his hand through the mass of dark waves as he evaluated his concern for Addison's condition. Then decidedly he pronounced, "Therefore, I say we go back to the parlor and give Addison some time to rest. Besides, we need to join our lovely partners. We'll resume this deliberation tomorrow."

Without agreement Gerimee turned and led Addison towards the door, leaving Donae' standing alone with one more question on the tip of his tongue.

When the three walked into the sitting room, Patricia was about to carry Cleo out the French doors to the patio. Carol and Sharon where both lounging on the davenport laughing. Patricia turned and gave them a quick smile as she waved and closed the door behind her. Carol and Sharon turned their heads around to greet the men as Gerimee asked, "Can I get anyone an after-dinner drink?". Carol had abruptly stopped her laughter and immediately stood up. Concern covered her face, and she swiftly moved over to where Addison was and wrapped her arm around his shoulder. Her voice was full of anxiety when she nervously asked, "Sweetheart, are you okay? Do you need your medicine? Maybe you should sit down?"

"No, Carol, I don't need anything except you, my dear, and, of course, a good night's sleep wouldn't hurt either."

Gerimee immediately moved to lighten the mood. "Ladies, please forgive us. I guess our business ran a little longer than we anticipated. And unintentionally we kept you sweet ladies unfairly waiting."

Even if Addison had tried to dismiss his weariness, Carol was well aware of the strain on her husband's face and chose to ignore Gerimee's offer. She sternly took charge of the situation, "My dear, of course you are forgiven, but your weariness is apparent so that is why we must be leaving. Sharon, you and Gerimee will surely forgive us if we depart a little earlier than normal. I worry so about Addison's health and he's been working overly hard lately. Heaven knows, he wouldn't admit it, but I've noticed he's not been himself for the past few months. Consequently, I often have to take charge and insist he gets some rest."

Sharon's face was full of question and glancing over to where Gerimee was standing she gave him a searching look. When he said nothing, her eyes quickly moved to Donae's as she agreed with Carol. "Absolutely, of course we understand. And it's certainly getting later as we speak, so let me get Sergio to bring you your overcoats. We mustn't let our dear Addison wear himself into a frazzle."

All the while Sharon spoke, Donae' could hear the puzzlement in her tone. He watched while her eyes darted from his face then back at Gerimee's, and once again back to his. She was not buying the, I am tired, allegory. Her next move proved Donae's suspicion, for no sooner was the door closed behind the Hobarts then Sharon commenced to make a full turn of her slender frame to face Gerimee and Donae' head on. "Okay, boys, so lets' have it. What's going on?

What, what may I ask, has put our dear, sweet Addison, in such a dismal state of mind? Come on, Lawrence, what's going on?"

Both men immediately looked at one another and Gerimee guiltily chided,

"My darling wife, you are unquestioningly reading way too many of those god-awful detective books you seem to favor lately. I mean, it's difficult enough that your brother's a private investigator and we contend with his questionable behavior and lifestyle. Now I have a wife who's beginning to sound like a policewoman in an interrogation room. And further, if I may add, is attempting to cross-examine her own family members."

Good-naturedly, Sharon smiled as she admitted, "Yes, you're absolutely right. I'm sorry, I know what I must sound like, but I know something is not right here. And you, Lawrence, you are much too quiet for my comfort. I do hope you two haven't had a squabble." Eyeing them both she suspiciously asked, "You didn't, did you?"

Donae' immediately leaped to the aid of his brother-in-law. "Sharon, I am sorry, but I am inclined to agree with Gerimee. We are definitely going to hide your detective novels. You are showing signs of skepticism much too easily these days. And, of course, Gerimee and I have not had a quarrel. As a matter of fact, we are meeting for breakfast tomorrow morning. In truth, I think Gerimee is simply a little concerned about his friend. He did seem particularly stressed throughout our meeting." This truth relaxed Donae' and helped combat his sister's accusations.

Sharon searched Gerimee's, eyes, then Donae's, for a full ten seconds or more while she tried to decide for sure if all was out in the open. Finally, she determined that she was satisfied with her brother's explanation. But still doubting everything was out in the open, she suspiciously came back with, "Okay. Okay, you two win . . . for now, but you leave my true detective stories alone. Do you hear me? No one touches those books, not a one."

Suddenly a small wicked grin crossed her lips and she added, "After-all, you can never tell when a big brother might need help from his little sister to solve some vile and mysterious crime." As quick as her expression had changed the moment before a new one replaced it and her glim-

mer transformed into mischievous broad smile; and in her normal energetic voice she spouted, "Well, dear brother, let's go find that new sweetheart of yours and go for a swim. Earlier I asked Sergio to bring a pair of
suits out for you and Patricia. So, last one in buys dinner at Fletcher's,
Friday."

Donae' was not feeling at all comfortable with the fact that he was
hiding information from Sharon, especially since it might in some way
involve her. For this reason, he had to make an extra effort to keep his
voice light-hearted when he eagerly responded to the welcome change in
subject. "All right, now you're talking, and you, little sister, have a deal.
But first you must give Patricia and I at least a five-minute head start. For
as you are well aware, she is still in the garden walking that bedraggled little Yorkie of yours. So, I will need at least a minute or two to lay down
the ground rules for her."

Sharon put her hands on her hips as she cried, "Lawrence! You stop
picking on Cleo. She's not scruffy, and for your information she spent
the whole day at the Puppy Parlor. She only returned minutes before you
arrived and, of course Gerimee and I agree to your ground rules. Now,
let's synchronize our watches. Okay, on your mark, get ready, set, one,
two, three and g . . . ."

# CHAPTER 4

Donae' arrived earlier than was normal on the Tuesday morning following his dinner meeting with Addison and Gerimee. Now that he realized whom the newspaper article pertained to, he wanted to reread the piece and see the file. He searched Silvia's desk drawers for the old publication since it was nowhere to be seen on his or her desk. Eventually he found the folder, but it was empty, which indicated she took it home to work on. Displeased, he would have to wait for her to come in.

At eight o'clock, Silvia waltzed into the room and without so much a good morning asked, "Mr. Donae,' did you get to those files on your desk?"

"As we speak, Miss Perez, as we speak." He grinned then quipped, "and if you can get me the file on Jennifer Peterson along with a cup of coffee I would forever be in your debt."

Silvia laughed, "Okay, but you're already in my debt. Coffee, huh, must have been a long night."

He nodded his agreement, yet he noticed she didn't move. She stood there and waited until he grabbed the first file and began to read. Then she headed towards the coffee pot.

**Kevin Phillips.** Age, nineteen. Missing, Case unsolved. Donae' knew this case as he did all three. He was aware that the Phillips have searched fruitlessly for the past five years for their only son, Kevin. It was heart rendering. Donae' began to read the file again. Kevin disappeared at age nineteen. He had left the university he attended and hitched a ride homeward. It appeared he made it only ninety percent of the way. Bewilderingly, the last report sighted him nine days after he had left school and only blocks away from home. The police penned it as a runaway. This didn't make sense to Donae' that a person who traveled more than two thousand miles by way of thumb, would suddenly decide to lose himself the last few blocks from his final destination, although the file did indicate that sometime later the police did admit to suspecting foul play. Donae' was not sure he agreed with either indeterminate assumption, since there had been several sightings of Kevin during the five-year period. Donae' scribbled a big question mark and the words, **Mental Disorder? Amnesia???** Then he put the file aside.

Then there was the open file on Conrad Therman. This case was big news when it first hit the media. Therman disappeared close to ten years ago and from all indications he took seven million dollars from the bank vault of the large investment firm he worked for and departed for places unknown.

His family still, to this day, insists that he had been murdered and framed for the heist. The police had never been able to find one clue to support either theory. Donae' muttered, "It seems our friend dissipated into thin air."

The third file brought the slightest suggestion of a smile to his sea-blue eyes and he whispered, "And then we have you sweet Mildred." From all indications, Mildred Pritchess was a charming woman of sixty-five and had more money than she knew what to do with. This was entirely due to her husband's tinkering, who, it seemed, invented a gadget that everyone had to have. Shortly after his success he died, but soon it was discovered that months before he had passed away, he had invented another such gadget. This one was even bigger and better than the first contraption. What's more, he wittingly put the patent rights in Mildred's maiden name, therefore saving her from the crafty tentacles of the Federal Government and its inheritance taxes. Old Frederick Pritchess was not just an amateur tinkering simpleton. He was smart enough to outwit the federal government.

However, with this conveyance, plus the money Mildred inherited, she had become an extremely wealthy widow. From the police investigation, along with a letter Mildred supposedly had written, she had decided that she wanted more out of life than simply money and family and signed everything she owned over to her daughter, Eloise. Then Mildred, with a half a million dollars, disappeared. Not a soul had seen or heard from her in over eleven years.

Her sister, Beatrice, who had initiated the search, had feared from the beginning that Mildred's life was in danger. The daughter, Eloise, said that her mother was simply overwhelmed with her wealth and needed time away from all her greedy relatives, which, of course, she considered Beatrice. After months with no contact from the missing Mildred, Eloise had come to the conclusion, that her mother must have been murdered for the half a million she had with her.

Eloise blamed all of her mother's misfortune on the fact that her mother had little knowledge of real life, which, Eloise decided, ultimately led to her demise. But to Beatrice, none of this made sense. Mildred was devoted to her family and not at all an adventurer. She would not have deliberately wandered far from home. Donae' pondered, then determined, "Thus far Beatrice, I would have to say, I tend to agree with you."

"Is that so Lawrence?" Gerimee asked. He was thirty minutes earlier than their ten o'clock appointment, yet he confidently strolled into Donae's office. It was obvious he was in a much better disposition than he had been the evening before.

"Good morning, Lawrence, I'm sorry I'm so early, but I hoped we could get started before Addison arrives. I feel all this may be too much for him to cope with. In fact, it may be wiser for us not to include him in the investigation unless, of course, it is completely necessary and unavoidable."

"Gerimee, I don't think you understand. I have not decided to take your case. As a matter of fact, I am quite sure I am not interested. I am in no way enticed to collaborate with you and Addison in your scheme to bamboozle an innocent man."

"Lawrence, wait, you have to hear us out . . . . Please listen, your decision at this point is merely due to lack of specifics. And by not hearing us out before you make your decision, you're being unfair. I trust once you get past all the camouflage and hear the facts, Lawrence, you will change your mind. I know you Lawrence, well enough to know you will want to be involved in this."

"Fine, Gerimee, I will do my best to do as you ask and listen with an open mind. Although, at this point I promise you nothing."

Gerimee said nothing as he weighed what Donae' had said.

Donae' studied his brother-in-law, then pushed himself out of his chair and directed, "Gerimee, sit down. I'll ask Silvia to bring us something to drink. Tea?"

"No, thank you, coffee will be fine."

"Would you like anything with it?"

"No, nothing, Lawrence. I just want to get started."

Donae' cracked the door and asked, "Silvia, can you please bring me a pot of tea and a cup of coffee for Gerimee? Also, I am expecting Mr. Hobart. When he gets here, would you let me know? Oh! But, do not send him in until I am ready for him."

Donae' busied himself while he waited for Silvia. He pulled the Peterson file from the drawer in which he had seen Silvia file earlier. Then he pulled the blinds to dim the brightness in the room. Next, he emptied his earlier pot of tea into his cup and laid a thick pad of paper on his desk. Once he felt he was ready he pushed himself back against the cushion and said, "Now, Gerimee, I hope you are comfortable and ready to get down to some facts. Let me have all that you know about the case. And, Gerimee please, no more straddling the fence. To start with I would truly appreciate if you could begin with how you are so involved in this case in the first place."

Donae' watched Gerimee's demeanor change. He was seated across the desk in an oversized leather chair. Finally, he looked up and confronted Donae's question, his face was a mélange of emotions when he said, "God, Lawrence, it's been about eight or nine years since Brian became involved, even longer than that for me. I guess it's been close to eleven years now since Jen and I, as they say, were an item, but before we go there let me start from the beginning."

"Thank you, Gerimee, that would be quite helpful. No more bits and pieces, please."

Gerimee eyed the traces of sunlight that beat through an opening between the blinds. The room had fallen silent and Gerimee shifted uncomfortably; he felt awkward in the silence. After a minute or so he uttered, "Addison Hobart." Then fell silent again.

He coughed and sat up straighter before he stated rapidly, "Addison's was the first gallery that ever-showed serious interest in my artwork. Soon after we met, he asked me to show my work at an exhibition; then he displayed the work at his studio for a full month. The exhibit was a success, and instead of just showing my work at his studio, we decided to sign a long-term contract. By then we were friends." Gerimee positioned his body before he added, "A few months later, at the gallery's black-tie Christmas exhibit, Addison introduced me to his daughter, Jennifer. We hit it off from the minute we said, "Merry Christmas."

From the very first we were extremely attracted to one another other and spent the whole evening dodging other guests so we could spend time alone. At the time, Jen was in graduate school and was only in town for a few days, so we had what you could call a whirlwind romance. We did our best to fit everything we could into those first three days. And by the time Jen left to return to school we were already deeply involved."

He fell silent and shook his head gradually, then moved on, "I can still remember how awful we felt when we had to say goodbye. One minute we were higher than a kite because we knew we were in love. The next, we were lower than the Grand Canyon because Jen would soon be leaving for Berkley and wasn't due back till June. We were adult enough to realize that that was only six months away, but at the time it sounded like a lifetime. Anyway, after she left, we called each other almost every day and wrote just about every other. When Easter break came, I flew out to California for a two-week visit. By the end of that visit our relationship changed, and we began to talk about marriage. We decided that as soon as she came home in June, we'd set a date."

"You two were married, Gerimee?"

"No, Lawrence, her parents had other plans and getting married right away was not in their game plan. See, Addison and Carol thought we were rushing the relationship. They asked us to wait for at least a year before we set the date. They wanted Jen to establish herself in her career before marriage. They reasoned that since our relationship was built solely on phone calls and letters and that we needed time to get to know each other, one on one.

Well ... Jen loved her parents and respected them greatly, and by then so did I. So, we agreed to wait. We decided that as long as we were together, we could make the year."

Gerimee stood and walked to the window where he fixed the blind that had twisted open. When he turned and faced Donae' his voice teetered with emotion as he mumbled, "I suppose it was a good idea at the time, but Lawrence, if we didn't wait, I don't think any of this would have happened. I'm damn sure I wouldn't be here telling you this story. Sadly, I believe Addison often reflects to that period and regrets asking us to wait."

"Gerimee, you know what they say about hindsight, I don't believe there's a person alive who does not have something they wished they could change."

"Yes, I know, Lawrence, but, still ..." There was silence throughout the room for the next several minutes.

Donae' prompted, "Gerimee, if you can continue; we may finish this before Addison arrives."

Gerimee nodded but stayed silent. He moved back to his seat and stretched his long legs outward as he stammered, "Well ... well ... months lat ..., after Jen and I had been together for about a year and a half ...." Gerimee coughed and twitched. It was easy to see that the next truth was making him feel uncomfortable, so Donae' moved forward in his seat so he could listen more attentively.

"Well, we started to talk about marriage again; however, it didn't seem to have the same urgency as it did once before. This was about the same time Brian came into the picture. We first met him at the gallery. Brian was there to assist our CPA, who at the time was getting ready for a major audit with the state. See . . . , well, Brian works for a large firm that handled all the gallery's records. That day when he met Jen and I, he fell head over heels for Jen. From that moment on he pursued her even though we were engaged. Lawrence, Brian became obsessed. He was so damn persistent; it was as if Jen was his life preserver and he couldn't let go."

Gerimee grew agitated again and started to move around the room. "God, Lawrence, he would drop by at all hours of the day and every time he came by, he brought her a gift. Plus, he sent her flowers continuously. She was bombarded with flowers, at home and at the gallery where she worked part-time. Matter of fact, once he even sent flowers to the restaurant while we were having dinner. I couldn't believe his gall. His actions infuriated me, but Jen thought all his attention was simply a crush and would eventually burn out. But I could see she was impressed with him and all his antics. Of course, at first, she denied her feelings. Jen said she thought he was arrogant and that she planned to tell him so. Yet, when she told me this, it was easy to see her face held a hidden smile of plea-sure. Anyway, it wasn't too long after that night at the restaurant that Brian's assertiveness paid off. Plainly, he won Jen over and there wasn't a damn thing I could do about it."

"So, you split up?" asked Donae'.

"Yes, Lawrence, we split. But it wasn't like I thought it would be. I mean the breakup hurt but not as bad as I thought it would."

He rubbed his forehead then said, "Don't get me wrong, I mean I still loved Jen, except our relationship had changed over time. I imagine if it hadn't been Brian, it would've been someone else. Despite this, I still wasn't ready for it when it actually happened. The thought of her no longer being a part of my life was inconceivable."

The phone jingled and Silvia came through on the intercom. "Mr. Donae', Mr. Hobart is here. Should I send him in?"

Donae' thought, then said, "No, Silvia offer Addison something to drink and let him know that I will be with him in a few minutes."

Gerimee was still concerned for Addison's well-being and asked, "Lawrence, do you think maybe we should continue this later? I don't want to upset Addison."

"No, Gerimee, I want to hear it all now . . . If you don't mind, I would like you to continue."

"Okay, Lawrence, I will try to quicken the pace so as not to upset . . . Never mind, let's move on . . . ok. Let's see, well, not too long after the episode in the restaurant, Jen came and told me that she had fallen in love with Brian. She said they wanted to get married right away."

Gerimee shook his head as he confided, "Like I said, I guess I really did see it coming, but I don't know, Lawrence, when I actually heard the words . . . . Well, that was just a whole lot harder than I expected. I guess I was ready to deal with it in my mind; however, face to face was a different story. Of course, I accepted my fate, but I told Jen I still wanted her in my life. You see, Jen was more than just my lover, she was also my best friend. And I told her, Lawrence, if we could stay friends, I could live with her loving someone else. That is as long as she was happy, and she did seem happy."

"So, you stayed friends?"

Gerimee nodded yes, then went on. "Yes, but Brian wasn't happy about our friendship and he openly showed his disapproval. Yet, Jen stood her ground and we stayed staunch friends throughout her marriage.

Of course, the Hobarts were not happy with the change and they tried to talk Jen out of the relationship. This angered Brian and consequently he talked Jen into an elopement a few weeks after we broke up."

Gerimee suddenly became embarrassed and sat down on the couch across the room. "I guess this is the part that I really didn't want Addison to hear. You see, Lawrence it wasn't long after they returned from their honeymoon that Jen announced that she was pregnant. To tell you the truth, I didn't know if the baby was mine or not. I mean, we did take precautions, but it did seem to be too close to know for sure. Consequently, I fostered my doubts throughout Jen's pregnancy. I could have just come right out and asked her, but I didn't feel I should . . . I just couldn't force myself to put the question into words. So, I kept quiet and waited."

Suddenly Gerimee smiled. "That was about the same time I met Sharon at an auction . . . fund-raiser. Lawrence, I never met anyone in my life like Sharon. From the beginning we became good friends, and then we fell in love afterward.

I mean, I thought Jen was great, but I soon realized Sharon was the love of my life. Still and all, I needed to find out if the baby Jen was carrying was mine."

Refocusing his gaze on Donae' Gerimee said, "Lawrence, I want you to know that I was completely honest with Sharon from the start. I didn't want any secrets between us. And, of course, Sharon was Sharon. She didn't get angry, like I expected. She never felt threatened by Jen or the baby in any way. Sharon was just great, completely sympathetic; she understood how I felt. She is a most unusual woman, Lawrence. Instead of being jealous, she wanted to help.

After a short time, I introduced her to Jen and Brian and she and Jen became friends. But Sharon never cared for Brian. I never liked Brian, either, only I always figured it was because he stole Jen from me. Except, Sharon put into words what I always felt. She said, 'Gerimee, something's not quite right with that man. He doesn't seem to be real.' I remember I said 'WHAT, Mr. perfect!'

"That's when she hit the nail on the head and said. 'Sweety, I see that he does everything right. That's exactly what I mean, he does and says, all that is expected, but there's something missing. It's as if it's all for show, a performance.'

I can still see Sharon's face as her mind worked to find the right answer. Finally, she shot, 'Gerimee, I believe Brian is void of true feelings. That's why he doesn't come across as sincere. I think he is only play-acting. That's why he does it to perfection. I'm sure I read there are people like that.' Lawrence, that's when I realized Sharon had picked up on something no one else had. Brian wasn't what he seemed."

Donae' cleared his throat and started to speak when Gerimee burst out, "Lawrence, I know you would have to agree that your sister is quite perceptive. She usually arrives easily to the correct conclusions and I think you also have to admit that she does have the training to perceive such a behavior."

"Yes, that I will have to attest to, Sharon does have the educational background, if not actual training in the field to render such a personality. Yet, most cannot deduce this on a first-time meeting."

"Lawrence, I'm sure if Sharon could have been around Brian to scrutinize his behavior more closely, she would have still come to the same conclusion. But at the time, Brian was traveling on business quite a bit. So, we didn't get to see him often. It was rare when we saw him and Jen together and mostly at large functions. But again, Sharon's observation was always the same; she still thought him apathetic and self-serving."

"Maybe Sharon does have that intuition, Gerimee, but as far as I can see, this is all still speculation, nothing more."

"Okay, Lawrence, you win. I'll drop Sharon's conjectures, even though I do believe they are correct."

"Gerimee, if you don't mind, can we get back to where you left off . . . The baby?"

"Yes, of course. It was not quite nine months after Sharon and Brian married that the baby was born. Patty was beautiful. She was twenty inches and seven pounds of wrinkly pink flesh, although, from the beginning it was obvious that she was not mine. And by the time she was two or three months old you could see Brian in every feature she had. Still, she was special to me. I truly adored her Lawrence. Maybe because of all the doubt I harbored all those months, you know, with not knowing for sure if she was my daughter or not. Perhaps in my heart, I still thought of her that way."

"Anyway, soon after she was born Brian changed positions within his company. He took over supervising another region and he didn't travel as often or as long. Therefore, we didn't get to see Jen or the baby as often as before. Regardless, when we did spend time with them, we always got that same feeling. Something just wasn't right with him, and as hard as I tried, I couldn't make myself trust the guy. Neither could Sharon, and after he and Jen were married a time it was plain to see Brian had more of an incentive than love. Lawrence, I'm sure the man was an opportunist from the get-go, and he married Jen solely for her money. But now I know it was more than that; he also married her for who she was. See, Lawrence, Brian has an appetite for station, you know . . . a social standing. He was a status seeker and with Jen he hit the jackpot. It only took a short time before some of us began to notice this, yet Jen refused to see it, although I'm sure she started to suspect it eventually."

"Why do you say that Gerimee; did she tell you so?"

"No, not in so many words. But it was obvious that once they were married Brian became more pretentious with time. He loved to flaunt his new wealth and station. He was extremely pompous around Jen's friends. And, I say Jen's friends because in truth, Brian had none of his own. He only socialized with people he felt benefited him in some way. Not everyone saw this of course, but those of us who did made an effort to avoid him. Eventually this annoyed Brian, and he became obnoxious to the mass that shunned him. This behavior embarrassed Jen, though she continued to make excuses for him and his conduct."

"Gerimee, it is not uncommon that a woman defends her husband. That does not make him an unfit husband or a murderer. From what you said, most all thought he was perfect."

"That's true, that is exactly what Brian strove for, and that's exactly what the world saw. But it is only a show, what you see on the surface is not the real Brian. Lawrence, I swear there were times when Jen was afraid of Brian. Even though neither Sharon nor I ever saw Brian physically hurt her, I sometimes suspected he mentally abused her."

Donae's brow popped to a questionable scowl and Gerimee revised his last remark, "Okay, I admit, it could have been emotional strain. Still, his behavior wasn't typical. He was obsessed with wealth, and like Addison said last night, Brian makes good money and he always had. He should have been somewhat comfortable with prosperity. Yet, he seemed captivated by wealth and talked of it habitually. It didn't matter if we were alone or in a group of mere acquaintances; with Brian's wealth was always the topic of choice. Like I said earlier, he was fascinated with recognition far more than was normal." Gerimee sniggered as he added, "This, too, was an obsession, almost to the point of disdain. As a matter of fact, I know of several functions he plainly refused to participate in unless it was publicly noted that he was to attend. If a charity event or fund-raiser didn't mention that he and Jen were there, he would get extremely angry. Jen once mentioned how mortified she was, because Brian called the newspapers to point out the oversight.

Most thought it was humorous the way Brian chased after the news media. Fortunately, the news hounds didn't like him anymore than the rest of us, so they avoided him whenever possible. I guess eventually everyone, except Jen, recognized he was a social climber, even the media."

"Gerimee, are you sure you see Brian . . . ."

Gerimee raised his hand and interrupted Donae'. "I know, Lawrence, it sounds as if I am merely discharging my bad feelings or as Grandmother would say, defaming the man. But in spite of my feelings about Brian, Lawrence, if you could just disregard my emotional entanglements momentarily and simply look at the facts. I believe you too will identify and agree that some men are greedy enough that when opportunity for a large amount of inheritance presents itself, not to mention status, they can easily give birth to a dangerous, if not climactic plot. And with all Addison and I have learned about Brian, this does seem to be the case."

Donae' said nothing so Gerimee moved on. "Lawrence, you at least have to agree if we are right about Brian being incapable of having true feelings, plus his two most desired objectives fame and fortune, can create a precarious situation, if not a time-bomb."

Donae' pondered a minute before he settled on a determination. "I do accede to your point, Gerimee. Except, all you have is nothing more than pure conjecture and circumstantial evidence, which I have misgivings about. Secondly, I cannot help but doubt your motives. You see, Gerimee, taking in your emotional state from the time you and Brian met, which carried through the period of Jennifer's pregnancy and for some time after Patty Jean's birth, I do not feel that I should trust your opinion or suspicions of their relationship. After all, you yourself said that you never saw Brian mistreat either of them. You also said that he worked very hard to do everything perfect, and killing your wife and child certainly sounds contradictory to that type of behavior. Do you not agree?"

"Yes, I see your point, but there is more and as soon as Addison and I fill you in you'll see there was plenty of erratic behavior and it became more evident as time went on."

"All right, then let's get Addison in here, and if you two can show me there is a cause for doubt of his innocence then I will consider the case."

Donae' pushed the button on his telephone marked "front" and immediately began to speak, "Silvia, can you please have Mr. Hobart come in my office? And if you do not mind, will you please run to the deli and get us some sandwiches and sodas for lunch. Maybe, roast beef on pumpernickel with plenty of mustard and, Silvia, please do not forget the pickles."

"Of course not, Mr. Donae', but are you sure everyone wants roast beef and on that type of bread?"

"I am sure it will be fine with Gerimee. However, maybe you better check with Mr. Hobart; before you bring him in."

A minute later Addison entered the room. His smile was anxious when he said, "Good morning gentlemen. I see that you started the meeting without me. I do hope I didn't get the time wrong."

"Please let me apologize, Addison, I hope you did not mind waiting. Gerimee and I needed to clear up several personal issues before we got started."

"No, no. Lawrence, of course not. Don't worry about it; I understand completely. Matter of fact, before we get started, I'd like to thank you and Gerimee. It is kind of you to permit me to join you; it means a lot to me that we can all work together on this."

Gerimee eagerly answered, "Finding Jen and Patty Jean's killer means a lot to me too Addison and together we'll do just that."

Donae' noticed that Addison Hobart appeared to be more rested than he had last night but still Gerimee seemed concerned about him.

Gerimee could see without a doubt that the incertitude of this ordeal was beginning to take its toll on Addison, and he wondered if he had made the right choice by including him in this meeting.

Donae', too, saw the signs of weariness on Addison's face. Even if he did appear rested, the strain was obvious. He thought, *I will never get used to the facial facade that the murdered victim's family often wears. The aura, he thought, held such a sad solicitude. This same look often appears to resemble that of an abused child. They both carry the unwarranted burden of guilt in their eyes.*

At this moment Donae' decided he would help Addison and Gerimee; he would take their case. Hopefully with his help, the self-blame in Addison's eyes would lessen much sooner.

Donae' cast a re-assuring smile toward Gerimee, then turned back to face Addison and his stressed-filled eyes. Silently, he promised to do whatever he could to help this gentleman conquer his immense pain and grief. Out loud he announced, "Okay, gentlemen, let's get started. Addison, Gerimee, give me everything you have and please do not omit anything. No matter how trivial you may think it is, I need it all if I am to find the key to this mystery."

Gerimee glanced over to where Donae' now stood between his desk and chair, and for the first time since last night he felt optimistic. He could tell by the change in Donae's voice that he intended to take the case, and this pleased him immensely. Gerimee leaned over and gave Addison a pat on the knee. This reassured him that everything was going to be okay. At the same time both men eagerly grabbed their attaché cases, and each one pulled out a file. With new energy, they were ready to recap their memories of Jennifer and Patty Jean, along with their views of Brian and his unorthodox behavior.

Gerimee was the first to speak when he energetically asked, "Lawrence, should I start where I left off?"

Donae' nodded and Gerimee half smiled in Addison's direction, then began his story. "After Brian's territory change, he started to stay home more. This is when his brutish side presented itself. This was a side none of us had seen before. He became controlling. He wanted to know everywhere Jen was going and with whom she was spending her time. He would give her the third degree every time she walked out the door; then again when she returned. Once, towards the end, he even forced her to let him check her to see if she had had sex while she was out. Jen said she was mortified. She told Sharon that this was one of the most degrading moments of her life.

That was the first time Jen admitted that she had noticed a change in Brian's behavior. She acknowledged it started right after they got married, though it was so infrequent that she felt she might be hypersensitive or imagining it."

"Is that possible, Gerimee? You knew Jennifer, was she sound?" Donae' saw the immediate reaction on Addison's face and said, "Addison, I must ask if I am to learn all I need to know." Addison's face still registered pain, but he nodded his head in agreement. "Gerimee, please answer my question."

"Absolutely, Lawrence, Jen was absolutely on solid ground. That's one reason she continued to ignore his outbursts; she thought everyone was as sane as she was, so she rationalized his behavior. However, as time went on and Brian became entirely distrustful of her, as well as of her friends, it became much harder for her to ignore. Even though Brian was smart and very good at hiding his peculiar behaviors, Jen became more concerned and started to question if Brian had something seriously wrong. He kept her off-balance by doing flip-flops, back and forth, so it made it difficult for her to point out his faults to anyone. When he was around his co-workers, family or neighbors, he reverted to his old, perfect self.

However, as soon as they were alone something changed in him, and he would become erratic again. In Jen's words, 'Brian was like a robot, that could turn him-self on and off whenever he felt it was necessary.' "She said his demeanor was deceptive, and more often than not she would misread his mood swings and for this reason couldn't counter them."

"Sharon and I urged her to leave but she wouldn't hear of it. She said, she loved him, and divorce was out of the question.

I guess Jen tried several times to discuss the mood differences with Brian, but he always became angry and refused to admit there was a problem. He said, if anything, she had the problem. Several times he accused her of having low morals and said she was not an obedient wife. Later, when things were at its worst, Jen simply avoided him as much as possible. Yet, she still refused to consider divorce."

Gerimee paused for a period, then stood to walk over to the window and opened its blinds, he needed a distraction and a minute to catch his breath. The sun shined through brightly, but not as bright as it had earlier. Abruptly, he turned and acknowledged, "Lawrence, I understand that this is only hearsay or, more to the point, her side of the story. And it's hard to believe that if Brian worked so hard to be so perfect, how Jen penetrated that shield. The only thing I can guess is that with his immense ego Brian became sloppy, because Addison also witnessed Brian's behavior, not often, but on several different occasions."

Addison stood to approach Donae'. He stopped in front of his desk and admitted, "This is true, Lawrence. Nevertheless, I at the time was not privy to Brian's behavior so I missed the signs. And when I discussed it with Carol, we attributed most of his failings to insecurity or stress. Neither Carol nor I ever realized that there was a serious problem. However, at one particular point I did have my suspicions, a situation that happened right after Brian changed positions. Jennifer invited me to lunch. I can only guess that Jennifer must have thought Brian would be out of town. Anyway, when I arrived Brian was already angry with Jennifer. He felt she should have first informed him of the luncheon.

I thought it was merely because he wanted to join us. But then he began spouting dialogue, which I thought was degrading. He remarked that Jennifer was not as trustworthy as women in general were and she did not deserve his trust. He said more often than not women betrayed men, that this was one reason the military refused to let women on the battlefield, because they couldn't be trusted. Of course, he soon realized that I was uncomfortable with his accusations and he immediately changed his tune, and he said he was only teasing. But I saw Jennifer's expression, and she was really uncomfortable. She immediately apologized to Brian for her oversight and canceled our lunch date. She pretended to make light of the situation and asked if we could reschedule for a time when Brian could join us."

Shaking his head, Addison added, "Lawrence, I really didn't want to leave her alone with him. I tried to make my feelings clear, but Jennifer glibly dismissed Brian's behavior with, 'Oh, Father do not be ridiculous, Brian just gets this way sometimes. I think it's because of his military background. It's not like he's going to hurt me.'

"I was not sure Jennifer herself believed what she said, but she insisted that I go home and ordered me not to worry about her or the baby. As I reluctantly left that day she repeated, 'Daddy it's just his military training. It comes through every now and then, that's all. Brian doesn't mean anything by it, please, just forget it ever happened.'

"As I said, not being aware of Brian's behavioral pattern, I didn't recognize Jennifer's excuses as covering for him. Afterward I heard that that was usually the case."

Unexpectedly, Addison cried, "Lawrence, I trusted my daughter, so I didn't question her; I simply took her at her word."

Gerimee jumped in and explained, "Brian was in the Marines, Lawrence. As a matter of fact, that's how he got his degree and became a Certified Public Accountant. He used his G.I. Bill."

"Yes," added Addison. "But while he was in the service he was in the field and I guess he saw a lot of killing, far more than any young man should see at his age, or I guess any man should see at any age. But this is what Jennifer was referring to when she said the military made him that way. And in truth, maybe that's why I so readily accepted her explanation."

At that time Gerimee added, "See, Lawrence, that's one more thing, Brian knows weapons. He knows about guns, knives and killing people."

Donae' brought his hand up and sharply addressed Gerimee's accusation. "Hold on, Gerimee! Wait one damn minute. Thousands of men across the world have been in the service, as well as in wars. And as many have not killed their wives and children. So, let's try and not get carried away, I only want to hear facts, not hypothesizes and irrational allegations."

"I'm sorry, Lawrence. I can imagine what I sound like, but I know we're right about this. I know, Brian killed Jennifer and Patty Jean. For one thing, Addison and I both agree Party Bird wouldn't have sat silent while someone entered Patty Jean's room that night."

"Okay . . . wait. One more time, who? And what is a Party Bird? And how do you know that he wouldn't let anyone in the room?"

"A parrot," cracked Addison. "A huge, blue and green beauty of a parrot that talked up a storm. Patty Jean loved that bird and the bird loved Patty Jean more than I ever thought any bird was capable of."

Gerimee quickly added, "You see, Lawrence, when Patty Jean turned two, Sharon and I bought this bird for her birthday gift. We delivered him the day of her party, so she called him Party Bird. Anyway, the point is the parrot turned out to be as loyal and loving to Patty Jean as she was to him. Wherever Patty Jean went the bird went. And what was even more bizarre, if a stranger came near Patty Jean, the bird would screech louder than a train whistle and would not stop until someone he knew calmed him down."

"So where was he the night she was killed," asked Donae? "Why had no one heard the bird's screeching? Did he not make his noise to wake anyone? Why was Jennifer or someone from the house staff not wakened by his commotion?"

"Yes, my questions exactly," spouted Gerimee.

"Later when Addison asked one of the officers that question, the officer said in so many words, 'they didn't want to hear anything about a bird.'

"They refused to listen to our theory," Gerimee sneered.

"They said since Patty Jean was asleep that the bird was most likely covered for the night. Lawrence, we tried to explain to them that Jennifer rarely covered the bird. Besides, I don't think it would have mattered if Party Bird was covered or not. If he had sensed a stranger in the room that night, he would have screeched louder than a banshee, Lawrence. That's why I say it had to be someone he knew or recognized. And what is even more peculiar is Brian got rid of the bird within days of the killing. Why would you simply get rid of something Patty Jean loved so much? Wouldn't you agree that that was a little strange?"

"Gerimee, I see where you're going with this, but that doesn't prove Brian was the one in the room that night. It could have been any one of the many friends that Jennifer knew."

"I agree, Lawrence, but the Coroner said that Patty Jean must have been awakened just before she was killed. He also said she must have recognized the person in her room that night, since she didn't react frightened."

"Again, Gerimee that does not say it was Brian."

Suddenly, both men heard a choked cry and Addison moved over to the window. He stood without saying anything for several minutes and when he turned to walk back to stand in front of Gerimee and Donae' evidence of tears stained the corners of his eyes and cheeks. Unashamed, he wiped the dampness with the handkerchief he pulled from the inside pocket of his suit. Gerimee and Donae' watched in silence as Addison re-pocketed his handkerchief and commenced to speak between clenched teeth. They could barely hear his dispirited voice since it was closer to a hiss. "Lawrence, they said that her face held a peaceful look on it. And her lips held the slightest hint of a smile." His voice raised an octave and he concluded, "Lawrence, a child of four does not awaken in the middle of the night with a smile on their lips unless they know the person in front of them. Their mind doesn't work that way; they can't process thought that fast. But that night, in that room, Patty Jean knew her as-sailant. And in that instant her mind registered that she loved this person and *that,* Lawrence, *is who* she wore her final smile for. Not a stranger." Addison's voice had wavered and momentarily he choked before he went on.

"Then this same person, without a moment of vacillation, slashed her throat. Taking every bit of life, instantly, out of her tiny four-year old body. Then without so much as a minute spent on remorse, he walked away to do the same damn thing to her mother." Abruptly, Addison walked back to the window and turned his back to face his pain alone, while his two allies stood helpless in the middle of the room.

At last Addison turned back to face them and Donae' could almost see the pain that surrounded his portly frame when he admitted, "I know now that my daughter had become afraid of Brian and I realize that she tried to hide that from Carol and I, but . . ." Suddenly, Addison sucked in a loud hollow breath and wailed a rhetorical, "But, why didn't I see it? I should have seen it. I didn't see anything until it was all too late. But now . . . . when it's no longer important, I see everything . . . ." He cov-ered his face with his hands and wailed, "I should have seen it . . . . God, I damn myself for this. Why didn't I see . . ."

Overcome with emotion, Donae' waited several minutes before he spoke. He wanted to say the right words and convince both these men to see the truth. Gerimee, he loved dearly and could easily sense his pain. Addison, he barely knew, yet it was as easy to recognize his pain as Ger-imee's, and Donae' couldn't help but feel a deep compassion for their suffering. Nonetheless, neither would be of much help in their immedi-ate state of mind. It was imperative that they release their unwarranted guilt so they could help search for the killer or killers of Jennifer and Patty Jean.

Donae' shifted. He was uncomfortable with the task at hand. Once he recognized this, he moved to verbalize his thoughts, yet he did so slowly and with careful precision. "Gerimee, Addison, please sit down. We need to get something utterly clear before we go any further." He watched as neither man moved. Then he continued, "I do recognize that blaming oneself for the death of a loved one is a normal way of handling the pain. And I would imagine it would be even more so with two such cherished young lives. It is easy to see how much you both loved Jennifer and Patty Jean, although the guilt you both have allowed to fester these past few years is unwarranted and it will only hinder us in our pursuit for answers. We all should maintain a clear mind. Our quest must be filled with positive deeds. You can't have ghosts concealed in the back of your mind, for they will surely taint your facts."

Donae' moved closer as he added, "This is one reason you have not been able to get the help you requested from the police. Up to this point they have only seen two emotionally guilt-ridden men in search of retribution. So, in essence, they do not take you, or any of your episodes as facts."

Donae' waited; he hoped what he said would sink in. Neither Gerimee nor Addison reacted to his words, so he went on. "I appreciate that both of you are very intelligent and talented men. For that reason, I know you can see beyond this junction we are at. Gerimee, Addison, right now at this point in time I am asking you to leave your guilt behind, for it is not doing neither of you nor Jennifer and Patty Jean any good. So, please hear me when I say there was nothing that either of you could have done to save them. You could not in any way have foreseen something like that happening. Even if you did you could not have stopped Jennifer and Patty Jean from being a part of Brian's life. That was solely up to Jennifer to make that decision, not either of you. Therefore, I am asking once again that both of you as of this moment join me to work for a resolution and not waste another minute on self-indulging condemnation."

Donae' walked over to stand between Gerimee and Addison. "Now, I am quite sure you can see our plate is pretty damn full as it stands, in which case we have no room for guilt. So, if I have your word that we will concentrate only on the solution, then we can get started today."

Both men hesitated; they were not sure whether they could do as Donae' asked. It had been three long years since either had faced a day without first asking, "What if . . . maybe . . . and why didn't I?"

Addison, as well as Gerimee, was aware that they couldn't change the past or bring back the two people they both loved. But maybe back then, before any of this had happened, they could have been an instrumental part in preventing the catastrophe, if only they had recognized the signs.

Finally, Gerimee answered, "Lawrence, after the death of Jen and Patty Jean, I didn't blame anyone except the unknown assailant. At that time my anger was too great, and I was having trouble putting things into perspective. Then, almost two years later when I heard about Brian receiving two million dollars from the insurance company, plus Jen's trust fund, I begin to think about Brian and his greed. That's when I first started to get suspicious. Then when Addison told me that Brian had said that he didn't want to touch any of that blood money, I started to recall things that Jen had told me, although I still said nothing; I kept my suspicions to myself. That is, until a couple of months later when Addison mentioned that Brian said, 'he wished Jen hadn't insisted on the life insurance policies, in which case he wouldn't have the heartache of dealing with these companies now.' "At that moment, I knew something wasn't right because I remember when Jen told Sharon and I about the policy. She said Brian initiated the policies. He was adamant that she and Patty Jean take the physicals as soon as possible. Her reason was that Brian was security conscious. When I asked how Brian felt about his medical test, she said he hadn't gotten around to his test yet. Lawrence, let me ask you this, if Brian was only worried about his family's security, why would he put a million dollar life insurance policy on a baby and a woman who were both already extremely wealthy, yet, never get around to instating his own policy? That's when I started feeling guilty. That's when I realized I should have seen the signs, but instead my ignorance failed Jennifer and Patty Jean. I guess what I'm trying to say is I'll do the very best I can to do as you ask. But Lawrence, my guilt is not unwarranted; I deserve to bear it."

"As do I," Addison added to Gerimee's confession. "I feel a father's love is like no other. We know the pain and happiness our children feel. I should have insisted my daughter tell me why she was afraid of Brian at times. I should have questioned her on why she seemed to be happier when he was out of town than when he was home with her and Patty Jean. Instead, I did as Jennifer requested and closed my eyes and pretended all was fine. Maybe because I could not imagine anything so horrid ever happening to anyone in my family. But my simple-minded innocence is no excuse. In any case, Lawrence, I, too, have earned the guilt I endure, but as Gerimee conceded, "I will also do my best to bury my burden and concentrate entirely on the work at hand.""

# CHAPTER 5

The day after Gerimee, Addison and Donae's meeting that continued well into the night, Donae' began the chore of deciphering the information he had received. Both gentlemen eagerly bestowed a wealth of information upon him; he had to decide what was fact and what was emotional entanglement.

Donae's first impression as he read about the subject, Brian Scott Peterson was, *poor fellow*. His overall perspective was that Brian Peterson had little luck in retaining a family. Addison had said that Brian was adopted at the age of two and a half years. As far as Addison knew, Brian had no memory of his natural mother or father, and he never had a desire to find out about them as he grew older. From what Addison gathered about his adoptive parents, the Petersons were poor but a loving family. They lived in a small farm community in Wisconsin near the Michigan boarder. They had run their small dairy-farm as close as they could to their strong religious beliefs which included early to rise and long laborious hours, until early to bed, six days a week. The seventh day, Donae' imagined, was mostly spent in church.

Addison was told by Brian that the Petersons adopted him after their young son, Peter, passed away from a congenital heart condition. Other than that,

Addison said Brian never talked much about his adoptive family, only that, just before his eighteenth birthday, his adoptive parents had died in an unexplained fire. The entire home burned to the ground. Lucky for Brian, he was out that dreadful night with his girlfriend.

It was not long after the fire when Brian decided to join the Marines. From what Addison understood from Brian's account, he no longer felt he had anyone or anything to keep him in Wisconsin. He sold what little he inherited, the diary equipment and land, to a nearby neighbor and joined the Marines.

After factoring in what Donae' perceived was Brian's pattern and personality, he decided to check his past as far back as records would permit. The temperament Gerimee and Addison had described was not something a person developed overnight. Some medical journals go as far as stating it is suspected that the narcissistic personality, and this is the temperament Gerimee and Addison were suggesting Brian has, is passed on from biological parent to an offspring. As far as Donae' was concerned this type of personality was far too complicated to label without fully exploring. With this even being a possibility, Donae' felt it was imperative to get all available information on who were Brian's natural parents and learn why he was given up for adoption at the age of two.

Yet, before any of this Donae' determined: "I must first meet with Brian and if I do this early enough, before he gets wind of an investigator, I might acquire more information." Donae' pondered, *this should not be too great a task, since our family has so many business interests, which, of course, all generate immense profits. One could easily understand the need of an accounting firm. So,* he thought: *My cover will be . . . , I am in search of a new CPA firm to handle our family holdings.* "Yes," he said, "that will work just fine."

When Donae' stepped into Silvia's small cluttered office, she was among her new bureau and amidst the men who were redecorating her office. A man stood in front of each wall busily painting the trim. Wallpaper samples were lying everywhere, and Silvia was sitting on the floor in the middle of the mess with about fifteen cold-case files spread out around her.

Donae' immediately smiled at her tenacity, then cautiously requested, "Silvia, if you have a minute, I would appreciate your assistance on a few matters."

She started to stand up and he hurriedly pleaded, "Stay where you are, please; now that I see you are busy this can wait until later." Yet Silvia was quicker than he and she eagerly jumped up and shouted, "No! I'm free now, Mr. Donae'. What can I do to help?"

Silvia loved the opportunity to be involved in any case where she could play amateur sleuth. And, in truth, she was quite good at it. Donae', never told her, but he feared that one day she herself would become an investigator and he would lose the most efficient assistant he ever had.

He handed Silvia the folder that contained all the information on the Peterson case and immediately witnessed the excitement wash over her lovely Argentine face. Silvia hurriedly followed him into his office while she opened the file and scanned its contents.

Respectfully, Donae' waited a few minutes while she examined the contents before he filled her in. "The date you are reading Silvia, is the date Brian Peterson was adopted. If you note, it says, 'sometime, in September, Nineteen-twenty-four.' We do not have the exact day." Donae' thought for a minute, then handed her one more sheet of paper with another date and year scrawled upon it and informed her, "This is the date I have for Brian's birthday, January Twenty-second, Nineteen-twenty-two. What I need from you is all the information you can find in the adoption court records. If we are lucky, we will discover some information on who his natural parents were and where they came from, although there is a good chance you may come up empty-handed. Still, I am hoping that we can at least attain an address or some other lead to follow. Perhaps we can even find a clue on the personality of his parents in the records. Sometimes the courts do make notes on such."

While Donae' enlightened Silvia, she eagerly took notes as fast as she could write. "And while you are doing your magic, I will start checking his military records. I have several connections at the Pentagon. From what Addison said, Brian was in the Marines for six years. From the age of eighteen, through the age of twenty-four. With all that time in the service and in close quarters, I know someone had to see a little of that true individual Brian hides."

Silvia could not contain herself any longer, and excitedly answered, "Oh, Mr. Donae', thanks. I'll get on it right away and I'll get the information to you as soon as I can get my hands on it."

Again Donae' took pleasure in her excitement. He knew she would be diligent and do her best to find what he needed. She was always a great help with any case and the more involvement she had, the more excitement she exuded.

It was later that same day that Donae' attempted to reach Brian's secretary to make an appointment, but after several tries and all misses, he changed his focus to Brian's military records. Unfortunately, when he called the Pentagon, he was also unable to reach his contacts and ended up with a Miss Robin Blanch, who staunchly informed him, "Old files take some time to retrieve, Mr. Donae'. For that reason, you may not receive the information you request for six to eight weeks. Will that be a problem?"

Donae' understood that there would be a long wait but wondered why she asked if the timeline would be a problem since it would not have changed if it were. Yet, before he hung up, he implored, "Please do your best, Miss Blanch. If you make it sooner, this information may very well save a young woman's life." Donae' jotted a question on his pad-Allison P. Carter in danger???

After Donae' set the phone back in its cradle, he started a mental checklist. When his list reached Brian and his young life in Hurley, he stopped. Mentally, he circled the high school sweetheart's name, and on his notepad, he penciled, 'Find out how deep the relationship was.'

Donae' thought there was a good possibility that Brian's sweetheart, Christine, may have noticed Brian's mood variations before he left Wisconsin. From what he remembered of his studies on unusual behavior, this type of personality usually revealed itself in young adulthood. With any luck, if Brian indeed does lack empathy, which is a trait of several different personality disorders, including narcissistic, it may have shown its ugly face as far back as his teen years. Donae' tapped his pencil to the notebook as he evaluated his options, then determined, "Maybe, instead of beginning with Brian, I should start in Hurley, Wisconsin. That might be my best option."

Now that Donae' had a definitive direction he immediately set forth to implement his plan. Enthusiastically, he searched the desk for a map. After what turned out to be an intense pursuit, he found an old worn out map book in back of a file drawer. Eagerly he opened the book to Wisconsin and began to scan the pages for the town of Hurley. In Brian's hometown, he might have the opportunity to learn more about him, but also, he would have the chance to find out more about the Petersons and their untimely deaths and how it affected Brian.

Donae' dialed the operator for the number of the Hurley Chamber of Commerce. After several unsuccessful attempts, he finally ended up with the number for the one and only local newspaper which he called right away. He wanted to set up an appointment to research the old newspapers for Nineteen-forty, the time of the Peterson's deaths.

An old gentleman by the name of Mr. Randolph Ferguson answered the phone. Quickly Donae' introduced himself and hurriedly made his request known. He trusted this would keep the questions to a minimum.

Mr. Ferguson asked, "Fer what date ere ya lookin fer, young man?"

Donae' detected the accent and wanted to inquire on it but instead quickly explained, "I do not know the precise day. Only that it was around, February, March, April, or May of Nineteen-forty.

The kind old fellow laughed and said, "Sir, ya sure ere gonna be busy, with all that readin!. Whatcha lookin fer, anyways?"

Donae' clarified, "Mr. Ferguson, I need all the information I can find on the deaths of Mary Beth and Handoff Peterson."

Without hesitation, the old man divulged, "Well, Mr., whyed didant ya say tat in the firs place?"

Donae' was still curious about Mr. Ferguson's accent, it was undistinguishable to his trained ear. He tried hard to detect its origin while he listened carefully to the dialect that quite often came through in his friendly speech. "I caan getcha those publications, Mr. Donae'. I can hav it by Tuesday mornin, if ya wanta com in about eight-tirdy or so."

Donae' assured him the time he indicated was not too early. But the amiable Mr. Ferguson kidded, "All right, if tats the way ya want it. I thought I'd herd ya city folk like ta sleap in a bit." Laughing goodheartedly, he warmly said, "Good day, Mr. Donae'," and hung up.

Donae' called out, "Silvia. Can you come in here, please?"

After a few minutes, Silvia rounded the corner of the opened door and Donae' saw that her arms were laden with a huge box. It appeared to be filled with old newspapers and he saw what looked like a photograph that was dangling over the side. Hastily she informed him, "These papers are from the area where Jennifer and Patty Jean Peterson resided at the time of their deaths."

Donae' immediately jumped up to relieve her of the burdensome weight, and she continued, "I thought you might want to see some of the news releases on the case."

Plus, there are several copies of photos that were taken at the crime scene. Mr. Hobart dropped them off early this morning. He's such a nice man, Mr. Donae'. I feel so bad for him."

Donae' nodded his head in agreement as he scanned the box. "Splendid, this will certainly help my research. If you have a minute, I need you to make me some travel arrangements. I need to get to a place in Wisconsin next Tuesday or Wednesday. Try to get as close to a town called Hurley as you can, even if I have to take a train. However, I will be there for several days so I will need a car along with a hotel room. Oh, and thank you for the box, Silvia. I certainly will go through these items."

Silvia turned to leave and Donae', already distracted by the box and its contents, thoughtlessly said, "Silvia, close the door on your way out." After he said the words, he realized how rude he sounded and with an apology he added a second request, "Sorry, Silvia, but if you will, please see that I am not disturbed for the next few hours. I not only want to absorb all these articles but decipher any clues that I might come across. I also need to lay out my strategies for this case. After all, we have several areas in which we will be investigating simultaneously."

Silvia nodded and began to close the door behind her when she heard Donae' mumbling to himself as he pulled a new notepad from his desk. "We are going to have to be explicit in all of our maneuvers. There is much too much at risk not to be precise." Silvia smiled, for she knew this was one reason Mr. Donae' was so successful in solving his cases. He was always extremely dedicated to its victim.

Before Donae' began to note his approaches, he emptied the box on to his desk. The papers had obviously been handled a lot. The notes were worn, and newspapers looked aged and ragged. There appeared to be no order to the papers, so Donae' randomly began separating them. As he placed them into different piles in order of time elapsed, he noticed that one of the pages looked to be the front page of a magazine. The page showed the beautiful face of Jennifer Hobart. She was dressed in a magnificent wedding gown. It seemed that after her elopement her parents had thrown Jennifer and Brian an enormous wedding party. The party was held at one of the most elite hotels in New York.

Donae' could see the sweet, tender smile of bliss that covered her delicate features. She was indeed, as Gerimee had guilelessly described, happy.

Donae' set the picture aside and continued with his inspection. He went from one clipping to another and each drew him closer to Jennifer and her personality. She was a philanthropist and her actions showed this. It was also apparent that she was very well liked as well as respected. Donae' became aware that most of the articles said very little about Brian. Even though, Jennifer's popularity was clearly high on the social strata, Brian's appeared less so as Gerimee had indicated earlier.

He noticed one magazine's article described the newly wedded couple as being storybook perfect. And at the end of the critique they showed a picture of Jennifer and Brian taken at their three-month anniversary. The article stated that this was the newlywed's first Benefit Ball together, and that the beautiful couple had chosen this time to announce the proud news of their expectant parenthood. The originator of the piece was correct in his analysis because the glow of the couple surely showed them to be extremely handsome together.

Donae' studied the picture of Brian closely. He and Gerimee seemed close to the same in height, about six feet tall. They appeared to be the opposite in every other distinction. Gerimee's face displayed a strong handsomeness, but leaner structure that was sharply defined. Brian, on the other hand, showed a physiognomy of strength, yet in a full manner and was lighter in complexion and hair. His good-looking features seem to favor the ancestral side of a Viking, or the Norwegian sector. Donae' set the picture aside as he thought, *I can easily see why anyone who saw Brian and Jennifer together would think them picture perfect*. At that instant, he glanced at the next segment and recognized it was an announcement. He picked it up and saw the most angelic, healthy-looking baby he had ever seen. The paper was announcing the birth of Miss Patricia (Patty) Jean Peterson. She was, as all babies are most of the time, asleep in the arms of the proud new mother.

Donae' continued to sift through the papers and found another picture of Patty Jean. She was standing ever so lady-like, next to her grandfather, Addison Hobart. She was gorgeous and now Donae' could easily understand what Gerimee meant when he said he could see he was not Patty Jean's biological father, because this soft blond beauty's genes were definitely from her father, Brian Peterson. Her fine blond curls fell buoyantly around her angel-like face. Patty Jean looked to be about three years old at the time the picture was taken. It was apparent that she was the apple of her grandfather's eye.

Almost immediately after his appraisal, Donae' sat up abruptly and dropped the picture he held behind the one he had just admired. Patty Jean's face was surrounded by what used to be her lovely blond curls. The hair was now stained and matted down, by a mass of heavy dark blood. The miniature face showed nothing but the faintness of a smile and no signs of life whatsoever.

Next to Patty Jean's picture was another that showed her mother. Jennifer was lying on her back. Her face was a mask that was filled with her final guise of horror. This terror completely covered the once charmingly delicate face. It also showed she realized what was about to happen. Donae' studied the two pictures. It appeared that Jennifer tried at least for an instant, to fight off her attacker before he overpowered her and successfully made his deadly incision. Dolefully, Donae' observed the photos, and after several minutes his mind still fixed on how lifeless both bodies were. He thought, *What, kind of person could look onto these two precious beings full of life and radiance, then promptly eliminate their existence?* Out loud he asked, 'how? Then promised, "Jennifer, Patty Jean, I give you my word, you will have your day of retribution. This person, the last human being you beheld in your sight, will be punished."

# CHAPTER 6

The day before Donae' left New York for Wisconsin, he stopped by the insurance company that paid Brian the substantial amount of insurance money. He spent the next two hours explaining who he was and why he was investigating a policy that had already been paid. He was finally, although begrudgingly, introduced to a lovely and most efficient woman named Miss Sidney Barrister. She, too, at first listened dubiously to Donae's story. He finally concluded, "So you see Miss Barrister, I only seek to defray any notion of an illicit transaction and emend any unwarranted indemnity."

Earnestly, Miss Barrister agreed, "If there is any suspicion at all that an account has been paid erroneously. I am fully interested in a joint action to prove the deception, Mr. Donae'."

Right away Donae' detected that Miss Barrister's smile showed a deeper interest in him beyond the case he presented. And, of course, he immediately took advantage of the moment and asked, "Is it possible that I can see the records that concern the Peterson account?"

Again, Miss Barrister answered enthusiastically, "Well, let me see what I can find. Not all the records are on this floor; I may have to go upstairs to the record room."

Donae' watched as she eagerly searched, then pulled what records she could easily put her hands on. Afterwards, she and Donae' went from page to page absorbing the information. One report showed that the police verified that Brian had indeed been in Washington D. C. at the time of the crime. Donae' also noted that the insurance company investigator had made no implications in his entries. As far as the notes were concerned, Brian was never a suspect, nor was there any suggestion or suspicions that he hired an individual to commit the murders. When Donae' set the folders aside he asked, "Miss Barrister, is there any way to find out who first initiated the policy?"

Sidney Barrister instantly beamed as she answered proudly. "Yes, there sure is, Mr. Donae'. As a matter of fact, we have a procedure within our company called the Frappe chain. It has been in effect for about ten years."

"Frappe?" Donae' repeated.

"Yes. We named it Frappe, after a beneficiary. You see, Mr. Donae', our company paid a large claim to an individual we knew was unmerited. His entitlement was a sham. But since we failed to provide a proper paper trail, we could do nothing. The courts awarded the judgment to the plaintiff and we had no choice, except to pay the claim. So now every policy that is introduced into the system is followed by a complete reference file. This file not only has, *who*, but what, when and where."

"Do you mean you record the telephone conversations?"

"No! Oh, no, Mr. Donae', we don't go quite that far. But we do document each, and every call we receive.

And if a policy is initiated, we then provide a copy of the calls to the agent who will be handling the account. And, of course, they continue to add details from there on."

"Where are those records now, Miss Barrister? Can I see them or, better yet, is it possible to get copies of them?"

"Well, Mr. Donae', if it will help you in your pursuit you most certainly can, except it'll take me at least a couple of hours to track everything down. Oh, and Mr. Donae', I will need a copy of your private investigator license. I'll have to put it in the file."

Donae' without hesitation pulled his license from his jacket pocket and handed it to Miss Barrister. With a grin that matched hers he asked, "Miss Barrister, when can I pick this information up? You did say you could have it today, did you not?"

"Oh, yes. Let's see, it's now two-thirty. If you meet me here, say at . . . five o'clock. I should have everything located and copied by then." She hesitated then asked demurely, "Mr. Donae' if you don't mind, I'd love to buy you a drink. There's a cute little pub right down the street."

Donae's smile broadened when she asked, "And please, can you call me, Sidney?"

Tickled, although surprised by her assertiveness, Donae' said. "I would be honored and pleased to address you as Sidney. And as for your offer, it is quite appealing. Only, I dare say I have one better. Lets' say, I along with that drink I buy you an early dinner at the Four Seasons."

Sidney was delighted and her elation was brought to light when she giggled then happily agreed. "That sounds wonderful, Mr. Donae', simply wonderful."

"Sidney, you must call me Lawrence, if I am to buy you dinner."

"Okay, then, Lawrence, I'll meet you downstairs at five, okay?" She gave him one last radiant smile and hurried away.

Donae' watched as she walked away while he pulled at his tie to loosen its sudden constriction. *She is a lovely woman*, he thought. This was an unusual situation for the judicious Mr. Donae', and he was not quite sure how he should feel. Usually he did not take women he had just met out to dinner or any place else, for that matter. In spite of this fact, Donae' thought Sidney had been extremely helpful and he did want to thank her properly, although if asked, he would have to admit that he had noticed and appreciated how extremely attractive she was.

Donae' turned to move toward the exit but before he left the high-rise office building, he headed for the phone he had spotted in the corner of the entranceway. He decided to call Silvia. He not only wanted to keep her apprised of what he had learned, he also wanted her to know where he could be reached in case, she uncovered any new facts.

Donae' had barely finished his hello when Silvia burst in full of excitement. "Oh! Mr. Donae', I'm so glad you called. I already have several tips, but only one that will interest you right now. I received Brian's military records."

Surprised, Donae' asked, "Brian's military records? So, soon? In no way did I expect them this fast."

"Well, there's a note attached that reads, "crucial, matter of emergency," circled in red. So, whatever you told them, Mr. Donae', it certainly worked. I also have the sergeant's name that Brian served under, along with his telephone number."

"Great work, Silvia. I will take that information right now. I can call him while I wait for the insurance company's records." Donae' quickly wrote the sergeant's name and number down, then related what he had learned from Sidney, "I really want to hear the rest of what you have Silvia, but everything is going to have to wait until I return from Wisconsin. You may as well put the rest of that information on my desk for when I return."

As soon as Donae' hung up the phone, he picked it up again and dialed Sergeant Cox. The sergeant, he was told, was not in and would not be back from field maneuvers for several more days. The gentleman who was on the other end of the line added in a deep voice that was heavily shaded with a southern drawl, "Right after his return, sir, Sergeant Cox will be leaving for a five-day furlough. So, I don't expect you are gonna get hold of him for some time, since he won't be around for a while."

Donae' was disappointed by this news but left his number and a message for Sergeant Cox to return his call as soon as possible.

At five o'clock Donae' arrived at the high-rise to pick up Sidney and retrieve the information he had requested. Miss Barrister grinned openly with pleasure, her anticipation at what was about to come quite evident.

Donae's smile was equally bright; then it immediately filled with appreciation as well when he noticed her hands contained a full folder. He promptly took the bulging file from her arms, then accepted her jacket and held it while she slipped her arm though the first sleeve, at which time he noticed Sidney had changed into a beaded silk dress that was more alluring than the one she had worn earlier. Uncertain, he reaffirmed, "Is the Four Seasons okay with you, Sidney?"

She grinned and whispered, "Perfectly wonderful, Lawrence. Perfect."

As soon as Sidney was seated in the Jag she confirmed, "I love the atmosphere at the Four Seasons; it's so charmingly romantic."

Donae' simply grinned his agreement.

Sidney watched as he readied himself for the short drive. From her side of the car she determined silently, *He is truly handsome and apparently much richer than I thought.*

As soon as they pulled in front of the hotel Sidney noticed the valet's sudden alertness and her euphoria increased. She liked that the valet was impressed and when he was overly attentive as he opened the door of the Jag it likewise satisfied her ego. Smiling to herself, Sidney further aligned her agenda with another brief thought, *How, am I going to turn this into an all-night adventure and secure a future relationship?*

When they received their cocktails, Sidney handed the file Donae' had returned to her in the car, the folder contained the information he had requested.

He thanked her then asked, "May I read it?"

She nodded, then smiled as he quickly read through the papers. She was satisfied with herself that he seemed impressed. Once he had read the report fully, he commented, "Sidney, I must say, I am entirely impressed with this. It is very inclusive and verifies what my source has implied."

For a second Sidney looked confused, and Donae' reminded her of their earlier conversation. "If you recall, my source said that Brian was the one that originated the policy, whereas Brian proclaims that Jennifer did. From your file's documentation, it seems that Jennifer only filled out the paperwork. This chronicle shows everything else was carried out by Brian."

# CHAPTER 7

V ery early the next morning, Donae' was standing in a line at the airport. He was flying into an area not far from Madison, then char-
tering a plane to Marinette. There he would pick-up his rental car and
drive the rest of the way to Hurley. It was going to be a very long day.

The hotel was located in the center of the old town near the building
in which the newspaper office was housed. At the appointed time, eight-
thirty, Thursday morning, Donae' arrived at the office and Mr. Ferguson
was nowhere to be found. Instead, he was greeted by an elderly yet ro-
bust woman, who he soon found out was Mrs. Martha Ferguson. She
was extremely friendly and intent on spending some time in conversation.

Donae' soon discovered that she actually only wanted a hearing
board. At first her conversation dwelled entirely around several relatives'
birthdays and what gift she thought she should get each one. Once she
decided that was settled, she rapidly moved on to the next subject, her
nephew, Gerhardt. She expressed deep concern for his well-being, since
he planned to move away to the big city of Los Angeles, California.
"Have ya ever been there, Mr. Donae'?" Then without waiting for his
comment, she again changed the subject to her beautiful niece, "who,"

said, Mrs. Ferguson, "is not only our local high school principal but also a published author. I'd say a man can't ask for much more than that, can he Mr. Donae'?" Smiling she added, "Yes, a woman with substance and passion as well."

She drew in a deep breath before she went on, "Mr. Donae' if you get a chance, you gotta pick up a copy of her book, *Country Poems*, by Mary Ellen Ferguson. That's what it's called. You can get it at the drug store; we don't have a bookstore here in town, so the drug store carries a few copies. Mary Ellen's a lovely girl, Mr. Donae'. She just recently turned thirty-seven and is looking to get married. I guess she realizes it's time to settle down and have a family of her own."

Mrs. Ferguson hesitated as she eyed Donae' closely, then added. "Yes, I truly believe Mary Ellen's gonna make some lucky man a splendid wife. You know, she does all her own baking, plus she's a terrific cook." Then briskly she asked, "You aren't married, are you, Mr. Donae'?"

Again, without waiting for an answer she went on, "Of course, you're not married. If you were you wouldn't be wearing a wrinkled shirt; now would you, Mr. Donae'? How long did you say you'd be in town? I'm sure Mary Ellen would love to cook you some supper, Mr. Donae'."

Donae' could not think past the invitation so he was not quick enough to get out of it in any polite manner. His excuses where still stumbling around in his mind when Mr. Ferguson walked in. The first impression that registered with Donae' was the gigantic smile across Mr. Ferguson's face. Immediately he quipped, "Mr. Donae', ya will hav to excuse my Mrs.; she's ben tryin to marry off our niece, Mary Ellen, for nearly ten yers now. She means well, but no man's safe from her infringement and many that see her comin run the other way."

Mrs. Ferguson laughed lightly and quickly apologized for making Donae' feel uneasy. "Sometimes I do carry on." In defiance when she turned to leave the room, she gave Donae' a quick little wink and added, "Mr. Donae', don't you forget if you'd like to have a good home cooked meal, just give us a call. I'm sure Mary Ellen can whip something up in a jiffy." At this time Mrs. Ferguson gave him another wink and hurried away. It was obvious that she was pleased that she had had the last word before she left the room.

Mr. Ferguson shook his head along with Donae's hand as he lovingly surmised, "Don't ya mind my lil lady none; she's just a lovin aunt, that's all."

Mr. Ferguson laid his arm around Donae's shoulder and led him to the stairs. He informed him that the room that housed the records was up the stairs and all the way on the other side of the building. Once Mr. Ferguson opened the door, he said, "This is where we kept all our ole records." Proudly, he added," on microfiche. We might be a small town, Mr. Donae', but we do try to keep up with the boys in the big cities."

Donae' was more than just a little pleased to see this; in fact, he was grateful. As far as he was concerned nothing was worse than going through hundreds of dried-out pages of dusty old newspapers. He was also pleased that Mr. Ferguson had taken onto himself to pull out all the old data on the Peterson case. This would no doubt save him a lot of time.

"I do hope this will halp ya some and make yar lookin a little easier, Mr. Donae'." Mr. Ferguson turned to leave and Donae' quickly asked, "Sir, one question before you go, Mr. Ferguson were you around here about eighteen years ago . . . when the Petersons died?"

"Ooh yea. Me and the Mrs., we were runnon the paper back then, since nineteen thirdy."

"Did you know the Petersons?"

"Yea, ever one knows ever one around here, Mr. Donae'. That's just the way it is in Hurley. But the Petersons were not a sociable folk, if ya know what I mean. So, we just know em, to tip our hats and say good mornon, that's all." The old man scratched his head and said, "Sad thing the . . . .," he stopped in mid-sentence turned and hurried from the room, leaving Donae' befuddled and on his own to conduct his search.

Donae' looked around then scanned several old papers before he began to inspect the microfiche. Soon he was deeply engrossed in the old newsprint. Interesting enough, at first the police thought the circumstances surrounding the fire were suspicious. The fire, it seemed, ignited in the bedroom. Neither Mr. nor Mrs. Peterson smoked, so it was assumed a candle was the cause, although the investigating officer suspected that the fire was much hotter than a simple cigarette or candle could have generated. Nothing though was ever found to verify otherwise. By all indications, from the burned-out ashes and the position of the body indicated that Mary Beth Peterson attempted to escape the flames. But apparently, the smoke was so dense that Mary lost her sense of direction and fell over a stool that sat in the center of the living room, thenceforth hitting her head against the fireplace and passing out, which would have explained the crack they found in her skull. Ultimately, she burned to death.

On the other hand, Mr. Handoff Peterson was said to have never awakened from his deep sleep. He was asphyxiated from the heavy smoke. He probably never realized that there was a problem, though the coroner noted several unexplained bruises on his wrist.

After the police investigated the crime scene and could not find any definitive evidence, the case was closed and ruled accidental. There was a short byline that read. "The only legal heir to the, Peterson's earthly possessions is their son, Brian Scott Peterson. At the close of investigation, he inherited the small dairy farm along with a life insurance policy of $10,000." It said nothing else about Brian or if Brian was ever a suspect in the incident.

Later, Donae' found another section that gave the investigating officer as Kent Dolton. He jotted the name down and continued through the rest of the papers. When he finally turned the light off and closed the door to the storage room, Donae' felt a sense of disappointment. He really did not know what he expected to find, yet he had hoped to find more than just the name of the investigative officer and an obit.

Donae' searched several rooms. No one was in the front office. Then he went towards the back area before he finally found the Fergusons cleaning their presses. He thanked them for their courtesy and started to leave, then stopped and asked, "Do you know if Kent Dolton is still on the police force?"

Mrs. Ferguson jumped in, "Oh, he sure is, but he's now Captain Dolton. And, Mr. Donae', he's one of the nicest men you'll ever meet. I'm sure he'd like to help you out . . . if he can."

For the second time, Donae' thanked, Mr. and Mrs. Ferguson for their help and made several excuses for not accepting Mary Ellen's dinner

invitation via Mrs. Ferguson last request. But once he closed the door behind him, leaving Mrs. Ferguson and her solicitations, he breathed an unexpected sigh of relief.

Donae' hesitated before he turned left and hurried in the direction
that the Fergusons had indicated the police station was. He was hungry
but decided he'd have breakfast after he talked with Captain Dolton.
Even though his stomach ached with pains of hunger, he was more interested in answers than food.

On the two blocks walk to the station, he noticed most of the towns-
people recognized him as a stranger. All but a few said hello. Donae'
could tell that their eyes were filled with curiosity and not a one tried to
hide their interest. Donae' surmised!. With *this much scrutiny, Brian
should not have been able to get away with much without someone noticing.*

The police station was staffed in one of the town's oldest structures
and the plaque outside its door boasted as much. As soon as he opened
the glass doors, he was surprised to hear all the hullabaloo inside. The
area that surrounded the front desk, which he assumed to be that of the
officer in charge, appeared to be in a confused state. The jollity was loud
as the excitement danced around the room. It was clearly a happy celebration. So not to disturb the fun he did not move into the room. Instead he stood back and watched the commotion.

A short time later he could see that one of the younger officers held a
box of cigars. He was zealously handing each and every person who stood
around him the pink cylinder that held the tobacco.

After a bit Donae' made his way through the group and up to the
desk. Suddenly he was simultaneously slapped on the back and handed a
cigar. He turned to address the perpetrator and was greeted with a bois-
terous, "Hot damn, it's a GIRL! I got me a little granddaughter. Gosh
damn, can you believe it? Johnson, you did good." This came from one
of the older gentlemen.

Donae' smiled obligingly as he eagerly offered the man his hand in
congratulations. Almost instantly someone else pulled the new grandfather around and gave him another hug. Awkwardly, Donae' stood there a
minute before he asked no one in particular, "Is Captain Dolton in? If
so, do you know if he is available?"

The older officer, still chuckling in celebration of his new grand-daughter, twirled around to face him with a merry, "I sure am, mister. What can I do for you?"

Since Donae' thought he finally had Dolton's attention, he hurriedly went directly into an explanation. "Superb, sir. I can see that you are deeply involved right now; however, if you have a minute or two, I need to speak with you privately. It concerns a very old case and could possibly mean the difference between life and death." Donae' started to explain further, but Captain Dolton was again grabbed from behind and turned away by an attractive woman, who also laughed happily as she flirted then teased, "Hey, Grandpapa, come to Grandma. Can you believe our little girl is a Mamma? It makes me wanta cry."

Captain Dolton was again distracted and Donae' realized there was little hope of an answer to his immediate request. Promptly he attempted to shout over the loud group of excited officers who had now become a rowdy mob. "Captain Dolton! Captain!" Once Dolton turned to face Donae', Donae' quickly added, "If it is acceptable, Captain Dolton, I will come back in an hour or so, I really need to speak with you."

The Captain happily shouted, "That would be very much appreci-ated, sir."

The commotion was back in full swing when Donae' shut the door behind him. It was obvious that Captain Dolton had little else on his mind except his granddaughter and that warmed his heart. Family has al-ways been the focal point in Donae's life, and he vowed that will never change.

Once outside Donae' stopped to get his bearings and observed his surroundings before he saw the cafe down the way. Readily he walked across the street to the little diner where he was abruptly greeted by an overly thin waitress who suspiciously asked, "Is it only gonna be you?" Donae' nodded his head and followed the undernourished girl to his seat. She continued to keep her eyes glued on him all the while he drank his first cup of coffee. The coffee was good, although the strongest he had ever tasted. Still, when the waitress brought him his hearty country breakfast, he asked her for another cup. As Corrine (the name printed on her nametag) poured the coffee, she distrustfully asked, "You got jet lag?"

Donae' smiled and again nodded but said nothing since he decided it would not be beneficial to carry on a conversation with the woman. She was much too shy to speak freely and too young to remember much about a murder that had taken place almost twenty years-ago.

An hour later when Donae' returned to the station it looked like everything was back to normal. He could see through the glass door and Captain Dolton was not to be seen, so he assumed he was in his office. The young officer that Donae' had seen earlier and thought looked like Howdy Doody was now busy at his desk. He had to smile at the correlation when the young officer, Frank Collins looked up and said, **"Howdy**, you must be that stranger everybody's talking about. I understand you're here to see the Captain. Cap told me you were coming and said when you got here for you to go right on in." He pointed, then added, "Go right through that door over there."

Donae' entered the office and he could see Captain Dolton was still beaming. Yet, he could further see he was eager to get down to business and suspiciously asked, "Did I understand you, right? Did you say something about an old case I was on? What would a stranger like you have to do with any of my old cases, Mr . . . ?"

"Donae', Lawrence Donae', private investigator from New York." Donae' handed him his credentials and continued, "And the incident I am interested in happened around eighteen or so years ago, the Peterson case. I am primarily interested in Brian Peterson."

Captain Dolton immediately sat straighter in his chair, and by the light in his eyes, it was plain to see that Donae' had hit a nerve; he now had the Captain's full attention. Without delay Captain Dolton snapped, "Okay, I'm listening, but answer me this, what do you have to do with that case? It's been closed now near twenty years, Mr. Donae'."

"Yes, I realized that, sir. However, if you will first let me explain; I am sure you can help me find the answers I am in search of."

After Donae' finished with his account and suspicions about Jennifer and Patty Jean's murders, Captain Dolton stood up and rubbed his seasoned hands through the thickness of his salt-and-peppered mane. After some time, he finally groaned, "Sons of a bitch. I knew it. I always knew he did it. From the very beginning, I knew he had something to do with that fire. But, dammit, I was just a rookie and never could find any real evidence. But as God is my witness, Mr. Donae', I knew he did it. Unfortunately, no one else did, and by and by, my Captain said he didn't want to mess with it anymore. He didn't want to hear any more of my suspicions. He said he wanted the case closed, that he didn't want no open cases on his books. Consequently, he ordered me to clean it up and label the deaths as accidental. I tried to argue that I needed more time, but Harper refused to hear me out. Matter of fact, he not only said it, but he yelled, "Dammit Kent, close it and I mean NOW."

"So, that's what I did, but dammit, I swear I never felt I did those Petersons justice."

"It sounds like you knew Brian personally. What kind of person was he? Had he been in trouble with the police before?"

Captain Dolton studied Donae', then grumbled, "Well, yes, I knew him; we weren't friends or anything. It's just hard not to know someone in a small town. But to tell the truth; I never liked him much, and of course, that was no secret either; everybody knew it. That might have been one reason Captain Harper wouldn't listen to me."

Dolton fell silent and sat back in his chair before he said, "But no, Brian never was in any kind of real trouble before. Just kid stuff, nothing big.

Regardless, I tell you, Mr. Donae' something wasn't right with that kid. I knew it as far back as when he was a kid in junior high school. But I could never put a finger on it. Do you know what I mean? Just something wasn't right."

Donae' nodded and Captain Dolton went on, "Anyhow, Captain Harper reminded me every time I brought up my suspicions that Brian had an alibi. See, Brian said he was with Christine Kelly all night so there wasn't too much more I could do about it, and she did corroborate the alibi."

"Do you believe she was lying?"

"Christine? Naaa, I don't think so. I mean, I knew her parents were away at the time, just like she said, and everyone knew Christine had a thing for Brian, so it was in the realm of feasibility. Plus, earlier that night she had a few friends over for a party. All the kids that attended the party confirmed her story. They said when they left, Brian stayed."

Disappointed, Donae' said, "I see; so why did you think Brian had anything to do with the fire and deaths?"

"I don't know, gut feeling I guess."

"Yes," Donae' agreed. "I know and trust that feeling. Captain Dolton, do you know where Christine is now?"

"Oh, sure, she's married to Kenneth Caplain, a real nice guy; he owns Kenny's Garage on the other side of town. Christine helps out there three or four days a week. If you try right now there's a good chance you could catch her at the garage." Captain Dolton glanced at his watch and then continued, "I would go with you, Mr. Donae', but I gotta go visit my little granddaughter and namesake, Kendra. My daughter decided to name her after me and her, Kent and Sandra. This'll be my first time to see the little angel and I certainly don't want to miss it or disappoint my daughter."

Donae's smile was sincere and he nodded his agreement once again. From the onset of the meeting he could tell that he would like this man. He could see that he was a family man and truly genuine; there was no pretense about him. Donae' reached out and shook Captain Dolton's hand and said, "Congratulations again, sir. I can only imagine your anticipation and I agree you should not miss a single second of this precious time. I thank you for your help, Captain. I will do as you suggest and pay Christine a visit."

Donae' was excited when he headed for Kenny's Garage and Christine. The closer he drove to the address he was given, the stronger his anticipation grew. He had what Kent Dolton had called a gut feeling. This feeling was something he, too, felt was useful and always followed it, and right now his gut was telling him he was headed in the direction of something consequential.

Christine turned out to be a whole lot different than the girl Brian married. She was big boned and was to a large extent on the brassy side. She wore a full head of over-dyed auburn hair which was ratted high on top.

The instant Donae' walked through the door, Christine perked up and smiled widely. She openly looked him up then down, while her eyes paused momentarily where any well-mannered lady should not.

At this time, she commented in a loud, immodest voice. "Well, hot damn, I heard we had a stranger in town." Hungrily, she licked her full red lips and continued, "But I had no idea how scrumptious you'd be. So, tell me, what I can do for you, yummy boy?"

For an instant the hairs stood up on the back of Donae's neck and he had the urge to laugh. At the same time, he had an impulse to suggest that maybe she should avoid watching so much television; then, on the other hand, maybe a simple change in the programs she viewed could help. Whichever, she surely needed to lessen her vamp impersonations, although since he needed Christine's help, he said none of these things. He needed her to like him if he expected to get any helpful information from her. So instead of chastising her, he smiled pleasantly and said, "I can see by the name on your shirt that you are Christine."

Right away Christine leaped at the opportunity to invite a warmer relationship and in an exaggerated, yet seductive, tone she murmured, "You can certainty call me Chrissy, Sweet-cheeks. And ... what might I call you besides Sweet-cheeks?"

Again Donae' wanted to laugh but bit the inside of his cheek and hoped he came across as sincere when he said, "Chrissy; certainly, Chrissy it is. I am Mr. Donae'. A private investigator from New York ..."

Christine interrupted in the middle of his introduction. "Oh, my, what a fancy name and you looking so damn dapper and all, and handsome to boot, I thought you'd be a lawyer or something like that. Well you certainly are something, alright. A private eye, uh?"

Once again, she suggestively licked her lips and asked, "Don't they call you types, private dicks? What would a ..., private dick W*aaant* with lil ole me?" she asked.

Donae' did not acknowledge Christine's risqué remark and resumed "I need to talk with you about an old friend of yours, Brian Peterson."

Suddenly Christine's demeanor changed, and in a bored, distasteful voice she asked, "Brian, uh. So, what's he up ta nowadays? Besides breaking some rich girl's heart. Is her Daddy out to get his ass?"

Again Donae' ignored the question and went directly to the gist of his inquiry. "Christine, what I need from you is to learn everything you remember about the night Brian's parents were killed in the fire. Captain Dolton said Brian spent the evening with you. Still and all, the fire started sometime after one in the morning and I heard your party ended at eleven. More to the point, Christine, I wondered if Brian might have had the opportunity to set the fire."

"Yea, I know a few people suspected him. But Brian was with me at the party and after everyone left, he stayed. We had several more beers and a couple of chasers, then fell asleep on the couch."

"Christine, if you were asleep, how could you tell the police that you were with Brian at the approximate time of the fire? Clearly, if you were sleeping you could not have known if Brian was there or not."

"Yes, I'm sure he was there. Because when I woke up about three in the mornin, he was laying on the floor next to the couch." She giggled. "He was naked as the day he was born, so, see, I know he was there."

"But could he have left while you were asleep, Christine?"

"No! I mean, I would have woken-up if he left. I'm a real light sleeper, Mr. Donae', and I would have woken up. **Besides**, Brian was naked, and he wasn't about to go anywhere naked, now was he? Why, I even had to loan him a pair of my daddy's pants and a shirt the next day."

"Why was that, Christine?"

"Because he went and got sick on his own durin the night and ruined em."

"Christine, are you telling me that you were not awake when Brian got sick? And that you did not wake up until after three in the morning sometime after Brian's bout with sickness and removal of his clothes?"

"Well, no . . . I wasn't with him when he got sick and no, I didn't hear em when he got undressed. But that was no matter, becau . . ."

"Did you hear him get up, when he took his clothes off during the night?"

"Nooo, but . . ."

"But nothing, Christine. I want you to tell me how you knew he had gotten sick if you did not see or hear him."

"Because Brian told me so and that's why his clothes was a mess. He said he even tried to wash them by hand."

"Did you tell this to the police at the time of the investigation?"

"No, nobody ever asked."

"Let me see if I understand you correctly, Christine. You consider yourself a light sleeper?"

"Yea, I do."

"Again, Christine, do you consider yourself a light sleeper after you have had a couple or more beers, plus several shooters? And can you honestly swear under oath that Brian was there with you, **all night long?**"

"Mr. Donae', you can't be sayin what I think you're sayin. Because you don't know Brian; he was all broken-up over his parents' death. That's the main reason he left town and joined the Marines, so he could get away from all the bad memories and pain. It was plainer than day to see he took the loss real hard. Why, after that night, he was never the same person."

"How do you mean, Christine?"

"Well . . . well, he just wasn't, that's all."

"Christine, did Brian ask you to cover for him that night?"

'No! No, he didn't need to, Mr. Donae'. After-all, I was his girl and he was with me; there never was any question about it. He was with me and that's the truth and even if he wasn't, I trusted him. And if he told me he didn't do it, then he didn't do it."

"Christine, did Brian ever promise to marry you? Were you upset when he left town? And did he tell you that he would come back for you one day?"

"No, no, no. Mr. Donae', I knew what I was to Brian, and I wasn't his marrying kind. It was plain to see he was better than me. Most all the girls in this town liked him. I mean, he could've married just about any one of them, me included, but he wasn't interested. He set his sights way higher than any of us. He said he was gonna marry a rich lady someday and knowing, Brian, he would, too."

"Money was that important to him?"

Christine's face changed from the stressed expression to a disheartened look when she answered, "Yea, and it always was. It was all he really

ever wanted to talk about. Money and being important, that was Brian."
She perked up some when she added, "Brian wasn't being mean, Mr.
Donae'. He just had big dreams, that's all. He said time after time that he
was gonna be rich someday. No matter what it took, he was determined
to be better than he was. His favorite line was . . . ,"

Suddenly Christine's voice deepened as she attempted to imitate
Brian's. "I have no intention of being stuck in this one-horse town." She
laughed before she continued in the same voice, "I'm not going to work
my ass off for some nickel and dime company in some knit-shitten job."
In her regular voice, she finished, "That was his very words. That's why I
knew he'd never marry me, since I had no more than what he already
had. Nothing."

"For that reason, you never hoped he would come back for you. Is
that why you said you didn't feel the need to protect him?"

"No, no, that's not it at all. Sure, deep down I always hoped he would
come back for me especially right after he first left town, but he never
even wrote me a letter. I wrote him a dozen or more times before it finally
sank in. I was angry at first; then I guess you could say I grasped the
truth. Brian never promised me nothing, and that's what I got. So, it was
my own fault I got hurt. I was stupid for hoping. And, as for protecting
him, Mr. Donae', like I said before, there was never no need for me to,
because Brian didn't do nothing wrong. All he ever wanted was better
than he had and that ain't no crime."

Donae' smiled at Christine's goodhearted declaration. At the same
time, he came to the conclusion that she to her knowledge, was being
completely honest; she was not attempting to hide anything from him.
As far as she knew this was the whole truth. If Brian had slipped out of
the house that night, she was completely unaware of it.

After hearing Christine's summation, Donae' felt sympathy for her.
He now realized that she held little self-esteem. He suspected because of
her impulsive nature and beguiling innocence she had perfected herself
to be exactly what she determined most others perceived her to be. That
would easily explain her charade as a strumpet. With Christine's lack of
sophistication, she would be easy to exploit, a perfect pawn and alibi for
someone like Brian.

Donae' started to thank Christine for her time when the door flew open and a huge man walked in. Donae' noted immediately that the nametag attached neatly above the pocket of his shirt informed the world that he was Kenny, of Kenny's Garage.

Donae' eyes moved to take in the full scope of the man and a comparison immediately popped into his head, "Big John, Big Bad John," which Donae' recalled were the words from an old country tune he liked. In contrast to Kenny's huge burliness were his eyes; they were as tender as he was big. And the instant his eyes caught sight of Christine, they displayed complete and unconditional love for the woman. It was evident that he saw what few others had not taken the time to notice, Kenny knew there was a lot more to Christine than a shallow, brazen hussy. Sure, she was unrefined, but a warm-hearted lady all the same.

Kenny walked over to stand where his wife was and gave her a well-mannered hug, then introduced himself to Donae'. Afterward, he politely said, "I hope Chrissy has taken care of everything you needed, sir."

Donae' smiled over to where Christine still stood. She was leaning against the counter grinning up at her husband. She, too, was obviously in love and Donae' immediately smiled at his own gullibility. He himself had taken her at face value and fallen for her sultry act. He smiled at Kenny and answered his question, "Yes sir, I would say she indeed has. As a matter of fact, she has been far more helpful than she may realize." Again Donae' glanced over to where Christine stood. Her expression had changed and now she wore a puzzled look; she was detecting a new respect in Donae's voice and could not imagine why it was there. She wondered; *Did he mean about the information I gave him?* This was baffling, since she didn't see where her facts were any more helpful today than they were eighteen years ago, but, all in all, she always appreciated a compliment, so she giggled and threw an obliged grin his way.

Donae' tipped an imaginary hat and said, "Thank you again, Mrs. Caplain, for all your help and good-afternoon to you both of you."

When Donae' closed the door, he turned to get a last glimpse of Christine and Kenny. Christine's face still wore a slight inquisitive grin as they stared back at him, and again, he snickered at his own naïveté.

Kenny and Christine turned to face each other, and when their eyes locked, he turned and hurried back to his car. After a few steps his un-controlled excitement burst forward, and he quickened his steps a notch.

Unknowingly, Christine had protected Brian all these years. What was it she said? "Oh yes, *nobody ever asked.*" At the time Kent Dolton was too inexperienced to ask the right questions or to read between the lines . . . . if he had, would Captain Harper have listened. Probably not, he simply wanted to close the case, thus relieving Brian of any accusation and richer to boot.

Donae' recalled the look of doubt on Christine's face. She was con-fused on how her information had helped, but she was tickled it had. For an instant he also pictured Kenny's adoration for Christine and thought, *I am glad things worked out for her.*

He was sure Christine had no idea how much better off she was with-out Brian in her life. But, from the look on her face he would guess, the loss of Brian no longer mattered. "[*Love is grand, when you find the right person.]*" was his sister Sharon's eternal allegation. Well, it seemed he had just seen living proof of that hypothesis. "Yes, little sister, I would have to say, you are wise beyond your years."

The next day when Donae' was ready to leave the little town of Hur-ley, he felt that he had accomplished more than he had thought he would. At this point, he felt he was ready to face Brian Peterson and his allegedly precarious personality. He was convinced that with what he had learned in Hurley he would now be more readily able to read Brian's idiosyncrasies. Now that he had a deeper capricious understanding of what Brian was capable of and how manipulative he could be, he could see where Gerimee had reached his conjectures, whereas before he was not completely convinced that the vision he or Addison Hobart had painted for him was completely factual and truly the whole picture.

From the beginning Donae' had his doubts and thought that their image had been slightly tainted with revenge, resentment and remorse, but now for the first time he could accept their assessment without mis-trust and accede that Brain has narcissistic tendencies. '*As well,*' he thought, '*I can now admit that the young Brian was as intelligent, calcu-lating, and decisive as the Brian of today is.*'

Brian had known then and evidently now what kind of personality he possesses. Unfortunately, he also knows how to cover his tracks and always . . . to his advantage. In fact, it looked as if Jennifer Hobart was merely part of Brian's initial overall plan. Brian had known exactly what he was after when he met Jennifer and Gerimee. Yes, Jennifer was his rich girl and her beauty and celebrity status was an added plus. With Jennifer, Brian had hit the jackpot. *So why kill her?* The insurance and inheritance were immense. But did Brian desire wealth to the degree that he would take his own innocent wife and child down to reach his avaricious goals? Unfortunately, with the questionable deaths of his adoptive parents . . . this was a cataclysmic possibility. Donae' speculated, "At least I may be one step closer to an answer."

# CHAPTER 8

B efore Donae' boarded the plane for home he called Brian's office to make an appointment. The secretary assured Donae' that the earliest date was one week from the day. He diligently informed the secretary, "My family is in search of a new Certified Public Accountant to handle our financial circumstances. Unfortunately, I have been chosen to do the leg work and I will be interviewing several firms next week. Thus far, Friday is already nearly booked. Are you sure we cannot make it this Thursday?"

Donae' knew Brian was in high demand, per Gerimee, so he feared he might not easily get an appointment. Though now that he had been assured a time slot, he decided to be pretentious. Since he assumed Brian would know the family name and affluence he intended to be as haughty and difficult as possible so as to get his attention. This ruse was primarily since Addison said Brian most naturally would not take a new client unless he thought this person would bring him not only monetary advantage but publicity, as well.

Donae' knew his surname would fit this prerequisite. Yet, since he also discovered Brian was extremely attracted to extravagance, he added a tone of snobbery to his voice when he clarified, "A friend from Hyannis Port mentioned your firm and Mr. Peterson; I hear he has become familiar with managing businesses of our caliber, although it was suggested he might be overburdened with accounts. Nonetheless, I have no doubt that after we meet his monetary demands, he will be quite interested in representing a family of our notability."

Donae' felt uncomfortable coming across as pompous and affluent, but he knew this was what Brian would expect of a person of his standing and this assessment would be passed along to Brian, along with the appointment time scheduled.

Donae' heard the first call to board the plane and quickly dialed Silvia to let her know he was on his way back to New York. Silvia immediately became overly excited when she heard his voice and grew more so when she started to tell him about the news, she had received from the adoption courts. Her enthusiastic voice carried loudly over the phone lines. "Mr. Donae', you will not believe this; someone else had tried to find Brian Peterson. The court had been petitioned for his adoptive parents' name and address. Do you think it could have been his biological parents? Oh, this is going to be much easier than I first thought or maybe I'm just good at this," she added immodestly. "Anyway, Janet Cumbers, from the courthouse, is sending me some more information she found. It should be here sometime next week. Oh, and you received a call from Sergeant Cox. Boy, does he sound big. In any case, he said he would try to reach you again next week. Then Gerimee called. He wants you to call him as soon as you get back. Also, someone named Sidney sent you flowers. The note reads, 'Thank you for dinner last night. Sorry you had to leave so early; hope your business trip went well. Please call. Love Sidney' .... Who's Sidney?"

Donae' politely waited until Silvia finished her verbal effusion and then said, "Silvia, my dear, I believe you may be drinking entirely too much coffee for your own good. At any rate, you definitely need to take heed to what Sir Ralph Richardson once said, and I quote, "The most precious things in speech are pauses."

Silvia immediately burst into her usual hearty laugh and replied, "I'm sorry, Mr. Donae'. I know sometimes I get pretty mouthy, but I've been so excited, and I didn't have anyone to tell. That is, until you called, but anyway who's Sidney?"

"Silvia, your excitement is entirely permissible and most appropriately earned, although I still have a fraction of concern about your excessive coffee habits, which we will discuss at a later date. I would hate to see my amateur sleuth become physically disabled by a tongue lash, due wholly to the fact that she was hyped-up on caffeine. Furthermore, Silvia, my dear, you should not be reading my cards."

Laughing cheerfully, she asked, "When will you be in the office Mr. Donae? I missed you. Lately, you've been away more than you've been here."

"I will be in the office tomorrow at around eight o'clock. And ... I do not want to see you there, Missy. You have been working entirely too many Saturdays and I will not have it. In regard to everything I have learned in Hurley, I can most assuredly fill you in on Monday."

Donae' heard the last boarding call and hurriedly concluded, "Oh, and before I go will you please enter an appointment for me, for next Friday at two-thirty. I will be meeting with Brian at his Manhattan office, and also, while you are at it, please call Mitch Hauser and ask him to join me for the appointment. Tell him that I will call him Monday to fill in the details and let him know that I will need him on this case. Silvia ... you have a good weekend and by no means do you open a file or work on this or any other case. Do you hear me, young lady?"

"Sure thing, Mr. Donae'. Consider it done, and you have a nice weekend as well." Playing matchmaker again, Silvia slipped in a quick, "And call Patricia. You've been neglecting her way too much lately. See you Monday, Mr. Donae'."

Donae' laughed at Silvia's efforts as he placed his long narrow frame into his first-class seat. It was obvious she was worried that Sidney might be competition for Patricia. He smiled as he thought, *No one could be competition for Patricia.*

The conversation Donae' had with Silvia had relieved him of his earlier focus and momentarily his mind moved away from Brian. He decided; *She is good at diverting my thoughts, at the right time."*

Silvia had been working with Donae' for about seven years. He had admitted to himself long ago that he would not want to work without her. She had been his third hand more often than not. Completely thorough; that is how he described her. For each project he had ever assigned her was an endeavor she relished. He thought, S*he, is indispensable and an essential part of my proficiency and she knows this, as well as I do.* For a fleeting second her image emerged, and he thought, *I know so little about her personally.* In fact, if he was asked, he would have to say he did not even know her true age. He presumed her to be around thirty-five or so. But that was just a guess; she is so high-spirited and energetic it is hard to tell. It was no secret she came to New York from Argentina and that she lived with a distant relative while she finished her education. At that time, she decided to stay in America, New York specifically. He thought she mentioned once that she made that decision about fifteen years ago; that is how he concluded she was about thirty-five-ish.

Donae' shifted in his seat and pulled the plastic shade to block the sun. He closed his eyes and leaned against the back of the seat as he recalled when he first met Silvia. She had told him she was married for a brief period to a young military officer who died in the war. He remembered when she disclosed this private side of her life, she was very uncomfortable, and he saw the pain that filled her eyes. At that time, she also professed that she would never marry again. And to this day Silvia still lives alone in a large, modern apartment with a silly-looking cat named Six Toes, for which the name was evident.

Donae' guessed that with the multitude of friends Silvia had, she was rarely lonely. Even with denying herself a love interest, she seemed extremely happy. As she so often professed, "Six Toes is the only man I need in my life." Donae' chuckled inwardly as he pictured the cat framed on her desk at work. It is completely black, lengthy and straggly with feet twice the size of any normal cat and a tail as long as its body. His face is thin and awkwardly shaped, accompanied with two large protruding eyeteeth and a pair of yellow eyes that always held an extreme amount of mischief. Donae' smiled to himself. Yes, he decided, she is happy in her life, but I must make a mental note to learn more about her.

"Can I bring you something, Mr. Donae'?" The stewardess's voice interrupted his thoughts. Donae' nodded and said, "Yes, please, a scotch sounds good." Immediately after ordering his mind drifted back to Brian, and after he thanked the stewardess for the cocktail, he determined that he should check with the airlines. Brian would have flown to his destination the night Jennifer and Patty Jean were murdered. *Maybe*, he thought, *if I am lucky, I can find a loose end there.*

The next day was Saturday. Still, Donae' was in the office early; he wanted to check and see which airline Brian had flown the night he went to Washington. This information would surely be in his copy of the police report.

Once he retrieved the information, Donae' dialed the airline Brian had named in the report. The gentleman he was finally connected with said his name was Mr. Andrew Ruysky and immediately informed Donae', "All I can do for you right now is to take the information that you have. The first thing I need to do is to confirm that Mr. Peterson was on the roster. And I don't keep the flight lists in my office, and I don't have the time to track it down right now. I'll have to research it later when it is less hectic. Saturdays, Mr. Donae', are always crazy around here."

Donae' countered, "I fully understand and later will do just fine." Then he asked, "Mr. Ruysky, is it also possible for you pull the name of the stewardess that hosted that flight? I would really like to speak with her."

Mr. Ruysky came across as friendly, though his temperament was of an overly busy person, and he confirmed this when he sharply clarified, "I can do both, but, like I said I need some time. Why don't you give me until Tuesday, or better yet make it Wednesday? By that time if you give me a call, I can let you know exactly what I've found."

After Donae' hung up, he checked his watch before he involved himself further. He was not running late. He had plenty of time before he was due to pick Patricia Woodts up. They had set up an afternoon date, but it was not until two-thirty. Prior to that, he was supposed to meet Gerimee for a game of tennis, although that, too, was later, not until ten-thirty. Thus, he had the time he needed to stop by the police station and talk with Detective Lauwdry in homicide.

Lauwdry was one of the investigating officers who worked on the Peterson case. Donae' had known Detective Frank Lauwdry for years now. Sadly, the detective was never one of his favorite people. As far as he could tell, Lauwdry was and always had been a sloppy detective. He of-

ten failed to check all leads and more than once he had overlooked criti-
cal evidence, which had helped botch a conviction. This Donae' had witnessed himself firsthand.

Anyone in law knew what sloppy investigation could do to a case, yet,
this fact continued to elude Lauwdry. What is more distressing, due to
just such sloppiness; more times than Donae' would like to disclose, the
guilty party walked away without punishment. Unfortunately, many of
these cases had Lauwdry's name at the top of the final report.

Not long after Donae' had first met Lauwdry, the detective made the
mistake of bad-mouthing Mitch Hauser. For Lauwdry, this was a nasty
trait that Donae' had seen often enough to be aware of. Yet, this time
Donae' refused to stand by and say nothing, considering Mitch, before
he was forced into early retirement, had been ten times the cop Lauwdry
could ever be, a fact that Donae' immediately educated Lauwdry of.
Thus, after this incident the open animosity between the two had heightened and still continued to this day.

*However,* thought Donae', *I have to admit, Lauwdry in his own way is
very dedicated to the department. And, if I take that into consideration, I
can be sure he will be in the office this morning, Saturday or not."*

Donae' quickened his pace, so he would have time to speak with
Lauwdry before he and Gerimee's ten-thirty tennis match.

Thirty minutes later Donae' walked into Lauwdry's upstairs office.
The first words that flew out of the Detective's unshaven face were,
"God damn, if it ain't that rich boy. Hey, Mr. Capitalist, whatcha doin in
these parts and on a Saturday no less? Are you slumin it? Or maybe
someone finally got smart and called you in to take away your P.I. license. It seems that that is the least we can do for the public."

"Well, doing your least for the public is what you do best Lauwdry,"
quipped Donae'

"Oh, a funny man, real funny Donae'. So, one more time, whatcha
doin down here and where's your fucken black shadow?"

This was Lauwdry's nickname for Mitch. The remark was intended
in a derogatory manner to point out that Mitch is black and that he is
Donae's back-up. Lauwdry had a problem with most ethnic groups,

which Donae' liked to chalk up to his cretin mentality. And this was the main reason Donae' disliked him so much.

"It seems to me, rich boy, if I had half the money you had, I certainly wouldn't be hangin around here on no fucken weekend."

Grinning, Donae' retorted, "You see, detective, that is where you and I differ. Because I can not see you anywhere else except here on a Saturday morning."

"Ouch! I can see you're in your usual mood. So, what do ya want, Donae'? Why are ya down here harassin good cops? Don't you rich boys have country club things to do on the weekends?"

"For one thing, Lauwdry," said Donae', "as of yet I have not run into a good cop. And secondly, what you know about a country club would fill a pinhole. And thirdly, and most importantly, I need information on the Peterson case, Jennifer and Patty Jean Peterson."

"Oh, yea, Donae', you're in rare form today, and what the hell do you have to do with the Peterson case? It's not that crazy old man of hers again, is it? Fuck, he's just another damn rich boy who thinks he can tell us how to do our jobs. Well, you tell him we're doing the best we can to find the bastard who killed that little girl and her mother."

"I am sure he realizes that, Lauwdry. But you do have to admit, it never hurts to have a back-up plan, right? All I am asking is for a few minutes of your time, along with a couple answers, okay?"

"Like what? You know we can't tell ya what we've got so far. All evidence on the case has been catalogued and that's classified information."

"Come on now, Lauwdry, you know as well as I do, I already have most of that information. I merely need to hear what you think. I need to hear what conclusions the experts came up with."

The flattery caught Lauwdry off guard and he asked in a suspicious tone, "What kind of conclusions are ya talkin about?"

"Well . . . to start with, I know you would have checked the husband out first thing. So, what did you think? Is he a suspect or is he clear of suspicion?"

"He wasn't even in town and besides, everyone said they were happily married, and even if they weren't, he wouldn't kill his own kid just ta get away from the fucken marriage. Anyway, like I said he was miles away and has an alibi."

"Did you know there were substantial insurance policies on both victims?"

"Yeah, the husband told us, but the wife was the one who took those out, not the husband. I guess she was a little daffy about security."

Donae' knew better than this but decided not to share the information with the detective. Knowing Lauwdry, Donae' was pretty sure he would simply cast the information aside without a minute's review. Lauwdry never was very open to new speculation and usually wanted to stay within his original conclusions. Donae' was well aware that this was not conducive to good, thorough investigating, but as far as Lauwdry goes, he rarely went beyond the surface in any case.

"Well, Lauwdry, can I count on you to . . ."

At this instant Donae' was interrupted when Detective Sandy Bronson burst into the room. Lauwdry started to add something to what he had just said, then recognized the urgency that covered Sandy's face and stopped. Sandy spoke in rapid procession, "Hi Donae'. By the way, how's that gorgeous secretary of yours? Lauwdry, grab your gear, we're out of here. Big shooting on Barker Street. One suspect down. Snap to it, SWAT'S on its way."

The detectives scrambled around the room, each grabbing a few essentials and both shouting at the same time, "So long rich boy."

"Bye Donae', give Silvia my regards," as they rushed from the room.

Donae' waved at Sandy and thought: *Poor guy, he really has a thing for Silvia.*

Recently Sandy and Silvia had started to date, not often, just here and there. But, so far not too much has come of it. Silvia said she had already lost one husband in battle and was not about to go through that again by becoming involved with a cop.

Donae' guessed she was right, because he knew as well as she that a relationship with a cop, whose life lay on the line daily, often meant heartache. Still, he was sure Silvia cared for Sandy. He could see the excitement in her eyes, every time Sandy entered the office, but so far, she has not relinquished her protective armor. Maybe one day Sandy would have a chance to help her overcome her fears.

Donae' stood outside the police station evaluating his next move. He did not get the information that he anticipated he would; therefore, he would have to call and make an appointment to talk with both detectives. He especially wanted to talk with Sandy. He respected and trusted his educated speculation.

Sandy Bronson was relatively new as a homicide detective, barely two years. However, Donae' had known him for about two years prior to his promotion. Sandy, in all, had been with the force about ten years. Most of those years were spent on a beat before he was promoted to detective and assigned to homicide. It was about the same time Lauwdry's partner retired from the force, so the captain appointed Sandy to be his new partner.

From the beginning, Donae' felt that this was unfortunate for the new homicide detective, Alisander Bronson, known to most as Sandy, whereas, it was probably the best thing that had ever happened to Detective Lauwdry.

Donae' had always thought anyone who got stuck with Lauwdry as a partner would definitely be at a disadvantage, since he suspected his cases have far too many blunders not to be noticed. He hoped it wouldn't impair Sandy's career in any way. Donae' was sure the hierarchy had to be aware of Lauwdry's inept performances, but, for some reason, they choose to remain mute and apparently viewed him with a blind eye. Donae' had a theory that someone for years, had been covering for the detective. Why, he could not guess.

# CHAPTER 9

Monday morning Donae' was in the office way before his normal eight o'clock. And when Silvia came in, he was already on the phone with the hotel Brian had said he had stayed the night of the murders.

Mr. Banks, the night manager, was still on duty. Mrs. Gage, the day manager, had not arrived to begin her shift. Donae' explained that he wanted to speak with the manager or managers that worked on the date of September twenty-ninth, nineteen-sixty." He added, "I need information on a guest named Brian Peterson; he stayed at the hotel that night. I am not sure if I need to speak with the day or night manager."

Mr. Banks, with whom Donae' was speaking, immediately knew exactly what day he was referring to and simplified everything. "Either of us can help you with that, sir. Are you with a newspaper, Mr. Donae'? We had every newspaper in town in here at the time of the murders, but none recently. Has there been a break in the case? Is that why the papers are interested again?"

"No, Mr. Banks, I am not a journalist. I am a private investigator and you say either of you can help me?"

"Yes... since Mr. Peterson checked in that afternoon when Mrs. Gage was on duty. And then I took over later that evening. I, too, spoke with Mr. Peterson briefly. He called and asked me to make him a dinner reservation at Percy's."

"Percy?" repeated Donae'.

"Yes, Percy's Restaurant. He wanted the latest dinner seating available."

Donae' considered the self-importance he heard in Mr. Bank's voice. He sounded like a celebrity who wanted his credit noted. With that in mind he moved on realizing, he may be inclined to embellish the truth a bit.

Mr. Banks continued, "Mr. Peterson said he had a cold and wanted to lie down and rest before dinner. That's why he asked me to make the seating as late as possible. Mr. Donae', he was in such bad shape; his cold sounded awful. His throat was all raspy and you could hardly understand what he said. You even had to strain to hear him at times, the poor man was so weak."

"Mr. Banks, did you see him leave for Percy's?"

"No, I didn't. But, Mr. Dirkenson, our hotel general manager did, and he said so to the police when they called."

"Did anyone see him return from dinner that night?"

"Oh yes, sir, I did, and so did the bellboy."

"How did you know it was, Mr. Peterson? Would you know him by sight?"

"Well, of course I would, Mr. Donae'."

"Mr. Peterson had been one of our regular guests for several years. At the time, he would come in about every three to five weeks, and always stayed for several days, except for that visit of course, which was only for one night. But... yes, everyone at the hotel knew Mr. Peterson. He was known as a difficult guest and somewhat unpleasant. Yet he was especially generous with the staff he liked, which does tend to stick in one's memory."

"Yes, I understand. Did you happen to see Mr. Peterson leave the hotel after the police talked with him, Mr. Banks?"

"Why, yes, yes, I did, but he didn't stop at the front desk to check out. He was quite upset. Poor fellow, couldn't get out of here and home fast enough."

"Mr. Banks, you said Mr. Peterson *visited* your hotel regularly. Do you know if he was in town on company business or was it personal?"

"I can only assume it was business, Mr. Donae', although I never asked, and he never offered that fact. But I did notice he seemed to put in extremely long hours, so that's why I assumed it was business, although the gentleman that always picked him up may have attributed to those late hours. You know men out on the town, and such. Anyway, I say visited, because Mr. Peterson no longer frequents our establishment. Not since the murders has, he been back."

That afternoon Donae' filled Silvia in on all that he had learned about Brian and his life in Hurley; then he called Mitch. And rendered the same information he had provided Silvia minutes before. "So now, my friend, I meet with Brian on Friday, at which time I hope to evaluate his personality. With a bit of luck, I can see for myself what type of traits he harbors. And . . . if he is indeed capable of what we all suspect him of. This is, of course, why I want you at my side, Mr. Hauser."

Mitch Hauser's background included several years as an orderly in a mental hospital while he worked his way through college. This was the first reason he and Donae' became friends. They both trifled in mental disorders. Although Donae's participation was of a more formal mode, he nonetheless trusted and respected Mitch's ability to recognize anomaly. In this particular circumstance he was hoping that together they could identify any signs Brian might unconsciously exhibit, thus betraying his cover.

"Mitch," Donae' ended his summation, "I know you will be extremely helpful in this evaluation; together I believe we can certainly ascertain if Brain has narcissistic tendencies or not."

Mitch humbly agreed, "Especially since my assessment will come from the gut and yours from an educated vantage."

"So, you are in?" asked Donae'.

"You know you can always count on me, Donae'. So, what's the plan? Am I your bodyguard or what?"

"Actually, you are going to be my secretary."

"Whoa! That's a new twist for me. I'm telling ya right up front. I don't sit on laps and I don't do anything kinky."

"Funny, Mitch: I can assure you you are safe with me, and if you don't believe me just ask Silvia. Never once have I misbehaved, and she is definitely a lot prettier than you, my friend. Besides, you are much too awkward for my taste, so for that reason alone you can comfortably let your guard down."

Mitch laughed at the ridiculous picture that they had conjured up. Then quickly he moved back to their prior business and a more serious tone. "Well, lets' devise a solid plan for this upcoming performance. If Brian is as smart as Gerimee believes he is, then he won't easily be fooled by any half-assed show."

"That may be true, Mitch, but then we have the element of surprise on our side, considering up to this point Brian has no idea we are investigating him. For that reason, I expect his guard will be completely lax. Therefore, he will accept us at face value and hopefully speak more freely."

It was late Tuesday when Silvia rushed into Donae's office. She was bursting with excitement and enthusiastically she thrust a handful of papers and an envelope towards him. Momentarily, she stopped while she attempted to catch her breath, then rapidly announced, "This is it. This is what Janet sent me from the courthouse. I can hardly wait to see what's in here. I didn't expect it to come so fast. This may really be helpful, Mr. Donae'. I mean, maybe we can find out what kind of family Brian came from."

Silvia impatiently watched as Donae' opened the envelope and begin to read. He studied the paperwork for several minutes without comment. Finally, Silvia yelped, "Well! Tell me, is it good?"

Donae' raised his hand slightly to let her know he was still interpreting the writ. Disappointed, she plopped herself heavily onto the chair in front of his desk and waited quietly until he was ready.

Donae' noticed a family member had attempted to find Brian, right after he was adopted. But since the adoption was already final, all information as per the law at that time, was sealed and unattainable. Now, with the new adoption laws, the seal on old adoptions has been reversed and information released to just about anyone who has requested it. He deemed: *The new change has allowed many adopted children to attain a copy of their original birth certificates, thus, obtaining the names of their biological parents. Biological parents were, as well, free to attain information on the adoptive parents and their child's new identity. Intriguing to say the least.*

Donae' read further. The person who had requested the information originally was the biological father, Harry Van Murck. After notification that the files were sealed then all contact had ceased. Years later when the courts had notified him that the information was now available, someone wrote back and informed the courts that Mr. Van Murck was deceased. This was several years ago. Since then, no new request had been added to the file.

Donae' was dissatisfied with what little information the documents contained. Disheartened, he released a deep breath and read out loud what he had just reviewed. Silvia could see his disappointment and jumped in, "But there's more, Mr. Donae'." She pulled one more sheet of paper from another envelope and shoved it towards him and announced, "See. Janet, sent this separately because she didn't want it to be lost in the stack of adoption papers."

Quickly he read it, then said, "This is certainly good news." Suddenly, he lost all control and gave a loud Bronx-cheer, then added happily, "Silvia, I absolutely adore you."

Silvia promptly laughed with pleasure as she excitedly replied, "I thought you might, Mr. Donae', and I would like you to keep that in mind the next time I ask for a raise."

Donae' was already re-reading the document and absentmindedly answered, "Indeed, indeed I will. Anything you want is yours." A minute later he whispered, "Damn . . . this is too good to be true." Then he grabbed for the phone as he said, "I have to talk with Mitch right away."

When Donae' finally tracked Mitch down, he practically spurted into the phone, "Plans for Friday have now changed. Mitch, you are going to be out of town, and you have to leave right away."

"So, you're going to meet with Brian alone? Damn, I hope wherever you're sending me is going to be as much fun. Can I ask where I'm going?

"Windy City . . . my friend . . . Windy City. Can we meet, I need to show you something and fill you in?"

Donae' knew the change in plans was not the ideal situation; it would have been a tremendous help if Mitch could have attended the meeting with Brian. But, right now, going to Chicago was of the utmost importance and might very well be the key to solving this puzzle.

The next day before Donae' had time to call Mr. Ruysky at the airlines, he received a message that Ruysky had called while he was out and asked if he could return his call. Once he returned his call, Mr. Ruysky told Donae', "I can't see you today, but you can pick up the information you requested tomorrow at three o'clock, although before I can release that information, I'll need to see your credentials, so please bring a picture I.D. and your license."

Donae' assured him he would have all necessary identification with him.

"Very good Mr. Donae'. Sorry for the inconvenience, but this is required whenever we release any data to anyone other than another employee. If the F.A.A. ever got wind that I didn't ask for proper identification . . . , well, I'm sure you understand."

Before Donae' hung up he reassured Mr. Ruysky that he would have all the proper Identification and that he certainly supported the process and requirements of the Federal Aviation Administration.

At this point he noticed another message on his desk. He could see it was from Sergeant Cox. Hurriedly he said his goodbye and eagerly scooped up the message. It said Sergeant Cox wanted to meet with him next week, that he would be in town the entire week and to call him at the Holiday Inn. Then he would let him know when he would be free to see him. "Perfect," mumbled Donae' . . . ., "Perfect."

# CHAPTER 10

D onae' was early for his appointment with Mr. Ruysky; he hoped to get the information and get out of the airport before the heavy business traffic began. Mr. Ruysky, on the other hand, had different ideas and made them clearly understood when he said, "Mr. Donae', sit and make yourself comfortable, because I have several duties that need my attention before I have time to spare." Respectfully, Donae' nodded and did as he was ordered.

Mr. Ruysky, who was a skinny man of about fifty, came across as unassuming, but Donae' could tell he was very secure in his position with the airlines. He had very little left of his dark brown hair, which was a contrast to his smile and face, both revealed a happy and youthful looking man. However, soon Donae' understood why he was so thin. The man continually moved around the room, which, Donae' decided, dispersed vast amounts of nervous energy, along with as many calories. He could also see that Mr. Ruysky was lonely; he had no other offices near his and was noticeably isolated. Donae' wondered if he had any foot-traffic. If not, he would be deprived of normal chitchat throughout the entire day. With this thought in mind, Donae' braced himself for a longer visit.

Donae' continued to sit in silence while he observed Mr. Ruysky's office. It was roomy, nonetheless cluttered and messy, and displayed several pictures of which Donae' assumed was his wife and children. His guess was soon verified when Mr. Ruysky noticed Donae observing the portraits and moved his chair to sit across from him as he boasted, "This here is my beautiful wife, Peggy. We were high school sweethearts; she is my one and only. This one is our son, Charles. He entered NYU last year and here is our lovely daughter, Nancy. She's a junior in high school and the spitting image of her mother; don't you agree, Mr. Donae'?" Mr. Ruysky opened his arms to acknowledge all the photos as he said, "I'm very proud of them as you can probably tell. You know, teenagers aren't as bad as people say, we really enjoy ours. And we haven't had a bit of trouble with either. Course, Nancy hasn't started dating yet, but that's another story."

Donae' smiled and replied; "You most certainly should be proud, Mr. Ruysky." While his mind unveiled an image of Jennifer and Patty Jean, he expressed, "Yes, a wise man enjoys his family; life with them is extremely precious and passes quickly."

Andrew Ruysky answered with a laugh. "Yes, I can attest to that. They do have a fondness for growing up, don't they?"

Donae' nodded and once Mr. Ruysky was satisfied with Donae's papers, he began to look at the information that Mr. Ruysky had just handed him. Afterward he asked, "Do you think I can speak with the stewardess you have listed here on the roster, Barbara Baxter?"

"I don't see why not; I will have to check out when she will be in town and available, but I don't foresee any problems. Suddenly, Donae' stopped . . . his eyes locked on a specific piece of information and after he studied it, he asked, "Mr. Ruysky, are you entirely sure about the accuracy of this information?"

Andrew Ruysky sat up straight to show his confidence when he answered, "Well, Mr. Donae', I'm as sure as anyone could be. Why, what seems to be the problem?"

Donae' pointed at the booking date. "Well, looking here, Mr. Ruysky, it shows the date of September Eleventh."

"Yes, I see that. So, why would that be a problem? Our data is most of the time extremely accurate, Mr. Donae'. But, if you see something wrong with it, let me know. I can always recheck it."

Donae' lingered while he tried to recall the facts, he had read in the police file he had. He wished he would have at least brought his case file so he could go over his notes, although he was pretty sure Addison and the police report said that Brian had been called out of town *suddenly*. It was not a planned trip.

"Is there any way we can recheck the information here and now, to make sure the booking date is correct?"

Mr. Ruysky took the data sheet from Donae's hand and looked at another area on the paper, then said, "I don't think that'll be any problem at all, Mr. Donae'. It looks like our Mr. Peterson paid for the ticket by credit card. If you want to wait a few minutes, I should be able to get the information from Fran in accounting. While I'm at it, I can also check with Horace Taylor. He'll know when Barbara Baxter will be available for you to speak with."

"Excellent, Mr. Ruysky, and I will wait as long as it takes. I appreciate your cooperation."

His eyes sparkled when he smiled and said, "Call me Andy; most people do, Mr. Donae'." Andy grabbed the data sheet and headed for the door as he stated, "Please make yourself comfortable. There's coffee over there on the credenza and I'll be back as soon as I can."

Donae' could see that Andy's disposition had now changed. He was beginning to feel a moral responsibility and was eager to do what he could to help solve the old crime. His eagerness, Donae' decided, was refreshing. As of late he had noticed that this was a more common reaction. He thought: *this new enthusiasm, I must be attribute to Sean Connery and his new movie. The public has gone mad over the character he plays, a distinguished maverick called James Bond, 007."* Donae' laughed as he admitted since its release it had made his job much easier.

It was approximately thirty-five minutes later when Andy excitedly marched back into his office. A pretty blond lady around twenty-five to thirty years of age walked next to him. She was easily a half foot taller than Andy and it was apparent that she felt a good deal of self-confidence. Donae' could establish this in the way she squarely carried herself.

As soon as Andy entered the room, he immediately handed Donae' a slip of paper. At the same time, he said, "See, it's been verified; the information I gave you was correct. Here, this is when it was booked. And look," he indicated a section highlighted and circled in red, "it even tells you by whom. Which, if you notice, Mr. Donae', was Mr. Peterson himself." Proudly, Andy announced, "We even have the date we billed the credit card company, plus when the credit card company paid it." Andy stood there a pinnacle of pride, while Donae' read the information. All of a sudden Andy remembered he wasn't alone and quickly explained. "Oh, Mr. Donae', let me introduce you to Barbara Baxter. Many of the stewardesses are not flying today; they are here attending a safety class. I can only say you are one lucky guy, Mr. Donae', because usually it's pretty darn hard to catch up with a flight attendant."

Donae' was pleasantly surprised and this was noticeable when he said, "I can't thank you enough, Andy; you are being particularly helpful. Please, if you and Miss Baxter will simply call me Donae' and forget the Mister, I would appreciate it." Donae' smiled warmly as he politely stood up and aside to offer his seat to the confidently composed Miss Baxter as he admitted, "It is certainly a surprise and pleasure to meet you Miss Baxter, and let me thank you up front for your precious time."

"Well, thank you, Donae'" said Miss Baxter. "Your luck is good, although not untarnished; you see, I can't stay. I have to get back to class., I only wanted to set up a time to meet with you."

"Oh, I see, when does your class end, Miss Baxter?" inquired Donae'.

"I have two more hours, then I'll be free."

"Can we meet after that? I can meet you here, if Andy will permit it."

Pleased to be included in the conversation again, Andy smiled and said, "Okay with me, Mr. Donae'. But I'll have to stay to lock up, I hope that won't be a problem."

Donae' looked down at the sheet he held, then absentmindedly muttered, "No, no problem, Andy, that will be fine." He fell silent for a minute while he evaluated the information in his hand. Then he continued, "So, I will see you at six-thirty, Miss Baxter?"

Barbara Baxter nodded and turned to leave. Abruptly Donae' asked, "Miss Baxter, can I ask you one question before you go?"

"Sure, go right ahead . . . , but please make it short and to the point."

"Certainly. Miss Baxter, I have read the police report and I do not re-call your statement. Have the police ever contacted you about the Peter-son case?

"No, Mr. Donae,' and I really have to run; we can talk more later."

Donae' drove to the police station post-haste. He did not have much time between now and his six-thirty appointment with Barbara Baxter, yet he felt a strong inclination to speak with the detective in charge of the Peterson case. He still could not believe that Detective Lauwdry had not questioned Barbara Baxter. It would have been simple police procedure to check the airlines. The oversight was inexcusable and angered him. For this reason, Donae' decided not to wait to speak with Detective Lauwdry, he wanted do it before his interview with Miss Baxter.

When Donae' arrived at the police station, he ran the complete dis-tance from the parking lot to inside the front entrance and up the stairs, at which point he took a deep breath and threw open the door.

Lauwdry was sitting on the table next to the window; immediately a scornful grin covered his face, then he asked, "So rich boy; what gives? What's the big fucken deal? You in a hurry to put out a fire or some-thing?"

Donae' was still angry but paused long enough to throw a quick glance over at Sandy, who stood in front of a battered old file cabinet. When Sandy looked up to see what the commotion was, he recognized that Donae' was angry. Donae' gave him a quick nod. Sandy's expression quickly changed to confusion and he asked, "What's up Donae'; what can we do for you?"

"Good afternoon, Sandy. I need to speak with you and Lauwdry, im-mediately."

Again, Lauwdry started in. "Hey, rich boy I saw ya runnin across the parking lot. What's goin on, what gives, why the panic?"

Donae' turned to face the detective, then accused angrily, "You said you checked Brian Peterson out. You said, he was no longer a suspect for the carnage of Jennifer and Patty Jean. You said he was not even suspected of a contract hit to kill them."

Lauwdry stood and turned towards the table that held the coffee pot next to where he sat. When he started to pour himself a cup of the brew, he answered, "Oh, that shit again. What the hell do you want from us, Donae'? I told you he wasn't even in town. He was called away earlier. He had to see some customer in Washington, or somewhere. I don't remember where, but he wasn't in town."

"So . . . you never checked it out?"

"Sure, we did. But, first of all, we know he was where he said he was, because that's where we called him to tell him about his wife and kid."

Snidely, Donae' remarked, "Lauwdry, even if he was where he said he was, what about hiring someone else to do the job?"

"Dammit, Donae', I told you before they were a happily married couple. And besides that, for the umpteenth time, he was called out of town suddenly. Do you understand the meaning of *suddenly*?

"Fuck, Donae', what do you think, Peterson just got out the phone book and called Dial a Murder or, better yet, Hit man for Hire? Dammit, Donae', get a brain. A person just don't get a call to go out of town, then decides today will be a good time to kill the wife and kid. Shit, Donae' what the hell ya think'n?"

When Lauwdry realized what he had said, he suddenly burst into laughter and choked, "Hey, that was pretty damn funny, uh, Dial a Murder."

He snickered, then snorted, "Hit-man for Hire. Damn, I'll have ta remember that one."

Suddenly his expression changed as he evaluated whether he got one up on Donae' or not. He grinned because he believed he had.

Donae's angry glare never faltered as he breathlessly asked, "Did you check with the airlines, Lauwdry?" Not waiting for the answer, he already knew he continued. His teeth, still clenched, tightened, "Did you think to follow up on every damn lead that was given to you? Did you, Detective Lauwdry? Or were you sloppy again?"

Lauwdry finally had had enough. Irate he began to bellow, "How many goddamn times do I have to tell you, HE WAS THERE,

DONAE'? We didn't need the airlines to tell us that. The goddamn hotel people confirmed when he arrived."

Lauwdry's voice was loud and it echoed out the door and down the halls. His words could be heard all over the building, yet when he threw his hands up and added more, it was even a louder roar; "WE TALKED TO PETERSON HIMSELF HE WAS THERE THAT NIGHT WHAT OTHER PROOF DO WE NEED! TELL ME THAT, MR. RICH BOY . . . HUH?"

Donae' inhaled a deep breath so he too could raise his voice an octave higher. He wanted it to be heard loud and clear when he informed the detective, that the reservation had been booked three weeks in advance, not the same day as Brian Peterson wanted everyone to believe. A second thought, though, prompted him to bite his tongue and he halted his words before they were spoken. The one thing he did not need was Detective Lauwdry muddying the water by going to Brian and mentioning his suspicions. Instead, Donae' decided to keep the information to himself. And suddenly he laughed at his own ignorance as a new thought shot across his mind. *I have always known about Lauwdry and his lax detective work. So why am I surprised?* For a full minute Donae' glared openly from one detective to the other, then turned on his heels and hurried from the room. As he rounded the corner, he heard the bewildered Lauwdry ask Sandy,

"So, who do you think put a feather up his wealthy ass?" Then Lauwdry muttered under his breath, "Damn jerk; who does he think he is anyway?"

Donae' was so disturbed that this cop always looked for the easiest solutions and because of his laziness, Brian could very well walk away scot-free.

The simple fact was the longer a case lay dormant, the harder it was to find clues and prove their solidity. This, consequently, was why Donae' had no intention of sharing his newfound information. There was no way he was chancing the information being botched up by Lauwdry and his slothful negligence.

Barbara Baxter arrived precisely at six-thirty as did Donae'. When both were seated comfortably and after Andy poured had each a cup of coffee, Donae' summarized, "Miss Baxter, the Peterson case I mentioned earlier was a double homicide that happened a few years ago. September Twenty-ninth, Nineteen-

Sixty, to be exact."

"Yes, I know. Andy filled me in."

"Good, very good. Miss Baxter, you said you were never questioned by the police about the murders."

"Yes, that's correct. The police have never contacted me. I've never been asked anything about it. And to tell you the truth, Donae', I don't know anything anyway, except what I've read in the newspapers, of course. So, I didn't expect them to. And due to that fact, I'm not quite sure why you want to speak with me now."

Donae' ignored Miss Baxter's negative response and continued with another question, "Am I understanding you correctly? Am I safe in assuming that you do not remember anything about that afternoon, Miss Baxter? You do not remember a passenger named Mr. Brian Peterson?"

"Well, of course I do, I didn't say that. I meant things like murder don't happen very often, not in my world, anyway. So, it would be ridiculous to think I wouldn't remember the incident."

"And so, you are saying you do remember checking Mr. Peterson into his first-class seating?"

"Yes, yes, of course I do. I even remember how miserable he felt that day because of his cold. You know, flying and a head-cold . . . Well, I don't know if you realize it, but a cold can make a head feel like it's going to explode. I remember I tried to make Mr. Peterson as comfortable as possible, but I wasn't very successful."

"Miss Baxter, you sound like you know Mr. Peterson. Do you know him personally?"

Suddenly, Miss Baxter looked sharply at Donae'. Her expression changed as she studied him. It appeared that he had insulted her, and Donae' could see that she was evaluating his comment. Yet, he was bewildered on how his words might have upset her.

The room remained silent for some time while Barbara Baxter determined whether she liked the way Donae's question sounded. Finally, she dauntlessly replied, "Mr. Donae', I know some stewardesses do go out with some of their regular passengers, but I hope you're not suggesting I had anything going on with Mr. Peterson. For I can assure you, Mr. Donae', that I only knew him as one of our monthly travelers and nothing more."

"Miss Baxter, I am truly sorry. Please forgive me. I did not mean to imply anything. I simply wondered if you would have recognized that this traveler was indeed Mr. Peterson and not another passenger."

Miss Baxter paused before she conceded, "Your apology is accepted, and I'm sorry if I come across as sensitive. But we stewardesses do at times get a bad rap. And yes, I did know Mr. Peterson by sight. And it was him I checked in that day, even though he wasn't in the best of health that afternoon and we didn't talk much."

She hesitated again, then clarified, "You see, Mr. Peterson could barely talk. His throat was so sore he was in no mood to socialize. To put it bluntly, he was a little grumpy and came across as rude and unfriendly. He's never been an overly friendly passenger, but that day was. Well, anyway, as soon as he boarded, he asked me for a blanket. Then immediately after take-off he covered himself and slept all the way to Dulles. At which time he scurried from the plane without so much as a goodbye. To tell you the truth, Mr. Donae', that is all I know, other than what I have read in the local newspapers and I have not seen Mr. Peterson since."

"Thank you, Miss Baxter, you have been very helpful . . . . And again, I am sorry if I offended you in any way."

Barbara Baxter smiled, then nodded her goodbye and hurried from the room. Donae' studied his notes before he remembered he was not alone and looked up. Andy was waiting quietly at the door with his key in his hand. Donae' read the look on his face. It was easy to see he did do not want to play detective any longer; he wanted to go home.

# CHAPTER 11

When Donae' left his office to head for the Peterson meeting, he began to experience an unnerving tension deep within, a feeling which soon moved closer to a premonition. He closed his eyes and for an instant and he could see himself stepping into a heavy foreboding mist. It took him several minutes to shake the eerie sensation, but soon his enthusiasm returned, and the thought of confronting Brian became more electrifying and less menacing.

After Donae' pulled up to the extraordinary and quite notable high-tech structure, he sat staring as he marveled at its exotic outline. The building was obviously superior to all others surrounding it and it stood arrogantly towering the rest. Still in awe, Donae' moved to open his car door when he noticed the valet, whose smile was as wide as was physically possible. He briskly approached the car and asked, "Good afternoon, sir, are you going in?"

Donae' jumped out of his car and handed the keys to the attendant, along with a twenty-dollar bill. He witnessed the instant desire that entered the young man's eyes when he took the keys. It was as if Donae' had just handed him the cup at Wimbledon. "Yes, I most certainly am going in. Do you think you can park her somewhere safe?"

"Absolutely, no problem, sir. Most of the cars I park all day are Cadillacs, Lincolns and an occasional Thunderbird, but nearly never a Jaguar. These cars make my heart pound and someday I intend to have one of my own."

Donae' smiled and goodheartedly offered, "You, young man, are welcome to take her for a spin around the block a few times."

From the grin on the valet's face, it was like Donae' had offered ownership of the car. And he squealed, "Hot damn," and leaped into the front seat. "Thanks, sir, I promise I'll take great care of her, I promise."

Donae' smiled as the valet finished his last, "I promise." While at the same time slamming the car door his *screeeech* was loud and sharp as he pulled away from the curb.

Instead of being angry, Donae' laughed at the young man's fervor, then spun around and headed for the doorman who sedulously held the door wide open for him to enter. From afar Donae' heard another screech of the Jag's tires. And he laughed out loud as he shook his head at the doorman, who in turn smiled and welcomed him warmly, "Good afternoon, sir. He's a good lad, sir. I can't promise you, but I think you'll get it back in one piece." Donae' tipped his imaginary hat and entered.

Once Donae' entered the grand building his anxiety reared its ugly head again. Yet, by the time the elevator doors opened, he could feel the strength of his convictions and his confidence returned; he was ready for Brian. *This*, he thought, *is a necessary meeting. It must be done to observe Brian while he's still unsuspecting. For, once his guard is up, he will fall back into Mr. Perfect.*

Donae' entered an enormous antechamber that was lavishly decorated extensively in expensive antiques, some of which Donae' noticed were exquisite copies, but admirable all the same. Once he completed his eyeful appraisal, he concluded that the pieces could easily go undetected by the untrained eye. After critiquing what he could see of the building and its occupants, Donae' decided his fundamental scrutiny of the company was correct. The accounting firm that employed Brian was indeed very successful and impressively flaunted such.

Donae' introduced himself and stated the reason he was there to the very professional looking receptionist, who immediately proved to be as proficient as she looked. Without a word, she handed him a sheet of paper that held several questions, plus a slot for the name of the person he was here to see. Donae' started to say that he was here only to speak with Mr. Peterson and nothing more.

Suddenly she pushed her hand forward and pointed as she said sharply, "Everyone who enters this building fills out this information. If you don't sign the waiver, you don't enter. So, if you will ... *please* ... fill out the data requested."

Perplexed, Donae' nodded and she continued, "I will let Mr. Peterson's secretary know that you are in the lobby, Mr. Donae'."

Again, Donae' nodded.

A few minutes later when he handed his completed worksheet to the young lady whose nametag read, Miss Rachel Moore, he noticed her demeanor suddenly changed. She smiled sweetly and in a newfound congenial voice she informed him, "Mr. Peterson will be with you in a few minutes, Mr. Donae'. Please, take a seat and there's coffee on the table to your left." Quickly she muttered, "Excuse me," then handed a message to a gentleman who started to pass her desk. Then she continued, "We also have several different cookies, if you would like to have them with your coffee. They're right next to the coffee. Please feel free to help yourself."

Suspiciously Donae' moved away from the reception desk as he asked himself; *"How long is a visitor expected to wait, that he would have time for coffee and cookies?"*

Dubious, Donae' sat down in a copy of a Victorian John Henry Belter armchair. After a bit, he learned the answer to his earlier question. It was a good twenty minutes before a tall slender woman of about forty-five walked up to him and asked, "Mr. Donae'?"

When he confirmed that he was indeed the person she was looking for, she stretched out her arm and offered her hand in a warm hello. She said, "Mr. Donae'. I'm Shirley Kelp, and if you will follow me, I'll show you to Mr. Peterson's office. He is expecting you."

Shirley signed for a visitor's badge, then handed it to Donae' and waited for him to pin it to his jacket before she said, "Okay, please follow me." She smiled once more, then took off in a gait that almost instantly turned into a dead run. Donae' stretched his stride while he hurriedly attempted to keep up. He followed her across the large entrance and out the door to a stairwell, then up two flights of stairs to an even more lavish sector of the building.

Donae' was still trying to catch his breath when Shirley said while pointing to the office door in front of them, "This here is Mr. Peterson's office and you can go right in. Can I bring you anything to drink or eat, Mr. Donae'?"

He shook his head no to the offer and took one last deep breath. Then he opened the door into one of the most opulent rooms he had seen in some time. Immediately, he remembered what Gerimee had said about Brian's desire for wealth and notoriety. There was no inaccuracy in Gerimee's indubitable assessment. From what Donae' could see of the room, Brian definitely wanted anyone who entered to recognize that he was affluent. Even though audacious, Donae' had to admit the decor was exquisite; the furniture showed a boldness that was almost overbearing. Not everyone could be comfortable in such an office. Nevertheless, it was obvious that the gentleman behind the huge Victorian desk felt comfortably at home.

Donae' thought: *With such an apparent display, Brian must have a compulsive need to compete. This is good to know. The degree appears acute. This I trust will come in handy in my investigation.* Donae' hoped, if needed, his insight would put Brian at a disadvantage.

He moved further into the room and Brian stood up to greet him. Donae' was surprised at the sight of his full structure; the newspaper pictures had not done Brian Peterson justice. The man was easily six foot three or more and had the physique of a Greek statue he had once seen in a Las Vegas hotel. His full head of luminous blond hair was almost white and had a slight wave to it. His features were nearly too prominent, yet he was still unmistakably handsome.

Donae' pondered: *I wonder if Brian puts most men on guard, since I can guess that with little or no provocation, he could easily sweep a woman off her feet.* Then again, his knowledge of women and their preferences was quite limited. *But still*, he avowed, *I would guess Brian's looks could easily melt away any barrier a woman might possess.*

Donae' clasped the hand Brian offered when he introduced himself. "Good morning, Mr. Donae', I'm Brian Peterson." When Donae' smiled and looked into Brian's eyes he was once again surprised. Brian was all that he had feared. Addison and Gerimee were right. This man held feelings for no one except himself. Yes, Brian's eyes were as cold and distant as the statue he resembled.

Some might attribute his impassivity to operating in the fiercely contested business world he so obviously existed in, only Donae' knew better. Brian's eyes not only lacked passion or empathy, they showed nothing more than cold emptiness. He would guess this man did not possess a normal measure of conscience.

Unhappily, Donae's' minds 'eye pictured Jennifer's sweet smile. Then moved directly to the innocent trust on Patty Jean's face. It was nothing more than a flicker but enough to momentarily stun him. Quickly his thought went to something he read years back as a child: *I am here to face the fire of the demon.*

With this thought in the forefront of his mind, Donae' began his performance as an impossible client. He wanted to portray himself as a tyrant who was as contemptuous as impossible an individual who felt this, or any firm would benefit vastly by representing his family's business. Categorically, he was playing a snob. This he hoped would push Brian towards his malicious side.

Luckily for Donae', if money and power impressed Brian., then that is exactly what he would attain from his affiliation with the Donae' name and business.

However, Donae' only intended to let Brian anticipate this prospect. Meanwhile, he would play a little cat and mouse and characterize his temperament. Without a minute wasted on colloquy, Donae' began to complain. "The wait, Mr. Peterson, was excessive. Is this what I am to expect if I decide to select you as the representative of my family's financial interests? And, by the way, what is this ridiculous habit of offering cookies and coffee? Was this supposed to appease me? I dare say it is insulting, if not repugnant. Imagine, handing out cookies."

Brian started to apologize and Donae' promptly interrupted, "Well, never mind about that right now; let us get down to business. Enough time has lapsed and been wasted on naught the way it is."

It was easy to see that Donae' was on the right track for he could now see a spark in Brian's eyes. He was already fighting for control. It was apparent he wanted to explode and lash out at him. Donae' added to his mental list: *short tempered*; *very beneficial for me though not for Brian.*

Donae' suddenly felt an incredible sense of pleasure. Yet, as quickly as Brian lost control, he soon regained his composure. His struggle diminished and the fire in his eyes lessened. Soon he succeeded in masking his anger, and in seconds Brian completely recovered his disciplined manner and his pleasant camouflage was back. Again, Brian was ready to deal with the overbearing cantankerous Lawrence Donae'.

Donae' recognized the change immediately and attempted once again to throw Brian off balance. In an exasperated tone, he asked, "So, where do we sit?" Condescendingly, he said these words as he looked around the room. "I suppose you do own a conference table or something to sit at, at least? Oh my, what an exquisite Victorian sideboard, positively unique. As a matter of fact, Mr. Peterson it is so exquisite, I question its authenticity."

Donae' fought a grin when he saw Brian flinch, then quiver with anger. "So, Mr. Peterson, where do I put my papers? Come on, Mr. Peterson, let's not dawdle; my time is of great value." Donae' stopped to take a breath while he opened his briefcase and pulled out his paperwork.

At this time, Brian finally received the time he needed to get a word in. His anger was well hidden, although Donae' could see his fists, as well as his jaws, were tightly clenched.

Sharply, Brian said, "Mr. Donae' please pardon my manners. I truly apologize for the wait. I hope you understand our clients are very important to us and that alone is why I had to keep you waiting. You see, Mr. Donae', one of our clients had a particularly unfavorable decision to make which involved a possible loss of millions of dollars, and the decision had to be reached immediately. It could not wait, so of course and rightfully, the client insisted that he speak with me about the action. Nat-

urally, no one else would do and I must confess, Mr. Donae', if this gentleman had not done so, it would have caused him ruin."

Donae' gave Brian a disinterested glare and Brian hurriedly added, "I
hope you can see that this was a case of great urgency. I'm sure your family would expect the same concession."

Donae' said nothing, and nervously Brian mumbled, "Mr. Donae' if
we can move to this side of the room, we will be able sit at the conference
table."

The bewildered Donae' looked at Brian in confused surprise for he
saw no conference table. By this time, Brian was in the process of reaching over and pushing an ornate knob on the wall next to his desk. Suddenly, a large bookcase that covered half the wall opened inwardly and an
ample size meeting room appeared. This room was also decorated in the
same antique furnishings.

Donae' smiled and said, "Quite impressive, Mr. Peterson. Quite impressive, indeed." Donae', without further ado, moved to sit at the head
of the table. The chair he chose was covered in a rich paisley design and
was comfortably overstuffed. As Donae' viewed the room, Brian read his
smile that showed he liked what he surveyed. At once Brian beamed with
self-indulged pride; he had finally impressed the impertinent Mr. Donae'.

"Before we get started, Mr. Donae', can I get you a drink or something to eat?"

"Again, with the food, Mr. Peterson? My answer is still no! I would
prefer to get started, if you do not mind. No more dallying, Mr. Peterson."

Snidely, Brian countered, "Sorry, Mr. Donae', I will refrain from offering you more repugnant comestibles. Where would you like to start?"

"Appropriately, Mr. Peterson, I have previously checked you and
your corporation out . . . and thoroughly, I might add. Anyway, I was
impressed with the company's standing, not to mention what seems to
be boundless assets. Plus, I must also say, although I was surprised, I am
impressed by your personal success as well. Frankly, I mention this because you are not from a family of any kind of means. So, I can only assume you did this the old fashioned way and earned it, which, of course,
shows you are not only smart but tenacious as well. It is irrelevant and
not at all consequential in my decision, but interesting all the same."

"Thank you, Mr. Donae'. I trust together we can enrich you family's interests."

"However, Mr. Peterson, my family is from very old money and I see your company has only been around for about twenty-five years, although I have considered that it has survived some of the hard times . . ." Donae' prattled on adding one insult after another. He did this wholly so he could observe Brian's reactions to disdain. "Nevertheless, Mr. Peterson, in all honesty I question the family's decision on this move. Our funds are currently with a well-established house which has been around with much success for about a hundred years. I myself surmise that this move is a step down, but Grandmother has decided that we must make the move and who am I to oppose her preponderance."

"Mr. Donae', I do respect your concerns, although I can assure you, we are a secure establishment. Our clientele can vouch for our stability along with our dependability. We are completely loyal to our clients as they are to us. And as for our company's standing in the financial world, we have a much higher rate of vantage than most of our competitors."

Donae's smile was condescending when he said, "As you say, Mr. Peterson, as you say. Yet, I know as well as you, that at any point in time numbers can be made to look any way one might want them to look."

Brian's confidence had begun to grow as soon as he heard Donae's confession that the decision to change investment companies was his grandmother's and not his. Thereupon, he retorted pointedly, "Ah, and, Mr. Donae', I would have to admit that that particular accomplishment is one reason, our clients are so completely satisfied with *me,* not to mention our company, and I am sure you will be as well, sir.

"Now, now, Mr. Peterson; let's not get ahead of ourselves. First, let me show you some of my family's present holdings and what interests we are currently working with. Then after that, Mr. Peterson, we can further discuss if you and your company are a suitable match for the Donae' family. Then, if, and when that is decided, we can also talk consummations."

"Excellent, Mr. Donae'. That, I say, is a reasonable directive." Brian nodded towards the folders in Donae's hands and indicated, "I noticed you have several files in front of you, so let's see what you brought me today. Then after that, Mr. Donae', I will be able to answer all of your questions and hopefully put your mind at ease."

Donae' handed the files that contained copies of about half of the family's holdings and watched without comment while Brian read the numbers. Donae' already knew this would impress, if not arouse his greed.

Almost immediately Donae' could see he would not be disappointed. He was rewarded when Brian looked up and smiled a desirous little grin and asked, "Mr. Donae', you don't happen to have a sister, do you?"

Donae' pretended he did not get the jest of what Brian implied. "Well, yes, I do. Why do you ask, Mr. Peterson?"

Brian looked thwarted then started to answer.

Donae' continued, "Oh my, I get it; you are making a joke. Well, I am sorry, dear man, but she is blissfully married to a wonderful gentleman of her own station."

Brian's face registered dislike yet he said a cordial, "What a shame . . . . I mean for me."

"Oh, are you not married, Mr. Peterson?"

"No, I'm not. But I will be in about three months. Matter of fact, you may even know her since she does travel in you circle."

"Oh, really, in my circle?"

"Yes, Mrs. Allison P. Carter. She is currently a widow and a very wealthy one, if I might add. I believe her family has been here since the Mayflower or thereabouts. The Pierce family, they are very prominent and are extremely active in the community. Do you know them, Mr. Donae'?"

Ignoring Brian's tasteless remark about being a wealthy widow, Donae' continued the conversation. "Of course, I have heard of the family. And, I would venture to say, at one time or another I have run across each and every one of the Carter relations. But, to tell you the truth, Mr. Peterson, I cannot recall when or with which family member. Is this your first marriage, Mr. Peterson?"

"No, no, I have been married before though for only for a short time."

"Oh, I see, how sad. Well, unfortunately divorce has become entirely too common these days. Would you not agree, Mr. Peterson?"

"Well, yes, I guess I would have to agree with you, Mr. Donae'. Now adays, it does seem to be the trend. However, in my particular circumstance, that does not hold true. You see, my wife is deceased; she expired suddenly a few years back. It was very sad. We were completely devoted to one another."

Donae' was taken aback by Brian's tone of voice. There was not a hint of remorse or sadness in his speech; his face simply registered indifference. In essence, he sounded as if Donae' had just asked him about the weather and he was merely relating what the status was outside.

Donae's next thought was to ask if there had been any children. Yet, he feared Brian's answer, for he felt sure he would deny her existence and Donae' could not bear to hear the innocent child's life disavowed. Instead, he first politely said what is customary and expected in any such circumstance, then added, "Hopefully you have children to ease your grief."

Brian gave a sudden laugh as he chided, "Children, Mr. Donae', have never been a priority or one of my desires."

After listening to Brian's apathetic avowal, Donae' not only felt appalled, he decided he had enough to conclude that Gerimee and Addison's theory was correct. Brian was dispassionate and his demeanor affected Donae' profoundly, and for several minutes after he simply sat silent and studied Brian's impassiveness. He was completely composed and placid as he continued to go through the folder Donae' had handed him.

Finally, Donae' contemplated; *I thought I had worked with every type of personality during my brief medical tenure. And I would have thought whatever I missed there I would have run across while with the District Attorney's office. Regardless, no one I have ever met has been as dispassionate as this individual.*

Brian's personality was quite unsettling and after a time Donae' abruptly stood up and started to gather all the files that were scattered around the table. He felt somewhat rattled as he slipped the folders back into his briefcase, then snatched the last file from Brian's hand and announced, "Mr. Peterson, I will have to cut this meeting short. My lengthy wait in the lobby has set me a bit behind and I have another scheduled appointment across town. At my convenience, I will go over your data and will get back with you in a few weeks."

Brian immediately jumped up and asked, "Can I call you next week? I would like to make sure I've answered all your questions and abated any of your concerns."

"I am sorry, but that will be impossible Mr. Peterson, I am leaving the country on business and will not be back for several weeks. If I do think of anything, I am sure my secretary can give you a call. Now you will have to excuse me; I do need to be on my way. Good day." Promptly, Donae' turned and headed for the door.

Brian hurried around the table and made one last request, "When you get back from your trip, Mr. Donae', perhaps we can get together . . . socially . . . I mean. I'm sure Allison would love to have a small dinner party, just her, you and I and, of course a guest of your choosing. I'm sure you and she would have a great deal in common. Hopefully, at the same time we can discuss a few business details. Maybe even conclude this one."

Donae' did not answer; he simply smiled slightly as he closed the door behind him. It was clear Brian was once again attempting to insinuate himself socially with an individual he hoped could be beneficial to his social standing.

While Donae' waited for the elevator he realized his anxiety had slackened. Now that he was out of Brian's presence, he was feeling less anger, and a calmness trickled down his spine. Relieved, he released the breath he had held and started to inhale and exhale at a steady rhythm. *Unfortunately*, he thought, *I still have several questions.*

Donae' was sure if he had only let the meeting go on, he would have gotten the answers he needed. *But*, he thought, *that was near impossible.* Throughout the entire meeting, his mind kept returning to Addison and his description of his granddaughter's last minutes of life. This picture stood out so vividly in his mind that at one point he thought he could reach out and touch the beautiful four-year old's face. *Patty Jean smiled at her slayer*; Addison had said. *It had to have been a person she loved and thought she could utterly trust.* These words haunted Donae'. Swiftly, his mind moved to another image. *There, without an ounce of emotional identification, that same person stabbed a knife into Patty Jean's tiny little throat.*

Since he had found Jennifer's and Patty Jean's pictures from the murder scene, these thoughts and images had continually crossed Donae's mind. And again, he cursed his inclination to flee. *Dammit, why did I run? Especially if I feel Brian is Jennifer and Patty Jean's brutal killer?*

The elevator door opened, and as he entered, he hissed, "Dammit, Donae', stay focused. You must not let Brian, or his callous behavior flaw your investigation. You have made a promise to Jennifer and Patty Jean and this should be your focal point, not your emotions."

Although Donae' still harbored an urge to run, he knew he would stay and fight for justice. Yet, despite his strong convictions the entire time he waited for the valet to return with his Jag, he had an awful yen to speak with someone who was absolutely normal, someone who could help him get his feet back on the ground. And as soon as he hopped into the front seat of his car, he quickly maneuvered the vehicle in the opposite direction, a direction in which he knew he could find just such a person.

As soon as he entered the gates and started down the long driveway, he felt his disoriented mind begin to relax. Immediately he pressed harder on the gas pedal so he could be in her presence a fraction of a second sooner.

Her smile was wide, and her greeting was warm as it was each and every time, she welcomed him home. "My dear, sweet, Lawrence, what a wonderful surprise. Come and give your dear old Grandmother a great big hug."

He hurried across the floor and encompassed her fragile form. After an embrace that lasted longer than usual, he whispered, "Grandmother, you cannot imagine how much I needed to hear your voice."

When his grandmother pulled away, she looked at Donae' questioningly, and for an instant he thought he could feel her move about his mind. Immediately, he felt comforted by how well she knew him. He marveled at how easily she had always been able to read him and his moods.

Donae's grandmother's smile was full of concern and she took his hand and asked, "Do you have time to walk with me, Lawrence? I was just about to take my evening stroll in the garden. I am sure it will do you a world of good." She winked and added, "A walk does tend to clear the cobwebs." She kissed his hand; then without lingering for an answer she opened the French doors.

In that instant his troubled thoughts vanished, and he entered a contrasting world. This realm his grandmother called her piece of heaven. At once the fragrances were abounding and tantalizing as the chirps from various birds were consoling.

Grandmother Donae' loved her garden and had always insisted on a variety of healthy scented wildflowers much to the dread of her horticulturist who always pushed for a simpler formula. Yet, for Grandmother, the stronger the bouquet, the happier she was.

Donae', with his arm through his grandmother's, ambled past a multitude of incomparable shades of roses. Then they moved to the daffodils which were one of her favorites. Straight ahead was the hearty resiliency of the purple crocus, plus a large diversity of colorful tulips which seemed to have spread everywhere throughout the cultivated area.

In silence, Donae' and his grandmother continued on the promenade and paused only here and there to admire a patch of flowers along the path. Neither one needed words to fill the space for they were both completely at ease with each other and this world.

Finally, they stopped to sit on the ancient rococo bench. It had sat in the middle of these colorful blooms for as long as Donae' could remember. She squeezed his hand to her chest and said, "My dear, sweet grandchild, you have always felt far more than you should, and being in the business you are in, well . . . ." His grandmother stopped her dialogue and for a minute Donae' could see that she was in search of the right words, although he also had a suspicion that she was also reliving the many years they had spent together on this very bench. Silently, she continued to search to find the right relevance, and finally he saw her face change and it revealed that without words or explanation she understood. She had determined there was no use aching for him because he was, what he was, and he was not about to change. Accepting this, she quietly said, "I guess I sometime wonder, Lawrence, if it will all be too much for you one day." Then she gave a tender laugh as she squeezed his hand and proclaimed, "Pray tell, I sound like a worrisome old grandmother, and one that dotes entirely too much on her grandchildren. I suppose that I see each and every tribulation more climacteric then it truly is. Do forgive me my dear."

Donae' kissed her cheek and teased, "Grandmother, you will never be old, and as for your worrywart nature . . . well, what can I say?" His weariness bled through his banter and this worried her; he was usually in much higher spirits.

Suddenly his manner became serious and he stood and paced several times before he sat back on the bench. "Grandmother, at times it does hurt to see all the pain that is out there. And yet, I realize my vocation puts me in the center of all that. Still . . . I . . . . Well, there are just so many kinds of pain to deal with and so very much heartbreak."

Donae' inhaled a deep breath, then decided to let his pent-up anguish flow. "Grandmother, I try hard to keep in mind that I alone cannot prevent depravity. I . . . . but . . . . when I see someone, who is so truly evil . . . . and he is out among the innocent, I guess I sometimes fear that maybe I will not stop him before he causes further pain. And, well . . . well, I guess sometimes the thought of that, is just too much to deal with alone."

"Then that is when you come to me, child. That is what I will always be here for, Lawrence."

"I know, Grandmother, and that alone is why I am here today, so I can feel your strength and your goodness" He gave her a light laugh, then added, "Before I go out into that mean ole world and slay those wicked ole dragons."

She laughed out loud at his witticism. "Oh dear, Lawrence, you will stay for dinner, won't you? And since it is Friday, you could certainly spend the night, can't you? I can easily have Kim pull the covers down on the bed in your old room. We could stay up most the night and if you insist, I will even play Monopoly with you *and* let you win. That is, as long as we can reminisce about the good old days."

Donae' continued where she left off, "Those wonderful days when life was straightforward, and my mother and father, as well as grandfather were still with us."

Again, she laughed at how well they knew one another and answered, "Yes, yes, I have to admit, I still miss them terribly." Her voice lightened and she added, "So, what do you say? Are you game, my boy?"

"Grandmother, I will be delighted to stay. It all sounds wonderful and I am yours to do with whatever you wish. That is until tomorrow at noon."

They clasped arm and arm and hurried back towards the house as his grandmother teased excitedly, "I must hurry and warn the staff of a visitor. We certainly do not want to upset them. Oh, and let's not forget to remind them to place another setting at the dinner table. I wonder if it is too late to make your favorite dish."

Donae' looked at his grandmother and nodded his agreement, and she gave thanks that his eyes were full of new enthusiasm. She loved her grandchildren for they were such an extraordinary treasure. She felt his gaze and smiled; then without meeting his stare she warmly patted his hand and he squeezed hers in return. And he too smiled; because he knew what she was thinking for she had always truly cherished her grandchildren.

# CHAPTER 12

Following the night at his grandmother's estate, Donae' picked Patricia up for a drive in the country. Later that evening they had a superb dinner at a unique old-fashioned restaurant called, The French Bistro, which was hidden deep in the countryside. This restaurant was Donae's favorite dinner house and one of the most popular around. A reservation was positively required, since they only served twenty guests per evening. And it was strongly suggested that one secured a table as early as possible for special occasions since every night was booked far in advance. This bistro always amazed Donae'; for no matter what the weather, it was always full. The Donae' family had a standing-reservation since before his parents' deaths over twenty years ago. The current proprietor, Kyle, took over after his mother, Charlene, the original owner, passed away. Kyle was also an old client. Donae' had assisted him in a search for his biological father. Kyle's mother had never revealed this fact until she was on her deathbed. At that time, she confessed that the man he had known and loved as his father was only so on paper and Kyle was the outcome of a wartime love affair.

Apparently, Kyle's biological father had left France unaware that Charlene was three months pregnant when he was wounded and sent stateside. At that time, they lost contact with each other and he was never informed of Kyle's birth. With Donae's help, in the end all turned out well for Kyle and his natural father, for which Kyle has always been magnanimously grateful.

Tonight, the bistro glowed in the evening's crisp, clear air and when Donae' looked across the table unto Patricia's enchanted face he smiled with pure pleasure. He could see, she too, was captivated by its delightful character and this pleased him. Patricia grinned across the table at Donae', her smile held obvious gratification and she declared, "Lawrence, you have outdone yourself this time. I love the Old French ambiance; the evening's been perfect in every way."

Her comment delighted him immensely, and by the time he kissed her good night they decided Kyle's would always be their special place.

By Monday morning Donae' was once again in a hearty frame of mind, he was ready to take Brian down and he hoped it would be soon.

As soon as he closed the office door behind him, he knew something was up for Silvia was about to burst with uncontrolled excitement. She jumped up and ran from behind her desk as she yelped, "Hey, good morning, Mr. Donae'. Boy, I sure am happy to see you. Mitch just called and he said he's on his way back; he said he would be here around three. He also said to make sure I tell you that you made the right decision when you sent him to Chicago. And that you're not going to believe what he found. He didn't go into any details, but I think we may have some good answers on the way."

"Silvia.... pleaseee take a breath..., now relax. I agree that does sound like good news, but if I lose you in the course of things, it tends to slacken the significance of its tidings."

She laughed at her own eagerness and Donae' continued, "Okay, since we are on a roll, let's see if we can get Sergeant Cox on the phone."

"Oh, no, I mean, he already called early this morning. He'll be in town Wednesday. He set a one o'clock appointment to see you."

"Then let's get Gerimee on the line. I need to fill him in on where we stand thus far."

"Oh, by the way your brother, Michael called, and he asked if you would join Shelia and him for breakfast tomorrow morning around ten at the club. I told him it looked like you were free, as far as your calendar shows anyway, and that you would be there. That is, unless I find out otherwise. Then I would call him and cancel."

Donae' smiled and suggested again, "Breathe, Silvia, breathe, and breakfast tomorrow will be fine. I need to fill Michael in on a few issues, anyway. My chat with Brian last Friday concerns him."

Silvia tilted her head and her face registered a question. Yet before she was able to ask it, Donae' continued with the answer, "Since Michael does handle the books for the family businesses and since I am using our businesses bookkeeping as a cover, I feel he should know about the ruse. I do not want him hearing it from someone else and taking it wrong."

"But, how can he, Mr. Donae'? Brian would be the only way and that is unlikely."

"Maybe so, Silvia. Then, on the other hand, Brian seemed overly eager to involve himself in the Donae' affairs. So, I would not be at all surprised if he took it upon himself to follow up with a phone call. And, of course, if he does that, his call would be forwarded directly to Michael. With this a possibility, Michael needs to be aware of the chicanery."

Silvia handed Donae' several more messages and declared, "Well you sound like you figured out Brian's character. Was Gerimee's intuition correct? I mean, is Brian dangerous, Mr. Donae'? Are you in jeopardy if he realizes what you're up to?"

"Silvia, let us not worry about me right now. Let's say we concentrate solely on solving this crime. When Brain is behind bars, where he can never hurt anyone again, we will all breathe a little easier."

Silvia's face registered uncertainty, but she said no more on the subject. Instead, she moved to matters at hand. "I left several other messages on your desk. By the way, Mr. Donae', how was your weekend? You certainly look better than you did Friday. I was beginning to worry that you've been overdoing it again. You know, with all those late nights with your files . . . that sort of thing. Besides, your Grandmother called this morning and she told me to make sure you have a good day. So, see . . . I'm not the only one who's been worried about you."

Donae' shook his head and Silvia turned her attention back to her typewriter, although before Donae' could make a safe exit, she added, "And, I hope you spent some time with Patricia this weekend."

"Thank you for your concern on my being overworked, Miss Perez. But today everything is back in perspective. So, please do not concern yourself and it's none of your business but the answer is yes, Patricia and I had a wonderful weekend."

Silvia laughed at his all but subtle message. She was forever playing matchmaker, and he was incessantly fighting her efforts.

Now that Donae' felt he had his feet back on solid ground, he decided to go back over his earlier field notes once more. He also pulled the files that Addison Hobart had dropped by and reread several articles that were written after the murders. But soon his mind returned to Hurley. He had a gut feeling about Brian's adoptive parents and their deaths. He thought their demise might have some correlation other than the obvious, inheritance, yet that did seem to be the pattern. Could Brian, as far back as then, have been developing a plan for future privileged circumstances? Was Jennifer . . . . Donae' shook his head; he did not want to move to Jennifer just yet. He wanted to stay focused on Brian's earlier family life and Hurley. Then again, if Brian did indeed kill Handoff and Mary Beth Peterson for the ten thousand dollar life Insurance, then years later killed Jennifer and Patty Jean for the two million plus, it would be wise to presume his soon to-be wife, Allison P. Carter, should unquestionably be on guard. "Yet" . . . .Donae' rubbed his chin and leaned back against his chair as he felt a feeling of despair. He was aware that most people in this type of relationship tended to be naïve, and more often than not they chose to believe the perpetrator. Even if forewarned, they were less apt to believe there was any threat than most. The innocent was more often, a person who would trust readily, therefore easier to beguile, as did it seem Jennifer Hobart was.

Donae' looked at his notes and sighed. Jennifer never asked Brian why he insisted on so much life insurance, not even when he wanted the same million-dollar policy on the baby. She never questioned that if he was so worried about their well-being why he had never initiated his own policy.

Donae' had checked, and Brian had never made any attempt to schedule an appointment for his pre-insurance physical. Consequently, his insurance policy never became effective, quite contrary to a person who was so worried about his family's security.

Gerimee said Jennifer had also mentioned mood swings. Although Jennifer complained to Sharon and Gerimee, she never made the effort to seek help.

Donae' scribbled the idiom his favorite professor so often repeated. "Sometime people simply do not do what is good for them." As so it appears was the path Jennifer had chosen.

Brian was not the only one who had hidden behind a false face. Jennifer had let her family and the world believe she and Brian were happily married. Most all trusted what they perceived since Jennifer Hobart was intelligent, plus she had two wonderful parents to lean on, so they believed nothing as awful as spousal abuse could happen to her. This was one reason Addison and Gerimee felt so guilty and questioned how this could have happened in plain sight without their awareness. *Sadly*, thought Donae', *we have so much more to learn about people and their psyche as well as why they so often do the opposite of what is good for them*. Jennifer had been extremely loved all her life and from what Donae' could gather, she had been slightly over protected. She had been completely unaware that people with Brian's personality even existed which, of course, only made it easier for Brian to take control and manipulate her. Donae' doubted Jennifer had ever realized she was in danger, since she had done so little to resist Brian's debauchery.

Then again, he should keep in mind that Brian was a master at suppressing his real personality for most saw him as a wonderful husband and father, a pillar of the community. He pondered. *Curiously studies show that wealth and prominence are rarely ever associated with abuse.* Even though, according to Addison and Gerimee, Brian was openly obnoxious at times. However, everyone chose to overlook his behavior. That sadly was primarily for Jennifer, who in essence, needed the contrary.

Brian was a successful businessman, yet without Jennifer he would not have so easily penetrated her social stratum. And this, according to his old flame, Christine, had always been Brian's goal.

From what Gerimee and Addison had observed, Brian's social standing was a burning desire that seemed to be insatiable. Still, there had to be more, something else that linked the murders in Hurley to Jennifer's and Patty Jean's . . . . Something tha . . .

Suddenly, Donae's thoughts were diverted as he heard a heavy knock at the door. Then Silvia pushed it open and peeked in. "Mr. Donae', Mitch is here. He just ran to the deli to pick up a sandwich. He hasn't eaten lunch yet. I told him you already ate and you wouldn't mind him eating in front of you. But I did remember to tell him to bring you a couple of pickles back."

He thanked her for her thoughtfulness, and laughed at the fact that she knew how much he loved pickles but yet still insisted on addressing him as *Mr. Donae'*, instead of Lawrence or simply Donae', as he had asked her repeatedly to do. Her comeback was always the same. "I'm from the old country and was taught to show respect for my elders."

In truth, he knew it was purely that protective barrier she always kept between her and the men she cared for.

A few minutes later when Mitch walked into the room, he carried a bag large enough to feed two to three hungry men. But knowing Mitch as Donae' did, it would be just the right size for Mitch's hearty appetite.

Mitch was a big burly guy, the kind the world would describe as heavyset, whereas to Donae' he always reminded him of an oversized teddy bear, sort of like Roosevelt. Aside from being his best friend, Mitch was the most lovable man Donae' had ever known. Most people liked him right off, that is, except Lauwdry. And Donae' had a notion that that was purely because of Mitch's dark skin. But Mitch's warm friendliness was what most people noticed, and Donae's intellect told him that was why Mitch was so successful with his job. Frankly he guessed, it was just too difficult to hold back information from anyone who resembled a huge teddy bear.

Mitch threw Donae' a big grin and pitched the small bag that contained the pickles on the desk in front of him, then teased, "Here, you look like you need these, bub."

Chuckling, Donae' thanked him and cracked, "You know my one and only vice is pickles. Mitch, I hear your trip went rather well."

"I'll say. You won't believe how much an ex-wife can talk about an ex-husband, especially when a little animosity lies between the two. Of course, he wasn't there to defend himself, so it was purely one sided."

"Well, Mr. Hauser, I suggest you take a comfortable seat and tell me just what you seem so elated about. You, my man, are obviously holding back a big revelation, and you appear to be near the point of eruption."

Mitch took a huge bite of his ham sandwich and chewed it a few times while he evaluated Donae's remark. After he swallowed; he grinned but said nothing. Donae' could see he was satisfied with the sandwich as well as himself and he knew what he was about to disclose would placate Donae' immensely.

However, before he answered the question in Donae' eyes, he took another bite of sandwich and with his mouth full he said, "Okay boss, but you better get your notepad ready. I think this is gonna be pretty damn good and you're not gonna want to miss a thing."

Donae' loved this man, but at times he could be downright mischievous when he wanted to be. "I have everything I need in front of me, Mitch so stop tormenting me and shoot."

Mitch continued to needle Donae'. "Ya know the letter you gave me to check on?"

Yes, Mitch, I remember the letter."

"Well, you were right; it was important."

Donae' threw Mitch a look and finally he responded, "Okay, okay, you were right; it was from a relative, of sorts. It was the ex-wife of the son of Mr. Van Murck. Ya see, when Mr. Van Murck died, she, Diana, had all his mail forwarded to her address. That was just about the same time she started her divorce from Van Murck's son, Eric Van Murck.

When Diana got the letter explaining that the information Van Murck had requested years before was now available, her husband wasn't around. Anyway, after she opened the letter and saw what it said, she went ahead and notified the courts of Mr. Van Murck's death.

Her ex-husband, Eric Van Murck, apparently knew nothing about this other kid, because when she gave him the letter sometime later, she said he freaked.

From Diana's view and from what information she had been given throughout the marriage, she knew that her late mother-in-law, Opal, was not Eric's natural mother. But nobody ever talked much about his real mother or mentioned any other kids. So, for that reason, she had no idea if Eric and Brian had the same mother or not. She said she didn't even know for sure if Eric's natural mother and father had ever been married. But she did remember his father said that he had been married a couple of different times, so he could have been married to her."

Mitch pushed his chair back and put his booted feet on Donae's huge desk as he took another bite of his sandwich. After a minute, he continued, "Also, get this, Donae'. Eric's biological mother killed herself when he was a baby.

Diana didn't know what age he was at the time of the mothers' death. But she thought he was about one or two years old, although he could have been older. She also said the father was in the service at the time of her suicide. And by the time he heard about it, Eric was already in a home ready to be adopted. Donae', do you think that he was too late for Brian? Do you think these two are fully related brothers, that Harry Van Murck fathered both, Eric Van Murck and Brian Peterson?"

"That, I could not guess Mitch, though I do think it would be wise to find out."

Mitch choked down a swallow of soda before he added, "Well, I guess it really doesn't matter; they would still be related since they did have the same mother . . . .or, I think they had the same mother. What if they didn't . . . . Geezsus, Donae'."

Mitch swallowed another gulp of soda then spurted, "Oh, and Diana was told that Eric's mother was a little loony and got depressed a lot. Diana figured that was why she killed herself. I guess she must've been bad off because Harry once told Diana he wasn't at all surprised she killed herself. Harry said the girl's mother did the same thing when she was just a kid, about ten years old or so. So, she grew up alone. Maybe that's why she was a little loony, do ya think Donae'?

"Could be, although I doubt it. It could be a genetic trait, though."

"I thought of that too, Donae'. But if that's a possibility, the gene skipped Eric because he's not like Brian. From what Diana said he's always been in and out of trouble with the law but nothing big and he's a decent father to his son. Not a real affectionate guy but not mean, either. Supposedly, he's generous with the kid and pays his child support on time. So far as I can see, he's responsible. Diana said even more so now that they're divorced."

Mitch tossed his empty sandwich bag in the trash, then announced, "I couldn't tell for sure, but I got the feeling Eric frightened Diana. So, I don't know for sure how much she said was sugarcoated. At times, I could see she wanted to say more, yet that's all I could get from her."

"That in itself; is not surprising, Mitch. This seems to be the typical pattern for such cases. Most people who become involved with this type of personality usually end up being intimidated by their aggressiveness. What's worse, they regularly protect the same person they fear, primarily because of repercussions they may suffer if they do not. From my research I have learned this type of personality very often demands complete loyalty from their partners. They generally are responsible individuals who work extremely hard to appear completely normal. One of the idiosyncrasies is an overburdening need to show everyone that he or she is as perfectly sane as the next person. So, in other words, their persona is as fake as they are."

Donae' scratched his chin as he silently considered his first impression of Brian and what Mitch had said of Eric thus far. After he concluded his evaluation, he decided he needed much more to get a complete picture of either man. "Mitch, you said Eric insisted on loyalty, but I need more from Diana. I need to know when she and Eric were married was, he a person that felt overburdened with anxiety? Did he work unduly hard to appear successful? Did Eric strive for recognition and insist on excessive allegiance, even if it was not warranted? Moreover, was he at times an anti-social individual? Did he have a hard time integrating himself with others especially other family members? Did he avoid functions? Was he ever physical or abusive in any way towards her or the child? I know Diana might not readily release these answers, but they are truly important, Mitch."

Mitch pulled his long legs inward and sat his feet back on the floor before he sat forward and said, "At this point, I already have a few of those answers. One, Diana said he wasn't physical with her. But, on more than one occasion he came very close to it. She also said he was rigid and inordinately strict. From the gist of it, Eric was essentially hard to live with. It seemed no one could live up to his standards, even himself. He felt most people were less than he was, so most of the time he didn't feel the need to be social.

"The main reason Diana got divorced was because Eric continually tore her down. He habitually told her she was stupid and as time went on, he became extremely foul mouthed. She didn't think this was good for Billy, so she stood up to Eric and filed for a divorce. He fought it, but eventually she won the decree. Donae', I'm not sure, but if I recall accurately this next bit of information is going to sound familiar. Diana said she blamed the bad language on Eric's military stint and the strictness of the Army Ranger unit that he was with during the war. Supposedly, his training was so rigid that it became deeply seated and a habit. And he expected everyone to live up to those same ideals. Same conclusion Jennifer Hobart came up with, right?"

"That is indeed the same rationalization. All this is extremely helpful, Mitch. Yet, what I think is most interesting is that Brian and Eric both had special training while in the service."

"Yes but get this Donae'. Eric was an expert with a knife and bragged of it often. He even halfway threatened Diana once."

The question was on Donae's face before he spoke the words. "What do you mean, half-threatened her?"

"Well, during their last argument before the divorce, Eric explained in detail how easy it would be to shut her up. He said all it would take is a single slash of a knife. Diana said she was never so scared in her life. Right after she mentioned this, she became frightened and changed her story somewhat. She attributed his behavior to the divorce and its stress. But Donae', I saw the fear in her eyes, and it was very real."

"Did you get to speak with Eric?"

"No, it seems he's one of those guys that you really can't pin down. Diana said he's always taking off and he can be gone up to a month at a time. Then suddenly he reappears out of nowhere. I asked what he did for a living and she said he was a new car salesman. Tell me, Donae', how do you think he can afford child support payments and all that travel? I thought car-salesmen worked on commission, and if he's gone a lot that would mean he's only working part time. Do you agree that this just doesn't add up?"

"I do, I do indeed agree, my friend. Yet, that is merely one more piece of the puzzle we need to find."

Donae' became thoughtful, then asked, "Is Diana going to contact you when Eric is back in town?"

"Yes, she is. She said she usually sees him around the time child support is due, which will be in about a week-and-a-half."

"Mitch, did you check on the mother to see if Mr. Van Murck was the father of both Brian and Eric?"

Before Mitch could answer Donae' continued, "Hell, Mitch, we also need to find out if *she* was the mother of both boys. One of the boys could even have been Harry's from another relationship. You did say Diana mentioned he was married several times."

"That's true, although so far I haven't been able to locate any information at all on the mother. I think she might have changed her name when she met Harry Van Murck, because Diana thought she went by the name of Shirley Phillips and I can't find a damn thing on her before the adoption. It had to be an alias. But I have a friend who for a price can get me a copy of the original birth certificates for both Brian and Eric. That way we can see who she put down as the father or fathers."

"Or if she was even their birth mother, Mitch."

"Yeah, that too. In any case, Rives, said it'll take some intense research, but he'll find the answers we need. Only it'll take a hefty sum of money, like I said."

"Great, tell him to name the price and just pay it. We need that information, Mitch. It will help us find out what kind of psychopath we are dealing with. And as soon as you do hear from Diana, please let me know.

If you can, Mitch, it would help a great deal if you would go back to Chicago and meet Eric, and I guess I do not have to tell you the sooner the better."

"No problem, boss. I think that's all I have right now, Donae', so why don't you let me buy you a drink? We can go over to Keely's, okay?"

"You have yourself a deal, Mr. Hauser. First let me quickly brief Silvia. Then I will meet you there . . . say in about . . . thirty minutes."

Mitch nodded his agreement and Donae' added, "Mitch, my friend, you likewise are going to be surprised, because you are not the only person who's been busy. And I will happily clue you in over a couple of strong scotch and waters. Plus, I have my evaluation of Mr. Brian Peterson himself, and it will knock your socks off, not to mention curl your hair."

Mitch gave a hardy laugh before he replied, "Shoot, Donae' this is really getting good."

The next morning Donae' was running late. He ran all the way up the stairs to the entrance of the country club. By now, he was sure, Shelia and Michael would be seated and in the middle of their first cup of coffee.

Yet after entering the large foyer his immediate view completely astonished him. Brian Peterson was crouched over Michael and Shelia, clearly deep in discussion. Donae', in hopes of hampering any conversation that might be headed towards the family's financial situation, rushed over to their table. He was further caught off guard once he approached the group and Michael leaped up and grabbed his hand, then began pumping an exaggerated handshake that lasted far longer than necessary. The warm welcome was genuine, but the handshake, Donae' realized, was anxious. Michael's expression was full of question as he immediately shouted, "Hey here's my good brother now. Boy are we glad to see you."

Brian turned and instant surprise spread across his face as his eyes registered suspicion and his temples began to twitch. Immediate paranoia crept into his voice when he incredulously avowed, "Oh, I see you're back from your business trip, Mr. Donae'. How was the . . . where abroad did you say you were going? It looks as though you had to cut the trip short, or did I misunderstand and there was no trip at all?"

Brian's attitude immediately annoyed Donae', and in a disdainful approach he replied, "Actually . . . I never went, Mr. Peterson. I decided to wait a couple of weeks before I make the journey. I have more important issues to deal with right here at home. I am sure you realize that a man in my position has many interests to contend with . . . other than our simple action."

Without further ado Donae' changed the subject. "I see, you have met my brother, Michael, and his lovely wife, Shelia. I would invite you to join us, Mr. Peterson, but as you can imagine we have private matters to discuss, so if you will excuse us . . . ."

In the process of placing a kiss on Shelia's cheek Donae' turned his back on Brian; it was an obvious act of dismissal, though Donae' noticed Brian appeared to not get the crux of his rebuff and remained where he stood.

Donae' imperiously and stiffly explained in a more forceful manner. "As I said, Mr. Peterson, you will have to excuse us. Have a good day." All the while he spoke, he kept his back to Brian and remained so until after he walked away, then Donae' sat down.

It was obvious to Michael and Shelia that Donae' was deeply annoyed by Brian's intrusion, although from Brian's expression he was even angrier than Donae'. Everyone could easily see he was infuriated by the obvious brush off. However, Brian and his psyche were not Donae's concern right now. All he wanted was for him to go away and to leave his family alone. As far as Donae' was concerned this man was frighteningly dangerous, and Michael and Shelia were entirely naive of the pitfalls that might arise from such fraternizing.

After Brian had finally muttered his quick goodbye and in a huff moved away from the table. Michael waited only a few seconds before he exhaled a, "Lawrence, do you think he's out of hearing range?"

Shelia burst in, "My lord love a duck, what in Gods' name was that all about, Lawrence? That man is utterly spooky. Do you know he badgered us?"

"How long was he here and did he say anything to you about our family or the business?"

Michael's voice was a mere whisper when he said, "He started to, but you interrupted him. He was only here for a minute or two. Why do you ask? What's going on, Lawrence?"

Instead of answering their questions, Donae' asked Michael, "Do you know Brian Peterson?"

"Only briefly through mutual acquaintances, but he seemed to think we should have known him a lot better. He also seemed to think we should have known you were out of town and that he was waiting for you to give him a decision on some business thing. Rudely, he brought up our family's business and investments several times. What do you think that was all about?"

Donae' moaned, "Oh, Michael I do hope you did not say anything."

All at once, Shelia and Michael burst into laughter and Michael choked and sputtered, "Oh . . . Lawrence, I'm sorry Lawrence, but this is priceless, and you should see your face. You look downright comical. I would wager you just saw your life pass before your very eyes."

Donae' whispered, "It was more like me seeing your life pass before my eyes."

Again, Michael laughed and teased, "Yes, yes, this is hilarious."

Donae' was bewildered, though he did understand that Shelia and his brother loved life and thought everything was amusing, and one should each day as it were a party. But, their reaction to Brian was confusing and Donae' watched them as they continued to chuckle, finally he crossed his arms and raised a precarious eyebrow and asked, "What is going on? What is so funny, and what are you two up to now?"

Still amused, Michael explained, "Lawrence, as soon as Brian Peterson spoke to us, we knew something wasn't right because he was far too friendly for a mere acquaintance. And when he told us he was about to take over the family's business interests we were satisfied that our assumption was correct. So, being as keen as we are, Shelia and I figured you must be involved in this one way or the other. We knew it had to concern a case you're entangled in, and Brain must in some way be caught up in it. Any which way, we made sure we did not say a single word that would hinder your position in any way."

"How could you possible know what would impede my case or not?"

"We didn't, so we didn't say anything. We just nodded our heads and smiled a lot."

At that precise moment the waiter approached and asked Donae' warmly, "How are you this morning, Mr. Donae'? Can I bring you your regular Earl Grey, or would like coffee today?"

Relieved, Donae' declared, "Good morning, Ross, and no tea today. I think it will be a round of mimosas, for we are celebrating family and their faithful allegiance today. What do you kids say, are you game?" Both, Michael and Shelia eagerly nodded their heads in agreement and Donae' continued, "And as a thank you, breakfast is on me."

Shelia giggled as she purred "Ooooh . . . mimosas, Michael and breakfast to boot. Lawrence sure does know how to keep a lady pleasantly pleased."

Again, she giggled with an added tease, "Not only with life's simple little pleasures but also with his never-ending escapades. I do wish you would include us more often, Lawrence. We do love a good adventure."

"My sweet, you are not included this time, either, so I suggest you take your pleasures from your breakfast and be satisfied."

# CHAPTER 13

Wednesday was cold and drizzly, yet Donae' was in his office hours before his normal time. He was excited and couldn't sleep, so he decided it was best to go back to work and prepare himself for Sergeant Cox. This anticipation had been building since Silvia had informed him Sergeant Cox would be in to meet with him today. Donae' had a hunch that this man knew something about the personality of Brian Peterson. After all, he had spent six years in the same close quarters. He had worked with him almost daily, so it would be inconceivable to think that he would not have seen something along the way. As good as Brian was at hiding his true self, no one was good enough to hide it twenty-four hours a day.

When Sergeant Cox entered the room, Donae' could feel his presence bigger than life. He resembled what most perceived a Marine to look like, but yet there seemed to be more than just his outer physical strength. It was as if one could almost see physically that he was a man who had a great deal of integrity. It was plain to see he was very proud to be a Marine and his carriage confirmed this. He stood tall, though Donae' doubted he was six feet. His jaw was stern, and he had a neck as wide as his head, which nourished a full head of light brown hair, cut short and high above his ears. His handshake was severe, however respectful, and behind his intense slate colored eyes was a twinkle that showed he enjoyed a good time. Donae' knew he could like this guy, but more, he could respect him.

Subsequent to the customary pleasantries, Donae' eagerly entered into the conversation about Brian Peterson. "Sergeant Cox, do you remember a Brian Peterson? He was in your Special Forces Unit about nineteen years ago. I believe it was 1940, until about 1946 or so, when he served under your command."

"No, Sir."

For an instant Donae's face registered disappointment, then Sergeant Cox moved on. "When Miss Perez first gave me his name, I didn't recall him at all. I needed to pull his records first and, yes, at that time I started to recall him. After thinking on it, I now remember him and his tour entirely."

Donae' relaxed and sat back to listen.

"We were what you or a layman might call a front runner. We were part of a recon unit, what is known also as a scout, slash, sniper unit. We did the dirty work, whatever it took to make sure our boys would be safe when entering a hostile area."

"Sergeant, how does one become a part of such a unit?"

"Well, for one thing, it takes a certain kind of man, a man who has a strong attitude along with discipline. Not everyone can do the job. It's not only difficult, it's brutal, and many more drop out than complete the course."

"How did Brian become part of this unit? It seemed it would take an expert shooter."

"Yes, sir, it sure does, and Peterson was just such an individual. He requested to join the unit and worked harder than anyone I had ever seen. He was determined to be the best sniper in the unit."

Donae' said more to himself than to Sergeant Cox, "So he was that good, huh?"

"What was that . . . Sir, I didn't quite catch that last question.

"I only wondered if Brian was good at his job, Sergeant."

"He was more than just good, Mr. Donae'. He thrived on it. I mean, if anyone was ever born to do a particular job, Peterson was for this one. His dedication was almost fanatical."

"What do you mean, Sergeant?"

"Well, the men that do this type of job need to be able to control their feelings and realize it's just a job. You know ... when you're a shooter it's nothing personal. Some men have trouble with this and some master it. But Peterson ... he enjoyed it. That's what was scary."

"Do you mean he liked the job or to kill people?"

"Both. He liked what he did and how he did it. He never tried to hide that fact."

"Do you remember when he first came into your unit?"

"Yes, sir."

"What was his frame of mind?"

"Like what do you mean, Mr. Donae'?"

"Was he depressed? Since the situation with his family was shortly before he joined the service, I wondered if his mental attitude was stable. Did he have any trouble adjusting to rules and regulations, et cetera?"

"As I said, after I went back through my records, it brought back all kinds of memories. But no, Mr. Donae', I don't remember him being upset, especially about any family members. And as far as I was told, Peterson didn't have any. I mean, he said he was an orphan raised by the state, and as soon as he turned eighteen, they just threw him out on the street. He said, that was why he didn't have any choice but to join a branch of the service."

"An orphan?"

"Yes, sir. Maybe that's why he was right at home in the service, since he was raised in an orphanage. I mean, I'm sure they also had strict rules he had to follow. I guess if you stop and think about it, there wasn't much of an adjustment for him to deal with. Wouldn't you agree, Mr. Donae'?"

Donae' was speechless for several minutes as he tried to figure out why Brian would want to lie about his parents. What benefit would it be for him not to have parents, to be known as an orphan since birth instead of just recently? Obviously, these were questions only Brian could answer. Yet, after some thought, the only explanation Donae' could determine was with no family Brian had fewer questions to answer. Therefore, no explanation was required about their untimely deaths. With no questions, there would be no chance for mistakes.

"Sergeant Cox, did you ever notice that Brian had mood swings or any personality variations?"

"Some, but he seemed to be able to control himself pretty well. But it mostly showed up when he failed at something, which, I think you would agree is normal, wouldn't you say, Mr. Donae'?"

Donae' did not answer, so Sergeant Cox moved on. "Peterson was hungry for praise. Always wanted to be recognized, and if he wasn't the center of attention, he felt he was being treated unfairly. Damn, I recall several times when someone else in the unit did better than him at a rifle competition." Sergeant Cox shook his head and continued, "Peterson was just downright pissed and once, when he didn't get a promotion and another fellow in the unit did, Peterson immediately claimed that this person was shown favoritism. Yes, Mr. Donae', Brian Peterson was always fretting about who was getting more credit or attention than he was. Plain and simple, he just wasn't much of a team player. He hated to share success with the unit; Peterson wanted all the glory for himself. That was one of the reasons he wasn't really liked by many of the men in the unit."

Donae' contemplated whether he should or should not explain Brian's, narcissistic personality to the Sergeant, yet he was not one hundred percent sure this was indeed Brian's state. And since he himself was not an expert in the science of mental disorders he felt hesitant about labeling Brian's condition.

Although Donae' had completed his studies he still had only interned shortly while he studied law. And now he only dabbled in it as part of his investigative evaluation of suspects. Still and all, he had enough background in the field to suspect that Brian might have more than one mental disorder. Donae' was not certain how probable this was. However, it did seem Brian Peterson leaned in that direction. He displayed a detached nature along with many negative personality traits. From what Donae' had assessed thus far, Brian's mental attitude suggested several idiosyncrasies that pointed to an, obsessive compulsive personality disorder, on top of his narcissistic personality.

Donae' examined his notes. Then still uncertain, he asked, "Did you personally like Brian, Sergeant Cox?"

The Sergeant moved slightly about in his seat. His demeanor showed the question made him feel uncomfortable. This was not Donae's intention; he only wanted to put the Sergeant's answers in perspective. After a minute or two of silence, Donae' saw that the Sergeant had come to terms with the question and relaxed, and once Sergeant Cox began to answer he leaned forward to impress upon Donae' its genuine significance. "Well, to be honest with you, sir, Peterson wasn't one of my favorite people. From what I remember, he never had any true friends and appeared to use people to his own advantage. Even with the women he occasionally dated he always had a reason for the relationship. It was pretty damn clear as far as I was concerned; Peterson just didn't respect other people. He was never happy for others or their achievements. He felt he could do better and said so more often than not."

Sergeant Cox shifted in his seat once more, then crossed his legs to get more comfortable before he added, "Mr. Donae', most all Marines stand proud and work hard to achieve their very best. But their unit is their family, so they also strive for a collective best . . . I mean, certainly they always want to do their personal best, but they also want their team to do as well. But, for Peterson it was different. He always wanted himself to be number one and the outfit second. He was extremely egotistical and not easy to get along with."

"Did he earn many merits?"

"He did well, but he could have done better if his attitude was more contributory to his unit."

"Do you remember if he had any buddies that he may have confided in?"

"No, like I said, he wasn't the most likable guy and mostly he stayed to himself. He was very reserved, treated people like they were below him. I tell you, Mr. Donae', if I didn't know he came from an orphan home, I would've thought he was a snob."

"Sergeant Cox, you said Brian was an expert in weaponry. Did that include knives?"

"He knew knives, but he wasn't as expert at it as he was with a rifle."

Donae' stood up and walked around the huge mahogany desk. He was very conscious of his thin frame next to this more than healthy individual. Playing tennis and golf was his primary exercise and he had a hunch that this brick of a man would have laughed at the suggestion of something so tame.

"Sergeant Cox, I want to thank you for your time. I am extremely grateful that you were in town and we had this opportunity to talk. You really have no idea how much your information has helped. Will you be in town long?"

Donae' was pleasantly surprised by Sergeant Cox's answer, "Only for one week, sir. I'm on the Marine Golf Team and we're playing at one of the country clubs nearby. Do you play?"

"I am sure not as well as you, Sergeant Cox, for no one has ever asked me to play on their team. As well, it's rarely easy for me to find a partner so I can only deduce it's because most do not want to be humiliated on the course."

Sergeant Cox gave a hardy laugh and shook Donae's hand while he patted him on the back. "Well, I guess we all have our expertise, Mr. Donae', so don't let it get you down."

Both men walked towards the door, and Donae' gave the Sergeant's hand one more shake. Before Sergeant Cox said goodbye though, he awkwardly asked, "Mr. Donae', I know you can't tell me anything right now. However, I really would like to know what's going on, so do you think when whatever you're doin is over, you could fill me in? I would hate to never know why you had all these questions or how my answers could've helped you."

Donae' laughed out louder then he intended as he thoughtfully answered, "Indeed, I understand completely. And I most certainly will let you know the entire story after the case is closed. Only, for now I hope that you will understand that obscurity is of the utmost importance and is the only way to keep my clients safe."

"You have my word, Mr. Donae', my lips are tightly bound. Oh, and one more thing before I go, Mr. Donae'. Is Silvia married or is she going out with anyone, because I'd love to ask her to join me for a drink later."

"Silvia? No, no man is in her life, Sergeant Cox. And I wish you all the luck in the world, Sergeant, for I'm afraid you might need it. Silvia, I am afraid, protects her solitude like a bulldog does his bone."

Donae' gave Sergeant Cox an encouraging smile and stood back to let him leave the room and to enter where Silvia sat smiling up from her desk.

Donae' closed the door and stood behind it for a minute. His inborn inclination was to put an ear to the door and listen to Silvia's answer, but suddenly he felt the presence of his grandmother and he thought he heard, "LAWRENCE! How dare you!"

Donae' looked around briskly, then moved back to his seat. He felt as if he had been caught in the act of doing something wrong. All this, because he knew what his grandmother felt about his eavesdropping. Yet snooping was his job, not to mention in his blood. His father also investigated unsolved crimes and wrote about the mysteries until his own mysterious death some twenty years back.

After he studied all the documentation he had compiled, Donae' decided that it was time for another conference with Gerimee and Addison Hobart.

*This should happen right away before I move closer to any final decision. I am sure I am close, but how close?* He contemplated. *Something is missing, but what? A mental disorder in itself . . . does not kill. Yet, I am quite sure Brian is responsible for the carnage of Jennifer and Patty Jean. With all I have, is it enough to be incriminating?"*

With his evaluation and what evidence, he had accumulated, Donae' hoped that he could soon openly charge Brian with the murders, but he had a way to go before he had solid proof. The meeting he planned to have with Gerimee and Addison was merely to give them ample time to ready themselves for the jolt of its publicity, as well as to prepare Sharon and Carol for the shock in the event there was indeed an arrest.

It was Friday and storms were predicted for later that afternoon. The three men sat in Addison's library sipping a snifter of brandy. Every now and then they could hear the wind as it began to pick up its velocity. Donae' appreciated that the comfortable room was more than a little agreeable to the inner soul as the fire burned softly in its hearth, and he thought, *this room is grand.*

Its colors were warm and full of earthy hues that fully enhanced the Oriental motif. The expensive artwork that hung on every wall showed large peacocks in brilliant dissimilar colors. They were accompanied by mosques and colorful florals. The golds and silvers throughout the decorative art only further embellished the warmth of the enormous but splendid room. The flicker of the fire plainly adorned the all-round pleasure while effortlessly putting everyone at ease.

The three men sat quietly as they waited for Carol to exit the room. She was busily bustling from one side of the room to the other, trying to assure herself that everyone was comfortable, and all had what they needed for the parley.

Addison's face showed the strain that he was trying unsuccessfully to hide from his wife. Finally, Carol turned to Mary her servant and asked, "Mary could you please take over from here, dear? Check now and then to simply make sure the gentlemen have everything they need."

She looked over towards her husband and smiled. Donae' could see her smile was burdened with worry, though her voice attempted to hide it when she informed them, "Gentlemen, you must excuse me while I take Corey for her walk before the rains."

She looked over towards Addison and continued, "Dear, if you need me just send Mary; she knows the route I usually take. We shouldn't be too long, especially with the storm on its way."

Once again, she turned to Gerimee and Donae' and added earnestly, "You two, please don't exhaust Addison. He's still not his full self yet. And Gerimee, you know as I do, that he's not as hardy as he wants us to believe."

As soon as Carol was satisfied that all was said and everything was in order, she scooped up her black terrier and headed out the door.

As the door closed behind Carol, Donae' looked over to where Addison sat and asked, "Are you going to be okay through this, Addison? We need you healthy if you are to be involved with this investigation. We cannot take a chance on impairing you and your health in any way."

"Thank you, Lawrence, for your concern. It is noted, as well as appreciated, but I am fine; my wife tends to worry a bit too much. I'm afraid she fears that she will lose another person she loves, and I don't think she could handle that . . . not quite yet, anyway."

With an eagerness that was evident in his tone, Gerimee enthusiastically opened the conversation to the subject at hand. "You found something, didn't you Lawrence?"

"I believe I have, my friend. I think we might be very close to several answers. And, I have learned that our friend, Brian Peterson, is more than he wants to show us . . . or the world."

Addison leaned forward and a new zest presented itself. His face was ripe with interest and he held his breath for an instant before he asked, "What are you about to divulge, Lawrence? What have you learned? We were right, weren't we . . . Brian killed my daughter and grandchild?"

"I cannot say that he himself killed them, but I have come to the conclusion that he had something to do with the murders. I believe he may have paid someone to free himself of both his wife and child."

Donae' stood and moved to stand in front of the warmth of the fireplace. After he pondered his thoughts he added, "Gerimee, Addison, do not misunderstand me. It is not that I think he is not capable of such a task. I merely think it was easier and much cleaner for him this way."

Addison's face looked even starker than it had earlier. Yet he stood and moved closer to where Donae' leaned against the fireplace and asked, "Lawrence, will you fill us in? Please tell us how we can help."

Gerimee threw in, "Yes Lawrence, there's got to be something we can do to help."

"Patience, Gerimee, Addison, all in due time. But for now, what I need from you two is more information on Brian and his past whereabouts."

"What do you mean? We told you everything we know."

"That may be true as far as you know. However, you may unconsciously have something and not be aware of it. With the new information I have on Brian's earlier behavioral pattern, I have a sneaky suspicion that Jennifer and Patty Jean were not Brian's first victims, and I want to make sure there were no others along the way."

"What! Lawrence, are you trying to tell us Brian killed others? Who, when? Come on, Lawrence tell us, tell us everything." Addison begged, "please, Lawrence, I need to know."

Donae' looked from one face to the other before he answered, "I am almost certain he killed his adoptive parents, although that case will probably never be proven. It has already been stamped accidental; case closed. However, I am confident we can stop this from going any further."

Gerimee sat dumfounded on the sofa; his eyes were glued on Addison's stunned expression. There was complete silence in the room. After several minutes the whirl of the wind banged a tree branch against the windowpane, and it startled all back to reality and to the words Donae' had just spoken.

Gerimee released the breath he was holding and asked, "More, he killed more innocent people?"

Donae' did not answer, for he believed it was nothing more than a rhetorical question. Instead he said, "First, I want your assurance that for now we will continue to do this investigation without any assistance from the police. I trust it is likely that they will not accept what we have as evidence and this could be detrimental to our case. I am quite sure they would brand what we have as circumstantial and disregard it. So, once again for the time being, we must keep this to ourselves and involve no one else."

Addison and Gerimee nodded in agreement and Donae' went on, "Okay, then let's move on. I need answers to several new questions that have arisen."

Gerimee spoke first, though his voice quivered then cracked with his opening word. "Whaa . . . at, what can we tell you? Just ask away."

"Addison, did Brian ever talk about his parents and their deaths? Did he mention he had a brother or any past relationships, maybe even a marriage?"

"Marriage? You suspect he's been married before?" Questioned Gerimee?

"What? Why are you asking such a question?" Asked Addison.

"Addison, Gerimee, please let's not lose track. There is a lot we do not know about Brian. And I am merely examining all avenues. Please, can you simply answer the questions?"

Again, Addison asked, "He has a brother? Brian has a brother?"

"Addison, please!"

"I'm sorry, Lawrence, but I had no idea: he never mentioned that. As a matter of fact, Jennifer at one time brought up tracing his biological parents. She wanted to see if maybe he had family somewhere, but Brian was adamant about "leaving dead dogs lie". His words, not mine. And as far as his adoptive parents went, it was like pulling teeth to get him to discuss them. At first, we asked all kinds of questions about his life before he and Jennifer got married. But he stayed close-mouthed about his past and only wanted to talk about his life today.

"And another marriage? There was never any mention of one. But, like I said, he wasn't very talkative about his past. He only told us what he felt was necessary, I guess. Just enough to keep us happy and off his back."

"He never slipped and told you something that did not fit his earlier story?" asked Donae'.

"No, he only furnished us with what I would guess was ambiguous information. He never journeyed deep into any portion of his life. Wouldn't you agree, Gerimee?"

"Yes, I do agree. I don't remember Jen telling me much about his past, except about his time and life as a Marine, which of course, Brian was extremely proud of. If I remember correctly though, Jen did mention that he had only dated a few women here and there. I guess he had told her that he was so busy putting himself through school and advancing his career he didn't have time for women. So, I don't think there was another wife, but I can't be sure."

Gerimee hesitated and stood up as he incredulously asked, "Lawrence, did I hear you say something about a brother? I'm absolutely sure Jen never mentioned anything about a brother or any relative. All she ever mentioned was the adoptive parents. Are you saying Brian has a brother and he never mentioned this?"

"I do not know if Brian was aware of his brother. At this point any-way, I do not think he did. It does not look like it, anyway. I only wanted to check and see if the brother ever contacted him after he was informed of Brian's existence. I should be learning more about the brother in a week or so. As of now, all I know is that he and Eric are related, yet, I do not know if he is a half-brother, or what. But when I find out you can be sure I will fill you in. As for right now, all I can do is wait and Mitch Hauser will let me know when I can speak with, Mr. Eric Van Murck."

Addison moved about the room. He stopped momentarily to look out the window and whispered. "This is all so incredible, Lawrence. These pasts few years have been so unreal. It's as if it all happened to someone else, and we are merely spectators. Then there's the pain, and that brings you back to the here and now, and the reality is overwhelming."

"I can only imagine how true that is, Addison, but soon we will have more, and you will have your answers.

Donae' laid his arm around Addison's shoulder and then informed him. "Mitch Hauser and I are working on attaining copies of the birth certificates for Brian and Eric. We should have them any day now, and hopefully with these in hand we can learn more. For right now, all we know for sure, is that his mother committed suicide when they were very young. We do not know if she was truly their biological parent or not; the same goes for the father."

Suddenly Donae' heard Carol close the front door and hurriedly added, "If either of you run into Brian, please go about as if nothing has changed. This will be extremely helpful. We do not want to raise his suspicions. This will only alert him and make my job more difficult. The less he suspects, the easier it will be to get him to open up to me. So far, he is very eager to be my friend. I would like to keep it that way as long as possible."

Gerimee and Addison nodded their heads in agreement, as Addison solemnly avowed. We'll do our damnedest to abide by your wishes, Lawrence. As we told you in the beginning, we'll do whatever it takes to take Brian down."

# CHAPTER 14

I t seemed Diana knew her ex-husband fairly well, since he showed up a week and a half-later, as she had predicted he would. When she called Mitch, it was early in the morning, and he was in the middle of his first cup of java and not quite awake. However, with the sound of Diana's excited barrage of words, he was soon open-eyed and alert.

Diana sounded breathless when she quickly stated, "Mitch, if you still want to speak with Eric, you better hurry. Because he just got back in town last night, and now he's talking about leaving again, this time for an extended vacation, maybe for several months or more."

After Diana's call Mitch didn't waste any time; he didn't even stop to call Donae'. It was Saturday and he didn't have time to track him down before the next plane left for Chicago. He grabbed his satchel, threw a few personal articles in it and stuffed all the files he had on the case on top, then headed straight for the airport.

When he exited the plane at O'Hare, the sight of Diana surprised him yet pleased him enormously. Puzzled, he asked, "What the ... what are you doing here and how did you know when I was coming in?"

She smiled good-naturedly and answered, "Now ... is that any way to greet your ride? Besides, I needed to talk with you as soon as possible.

Right after I talked with you this morning, I spoke with Eric again. He dropped by about a half-hour after I talked with you. He asked me if I knew anything about some guy who was looking for him. I guess you left some messages that you wanted to speak with him. Anyway, when I said you dropped by looking for him and the only thing, I knew was you were from New York, you should have seen the look on his face. I tell you, Mitch, he freaked out. The way he reacted I didn't know for sure if he would stay around much longer. I was worried you wouldn't make it back to town before he left again." Diana stopped to search her purse for her keys and parking stub, then went on. "So, I called your office and your service answered. They said you would be out of town for a few days. Then, as the saying goes, from pure deduction I figured out you were on your way here. In any case, I called and found out when the next flight was due in from New York and took a chance that you'd be on it. See, you're not the only detective in town, Mr. Hauser."

"Well, I'm very glad to see that you're so good at tracking people, Diana. Where is Eric right now; do you know? I'm not too late, am I?"

"No, no, Mitch you're not late at all. And yes, I know where he's at. He took Billy to the midget-car races, and he won't be back until around seven o'clock tonight." Diana checked her watch before she continued, "So, that gives us about three hours to kill. How about an early dinner?"

Mitch's smile revealed pure pleasure, and he openly responded with ease. "You're on and any place you feel like, is fine with me; I love to eat."

As he took her arm to help maneuver her through the crowded airport, he thought how much he liked this lady. She was a person he had felt comfortable with from the get-go. He decided that it had to be because she was so real, a natural woman with no false fronts, and he doubted she ever noticed he was black.

After they took several steps towards the exit, Diana asked, "Do you like Italian? I know this great little place; it has red-checked tablecloths, a violin and some of the greatest Italian food you'll ever eat."

"Sounds good as long as it's on me."

She smiled her agreement and took his hand so they would not be separated as they exited through the crowded doorway.

Once Diana started the car and pulled from the parking-space, Mitch opened the conversation again. "You said, Eric told you he was leaving town?"

"Yeah, that's what he said all right."

"That came about after he found out I was looking for him, huh? Are you sure he wasn't planning this trip before that?"

"No, he's never said anything to me about any extended trip until last night."

Diana hesitated and Mitch watched as she carefully considered her next words and when she started to speak, he could tell she was uncomfortable with what she had to say. "Mitch, I want you to make me a promise that you won't let Eric know that I said anything to you. Eric can't know that I called you. Just tell him you took a chance on him being in town. Or you were already here on some other business. Tell him anything, except that I called you. Do you understand? I just don't want any trouble; I don't need Eric going crazy on me because he thinks I betrayed him. He can get pretty rowdy sometimes, especially if he thinks I'm not being loyal to him. That really pisses him off and anytime I can avoid his wrath, I'd like to."

Mitch could see the fear in Diana's eyes and tried to alleviate it. "Don't worry, Diana. Eric's not going to hurt you or Billy."

Later that evening Mitch recalled these words as they sat in Diana's living room waiting for Eric to bring Billy home. It was after nine and she was becoming frantic. She kept repeating, "This is not like Eric. I mean, not to call or anything. I mean he knows I worry; it's just not like em. Mitch, something has to be wrong." Wringing her hands, she added, "Maybe I should start calling the hospitals or something, cause this just isn't like Eric."

Mitch was also starting to worry. His instincts told him this was going to get worse and he didn't know how to tell Diana this. Finally, he asked, "Diana, do you mind if I leave you for a few minutes? I need to make a phone call and I don't want to tie your line up."

She looked frightened but answered, "I'm fine, Mitch. You go ahead; I'll be okay. There's a phone on the corner by the cleaners."

Mitch, discouraged, dialed Donae's number. When Donae' finally answered after about ten rings, Mitch could tell that the jingles had awakened his sleep. Mitch had completely forgotten how late it was, yet it wouldn't have made any difference; he still would have called his friend for support.

Without any preliminary, Mitch went straight to the issue and filled Donae' in on everything that had gone on since Diana's first call early that morning. Finally, he took a deep breath and asked the question he dreaded, for he feared he already knew the answer. "Donae', do you think that I'm overreacting, or do you think we better get a couple of your friends here in Chicago to start looking for Eric and Billy?"

Donae' could hear the tension that accompanied the fear in Mitch's restrained voice. He knew this man's instincts were rarely wrong, so he quickly responded to his friend's obvious concern. "Mitch, see if you can get a picture of Eric and Billy. In the meantime, I will get Carl Lansing on the line and we will see what we can do. And Mitch, you are going to need to get that picture and a good description of the car Eric is driving into the hands of the police ASAP; get that info downtown as soon as possible. But first give me the number where I can reach you, and I will call you back as soon as I finish with Carl. It will not be too long Mitch, And . . . Mitch do not worry. We will get Billy back safe."

The minute Donae' hung the phone up, he grabbed for his personal address book and dialed Carl at home.

After a few rings, the gravelly voice of Captain Carl Lansing came on the line with his gruff, "Yello."

Donae' smiled to himself and said, "Hello, old man. How are things in the Windy City?" He heard Carl's sudden intake of breath and Donae' knew it was a sign of recognition. Then, immediately, the man happily shouted into the mouthpiece, "Dammit, Donae', it's damn good to hear your voice, even if it is close to midnight. How in God's name are you, anyway?"

Before Donae' could answer, Carl went right on. "Well, I would guess not good because you wouldn't be calling me at this god-awful hour of the night if it were otherwise. Am I right?"

"You are indeed right, as usual sir."

"Oh, knock off that shit, Donae'. Don't waste your time trying to butter me up with that damn, sir stuff. Just tell me what in the hell I can do for you."

Smiling at Carl's gruffness, Donae' moved on to the problem at hand. And without a new breath, he went through his brief but accurate scenario of the Peterson case and ended with why Mitch was in Chicago with Diana. Then he moved directly to what Mitch had called to tell him. He finished with, "Carl, can you help us?"

"Sure, you know anything you need, you got. I'll get dressed and go down to the station. Meanwhile, you have Mitch get that picture of the kook and tell him to meet me at the precinct. It shouldn't take us too long to find this guy, especially since he's only been gone a few hours."

Donae' hung up and called Mitch to explain what Carl had said. When Donae' said goodbye, he could hear the relief in his friend's voice and as he hung up the phone Donae' wondered if Mitch blamed himself for this unexpected change in events.

Up till now Donae' had avoided the obvious; he couldn't help but think of Brian and his lack of compassion. He sighed and whispered a quick prayer for Billy that he would be home safe in his mother's arms very soon. He ended it with *Please, God, do not let Eric have the same tendencies as his brother Brian.*

Diana had an old picture of Eric and a new one of Billy. Mitch took these, along with the description of Eric's car, and headed downtown for the police station where Carl was captain.

Mitch had first met Carl years ago; at the time Carl's brother had worked with Donae' in the district attorney's office. Then once again a few years later, after Donae' helped him locate the remains of his niece who had vanished a few months before. It seemed the young lady had the misfortune of being in the wrong place at the wrong time and a couple of thugs took advantage of the fact. They saw the pretty twenty-four-year-old waiting at the bus stop after her hard day's work at a local clinic.

The two slime balls had sat and watched her from the diner across the street where they had been slugging down beers since noontime. The punks told police that before they left the diner, they decided to spend the night partying with the girl. They confessed dismissively, "We never been with a real lady before, so we figured that this night was as good as any to taste the forbidden fruits. All we wanted was to see if a lady was any different than the street girls we hang with. But, damn, she was a real spitfire and all she wanted was to fight. We just wanted a little fun and the bitch wouldn't even give us the time of day. But we damn well showed her."

The captain's niece apparently ignored their advances and that angered them. "No", was not an answer these creeps accepted readily. So, they grabbed her and forced her into the back of their van. Later that night the captain's niece made a big mistake. Hysterical, she screamed at her perpetrators that her uncle Carl was a police officer, and he would track them down and kill them for what they were doing to her.

Unfortunately, these two thugs already had several priors which happened to include a couple of assaults along with one armed robbery, but what made it worse for the girl, they both hated cops. That accompanied with the thought of prison again further panicked them, and in minutes after her disclosure, the young girl lay dead at their feet. Now the charges would not only be abduction and rape, but murder as well. Terrified, the punks hid the girl's body in the trunk of an old abandoned car in a junk-yard, then went about their illegal business as if nothing had ever happened.

Several months of investigation brought the police no answers, and eventually they gave up. The file read: **cold, no trace, no leads**. That's when Donae' stepped in. It was his first case and he broke it wide open within two months'. Carl and his family were completely grateful to him and said they would always be there if Donae' ever needed their help in any future action. It turned out that Carl was true to his word and had proved it many times in the past years.

Carl stood patiently at the front desk as he waited for Mitch. He read and reread Eric's rap sheet, trying to get a feel for the perp. The guy was a nuisance, but it seemed that was all, mostly just domestic squabbles in which the charges were always dropped. Plus he had a couple of brawls at a local tavern but those, too, were dismissed.

Just about this time Mitch walked through the front door of the police station and Carl set the file aside and hurried over to greet him. He grabbed Mitch's hand for a quick handshake, then slapped him on the shoulder and said, "How are you, Mitch? Did you get the pictures? What about a description of the car? We need to get it on the streets as soon as possible. Eric already has a pretty good head start." Carl recognized the concern on Mitch's face and gave him another slap on the back.

Carl's confident manner immediately helped Mitch calm his imagination which had been fueling his fears up to this point. He returned the slap on Carl's back and said, "I'm glad you're with us on this, Carl. It's so different being on this side of a case."

Carl nodded his mutual understanding and Mitch moved on. "I don't know if Donae' filled you in on what kind of nut case we might have here. But I have to confess, Carl, I'm scared. I just don't know what Eric's capable of and Diana, the mother, gives mixed messages. I don't know if she's completely open with me; I think she's scared of her ex."

"From his rap sheet, I can see why. It seems he's a big man when it comes to women, but from his wife's prudent interpretation, he was more mouth than anything else. I, myself, have my doubts but don't worry about the kid Mitch, we'll get em back and he'll be okay."

Mitch felt better once the description of Eric and his car hit the streets. He paced the station's floor as he clung to Carl's reassurance that everything would work out and soon Billy would be back, safe in his mother's arms.

By early morning Carl received a call from an officer who said he was from the Freeport area. He reported, "I spotted the boy and his father, Eric and Billy Van Murck. They just left a Motel Six and I followed them to a pancake house. It looks like the father feels pretty safe because he and the kid are having a leisurely breakfast."

Carl asked, "Does the kid look okay?

Officer Mac Brick paused, and Carl could hear the line scratch and crackle before he answered. "From where I stand, and what I can see, he looks fine. Captain, right now I'm waiting for my backup to get here. Then I think I can have Billy out of harm's way in a matter of minutes. I'll give you a call as soon as everything's under control. Then we can set up a meeting place for the transfer. Oh, and Captain, if it's possible, it'd be good if the mother was there for the transport. I know how kids that young can get pretty scared; I have a couple about the same age."

Mitch was on the phone calling Diana before the officer could reply to Carl's ten-four. After she screamed her delight, he told her that she should get ready; he would pick her up and they would go get Billy. When Mitch arrived, Diana was so grateful she couldn't hold back her tears of relief. She thanked Mitch, then Carl, and then Mitch again.

During their trip and in spite of her hiccups and tears, Diana explained to Mitch and Carl, "I've always feared something like this would happen. I guess in a way that makes this my fault. I shouldn't have always tried so hard to appease Eric and his whims. See, I never knew for sure how to react to his crazy moods. So, I just didn't fight him. But, let me tell you Mitch, fearing the inevitable and actually living through it are very different. And I will never put Billy in harm's way again, never, and I have you to thank for my second chance." Diana squeezed Mitch's hand and added, "I'll always be grateful to you both."

As they moved closer to the stationhouse in Freeport, Illinois, where Eric and Billy awaited them, Mitch noticed Diana started to nervously bite her nails. Finally, she asked, "Mitch . . . was I wrong? I kept Eric in Billy's life because I really thought a boy needed his father. But with Eric's irrational behavior, maybe I shouldn't have. I tried to make sure Billy was safe. I kept their visits short and usually in a controlled environment. I also worked so hard not to upset Eric before a visit so Billy wouldn't have to put up with his tantrums."

Diana took a deep breath and crossed her arms protectively around herself and acknowledged, "Still, with all this I lived in constant fear that something like this would happen. Mitch, Eric threatened that one day he'd take Billy from me, but I thought it was only to frighten me, or for control. Eric loves to be in control."

Mitch wrapped his arm around Diana as he attempted to comfort her. "Diana, you were just trying to be a good mother. You didn't do anything wrong."

Diana studied Mitch's face for several seconds before inhaling another deep breath. Eventually she laid her hand softly on his knee. "Mitch . . . I know Eric and his temper, and in reality, I think this was bound to happen sooner or later. So please don't feel guilty; you didn't cause this to happen. It wasn't your fault. Please, understand that."

Mitch was happy to hear her words and to know Diana felt that way. He didn't want her to blame him for Eric's backlash to the news that he wanted to speak with him. Yes, it was nice to hear. Yet regardless of her words he still blamed himself for the pain she had suffered for the past twenty-four hours. However, he smiled and said, "Let's negotiate. I won't blame myself if you do the same." She smiled softy and squeezed his hand to let him know they had a deal.

By late afternoon Billy was back in his mother's arms. Mitch could see the young boy was a little confused. He didn't understand why the police had arrested his daddy or interrupted their trip to Canada. Nevertheless, Diana had him comforted and calmed down before they were on their way back to Chicago.

As soon as Mitch set eyes on Eric he knew he was a browbeater, which helped him understand Diana and her actions. And now he could hardly wait to get him back to Chicago and the police station, because he was itching to begin interrogating him. He wanted to know why Eric would react so irrationally to the possibility of speaking with him. Why did he feel the need to take Billy and leave the States? Above all, why did he look so frightened? In Mitch's opinion, this kind of reaction was obviously from a man who had something to hide. Eric's flight was a lot more than a simple retreat from his ex-wife and he intended to find out the whole story.

When they got back to the station, Mitch and Carl checked the contents of Eric's suitcases, at which time Mitch had one more interesting question. Where did Eric get all the cash he had stuffed to the brim of his suitcase?

Carl shook his head and asked, "Hell, Mitch, don't you think that's a lot of money? I mean, it certainly is a hell of a lot more than any car salesmen I know earns."

From the beginning, Eric was uncooperative. He refused to answer any questions at all for the police in Freeport and was pissed off that he had been picked up in the first place. Between his foul-mouthed tantrums, he insisted that he had a right to take his damn kid anywhere the hell he wanted and when it damn well pleased him.

When Detective Samuel, who conducted the interrogation with Carl asked, "Hey, Eric, where did ya get all that money? It's gotta be close to a quarter of a million dollars."

Eric flinched then shot back, "It's none of your fucken business." He grinned, then snickered sarcastically, "Why are you guys so interested in what money I have? Are you workin undercover for the IRS or something? Or maybe you're just plain fucken jealous that a guy like me has all that fucken money." Again, he snickered, "I'm cocksure, it's a hell of a lot more than either of you'll ever see in your sorry-filled lives."

The two officers listened to Eric's smart-ass remarks for almost an hour-and-a half. Finally, Captain Carl Lansing decided, "This is a bunch of bullshit, Get Hauser in here."

At once Carl recognized fear as it flickered across Eric's eyes, and when Mitch sauntered into the room Carl laughed and said, "He's all yours, Mitch."

Carl peered directly into Eric's remorseless glare before he moved around the table. At the same time, he slowly lit the cigarette that had hung from the side of his mouth throughout the entire interrogation. Eventually he stopped and took a long drag, then slowly blew a huge puff of smoke into Eric's impertinent face. Without another word he turned and walked to the other side of the room. There he leaned against the wall while he waited for Mitch to begin his first round of questions.

Mitch observed that either his entrance or the captain's show of anger had rattled Eric. For this reason, after Carl had leaned himself against the wall, Mitch persisted with what seemed to be Carl's effective stare, and with each step closer he peered boldly into Eric's contemptuous eyes. Slowly, he walked the rest of the distance around the conference table. After he planted himself firmly in front of the now provoked Eric. He stood there without uttering a word for at least two minutes. He waited stoically while he studied Eric's obnoxious expression which at the present displayed a nervous and ill-favored twitch.

The silence was clearly making Eric nervous. Now, Mitch grasped what Eric was about. He thought his foul mouth intimated people, thus giving him control, which at this time he feared he had lost.

Mitch continued to stand in silence while he tapped his six-inch pencil on the ledge of the table, hoping to increase Eric's annoyance and rattle his confidence even more.

Eric grumbled under his breath, "Damn asshole," then nervously shifted in his seat.

Mitch was instantly gratified with Eric's response. It had become obvious that only minutes before, Eric had felt intoxicated with power. Now that had evaporated into thin air. To Mitch, Eric's discomfort was what he had hoped to see. Eric no longer felt himself the intimidator, and he studied Eric's face while this notion diminished, and his obnoxious attitude became less conspicuous.

Eric's nervousness was due to the fact that he couldn't figure out who Mitch was. Why would anyone as important as Captain Lansing step aside and let another person question his prisoner?

Once or twice Eric cleared his throat, then coughed several times, and when he couldn't take it any longer, he jumped up and started to pace back and forth. At last he shouted, "So, who the fucken hell are you? And what the fuck do you want with me? I tell ya I didn't do anything; you can't keep me here, jerk off."

Mitch debated if now was a good time to learn how short Eric's fuse was. Immediately after this thought he decided to wait and let Eric get really steamed.

At this same time, Eric jerked his head around and looked at Captain Lansing. Angrily he shouted, "How many times do I have to tell you, I didn't do anything? Now let me out of here."

Captain Lansing remained quiet and ignored the request. Finally, Eric burst, "It's that damn bitch, isn't it? She's the one who put you up to this, right?"

He hesitated then mumbled. "The pig." His eyes suddenly lit up and he yelled, "And I can prove she's nothing more than an unfit tramp. She's not fucken fit to raise my kid. Yea, I can name ten guys right off that'll testify to that."

At this point, Mitch wanted to hit Eric because he was a good judge of character and Diana was no tramp. But instead he stayed calm and asked casually, "Do you have ten friends, Eric? I mean, ten friends that would lie for you?"

Frustration grew across Eric's face and at last he spat, "You probably fucked her too . . . . you black son of a bitch."

Mitch wanted to squash this cockroach. He was so close to mashing his fist into the big-mouthy punk that his restraint almost gagged him. Yet, instead of his fist, he chose to use the information he had. Mitch grinned and spat back, "Eric, why don't you sit your skinny ass down and tell us all about that brother of yours? I believe his name's Brian, isn't it?"

As soon as the words were spoken, Mitch was rewarded with a look of sheer panic that promptly washed the insolence right off Eric's despicable face.

Mitch watched as Eric cautiously moved back to his chair and fell onto the seat as he ambiguously denied, "Brother, ahhh, what, brother? I got no brother. What are ya talkin about?"

Mitch calmly charged, "Come off it, Eric. I know damn well sometime back Diana showed you a copy of a letter and it stated you had a brother. Are you trying to tell me you forgot something as momentous as that?" Again, Mitch felt a tinge of satisfaction with the trepidation in Eric's voice as he stumbled and stuttered, "Wel-well yeah, I remember. Bu-but but, that's got nothing to do with me."

"Are you telling me you found out you have a brother who was given up for adoption and it didn't mean anything to you, Eric?"

"Well, yeah."

"Uh-huh, I see. Have you ever met your brother?"

"No, and I don't want to, either."

"Why is that, Eric? Aren't you just a little bit curious about him? Don't you wonder how he looks and what kind of person he is? Things like that."

"Why should I be? And I'm not talkin to you no more and I don't have to either, asshole." Again, Eric looked over to where Carl stood and shouted, "I know my damn rights and I don't have to talk to you. Captain, I want my lawyer. And I want to go back to my cell now. You fucken jerks have no right to keep me here against my will and my lawyer is gonna sue your fucken asses off."

Mitch smiled and said, "Come on, Eric, you can do better than that. I'd guess we hear that from just about every perp that comes in here. Wouldn't you agree, Captain?"

Eric added nothing more and Mitch could tell he was finished. For now, they would not get nothing else from him. So, he walked over and flicked an imaginary fleck of dust off Eric's shoulder, and said, "Ya know, I'm really gonna love putting you down, Eric. I bet there's plenty you know about that brother of yours, but for some reason you feel a need to protect him. Why is that, Eric?"

Eric's expression went blank, then stoic. Mitch decided right then that he had to have had something to do with the murders. He felt it in his gut, though at this minute his only concern was to keep him locked up and away from Diana and Billy. Mitch looked at the officer who stood by the door and said, "Get this piece of scum out of here."

After Eric was back in his cell, the guard watched him pace nervously around the room like a caged animal. Meanwhile, Mitch was in the captain's office doing the same. Eventually, he asked, "How long can we keep him locked up, Carl? I mean, he does have joint custody, so I suppose he can take his son on vacation if he wants."

Carl jumped in, "No, no, he can't, Mitch. Eric doesn't have joint custody, so he can't take him anywhere, let alone across the state line, without his mother's consent, anyway. Just don't you worry; we'll keep him locked up for a while. You and Donae' just get the hell out there and prove he killed those two people. Then we'll be able to keep Eric locked up and away from his ex-wife and kid forever."

Mitch called Donae' from the airport, but he wasn't in the office, so he asked Silvia to relay a message. "Please tell him to call me this evening around eight. I should be back home by then. I really need to talk with him as soon as possible. It's imperative we move ahead with this case and soon. I've seen Eric's temper and without too much provocation I believe he could be dangerous. We were lucky this time, Silvia. We found

Billy and he's safe, but who's to say what the outcome will be next time? And I, for one, intend to see that there isn't a next time."

Silvia assured him that she would make sure that Donae' got the message as soon as he called in, then added, "Mitch you received a large envelope from a Chicago hospital. Do you think it may be the birth certificates we're waiting for?"

"Well I hope so. Maybe I'll stop by the office after I leave the airport instead of going home first. But you'll have to excuse the way I look. I've been wearing the same clothes for two-and-a-half days". He laughed while he added, "I pity the poor soul who has the seat next to me."

Silvia gave a soft laugh, then in the same concerned voice asked, "Mitch, are you okay? I hope you don't mind my prying, but you seem to have a lot of feelings for Diana. Do you like her? Is there more than a friendship developing there?"

Mitch thought for a minute before he answered. Yes, he had to admit, even if only to himself that he did like Diana. But he could see she was not in any way ready for a relationship.

To Silvia he said, "No, I don't think so. I just think the whole situation reminds me of when I was a kid. My old man was an asshole and my mother never knew how to handle him. He wasn't even living at home, yet he still ruled the roost and our lives. I guess I see the same fear in Diana's eyes that I used to see in my mother's when my old man was around."

"Oh, I'm sorry, Mitch, I . . . ." Silvia floundered then stated, "Mitch, you were too young to do anything about it then, but now you'll be able to help Diana and Billy. Maybe this will help ease some of your buried pain."

"Yeah, let's hope," he muttered.

"And, Mitch, don't worry about dropping by the office to pick up the envelope. Mr. Donae' won't be back until tomorrow morning and I'm leaving early to run some errands. So, after I finish with them, I'll drop the envelope off at your flat. Is that okay?"

"Sure, I'm dead tired, so the sooner I can get to bed the happier I'll be."

"Great, and if we're lucky, I'll hear from Mr. Donae' before I leave."

"Thanks, Silvia, maybe I can get a couple of hours of sleep in before I talk with him. See you later . . . and Silvia, thanks for being a friend."

That night when Silvia slipped the envelope under Mitch's door, she left a note attached to it. She told him that she had not spoken with Donae' and not to expect the eight o'clock call he requested. This, she decided, turned out for the best since he was obviously sound asleep. He never even heard the doorbell or her hard knocks. So, there was a good chance he probably wouldn't have heard the phone ring either.

# CHAPTER 15

The next morning Mitch was up and ready to leave his apartment by seven-thirty. On his way out he noticed and scooped up the envelope and quickly read the note Silvia had left. He banged the door shut to his flat and hurried to catch the elevator that had just opened for the elderly Mrs. Jennings with her toy poodle. Mitch nodded his head and asked, "Out for your morning walk, Mrs. Jennings? And how's Mitzi Rose today?" He scratched the poodle under her chin and winked at the elderly woman as he remarked, "Wow, Mitzi Rose, you sure look pretty today. Are you planning to see someone special at the park?"

Mrs. Jennings giggled, and the dog panted happily while she wagged her tail gaily. After a quick goodbye Mitch turned and headed in the direction of the parking garage and realized he felt normal for the first time in several days. He chuckled and read the note again as he stopped and bought a couple of donuts with his usual large cup of coffee. It was a long drive to Donae's office. But for Mitch, a good cup of coffee always seemed to ease the stress-filled drive through New York's heavy morning traffic. Therefore, this morning he wasn't the least bit distraught when traffic slowed and bogged down for more than an hour longer than usual. He sat back and munched his donuts while he calmly watched some nutty cabby throw a fit. The cabby had just rammed into the rear end of some guy in front of him. And instead of pulling off the roadway so he wouldn't block traffic, he chose to have his fit of anger in the middle of the street. All because, as far as Mitch could deduct from the cabby's tirade, the idiot in front of him had had the audacity to stop for the red light.

When Mitch finally arrived at Donae's office, he'd missed him by twenty-five minutes. However, Silvia held out a message from him as she smiled and said, "Good morning, Mitch, you look like you're in good spirits today."

"Yes, I'm past the melancholy stage."

"Good, very good, because Mr. Donae' would like you to meet him at Bergensten's restaurant near Brian's office." She handed him the address she had earlier scribbled on a sheet of torn paper and asked, "Was the envelope I dropped off last night the birth certificates for Brian and Eric?"

"I don't know. I haven't opened it yet. I was waiting to do so with Donae', only now I can't wait any longer; I want to know if they're brothers or not." Mitch ripped open the envelope he held in his hand and pulled out the papers. When he began to read, he stopped suddenly and looked at the second page, then studied the two pages together.

From Silvia's obtuse angle Mitch looked as if he were interpreting something in a foreign language. After he considered them for some time, he glanced down at Silvia who still sat at her desk and he said, "Holy shit."

Silvia saw the expression on his face, but she couldn't interpret it. She couldn't make out if he was happy about the news or upset about it. Finally, she whispered, "What . . . Mitch, what is it? Is it, bad news, what? Tell me. Is everything okay? Please tell me."

Mitch didn't explain; he simply turned and ran from the room towards the stairway. About the time he made it to the stairwell, he heard Silvia's desperate cry, "Mitch, please come back. You have to tell me. Please don't do this to me; it'll drive me crazy all day. MITCH, PLEASEEE . . . ."

Mitch didn't break any speed limits to get to where Donae' was, but he did push it to the max without breaking the law.

As soon as he entered the restaurant Mitch eagerly scanned the room to find his friend and colleague. When he finally located his table, he headed directly for it. Yet before Mitch could make it to the center of the room, a tall, professional-looking man walked over to stand in front of Donae' and his table. The man's frame cut off all view, so Mitch assumed it was business and slowed his walk so not to disturb Donae' and the gentleman. By the time Mitch almost reached the table, Donae' was already deep in conversation, so he stepped aside and waited. Eventually Donae' looked-up and saw Mitch and halted his discussion long enough to welcome him with a friendly smile. After a second or two he reached out to welcome him with a handshake and said, "Mr. Mitch Hauser, please . . . . come and join me."

Mitch moved forward and Donae' added, "Please let me introduce you to Mr. Brian Peterson."

Mitch automatically held out his hand to shake the hand Brian extended towards him. Donae' had seen the sudden change in Mitch's smile when Brian turned to face him. He was startled, then surprised. Now his usual strong features only held a vague uncommunicative grin, and Donae' could hardly wait to find out why.

After all the pleasantries were out of the way and Brian had excused him-self and walked away, Donae' spoke up. "Have a seat, Mitch, and I will buy you lunch." Donae' evaluated Mitch's expression as he kept an eye on Brian until he could see he was headed out of the restaurant. Then Mitch sighed, "Shit, man."

"Okay, Mitch, you have something and from the look on your face, I would say it is damn good. Come on, out with it. You, my friend, are about to erupt from holding it in and I am dying to hear, so give."

Mitch's face glowed with the biggest smile Donae' had ever seen; it had replaced his previous astounded look. Finally, Mitch threw the envelope across the table and blurted out, "Read it for yourself."

Donae' eagerly pulled the papers out and started to read the first page slowly, then grabbed at the second page and read it in haste. All the while Mitch sat there with the same stupid grin he had when he had handed Donae' the envelope. When he couldn't hold back any longer, he laughed out loud as he observed Donae' do the same thing he had done when it first sank in what he had just read.

Donae' shook his head in disbelief and then reread the information one more time. Gradually he pulled his eyes away from the pages and looked up to smile at Mitch, who nodded his head deliberately while he said, "Yes, it's true, they're fully related: same mother, same father."

Still surprised by the news Donae' asked dubiously, "But, twins, we have twins? Jesus Christ, Mitch, we have twins!" We never went there . . . . TWINS?

The people at the next table threw Mitch, then Donae', an inquiring glance. Then they returned to their cocktails, soon followed by a sequence of whispers and a round of laughter.

Both Mitch and Donae' laughed but lowered their heads self-consciously. Immediately after, Mitch couldn't help but give an exhilarated laugh that was full of relief. And finally, he burst in a controlled, but louder voice than necessary, "Twins, DAMMIT, Donae'. We don't just have twins; we've got IDENTICAL TWINS."

Donae' scooped up the paper once again and spurted, "Where does it say that? I did not see that."

"It doesn't, Donae'. But, hell, I just saw it for myself, with my own two eyes."

"What! Is it that obvious?"

"Identical, my friend, identical. I've never seen more identical."

"Tell me, Mitch. Tell me everything you know. Do they walk alike? Do they smile alike? Are they the same size? Is the hair color the same? Do they talk and sound alike? Tell me all that and more, if you can. Then tell me what you found out in Chicago. I take it that everything turned out well or you would not be here."

"Yes, everything turned out fine. Eric is locked up for now. And if we could prove he murdered Jennifer and Patty Jean, he'll be locked up and away from decent folk for the rest of his life. As for Brian and Eric, if they dressed in the same type of clothing, they could easily pass for one another. Eric's hair is a touch shorter and maybe a tinge darker, but not much, not that you would notice if you weren't looking for it. Or maybe it's just because it's shorter that it looks darker."

Mitch shook his head in disbelief. "Anyway, they both appear to be the same size and smile-wise, well, from what little of that I saw from Eric, it was pretty damn close. But on the other hand, the voices are noticeably different. And Eric certainly isn't as well-educated or refined as Brian just demonstrated. Aside from that, let me answer the question you're dying to ask. Yes, Donae', I believe some little girl that was just wakened from a deep sleep might have easily thought it was her daddy."

"Did Eric have an alibi for that night?"

"We never got that far. He's positively hiding something, and he's scared, but he's also not talking. Oh, by the way, guess what he was carrying in his suitcase when he was picked up?"

Donae' moved forward and waited. Mitch, satisfied by Donae's anticipation, spoke slowly, "About—thirty—thousand—dollars, short—of—a—quarter—of—a—million—bucks."

"Damn, what an idiot," established Donae'.

"My thoughts exactly," Mitch agreed. "Although he denies knowing his brother, it's quite clear he's lying.

The following day Donae' and Mitch made plans to fly back to Chicago to talk with Eric. Whether Eric killed Jennifer and Patty Jean or not, Donae' figured he had to know something. Especially since Brian was not generous by nature, he most likely would not have given Eric a quarter of a million for nothing. He had to have been paying for his silence, if not the murders. The question was, which?

Although, Donae'. suspected that they had the actual killer locked behind bars. He reasoned, "Mitch, now that we do not have to worry about another murder, let's concentrate more on Eric and less on Brian. For the time being, anyway, let's work on keeping Eric in jail."

Later that day when Donae' called Captain Lansing to inform him that he and Mitch would like to interrogate Eric again, he was surprised by his response. "Well, I was just about to give you a call, Donae'. Eric is very close to being released."

Donae's' disappointment trickled out between Captain Lansing's words as he muttered, "The damn fool hired one of the most double-dealing lawyers in town. Unfortunately, he's good enough to get anyone out of jail on bail."

Donae' asked, "Can you slow up his release until we can get there? We really need to talk with him before he talks to Brian. Or worse, leaves town for good."

"Well, Donae', I'll do my damnedest. I can't promise you anything, but papers can get misplaced at times. And with Eric's temper, I wouldn't be at all surprised if he wound up in some mishap with one of the guards, which might put a hold on everything. I tell ya, Donae', that guy doesn't have a lick of sense, and it's going to get em into trouble sooner or later. If you get my drift."

Donae' laughed and replied, "I do, and thank you Carl, for all your help. As usual, I knew I could count on you." Carl asserted, "That'll never change Donae', and you can stake your life on it."

"Mitch and I will be there as soon as we can get into the air, Carl."

Despite the scheme, Donae' was already too late to get to Eric before he had a chance to talk with his brother. Eric had bribed a guard earlier that morning with the two hundred dollars he had stuffed into a hidden pocket of his jacket. The guard accepted a hundred-dollar bribe for the unauthorized use of his phone. And took another hundred for five minutes of unsupervised conversation. Eric had lied and told the guard he wanted to call his girl and needed to speak with her in private. Instead of a girlfriend, Eric immediately dialed Brian.

When Brian heard Eric's voice on the line he yelled into the receiver, "You imbecile, what are you calling me here for? I told you never to call me at the office. We can't take a chance like this, you idiot."

As soon as Brian finished his rampage, Eric burst into his argument for the call. "You don't understand. They're after me, Brian. They're gonna find out and I don't want to go to prison for life. I don't like jail."

To keep control over his frightened brother, Brian chided, "Well, don't worry about it. You won't have to spend your life in jail; they'll probably give you the electric chair."

"Really, do you think so? I don't want to die in the electric chair, Brian. You said we wouldn't get caught. Now I'm gonna die in the electric chair; you gotta help me, Brian."

To appease Eric, Brian added, "Eric, you're an idiot and they never put idiots to death, so you don't have anything to worry about. Now, me, on the other hand, I may have a problem, but let's not worry about that right now. Why don't you just shut up and tell me what the hell you're afraid of and why?"

"I'm in jail, Brian, I had to pay some bull two hundred dollars just so I could call you."

"What? Why? I mean, what did you do? Why are you in jail?"

"I didn't do nothing. It's that Mitch Hauser; he did it."

"Mitch Hauser? Lawrence Donae's friend? What in the hell does he have to do with this? Did he mention Mr. Donae'?"

"Brian don't ask me so many questions and listen. This Hauser guy, came here a few weeks ago to talk with Diana, the fucken bitch."

"Just stick to the subject, Eric. You can curse Diana later. For now, tell me everything and don't leave anything out. As I said earlier, your life may depend on it."

"Oh, okay; well . . . when this guy Hauser came the first time . . ."

"What? He's been there before?"

"Ya, like I said, a couple of weeks ago, when I was out of town. He told Diana that he wanted to talk with me. He wanted to know about you and me being brothers, Brian. I don't know what she told him, but he came back the other day and wanted to see me."

"So, that still doesn't tell me why you're in jail."

"Well, Brian, when I heard he was coming to talk with me, I guess I got a little panicky. Maybe I overreacted, I don't know. Anyway, I took Billy and the money and headed for Canada." Suddenly, Eric's anger returned, and his remarks led him in a different direction. "But that stupid fucken bitch must have called the cops. Because, the next thing I knew, I was being arrested. And, Brian, they were throwing all kinds of questions at me and they gave Billy back to that fucken whore. Can you believe it, Brian? I'm gonna kill that bitch someday, the double-crossing bitch."

Brian almost screamed into the phone, "ERIC! SHUT UP, DAMMIT! And stop thinking about your own petty ass for once. Now . . . one more time, why did they arrest you, what is the charge? Never mind. Just answer me this; did Hauser say anything about someone name Donae'? Lawrence Donae'."

"Yeah, I remember I heard that Hauser guy tell the Captain that Donae's gonna want to talk with me. Why? Who's this creep, Brian, and who's Hauser? I don't trust him, Brian. I think he's out to get me. I think the black son of a bitch has been sleepin with Dia . . ."

"Eric, shut up! And never mind who they are. All you have to know is to keep your mouth shut."

To himself, Brian muttered, "That god damn asshole. He was setting me up all this time. I can't believe it! Damn, he had no intention of ever signing me or this firm; he was just setting me up."

Eric started to say, "Bri . . ." and was cut off immediately when Brian continued his own barrage, "Well, he'll be more than just a little sorry he ever messed with me. I can't believe I put up with all his shit for nothing. I can't believe he treated me like that. But he'll pay; you mark my words, brother. We'll show that snob who's better than whom and we'll rub his nose in it. That damn . . ."

"Brian! Brian, listen to me. Let's talk about me right now; you can get mad at Donae' later. I'm the one in trouble and I'm scared. And I'm sure, Diana's gonna try and use this to keep Billy away from me. Can she do that? Can she Brian? I don't want her to win, even if it means I get stuck with that damn kid."

Finally, Brian shot, "Forget about fucken Billy and Diana. They're not important, Eric. You said they found you with the money? You had the money with you?"

"Well yeah, and they put me in jail, Brian, for taking my own kid; isn't that against the law? They can't do something like that, can they? Can't I do something about it? I mean, isn't that police brutality or something?"

Again, Brian shouted, "Shut up Eric! Now listen to me you damn moron. Why did you have the money on you? It would be obvious to them that someone like you can't possibly get that kind of money legally. What did you tell them about the money?"

"Nothing, I didn't say anything, Brian. Honest."

Brian said nothing and Eric couldn't tell if he was still on the line or not. Then he realized Brian must be thinking and he waited in silence.

"Well . . . that's one good thing; you kept your mouth shut. Now, we're going to have to think of a good story, and you better stick to it. You better not mess up, Eric. You do, and you're on your own, so listen and remember everything I tell you. Do you hear me?"

"Yeah, Brian, okay, I'll do everything you say. I promise no matter how scared I get, I'll do it."

"Just keep in mind, Eric, if you mess this up, we're both going to be in prison for the rest of our lives. Do you understand? No screw ups!"

By mid-morning the next day Donae' and Mitch were landing at O'Hare. This was much earlier than Donae' or Mitch had anticipated since it seemed all flights to Chicago were booked and the weather was not cooperating in the least. Yet still, with all this working against them, they were sitting in front of Eric by three in the afternoon.

All eyes were firmly fixed on the irate Eric as he glared across the interrogation table. He held the same usual smirk that covered his face most of the time. Nevertheless, under that smirk his resemblance to Brian was almost uncanny, and it took Donae' several minutes to file Eric and his resemblance in a crevice in the back of his mind before he was ready to move forward with the questioning. Consequently, Mitch, Carl, Eric and Donae' all sat around the table. No one spoke as each evaluated the other. When Donae' stood and moved closer to the prisoner, he realized Eric's angry eyes held the same misfortune that cursed his brother. There was no mistaking it. Eric did not feel love, empathy, or even remorse; he would not see anything wrong with anything he did. Even if it was to take the life of two innocent people, it was not in him to do so.

Brian and Eric's likeness to one another astounded Donae'. The obvious lack of compassion he now witnessed in Eric's eyes was amazingly close to what he had beheld earlier in Brian's eye and for a brief moment the likeness had overwhelmed the private eye for in both these men he could see nothing but irrefutable emptiness. Finally, Donae' broke the silence with a light cough and a, "Good afternoon, Mr. Van Murck." Then he asked the first question, "May I call you Eric?"

Donae' was immediately taken aback when Eric, with no warning whatsoever stood up and bellowed, "You can't bully me into talkin; I'm not your prisoner and my lawyer got me out, so you better let me go and fucken now, . . . dammit."

Donae' could hear what Mitch meant when he said Eric and Brian sounded different. This person not only spoke with the vocabulary of a less educated person. He also had a speech pattern that seemed to be on the slow side. *But still*, Donae' thought, *if he didn't open his mouth he could easily pass for Brian.*

Donae' smiled in a friendly manner and walked closer to where Eric had just sat down again. His movement was so coarse the legs of the chair scraped against the floor and made a loud screech on the tile as it almost toppled over. Donae' continued to smile and pretended he didn't notice Eric's anger. When he stood in front of the incensed Eric he bent over his large structure and asked calmly. "Eric, I am sure you do not want to take the rap for something you had nothing to do with, do you? Even if it is for your brother, I am quite sure you are not that stupid. So why not simply tell us what we need to know, and you can be on your way."

Eric crossed his arms and his face held a stubborn pout when he muttered. "I don't know nothing, so leave me alone."

"So . . . I take it, you would do just about anything to help your brother. Am I reading you correctly, Eric? Is that what you are implying?"

"As I said before, I don't have a brother and I don't have to talk to you. I want to see my lawyer. This is plain police brutality against an innocent man."

At that instant it was too late for Eric because now Donae' could see the first sparks of fear in his apathetic eyes, and he quickly continued, "Eric, can you tell me where you were on September, twenty-ninth, Nineteen-sixty, say around midnight or so?"

"How the hell should I know. Probably sleeping, asshole."

"So, you don't have an alibi for that night?"

"In a childish sneer, he gnarled, "I don't need one, stupid; I didn't do nothing."

"Like what, Eric?"

Eric hesitated for a minute. He wanted to make sure he said things right; he didn't want to mess things up like Brian always says he does. Finally, he spewed, "Why don't you tell me, Mister Fucken Big Shot? It seems to me you think you know all the answers. So, shoot, give me the answer you want to hear. Tell me what you're huntin for." Then he mumbled more to himself then to Donae', "damn stupid cop. You think you can push me around."

Donae' did not respond right away. Instead he thought, *So, he is not as dumb as he pretends to be. His facade is mostly for affectedness and a way to hide his true self.* Donae' studied Eric and his expression for some time before he asked, "Eric, where did you get all that money you carry around in your suitcase?"

"It's mine. That's all you need to know, okay."

"Did you earn that money? Was it legal? And why have you not put it in a bank where it would be safe?"

"I don't like banks and it's my money, so I can do what I want with it and that's all you need to know."

"Did your brother, Brian, pay you to do something for him?"

"I told you before. I don't know my brother."

"Eric, we know that is a lie. So why not tell us the whole story before you get this complete rap dumped on you." Donae' glanced to where Mitch and Carl stood and Mitch nodded slightly. He could see Eric had become less sure of himself and he wanted Donae' to know he was headed in the right direction.

Eric continued to fidget with a pencil that lay on the table in front of him. He had become visibly agitated and more nervous with each question asked. And

Donae' wondered how much further he could push him before he became contemptuous and less transparent.

"Come on, Eric, did Brian pay you that money to do something illegal? Would you kill someone for that much money, Eric?"

"NO, and Brian only gave me the money so I could start my own business; he knows I'd be very successful and probably triple his investment."

"Sooo; it was a loan. What kind of business were you going to start, Eric?"

Again, with the fidgeting, then, "Well I didn't decide yet."

"You said you didn't know your brother, so why would he give you so much money to start a business? That does not sound at all like the Brian Peterson I know. Especially since you do not know him."

"Well, I do know Brian. I just didn't want to say anything to you."

"Why?"

Because Brian don't want anyone to know about me."

"Why is that, Eric?"

"Maybe because he's ashamed of me; I don't know."

Donae' suddenly got a hunch and decided to play on Eric's self-doubt. "Ashamed of you. Why do you think Brian's ashamed of you, Eric?"

"Maybe because I'm not smart like he is, and I don't have lots of money like him. Who knows? But I will, and soon, soon as I start my business. Then you'll see I'm as smart as Brian, maybe even smarter."

"Does that make you angry, Eric, angry enough to hurt him back?"

Eric did not answer. Instead he stared at Donae' with his mouth half opened and a look of surprise covered his face. This was a question Brian hadn't practiced with him and he searched his mind to find an answer on his own. He thought of Brian and his last piece of advice. He was supposed to be careful and not lose his temper. If he blew up, then he might say the wrong thing. Donae' was slick, Brian said, and right now, Eric agreed. Donae' was very close to making him say the wrong thing.

Donae' glanced once again over to where Mitch and Carl stood. Both held back a smile and Mitch winked his approval. Everyone could see Donae's last question had rattled Eric and for some reason it had made him extremely uncomfortable.

Donae' quickly moved on before Eric could think of an answer, "Come on Eric, why not tell us the real reason Brian gave you the money?"

As soon as the question was out, Donae' knew it was the wrong one to have asked. Eric's expression changed and his recovery was complete within seconds of Donae's last word. His face promptly registered a sneer and he sat back, comfortable with the query, as he smiled slightly when he decided he knew how to answer the question. Brian had been wrong. He could handle this shit head. Maybe Donae' wasn't as smart as Brian thought.

At the same instant Eric's expression had changed Donae' knew the question was wrong and suddenly he knew Brian had gotten to Eric before him. And Eric confirmed this suspicion with his answer, "Brian gave me the money so I could have a fresh start. He doesn't want to be ashamed of me anymore. He wants me to be more successful like him, and now I can with all my money. After all, Mr. Donae' you should keep in mind I'm all that Brian has. It's just me and Brian."

Donae' walked from one corner of the room to the other while he tried to figure out how Brian had got to Eric. When he recovered from his impasse, he turned and asked. "You and Brian have quite a relationship, then."

"Yeah, so what?"

"Simply an observation, Mr. Van Murck."

Eric's eyes registered a question, but he said nothing.

"Eric, can you tell me when the two of you became aware of each other? Moreover, how did you find each other? From what I was told, your father was not able to find Brian after he was adopted. So how did you manage it?"

"Well, it wasn't me. And Brian is a lot smarter than our old man was and he found me."

"When was that, Eric?"

"I don't remember."

"You don't remember something as momentous as meeting your twin brother for the first time?"

"Well, I do remember, but it don't really matter, does it?"

"No, not really, but it would help me understand how you two guys became so close."

Squinting as if it hurt to think that far back, Eric hesitantly answered Donae'. "It was . . . when I was about eighteen or nineteen . . . I guess, just before I joined the Army. That's why I joined the Army, because Brian was in the Marines. I wanted to join the Marines, but they wouldn't take me. I didn't pass their fucken test. They were fucken idiots. I would've been the best damn Marine they ever had, the idiots."

Donae' decided to utilize Eric's ego and volunteered. "Yes, but the Army is a good place, a place for real men. A place a man can grow and learn all kinds of skills. From what I hear, they only take the best. As a matter of fact, Mitch here . . . he was in the Army."

Eric was now relaxed and his interest in himself and the conversation grew. "Oh yeah, what did you do?"

Mitch recognized where Donae' was going and to help his plight he lugubriously remarked, "Oh, I didn't do much more than become a foot soldier. I guess I simply didn't have what it took to be anything more. I tried but never made the grade for anything else."

You could see the pride swell in Eric as he said. "Not me, I was the best I was an Army Ranger."

Mitch stepped closer and full of false admiration he said. "Nah, you're kiddin? Right?"

"Proudly, Eric sat up straighter and shot, "No shit, I'm not kiddin. I was one of the best."

"God, you guys got all the respect. Plus, you guys got to do everything, go everywhere. You must've been pretty damn good, I mean with your weapons and all, for them to take you into the Rangers. Yeah, you had to be damn good; hell, I'm impressed."

Arrogantly, Eric began to spout. "Yes, and you well damn should be. After all, I had to take care of you and all those other pussies like you. Yeah, I was the best."

"I bet it didn't matter if you were in the Marines or not . . . you probably still ended up being better than Brian," remarked Mitch.

Suddenly Eric exhaled and answered sadly, "No, I wasn't as good as Brian. I don't think too many people were." Unexpectedly, he perked up and proclaimed, "But I was damn good at teachin those dumb fucks how to use their weapons. I bet I saved more asses from being shot under fire than just about anyone." He thought and then added with disdain, "Brian's good at everything, especially shooting. He can shoot a peanut out of a bird's mouth a mile away. But he's no good at teachin anyone, not like me."

"What about knives?" asked Donae'. "I bet Brian was good with knives."

Again, Donae' could see he had gone too far. Eric's expression suddenly changed back to the same obnoxious smirk. He realized that the two had played him for a stooge. They were in no way his buddies. They just pretended to be so they could get more information from him. He mumbled under his breath, "Brian was right. I need to learn to keep my big mouth shut and not be so gullible."

Donae' asked, "What was that Eric? What did Brian say?"

With a laugh, Eric promptly looked over to where the captain stood and shouted, "Dammit, you let me out of here or my lawyer's going to raise some hell and sue your fucken ass off. No more games, no more questions, I want my release."

Donae' wanted to kick himself; he knew better than to ask about knives. Mitch's report said Eric was the one who was the knife expert. If Eric had answered the question, he would have implicated himself and that was not going to happen. He was much too smart for that.

Donae' quickly tried to change the course of their conversation in hopes of keeping Eric interested and rambling. He wanted a lot more questions answered, but one in particular, so he gave it one more shot before he called it quits. "Eric, you said Brian found you when you were about eighteen. How did that come about? How did Brian find you?"

Still angry and distrustful, Eric gave a smart-ass answer along with what Donae' had hoped for. "It's none of your damn fucken business, Mr. Fancy Ass Cop, but for your information, he found a letter. His god damn folks hid the letter all those years. Our old man had his lawyer send it years ago when he first tried to find Brian and get him back. But they never answered it and worst, they never said nothing to Brian, either. They even hid that he was adopted and everything. Stupid jerks. Brian hates to be lied to."

Mitch rubbed his hand through his hair as he surmised, "Boy, that's rough. I bet that really pissed off Brian."

Irritably, Eric gave Mitch a filthy look, then snapped, "I want out of here and now, or my lawyer's going to call the governor."

Captain Lansing turned to Donae' and said, "I think we're about finished processing his papers. If you're finished, we can get this so-called gentleman out of our hair."

Donae' wanted more, but he could see that Eric was not going to tell them anything else. Unhappily he agreed, "Yes, Captain, I'm finished for now." In defiance, he added, "As for you, Eric, I will be in touch."

Again, Eric gave them one of his uncomplimentary smirks as he mumbled, "That's what you think, asshole. If you even try to talk to me again, you'll be talking to my lawyer cause I'll sue your ass too. If you so much as look in my direction, I'll sue. There's laws against harassment, ya know."

Donae' and Mitch looked at one another, then smiled back at their new-found friend as Mitch flippantly asked, "Eric, you wouldn't do that to an old army buddy, would you?"

Mitch and Donae' laughed as Eric grumbled something angrily under his breath. He cast one last hate-filled look in their direction, then turned and in a huff stomped out of the room. The guard scurried off to catch up with his irate prisoner.

When Eric had cleared the room, Mitch turned to Donae' and asked, "What do you think?"

"I think Brian has gotten to our friend before us."

"I thought so too," Mitch declared. "So, now what do we do?"

"First thing I think we need to do is get Diana and Billy out of town. That way we know they are safe and out of the line of fire," said Donae'.

"My thoughts exactly."

"And secondly, Mitch, I want you on Eric's tail. I do not want him out of your sight for a minute. One more thing, Mitch. Let him see that you are following him. If I read Eric accurately, he should soon become unnerved and panic and when that happens, I think he will run directly to his brother for protection. Hopefully, that will not take too long and then he will be on our turf. That should make it much easier for us to deal with him, if he is in our own backyard. Do you agree Mitch?"

"I do, and I'm on my way, but first I'll call Diana and explain everything. As for Eric, I'll be on him like stink on shit. You can count on me, boss."

Donae' arched his left brow then, in an appalled tone, he challenged, "Mitch, can you please not forget yourself? And if in the future can you avoid such language, I would appreciate it. Definitely do not let it become a habit."

"Sorry, Donae', old Army habit. Eric brought back all the bad habits I had tucked away in the back of my memory bank."

Mitch laughed at his friend, then quickly added, "Hey, Donae', I would think you should be used to that kinda talk. I mean, with you hanging around police stations and Detective Lauwdry."

"You may be right, my friend, but there is a slim-to-nothing chance that I would grow use to that language, not to mention, Detective Lauwdry . . . . Both, disgust me."

Mitch turned to close the door behind him and Donae', and in a low badgering monotone he mumbled, "Candy ass."

They both gave a comfortable laugh, and Donae' chivalrously declared, "Touché, my friend, Touché'."

As soon as Donae' put the ecstatic Diana and her son Billy on a plane headed for Europe, he set forth to secure himself a ticket back to New York. He hoped by the time the two returned from their month-long tour, courtesy of the Donae' family, Eric and Brian would be behind bars.

The flight he secured was leaving within minutes of his booking, but before he boarded the plane, he made one quick call to Silvia. After several rings, she breathlessly yelled into the phone, "Yes, Donae's office."

"My dear Silvia, is that any way to answer the telephone?"

"Oh, hi." Then to someone else she remarked, "Its Mr. Donae'." Then back into the phone she said, "Sandy's here. He's taking me to lunch. I heard the phone ringing just as we were ready to walk down the stairs. I had to run back and unlock the office, and I was afraid I wouldn't make it to the phone before you hung up. How's everything going in Chicago?"

"Everything is coming along just fine. Now I am on my way back. Silvia, do me a favor and make sure Sandy does not hear or understand anything that I say to you."

"No problem, Mr. Donae'."

"I really don't want the police in on this matter, not yet anyway. We certainly don't need them to muddy the water with their interference."

"I understand, boss. Sandy said to say hello."

"You tell him hello right back and then listen carefully."

Okay, I'm ready, sir."

"Silvia, what I need from you is that you get on the phone to the Pentagon, or to whomever you need, and get copies of Eric Van Murck's Army records. Then I need you to set an appointment for me with Brian Peterson. I believe he is aware of who I am at this point. Regardless, do not let him know that we are aware of this fact, and if you can get the appointment set it for lunch at Sash's, the day after tomorrow. Yes, that would suit me fine. Did you get all of that?"

"Yes sir, but I have already anticipated your need for the records, and they should be here any day now."

"You are a jewel, my dear."

"Well, thank you, Mr. Donae', so I'll let Sandy know lunch is on you today."

"You can, indeed, and, Miss Perez, I will see you tomorrow."

# CHAPTER 16

The very next morning Donae' was sitting at his desk going through each page of information he had jotted down while in Chicago. The morning silence was always pleasing to him and a good time to get things accomplished. Suddenly the phone rang, and its loud shrill startled him before it brought him back to reality. It was Mitch reporting in. "Donae', Eric's going bonkers out here. He's been all over town looking for Diana and Billy, and with each miss he gets angrier. I certainly hope we get some answers before their return."

Donae' reassured Mitch, "Diana and Billy are safe, and they are going to stay that way."

Mitch said, "Thanks, Donae'",then bid a hasty goodbye and hurried off to catch up with his mark.

Donae' returned to the drudgery of reexamining every piece of evidence from Chicago to what Addison had dropped off weeks ago. He decided that with all that had happened since he had begun the investigation a few weeks before, this information might now view differently than it did when first scrutinized.

To his surprise, he realized he was unconsciously holding Patty Jean's photograph. He studied her last sweet smile for several minutes and asked, "Is Addison's theory correct: did Brian himself kill Patty Jean and Jennifer or is Eric the culprit? Addison had said a child would not smile to a stranger if awakened from a deep sleep. *Is this a fact?* he wondered, then decided: *Addison's theory must be correct; it has to be the truth.*

Donae' himself could not determine whether a child would smile for a stranger when awakened from a full sleep or not. He had not studied too deeply into the world of child psychology and he did not know many children. And those he did know; he was not close enough with to safely make a sound judgment either way. Again, he studied Patty Jean's face, then pulled Jennifer's photograph from her file and evaluated her expression. He determined what he saw was someone who was unquestionably frightened by her intruder. He asked a question he knew he would not hear an answer to, "Did you recognize and fear the person who did this, Jennifer? Was it, Brian or did you simply think it was Brian?" Donae' pondered: *Would a woman awakened from a deep slumber to see her husband standing over her, show this much fear?* He would not think so, since he would assume, she had awakened with him almost daily, that is unless they were not as happily married as most perceived or had been told. Donae' had his doubts that Jennifer and Brian's marital status was as blissful as many believed. If anything, from what he had learned of Brian's personality thus far, he would guess he would have been extremely hard to live with, much more so than what Diana had thought Eric had been.

The behavior he had witnessed with Eric showed many irrational traits, most minor eccentricities, but still in all, difficult. Donae' believed he would be a very demanding and a disrespectful husband. It seemed he possessed an irrational prejudice especially towards women. Donae's opinion was most women were unlikely to ever live up to Eric's standards.

And, if he remembered correctly, Addison had mentioned that Brian also thought women to be less worthy than men. According to Jennifer, via Gerimee, he repeatedly had said he did not trust Jennifer and was often disrespectful. So, in that sense, Brian and Eric were alike.

Donae' scratched his chin as he concluded his rationalization: *Since each had been raised by a different set of parents . . . this similarity can only be construed as an inherent personality trait.*

He again studied the notes he had jotted down when in Chicago and decided: *However, their personalities do vary somewhat.* Eric had seemed to hold a lower self-esteem; yet he was preoccupied with success. And from what Donae' had witnessed, Eric felt he deserved it as much as Brian did. This was not a surprise. Donae' knew this was a common idiosyncrasy for this type of personality. They simply feel they deserve what they want.

On the other hand, Brian held a grandiose sense of self-importance and a substantial need for admiration. He worked hard for his success, but he exaggerated or enhanced whatever he possessed, and, from what Sergeant Cox had said, he also inflated his achievements.

Donae' thought back to the day he had met Brian at his office. Even his office decor screamed the need to be noticed and admired.

Gerimee had said Brian exhibited an insatiable desire to be accepted by high-status people. That could be one reason he had pursued Jennifer so ardently. As far as Donae' could tell, she was the trophy for all his hard-earned efforts. She could make all his dreams come true and his trip to the other side much more attainable. Brian must have come to comprehend he owed Jennifer for his extreme wealth and élite status and this would have eaten away at his ego, and he would have grown to resent it. This would explain the change in his personality after they married and why he made his wife's life miserable.

Far worse, both Brian and Eric revealed a lack of empathy. They were unwilling to notice or identify that other people are entitled to their own feelings.

In their eyes no one would ever be worthy enough to deserve their love or respect; life was for the taking and others were only tolerated as long as they didn't get in the way of their wants.

Still and all, he felt Brian had the more severe personality disorder; he had only mastered hiding it better than Eric, which, in Donae's eyes made him more dangerous. Where Eric's obvious contemptuous personality would easily forewarn a person of danger, Brian's would not.

Silvia knocked softly on the door and his thoughts came to a sudden halt. He gave one last glance to Jennifer's and Patty Jean's last photos then, soberly laid them aside as he gravely called out, "Come in, Silvia."

Marching eagerly into the room, Silvia was holding a large brown envelope. She chirped gaily, "It's here ... Mr. Donae' we have the service records of Eric Van Murck." She handed the packet over the desk into his anxious hands. "Thank you, Silvia. I can hardly wait to see how long our friend Eric has shown his narcissistic tendencies."

Donae' ripped open the envelope and set the file wide open on his desk. He glanced up at Silvia with a look of confident expectation, yet he still hesitated. The prospect of what he might not learn was very real and he did not want to let anyone down. He truly hoped to find the right clue, the one that would point them in the right direction. Who really killed Jennifer and Patty Jean, Eric or Brian? Which one rendered that final act, or were they on the wrong track altogether?

At first Donae' had been convinced that Brian was the evildoer, but now after the introduction of his twin, he leaned more towards Eric. Yet, he still felt sure Brian was involved in some way.

Donae' smiled at Silvia, then requested, "Please sit. You deserve to hear it all." He inhaled a deep breath and resolved, "Let us see what we have here."

Silvia without a second's hesitation grabbed a chair and pulled it over to sit in front of Donae's desk. She watched while he read several paragraphs. Finally, he looked up and smiled, then went right back to what he was reading. Before long he jumped up and out of his seat. He slapped at the paper he held in his hand and yelped, "BINGO! Silvia, we got him; it is all right here in front of me."

Silvia sat forward in her chair and asked repeatedly, "What, Mr. Donae'? What do we have? Tell me, what? What, Mr. Donae' pleaseee."

"Section Eight, my love, we have a Section Eight for our number two twin."

"You're kidding, right?"

"I am happy to say I am not kidding, young lady. So, let us see when and why Mr. Eric Van Murck had to shorten his commendable career."

Donae' went back to the paper and continued to read for some time. When he completed each page, he handed it over to Silvia for her to read. This was not only for her own information, but also in case he may have missed something of importance. After about a half-hour, Silvia set the last sheet of paper back in the folder that still lay open on Donae's desk. At first neither spoke; they only looked at one another in amazement. Suddenly, they both jumped at the sound of Mitch as he barreled into the office. Mitch took one look at Silvia, then glanced quickly over to where Donae' sat. Suddenly he opened his arms outward and asked, "What, what's up with you two? You look like you just saw a ghost. Damn, did I get killed or something and just don't know it yet . . . . did I?"

Both Silvia and Donae' burst into laughter. "Mitch, what a ridiculous idea," Silvia declared.

And Donae' scoffed, "I certainly hope this means our suspect is here in town and that you did not lose him."

"Very funny, Donae'. Yes, Eric's here in town. It didn't take him long to decide to hightail it out of Chicago once he learned all the charges had been dropped and that Diana was nowhere to be found."

Mitch opened a gadget on his keychain and popped the cap off his Pepsi, then took a large gulp before he said, "So is anyone going to tell me what's going on? Why the dumbfounded look on both your faces?"

"Well, have a comfortable seat, Mr. Hauser and I will fill you in. Silvia can you order us some lunch?"

"You got it, sir."

"Mitch, it seems our proud Army Ranger, Eric Van Murck, was considered unfit for military duty about a year before he was due to be released."

"Whoa, you mean a Section Eight."

"I do indeed, my friend."

"Damn, well let's hear it. God, I just can't believe it, Donae'. What a surprise. I mean, I don't doubt it with his attitude, but I wonder why Diana never mentioned it?"

"Maybe he never said anything to her about it," answered Silvia in Diana's defense.

"I suppose it's something you wouldn't brag about, and that's one thing Eric likes to do most," replied Mitch. "You're probably right. Because if Diana knew, I'm sure she would've mentioned it. So, what's the scoop, Donae'? Come on; let's hear it all."

"Well, it looks like our trusted mate, Mr. Van Murck, had a slower evolution than Mr. Brian Peterson. From what has been reported and data recorded, I think I can discern that Brian showed his tendencies of the personality disorder around the latter part of his sixteenth year. Furthermore, from all indications, I suspect he killed his adoptive parents. I am certain it was not for the money, but for the mere fact that he believed they had betrayed him."

Mitch gave Donae' a questioning look and Donae' answered his unspoken question. "For concealing the fact that he was adopted.

"Oh, yes, Eric did say that angered him, but to that degree?" asked Mitch.

"This is all purely conjecture on my part, Mitch. And concerning that action, we may never learn the truth, since the case has been closed for years and most of the evidence has been destroyed. As for Eric, his coming out was later. He seemed to be like any other young man with a slight attitude until he joined the service. Although it was slight at first, things began to change rapidly."

Donae' scratched his chin then continued, "In the beginning of his hitch in the service, his records show he strove to be successful. He had always desired and pushed to belong to the Rangers; he put every effort into that goal. In spite of this fact his request for that assignment was continually turned down, primarily due to his increasingly offensive attitude. At one point his request was accepted and shortly after his training was completed he was assigned to a unit that was based overseas. It was about this time his traits started to emerge fully and he became egotistical, arrogant, and simply harder to deal with. It was not long after this assignment that he added to these characteristics. It was reported that Eric became hungry for command and was envious of anyone who had it. Several times he demanded to be awarded merits he had not earned and more often he fought for positions he was not qualified for.

At the time it was chalked up to his overzealous nature. But when he was not recognized for his fantasized accomplishments, he grew pugnacious towards his superiors. One time he even accused an officer of giving preferential treatment to a popular squad member. Eric charged that this soldier was awarded privileges for sexual favors. As you can imagine. this did not sit well with these particular gentlemen and their cohorts."

"For sexual favors," repeated Mitch. "What an idiot, I mean, in a unit like that, he was just asking for trouble."

"Yes, I agree, and as it seemed so did a few others. The record reads that someone eventually had enough of Eric and his allegations, and about a year-and-a-half before his tour of duty was to end several men got together and attempted to fix him and his attitude permanently. It happened one night after he left the bar where he had spent most of the evening; he was jumped and beaten. Records show that he was close to death. It took him several months to heal, and when they finally released him from medical care Eric was not the same man. His speech and actions were much slower than before. As for his mouth and attitude, they were on the rise. This is when he was given the Section Eight."

"Damn, I guess we found out a lot more than we anticipated, didn't we? Do you think he's worse than Brian?"

"That I cannot say, Mitch, but I have my doubts. I think Brian's just a whole lot smarter and better at hiding it than Eric is. However, I tell you I have every intention of finding out. Whatever it takes to get these answers, I will do."

"Well, as always, my friend, you can count on me."

Thanks, Mitch, that goes without saying, for you have always been a good friend and trusted counsel."

"Ah, shoot, Donae'. Let's not get sappy here."

"Lunch is here," shouted Silvia. "Who wants the corned beef on rye and who wants the ham and Swiss? And before you ask, yes . . . . I got extra pickles."

When Donae' entered Sash's the next afternoon, he was greeted by a warm wave from the lovely Margaret Sash as she seated a couple across the room. She and her husband Gordon were the proud proprietors of this grand establishment. The restaurant was one of the most highly regarded and most difficult to get in, and for some undiscovered reason it seemed the lunch hour reservations between eleven and two were the most sought after. Those who critiqued the restaurants in the area referred to Sash's as *the place to be*. Anyone who was anyone wanted to be seen at Sash's' at the noontime hours in hopes of their presence being noted the next day on the society page.

This is precisely why Donae' chose to meet Brian at Sash's. Since Brian had such a need to be seen at the right places and with affluent people, Donae' felt there was little chance he would not accept the invitation. He had feared that this was a great possibility if Brian was indeed aware of his and Mitch's current investigation.

Donae' looked around the room and observed all its celebrities. Jennifer Hobart, he was sure, would have been a part of this group and her status would have gotten her and Brian into Sash's with little or no problem. Yet, he would guess, Brian on his own would have a problem obtaining a table anytime, simply due to the fact that many thought of him as a user and were offended by his lofty and conspicuous manner.

Suddenly Margaret was upon him, and she threw her arms out robustly and hugged him to her. "Finally," she whispered. "My Love, I've missed you so. Where have you been lately?" Standing back to get a better view she studied him as she added, "I see Michael and Shelia regularly and occasionally Sharon and Gerimee will drop in, but you, my dear, are as scarce as anyone can be."

"I am truly sorry, Margaret. I can only shamefully apologize for my neglect of you and Gordon. I have been extremely busy on a new case and have had little time to spare, which sadly means I have had no time for visiting old friends and relatives."

"Oh, my, I'm very sorry to hear that, sweetheart. I think you really work much too hard for it to be any good for you or your health. You need to let yourself go and unwind every so often. I do hope you're making an extra effort to at least spend some time with your grandmother. You know how she adores her three grandchildren."

"Of course. I never miss my weekly visits with Grandmother; they are as significant to me as they are for her."

"Good, very good. Then I will not worry that she is being neglected by her very busy grandson."

"Now, Margaret, you know as well as I that it is impossible for me to ignore Grandmother, for it is not in her to let one do so."

She laughed affectionately as she kissed his cheek and reasoned, "Lawrence, I can see that I'm holding you up, my dear, I can get a little gabby some days. And, of course, I'm sure your guest will be here any minute so let me show you to your table. Silvia said you wanted something out in the open but still one of the better seatings so I could only guess that it has something to do with one of your cases since it is unlike you to want to be conspicuous."

She pulled the chair out for him to be seated, then kissed his cheek one more time and immediately turned and walked swiftly back to her podium to attend to her many other duties.

Donae' watched as Margaret moved towards the front of the restaurant; smiling, she graciously greeted several guests as she maneuvered herself between their tables. He chuckled as he thought how much she reminded him of his mother, and as always, a sharp pang of loneliness engulfed him.

While Donae' waited for Brian, he viewed the well-to-do clientele as they moved from table to table to greet friends and associates. He marveled at the success that his dear friends had accomplished with this handsome, but awkward building. The elegance and warmth the restaurant bestowed was breathtaking. Donae' wondered how Margaret was able to achieve this feat; afterall the room was overly large, yet it felt warm and cozy. He attributed this splendor to the colors of warm cream and light tints of greens that were complimented by the heavier dark beige that ran along the top of the ceiling. This, he decided, gave a false sense that the ceiling was lower than it really was. The room exhibited many colorful variations and the soft orange hues also contrasted the coolness of the high ceilings and huge crystal chandeliers. Yet Margaret brought even more elegance to the room with a vast array of gigantic vases from every corner of the world. They were displayed and filled with leafy greenery along with large, beautiful lilies, delphiniums, birds of paradise and various colors of snapdragon and stock along with the largest mums he had ever seen. These arrangements gave the room a soft, sweet smell throughout the day, and that too, added immensely to the interior's extensive radiance. Sash's success, he knew, was more than Gordon or Margaret had ever dreamed. To make the Gold List at Sash's was the goal of many elite, and, of course the everyday New York celebrities who continued to seek prominence.

Donae' sighed with relief since he did not have to bother with the effort. He could have a table at Sash's anytime even without notice; for he had known Margaret his entire life. She had been his mother's oldest and dearest friend and today she was as devoted to his mother's family as she had been to his mother before her untimely death.

At once Donae' became alert as he observed Brian entering the room. He was exquisitely dressed, as one might say to the tee. Donae' continued to watch as the arrogant Brian pushed himself to the head of a small group of businessmen. Donae' could see him clearly as he flamboyantly tried to introduce himself to the busy hostess. Unmindful, she immediately turned her attention to the group who graciously awaited their turn.

Donae' was not at all surprised that this angered Brian and when the girl walked back to greet him, she was bombarded by an incensed Brian who lectured her for not seating him promptly. Politely she listened without offering a single word in defense. Finally, she smiled sweetly and turned to show her charge to Donae's table. When she approached, she rolled her eyes back and made a face. Donae' grinned to show his support; luckily, she was where Brian could not see her face or Donae's wink.

As soon as they approached the table she asked, "Mr. Donae', now that your guest has arrived, shall I have your Wine Steward bring you a bottle of your regular reserve?"

Trying to hold back his laughter at another of her facial expressions, he immediately answered, "Yes, Nadine, thank you. That sounds like a marvelous idea." At the same time, he commenced to stand and greet the obviously aloof Mr. Brian Peterson.

"Sit, Mr. Peterson. I notice you are eleven minutes late. Was there a problem with the directions?"

"No, Mr. Donae', I know exactly how to find Sash's as you are probably very well aware of."

Donae' noticed the sarcasm in Brian's tone along with the mistrust in his eyes as he scrutinized him and the room full of people that surrounded them. Granting his lips stayed pasted upward in a false smile, he clearly had a dislike for his present situation and for a full minute he appraised Donae' and his circumstances.

Donae' sensed Brian's apprehension in the way he approached the table then firmly shook his hand. He could also see he was aptly pleased to be the center of attention, even if leery of his control. At this point Donae' decided it might be helpful to exemplify the snobbery he had been exhibiting since he had first met Brian. The restaurant, he was sure, impressed the status hungry Brian, yet Donae' still felt the need to engage attention to his own eminence. This, he was sure, was the only way to get Brian to trust him and break that barrier he lived behind. Indeed, all the lies and his deceptive persona were mastered for one thing and one thing only, so he could become affluent. Thus Donae' deduced this was the way to tear through that wall and catch Brian off guard. Anger was the only way to get him to lose that rigid control.

Donae' pretended to overlook Brian's annoyance and voiced gallingly, "Mr. Peterson, I hope you enjoy an excellent bottle of dry wine. This is a rare treat for most, as I am sure it will be for you. The wine you are about to taste is ordered by Sash's only for the Donae' family. This intoxicating beverage is from a small private vineyard in France that centers a small but lovely village that I am sure you would not recognize or know of, Mr. Peterson. These wines are only for a selected circle which, of course, includes the Donae' family. Undeniably, their wines are excellent, yet, alas, most will never savor them. So, I dare say, Mr. Peterson, this is your lucky day."

Brian's face simulated a smile as he tried hard not to exhibit his nervous anger while he feigned confidence. However, Donae' sensed that this was still a situation Brian was not sure he had control of. Finally, with a deep breath, Brian gave in to his discomfort and confessed. "Okay, I'm very impressed, Mr. Donae'. All of this is very impressive, indeed." As he waved his hand around the room to indicate its interior and the whereabouts of their table, then sarcastically added, "I guess you could say I'm overwhelmed and awestricken, Mr. Donae'. Afterall . . . this is Sash's." He bent forward when he asked, "Please tell me, how does one rate such attention from a place like this?" Then in a sardonic tone, he said, "And *please* tell me why in the hell I am here, Mr. Donae'."

Donae' played doltish. "Excuse me; I do not understand, Mr. Peterson. I merely thought you might enjoy our meeting at a less pretentious site. I mean, I am sure you are aware and will admit that whoever decorated your office did so in a rather garish, if not an obnoxious, overstated manner. And, if I may add, Mr. Peterson, business can be done effectively in a more pleasant atmosphere, especially if one considers the full negative effect an office such as yours can have on a person's psyche." Innocently, he asked, "Do you not agree, Mr. Peterson?"

Donae' saw the fire in Brian's eyes and he continued, "You know, Mr. Peterson, I truly believe that our surroundings exhibit a part of one's mind. You know . . . , whether it is healthy or not. And I dare say the person who bedecked your office . . . well . . . , I need not say more."

Rashly, Brian leaped to his defense. "Mr. Donae', I would like you to know that my office was decorated by one of the most well-known, respected and expensive decorating firms in New York, not to mention with my full supervision. Aside from that, I'm sure you are not only observant, but also completely proficient and knowledgeable enough to recognize that all the antiques are originals. So why don't you knock off your overbearing and detestable act because I am completely aware of who and what you are . . . . Mr. Donae'."

"Whatever do you mean, Mr. Peterson?"

"I mean, I know you're a private eye and I want to know who in the hell hired you and why. Why are you and Hauser investigating me, Mr. Donae'?"

Donae' raised his hand and pushed lightly at the air. It appeared as if he were brushing away Brian's obnoxious words and said, "Ohhh, that, Mr. Peterson."

Then instead of answering Brian's question, Donae' shot back in a mocked surprised timbre, "Mr. Peterson, am I to understand that you are no longer interested in representing my family's business affairs? Why, an individual such as yourself would greatly benefit by being associated with the Donae' name and our interests; just think of the accolades your reputation will gain. And as for my dabbling in the investigative world, it is nothing more than a mere hobby, Mr. Peterson, and has nothing to do with our dealings in any which way."

Donae' noted he had not yet convinced Brian, who sat with his arms crossed and seething, that he was his pal. But he also recognized he was getting his goat, and this pleased him. So, he moved on. "To help ease your mind, Mr. Peterson, Mitch Hauser, whom I do believe I introduced you to, is a private investigator. And I do join him occasionally for the sheer fun of it. One can never experience too much fun and excitement, and a good mystery does intrigue me. Other than that, I cannot tell you anything more because I had no idea that someone hired him to investigate you. Are you a suspect for something?"

Not waiting for Brian's answer, he threw in. "Although, now that you mention it, I do recall he did mention something about an unscrupulous brother, as they say, hidden in the woodwork. And if I remember correctly, it is he; Mitch is interested in, not you, Mr. Peterson."

Brian's persona immediately changed, and he asked in a doubt-filled tone, "My brother?"

"Yes, indeed. Although, I am sure if you have something to add to the investigation or you simply want to tell me what you know about . . . uh, Eric Van Murck, I am sure that would help alleviate any suspicions Mitch might have of your involvement in any crime. Of course, as I said, this is if he suspects you at all."

Brian sat speechless as he took all Donae' had said into consideration; still and all, he didn't trust Donae'. He knew the truth Eric had told him that Donae' had done most of the questioning when he was interrogated. However, Donae's act did persuade Brian that he was half-witted. This thought further persuaded him that he could beat Donae' at his own foolish game and he decided, *why not turn this to my advantage. Afterall, I'm damn sure I'm a lot smarter than this asshole sitting across from me.* It irritated him that Donae' sat there looking smug and pleased with himself.

Donae' knew he was getting through to Brian when he saw him nervously bite down on his lower lip. Consequently, he said nothing more and waited for him to conclude that he could outwit the dimwit.

A minute later Brian feigned innocence and admitted, "All right, I guess maybe you're right, and I apologize for overreacting. I hope you can see where I was coming from. I simply wasn't sure if your offer was bona fide or not. And as far I my brother goes; I really don't know how I can be of any help. After all I really don't know him very well."

Once the steward, had finished refilling their wine glasses and left the vicinity, Donae' said, "Well, Mr. Peterson, why not let me ask you a few questions? I am sure I can guess several of the areas in which Mitch would be interested. And hopefully, once Mitch's curiosity is satisfied, we can go on with our business and forget this ever happened."

"Sure, Mr. Donae', but first tell me what Hauser's investigating and then I'll be happy to cooperate. That's if I know anything that can help."

Donae' smiled slightly while he mused to himself: *So, I see where you are headed, Mr. Peterson. You are going to play the forthright and virtuous brother.* Donae' considered his options before going any further. Finally, he decided: *Let's see how damaging you can be against your own, Mr. Peterson, for I doubt that you would hold any more love or empathy for your twin than you did for your wife and daughter.*

"Excellent, Mr. Peterson. From what I have been told, Mitch is investigating the murder of your wife and child. And I remember that you told me that you did not have any children, but I can understand why you would do so. After all, I am sure you would rather not deal with all the curiosity and questions of such a horrid state of affairs, which, I can only imagine, arises every time you make an admission of the deaths."

"You're right, very astute Mr. Donae', and I appreciate your candid understanding."

"One should always try to be compassionate, Mr. Peterson."

Brian smiled his agreement and Donae' realized that Brian thought he was in control and that he, the dimwit, was playing right into his hands. Donae' hoped his knavery would give Brian the needed security to let his guard down even more. Although, Donae' could see this was not the time to move forward so instead he asked, "More wine, Mr. Peterson?"

"Please. It's unblemished as you promised, Mr. Donae'."

Donae' smiled and nodded at his opponent while he evaluated his next move. "Mr. Peterson, what do you think? Should we get these questions out of our way while we eat lunch? I do hope you won't mind, but I took the liberty and ordered our dishes before you arrived. They rarely prepare enough pheasant and usually run out way before they should. I am sure if I had not ordered it when I did, you would not have this opportunity to enjoy Sash's most favored and famous dish." Suddenly a touch of concern entered Donae's voice and he asked as an afterthought, "Oh, of course I am sure you like pheasant, Mr. Peterson. Do you not?"

Amused, at Donae's obvious attempt to get his goat, Brian chuckled. "It will do, Mr. Donae'."

Brian waited for the server to remove the dome and set the plate in front of him so he could take his first bite. He eyed Donae' while smiling slightly, and when he tasted the bird his smile broadened to show his pleasure. Inside, he was fuming, and Donae' could see it in his eyes as well as in the clenching of his jaws. He smiled to himself for he guessed Brian thought he was the most trying, self-important dimwit he ever met.

Brian thought to himself: *He thinks he's so much better than me. He has the audacity to think he can treat me like an errand boy. It's as though he's doing me some big favor by teaching me how to enjoy the finer things in life. Well, Mr. Donae' one day soon, you'll be very sorry. You and yours will never be able to look down your snooty noses at me again. And if I ever do take over your family's business accounts, I will do everything in my power to ruin you,* posthaste. *That, I'm sure will be an unrivalled pleasure.*

The tuxedoed wine steward stood straight-backed while he asked, "More wine sir? Steadfast he waited for his question to be answered. Slowly he bowed over slightly as he continued to look hesitant about interrupting Brian and his thoughts. Puzzled, he looked at Donae' for reassurance, then asked once again, "May I pour you more wine, sir?"

Annoyed by the steward and the interruption, Brian rudely nodded his head. The steward immediately poured and moved away.

Donae' asked, "Mr. Peterson, may I call you Brian?"

"Yes, of course, please do," answered Brian in a most pleasant voice.

"Good, and you may call me Donae', just simply Donae', no Mr. to it." This Donae' could see also irritated Brian for he was sure he knew his true friends called him Lawrence. This determination pleased Donae' immensely for he truly did not like Brian Peterson, not even in a negligible way. And he was sure Brian was far from the innocent brother he wanted to portray himself to be.

Brian watched Donae' as he played at being a simpleton detective who was unsure of where to start with his questions. This is exactly what Donae' wanted him to see. He hoped his apparent amateurishness would put Brian at ease so he would not police his answers.

Donae' hesitated before he asked kindheartedly, "I hope I do not upset you with my questions, Mr. Peterson. I am not very good at this, since it is only a hobby of sorts. But I am sure Mitch would want to ask you if you ever suspected your brother as the murderer. And if so, why did you not mention that to the police? Or, for that matter, why did you not acknowledge that you even have a brother?"

Brian held the snicker he so wanted to release and answered pensively, "In all honestly, Donae', I never gave it much thought. You see, my brother and I rarely talk, and we never visit, so at times I forget that he is my brother or that he even exists."

"Oh, really, is that so, Brian? So, you do not feel that he would have hurt you or your family in any way?"

"I didn't say that."

"Oh, then what did you say?"

"What was your question again, Donae'?"

*Clever*, thought Donae'. "I asked if you thought Eric could have hurt your family. Did he dislike them or was he jealous of them or you?"

"Why would you ask that, Donae'?

"Well, for one thing, he has never been as successful as you have been, and from what I have heard he is not as well-educated. Considering these factors, do you think that could have made him jealous of you and yours? Maybe he was envious or resentful of your wealth and status."

Donae' saw that Brian noted the validation of his wealth and he could see he enjoyed the expressed homage. Furthermore, instead of answering right away, he exaggerated the contemplation of what Donae' had said. Then after a respectful pause, he very meticulously answered, "Eric? You know, Donae' . . . I really never thought about it." Bogus doubt masked his face; then it was soon replaced by out-and-out fear. Donae' noted this masterful performance as Brian's voice trembled slightly when he innocently asked, "Do you think he is capable of such an act?" Brian shook his head in disbelief, then suddenly added, "I guess I knew he had special training in the service. And he does have a temper, but to kill my family? I don't know. Just the thought of it . . . ." Brian grabbed his glass and gulped a swallow of wine. Artificial skepticism covered his face as he added slyly, "But for what benefit, Donae'? I question that someone would do something like that, simply because they were jealous."

"That is exactly what we need to find out, Brian." Donae' thought: *Watch out Eric, he's throwing you to the dogs.*

Brian shook his head and said, "No, no, I just can't see that. Then . . ., like I said, I really don't know Eric that well." Brian became thoughtful again, then said, "On second thought, I don't understand how I could have overlooked such a possibility. Now that you have brought it to my attention, it's not at all out of the realm of feasibility." Brain rubbed his hand over his face and asked, "Could the answer be that simple and close to home, Donae'? Have I just naively overlooked the abhorrent truth?" His face showed dread, then alarm as the idea became a likelihood, and he murmured, "Oh, my God, Donae'."

Donae' thought: *He's good. He's damn good.* Then he cautiously asked, "Why do you say it sounds so feasible? Do you think your brother has the inclination of doing harm to others?"

"To tell you the truth, Donae', when the police first asked if I knew anyone who might be capable of such an act, I said no. I never thought of Eric or his background. I think he was trained as a sniper or something like that in the service. So, I assume he is quite capable of killing, but still I never put the two together."

"I see. I guess to some extent I would have to agree with you. Snipers do get trained to kill people." Donae' contemplated, then asked, "Has Eric ever threatened you before?"

"Well, not in so many words, but like I said, he does have a temper."

"Can you recall if he has ever asked you for money?"

"A couple of times, but like I told him, I didn't have any money of my own, only my insufficient wages. Everything else was in Jennifer's name."

This was the first time he had heard Brian use Jennifer's name and again he realized that his voice held no emotional attachment whatsoever.

"You did give him money eventually, did you not?"

Brian waited to answer Donae'. He picked up his glass of wine and pretended to sip it. Donae' could see he was trying to think of how he could answer this question to his advantage, and after a minute or so he finally replied, "Well, I did, but only to help him better himself. But that was some time after their deaths."

This time he did not say Jennifer's or Patty Jean's names, only, their deaths." This angered Donae' and he said, "After you received your insurance money, of course."

"Why, yes, how could you have known that?"

Donae' caught himself and promptly acclaimed,

"Mitch. He said Eric admitted that he had received a quarter of a million dollars from you. So, he checked with the bank and saw that you had withdrawn the same amount after you received the insurance money."

Donae' thought it was wise to watch what he said, since he did not want to alert Brian of Addison Hobart's involvement. It was best to keep him and Carol as far away from the investigation as possible.

Brian repeated, "He checked my bank account?" He shifted in his seat, then asked, "Is that legal?"

But before Donae' could answer he added, "The only reason I ever gave him money in the first place was because my father-in-law was after me to give it to some charity which I intended to do, but then I remembered how Jennifer had always wanted to help Eric. Of course, I always disagreed because I thought Eric was a user and would take advantage of her wealth."

Surprised by this statement Donae' interrupted and asked, "So Jennifer wanted you to help Eric?"

"Oh yes, she was a humanitarian."

"So, she knew Eric?

Once again Brian shifted before he answered, "Why, of course."

"She must have liked him. Were they close?"

"From what I could tell she liked him a lot, and that was why she wanted to help him any way she could."

Donae' knew this to be a lie, because Jennifer would have told the Hobarts or Gerimee about Eric. Jennifer had had no idea Eric even existed, and if she had he could not believe that she would have liked him.

Not the Eric he had met, no matter how much of a philanthropist she happened to be.

Brian continued while Donae' smiled his encouragement. "And like I said before, my father-in-law wanted me to give the insurance money to a charity and if you think about it, Eric was in need as much as any charity."

Brian played with his dessert fork while he weighed his next words. The server poured coffee in the empty cup that sat in front of him and asked if he wanted cream. Brian rudely waved him away without answering. Donae' remained silent as he pretended to pick at his white chocolate mousse. He did not want to give Brian any indication that he was overly interested in his dialogue.

Donae' glanced up when he heard Brian cough. Then he continued, "Inasmuch as I knew Eric's welfare was important to Jennifer, I decided she would have been pleased with my decision, so I choose to follow that path. As I told you earlier, she wanted to help Eric, and sadly, in a sense, now she has."

"I see. That was very kind and thoughtful of you, Brian. I am sure Jennifer would have been immensely pleased with your generous gift."

Virtuously he muttered, "Yes, so do I."

"I bet Eric was happy with your decision, since that certainly was a hefty sum of cash. I imagine now he can do just about anything he wants."

"I thought the same, but unfortunately, that is not so, he has asked for more several times. I've told him no, but I can't seem to get through to him that I am not going to give him anymore. Each and every time I see him, he brings up the insurance money. I guess he thinks that I should share more of it with him."

"How would Eric know the worth of the insurance policy?"

After he considered the question for some time, Brian innocently determined, "I can only guess that Jennifer confided in him. She and Eric did speak regularly on the telephone."

*Another lie.* Donae' thought. *It looks like Brian wants to set his brother up for the entire murder rap.* Donae' smiled inwardly as he deemed: *I am extremely glad I had the foresight to record this conversation. I trust Eric will be truly interested in what his beloved brother has to say about him and his involvement in the murders.*

Donae' waited, but Brian said no more. Therefore, he moved the subject in the direction of another unanswered question. "I understand that you were adopted, Brian. Were you and Eric adopted by the same family?"

"No, no, Eric was not adopted. He stayed with our paternal father after our mother passed away."

"How interesting. So, you alone were put up for adoption. How peculiar." Brian looked perturbed and Donae' swiftly asked another question, "When or should I say *how* did you and Eric get back together?"

Suddenly Donae' saw a glimmer of laughter in Brian's eyes, and immediately he answered glibly, "Well, I really can't answer your first question. All I know is Eric ended up with our natural father. As for the second question, Eric found me when I was in the service. I really don't have all the particulars; I think our father must have told him about me before he passed away."

"That must have been particularly exciting for you to suddenly, out of the blue, find out you not only have a brother but an identical twin. After all, if I recall, Mitch mentioned that you had lost your adoptive parents around that same time. Dreadful accident, I hear. It was, if recall, a candle that started the fire, was it not? "

Brian's eyes became dark holes, and they stared unemotionally back into Donae's. Donae' could tell his question had caught Brian off guard and he waited for an answer. Suddenly it was easy for him to read Brian's decision; he was not about to answer any questions about the deaths of his adoptive parents.

Brian frowned then sat forward and spoke slowly, "My adoptive parents have nothing to do with the here and now. Their case has been closed for years." And to himself under his breath, he muttered. *And as far as I can tell, I am free of any accusation. I no longer fear indictment. I'm free and clear, and Donae' is just trying to catch me off guard with his meddlesome inquiries.*

Donae' added to Brian's declaration, "That is true. It has been closed for years, but still in all, the fire was bizarre, if not suspicious. Do you not agree?"

Donae' was aware of Brian's sudden effort to control his mounting anger. While he gazed steadily back into Donae's eyes, it was as if he had never been asked the question.

Donae' surveyed Brian's unresponsive eyes and saw nothing but a sea of vacancy. He realized he was not going to receive a response, so he went to a less threatening matter. "When was the last time that you saw Eric?"

Immediately Brian smiled his relief and replied, "Jesus, let me think . . . . I did get a card from him just recently. That's when he notified me that he was being investigated for some family squabble. Funny thing . . . Donae', but now that I think about it, it seems your name was mentioned in that postcard."

He grinned at Donae' as if he thought he had him, then continued, "However, before that it's been quite a while since I've even talked with Eric. You see, we don't have too much in common and we haven't made it a habit to stay in touch."

"Interesting. I thought I heard Mitch say that Eric was in New York. Yes, I am quite sure Mitch said he arrived yesterday, and you say he has not made any attempt to contact you. What a shame that you two are not closer."

Brian's face registered surprise, although it was obvious, he wanted to suppress it, but it was plain to see he had no idea that Eric was in town. Once he realized what his face revealed he made an immediate attempt to hide it. Then, as quickly, he decided that it would be best to let it show.

Casually he sat back and replied, "Is that so? Well, like I said, we don't stay in touch. As a matter of fact, this is the first I've heard he's in town, and to tell you the truth I wouldn't expect him to call me. If you remember, I told you we don't have a whole lot in common. If it wasn't for Eric's money needs, we would have no contact whatsoever."

"That is truly a shame, Brian," declared Donae'.

"I don't feel bad about it at all. We were raised in two different worlds, and neither of us would be comfortable in the other's," defended Brian.

After Brian finished his declaration, Donae' could see Brian suddenly had an urge to leave their little tit for tat and be on his way. He could only presuppose that he needed to get to Eric before he fouled things up.

Thus far, from what he had seen and learned, Brian was the brains behind this callous scheme.

Donae studied Brian as he anxiously squirmed and glanced at his watch several times before he said, "Damn, I didn't realize it was so late, I really must get back to work. I hope you don't mind, but I have several appointments this afternoon and I can't be late. These particular clients are as demanding of my punctuality as you are, Mr. Donae'."

Brian busied himself folding his napkin and pushing his coffee cup aside. Then, inordinately polite for him, he excused himself. "Again, let me thank you for the pleasure of dining at Sash's. I do hope I've been of some help with Mr. Hauser's investigation of my brother, but still I must say I am completely stunned at the prospect of him being the culprit we've been looking for." At that minute his demeanor changed and Donae' could tell he had thought of something else that might further his case against his brother. "Then," he acclaimed, "again I am just a little frightened by this theory of yours, Mr. Donae'. I mean, since Eric is the sole beneficiary to my entire earthly possessions, I'm afraid the concept tends to render all sorts of images. Do you think I'm safe? Should I be on guard? Maybe I should change my will."

"Well, I, for one, would be extra cautious before crossing a street, especially with Eric here in town. Yes, you most certainly should safeguard your back at all times." Donae' grinned innocently and added, "It is simply frightening to think a killer is among us. Do you not agree, Brian?"

After Brian had left Sash's, Donae' sat and sipped a fresh brewed cup of tea while he tried to decipher Brian's words and their intended meaning. What was he up to? His last statement was out of character, for there was very little chance of him being frightened of Eric. Donae's background in psychoanalytic therapy led him to believe that Brian was the dominating personality in this relationship, not Eric. He also detected it was not in Brian to admit to being afraid of anyone, let alone someone he felt was so inferior, unless, of course, it was to his advantage to do so. Donae' pushed himself against the back of the seat and surmised . . . *There is no doubt in my mind that Brian perceives his twin as inferior. So, I am sure he has little or no fear of Eric's aggressive behavior.* For this reason, Donae' knew Brian was the one in control; he was the one who would have instituted the ingenious plan. *But which one carried out the deadly act, Brian or Eric?*

Without warning Donae' felt a trickle of fear for Eric when he concluded that he most likely would not act on his own. He could not see him doing anything unless Brian told him to. And from what he had observed, Eric did not come across as a person who had the confidence or the aptitude to work on his own. If anything, he seemed to depend heavily on a brother he supposedly did not know well. *Then again, Brian simulates a well-balanced normal human being but is more likely a live wire,* decided Donae'. *And there is no telling where he will wind up, or whom he will cast down before he is caught and grounded. On second thought, if in fact Brian did not know that Eric was in town, then maybe Brian had less control over his brother then he had thought. Or maybe Eric was simply showing a touch of rebellion.* "Either way," Donae' sighed, "this is good. Dissension in the ranks is always beneficial for the opposing team."

Abruptly he stood and hurried towards Margaret's office. He wanted to use her phone to call Mitch. It suddenly occurred to him that he needed to evaluate Brian and Eric while they were together, and he was sure that would be sooner rather than later. He was damn sure Brian was headed straight for Eric who at this point was completely unaware of Mitch's tail. This would be an opportune time to assess them both without their knowledge

Donae's last words to Mitch before he hung up the phone were, "I do not trust Brian. My intuition tells me that I am missing something vital. For some reason, I feel Brian wants to get to Eric and stop whatever is about to happen and we, my friend, need to do the same."

# CHAPTER 17

B rian knew exactly where Eric would be. They always met at the same resort. This establishment offered the privacy of a bungalow and was close enough to the city that a person could get there without haste. However, today was different and the traffic was horrendous, and he was getting angrier by the minute. His mind was reeling with questions and he muttered and cursed as he proceeded. Aggressively, he jerked the wheel to his left and passed a broken-down truck. As he heard screeches then horns that bounced off his Cadillac, he instantaneously answered them with an unfriendly gesture in the air. Again, Brian cursed at the idiots behind him and honked at the car that blocked his way in front. The only thing that mattered was getting to Eric before Donae' found him.

He cursed out loud as he said, "What the hell are you thinking? Are you trying to get us both caught? You imbecile, you have to be watched every damn minute, or hell; you screw things up." Frustrated he screamed, "SHIT! SHIT ERIC!" As he hammered his fist against the wheel and asked, "Eric, what the hell are you thinking coming to New York?"

Brian was very thankful that he had had the brilliance to play along with Donae's' game, which was what led had to the information that Eric was in town. Donae' had no idea just how helpful he was.

It took Brian almost two hours before he pulled up in front of the hotel's entrance, and by this time he was fuming. He handed his keys to the valet without a word and hurried to the front desk where he stopped abruptly in front of a gaunt and gray-haired clerk. The man stood so still that for an instant Brian thought he was a statue behind the enormous counter. Then the man blinked, and Brian realized he was a live person, even though his skin still favored death more than life. He was a perfect match for the gray and white veined-marbled countertop that he stood behind.

Brain never asked if Eric was a guest or not. He simply pounded the desk and barked an order, "I want to speak with Eric Van Murck, at once."

The clerk smiled in a friendly professional manner but sternly retorted, "I'm sorry, sir, but our establishment does not give out room numbers and I'm afraid I cannot call your party for you, but you're welcome to use the courtesy phones against the wall." He pointed and continued, "Over there; the operator will connect you. I'm sure you can understand our policy."

At that moment, Brian gave the clerk a look that made him step back away from the desk and for an instant he feared he might be in harm's way. Apologetically, he added, "I'm sorry sir, but I can't do anything about it. It's not me; it's the hotel's policy."

Again, Brian slammed his fist hard against the countertop, then turned angrily and walked over to the wall where the scarlet red courtesy phones hung. He grabbed one and immediately shouted into the phone, "Eric Van Murck's room, now . . ."

After several rings the operator came back and expressed regret, "I'm sorry sir, no one is answering in that suite. Would you like me to transfer you to another visitor's room?"

Brian didn't answer. He slammed the phone in its cradle and stomped in the direction of the hotel's bar. Not to his surprise, sat Eric. He was seated in the center of the room and appeared to be enjoying himself with a tawdry-looking barmaid. When Brian approached the table, he could see the color drain instantly from Eric's face and he stood up and moved away from the barmaid while he muttered, "Hi, brother. I was gonna call you. I just wanted to unwind before I did."

Brian started to speak when the waitress cut in. "Come over and sit here next to me." She patted the chair and in a more suggestive overtone expressed pleasure, "Oh, my heart be still, twins. Wow and what a pair. Do you suppose I can get two for the price of one? You know, sort of like bookends."

Brian turned sharply and snapped between his clutched teeth, "Get the hell away. If we want you, we'll call you. Do you hear me, bitch?"

The waitress' eyes grew wide, and the naked fear was evident as she backed away and almost tripped over her chair. Her face turned a fiery red as she stuttered, "Yes, yes, mister. I mean, I'm . . . , I'm sorry. Please, I didn't mean to cause any trouble. Let me get you a drink or something on the house. Please, I'm sorry. I didn't thi . . . ."

Brian sat down and without looking up he snapped once again, "Just leave us alone, dammit."

The waitress hurried away without another word. Her thought was to get out of their sight as soon as possible. She couldn't afford to lose her job over some angry guest. But as soon as she turned the corner another gentleman approached her and asked, "What did those guys say to you that scared you so much, miss?"

Still frightened, she stepped backward and tried to sound as normal as possible when she answered, "Ah, um, nothing at all. I, ah, they just wanted to be alone, that's all."

"So . . . you're okay?"

When she realized he was only showing concern she calmed herself and smiled sweetly as she nodded a thank you and walked away.

He smiled back, then turned and walked over to where the phones were lined up in the corner of the room. After he pulled out a pocket full of change, he began to plunk one after another into the shiny coin receptacle. Mitch let the phone ring a long time before he hung up. Then he dialed Donae's office it was late but with Donae' one never knew. Sometimes he worked odd hours. At times he even stayed and work most of the night, then slept on the office couch. Finally, on the fourth ring, Donae' grunted a loud, "Yes, hello."

"Are you okay, Donae'?"

"Oh, good evening, Mitch. I am sorry; I was so deeply involved in these damn files for a minute it did not register that the phone was ringing."

"Maybe you should call it a night."

"No, Mitch, I know there has to be something I have overlooked. I just have this feeling."

"Well, we all know about your feelings and how sound they usually are. But, for right now, my friend, I would say that is going to have to wait."

"Oh, and the reason is . . . ?"

"Because right now I think you need to get over here to the Centurion and quick. Brian just got here, and if you ask me, he doesn't look very happy with his brother."

"I am on my way. Keep an eye on them and do not let them leave, Mitch. Even if you have to blow your cover, keep them there. I think my observing them together will help immensely. How they interact with each other may be the key in understanding their relationship better."

Mitch ordered a tall mug of beer and sat himself in the corner of the bar where he had an open view of the room along with good visibility of his two subjects. In spite of this, he was well hidden from sight due to the widespread protection of a large potted tree. He kept himself from being bored by scrutinizing the mannerisms of both men. He could clearly see that Brian was angry. It looked as though he was lecturing Eric more than adequately.

Eric appeared as though he was in some kind of trance, and his mouth hung open while he gawked awkwardly at his incensed twin. Mitch wished he could hear the tongue-lashing that Brian was so obviously bestowing upon his mutinous brother. Finally, Mitch grabbed a few napkins and started to jot down some notes. His hand began to move faster and faster and several napkins were soon filled with his observations. He wrote, "How strange it is that they're so much alike, not only in appearance, but body gestures as well. They seem to move in the same manner and unconsciously they even tilt their heads the same way." He gazed in bewilderment as he asked, "How can that be?" After all, they were raised by two different families. They didn't even know each other until they were young adults and even today, they claim not to know each other very well. So *how could they be so much alike?* He wondered, as he scratched his forehead.

He remembered that once he had read that twins could sometimes have an unusual connection, the kind of link that regular siblings didn't hold. He mumbled under his breath, "Well, as far as I'm concerned, Brian and Eric are living proof of that theory." *Well, at least proof enough to change my skeptic mind*, he mused.

Mitch continued to scrutinize the two; they seemed to be arguing hot and heavy. Once again, he wished he could get closer without them spotting him. He stood and looked on every side. There was no way too get closer. "Damn, I really want to hear what they are saying." But he didn't see any way he could get closer without blowing his cover, so he decided he would have to be satisfied with the view he had.

Their argument lasted quite a long time and it gave Mitch ample time and opportunity to read both Brian's and Eric's distinctive body language. At the same time, it gave him a rare chance to see their true, unvigilant, emotional behavior. He wished Donae' was here and could have witnessed this from the get-go, but his notes were going to have to be sufficient for his evaluation.

"What the fuck were you thinking, Eric? Dammit, why do you do things like this? Why did you come to New York? Don't you know that someone must be watching you? And dammit, why didn't you call me as soon as you touched ground? Or better yet, why in the hell did you ever leave Chicago, you goddamn idiot."

"I don't care if someone's following me, Brian. I'm tired of being the one who has to take all the heat, and I can go anywhere I want without asking you for your permission."

"Are you crazy, Eric? Without me you'd be in jail right now, and you know it. So, don't give me any of your bullshit. Do you understand what I'm saying Eric? Do you?"

"Well, how do you know if somebody's tailing me or not? Mockingly he gave a quick glance around the room and laughed as he whispered, "I haven't seen anyone lurking around." Then he gave another impromptu laugh as he exaggerated a search around the lounge's perimeter. Suddenly he rapidly looked over his shoulder towards the hotel lobby, then snickered as he turned back to face Brian with a wide, sarcastic grin. He leaned inward and crooned, "See, Brian. We're the only ones here. What's the matter, brother? Are you startin to get scared? Have you been seein bogeymen? That's it, ah, Brian? This is all startin to get ta ya." Then in a heinous laugh he added, "Maybe you're seein ghosties. Yea, I bet that's it. I bet you're seein ghosts. Maybe, like a pretty mommy ghost and a little baby ghost." Suddenly Eric burst into laughter while he enjoyed the expression on Brian's face, as it changed from anger to total disgust, then quickly back to furious anger.

"Knock it off, you goddamn fucken smart ass. This is no damn laughing matter and you know it. And as for you being tailed, I know it's a fact. I had lunch today with Mr. Private Eye himself, and for your information he knew you were in town, which was a lot more than I myself knew. How else could he find out unless he had you tailed? God, you're an idiot, Eric. Your ignorance put us right into their laps."

Eric's smirk changed to fear and he asked, "Why are they tailing me, Brian? The cops let me go. I don't have any charges filed against me, so why are they following me?"

"Someone hired them to investigate you for the murder of my damn wife and stupid kid, that's why."

"They know we had something to do with that, Brian. How could they? We covered every base, just like you said, Brian. How did they find out?"

"We don't know that they have, you idiot. And our panicking will only benefit them, so try to stay cool, Eric."

"Did you miss something Brian? You said you covered all our tracks. Did you?"

"Dammit, I don't know, but even if they try to pin it on us, they're not going to be able to prove anything. And as far as I can tell they're only looking at you right now. So, as long as you keep your damn big mouth shut, they won't be able to make anything stick, not a damn thing."

"Brian, are you sure? I don't want to go to prison. Do you know what they do to baby killers in prison?"

"Like I said, Eric. If you keep your mouth shut, you won't have to worry about that or anything else for rest of your life, because next time I intend to give you a much bigger share of the profits."

"But, Brian, maybe we shouldn't hurt anyone else. Maybe we should leave Allison alone. Maybe Jennifer and the kid shouldn't have been killed. Then we wouldn't be in this fix."

"No, no, the damn situation would be far worse, and we would be living in some poorhouse while the bitch continued to live in luxury."

"But you don't know that for sure, Brian. She might not have really left you. Sometimes women just say things like that."

"Well, that's one problem I did not want to contend with. I've worked way too long and hard to give it all up because some bitch felt she made a damn mistake. Like I keep telling you, Eric. Keep quiet and there's no way they could prove a thing. I have my alibi and you have yours. So, one more time, moron. If you keep your fucken mouth shut and don't screw anything up, we'll be okay."

"But, Brian . . . ."

"Drop it, Eric. I don't want to hear anymore. Now, let's show the world we're merely two brothers out for an evening on the town. And Eric, wipe that damn panic off your face and try to pretend you're having a good time. That's if we can get the damned stupid waitress over here. Oh, and by the way, if anyone should ask, you called me at work this afternoon and told me you were at the Centurion. That's when we decided to have dinner together. And as far as anyone is concerned, we haven't seen each other in such a long time. Got it?"

"Okay, but Bri . . . ."

"There's no more to be said, Eric. Just drop it."

It took Donae' a little over an hour before he stepped up to the large brass doors of the hotel Centurion.

As soon as he entered Mitch rushed over to greet him. "No hurry, boss. I think they realize they're being watched. And now there're having a quiet dinner in the lounge. But for a while there it was damn hot and heavy. Now I think Brian has control over Eric and the situation again.

Follow me and I'll show you a good place to observe them. It'll blow your mind how much they're alike, Donae'."

The next day started off brutally early. With a large pot of strong coffee, Donae' deciphered Mitch's handwritten observations of Brian and Eric. He compared them to his own analysis then decided, as usual, Mitch was extremely perceptive when it came to reading people and their behavior. As a matter of fact, as far as he could make out, he was right on target with these two.

In Mitch's field notes he had stated that he saw Brian as the leader of the two. And that he was unmistakably the stronger and more dominant personality. He also thought that Eric was becoming harder for Brian to manipulate. Donae' also thought this was a possibility.

In Mitch's estimation, he thought Eric would be the easier of the two to break; or confuse enough to cause mistrust in the other. Donae' agreed. If they could create distrust between the two, it would give them an opportunity to divide and conquer.

Donae' glanced over to where his notes lay and read, "Brian, it seems, has less conscience than Eric, so he would be less apt to panic." *Yes,* Donae' thought, *Eric would be easier to convince his brother was capable of being underhanded.* But still he could not see him joining forces with them, even though Eric is still their best bet. He already harbored feelings of inferiority towards his twin. Brian, on the other hand, would more easily believe that Eric is weak and capable of selling him out.

Donae' added to his notes. "It has become obvious that Eric has begun to resent his brother's strong hold on him, and I doubt his feelings will lessen with time. If anything," he concluded, "Brian will see more rebellious behavior from his less clever twin."

Silvia walked into the room holding a cup of hot tea. She offered it to Donae' and asked, "Did you work all night? I talked with Mitch earlier and he said he left you at the office buried behind a stack of folders about one this morning. Did you find any answers?"

"No, not what I had hoped for, but I think you should call Mitch and ask him to accompany me on a visit to our friend Eric's temporary habitat. I believe this would be a perfect time to start our game of cat and mouse . . . .and to do so, we need to plant the seed of doubt. Tell Mitch to meet me at the Centurion at two o'clock. For now, I am on my way home to get a couple of hours of much-needed sleep."

"Good," said Silvia, "If you don't mind me saying so, you look pooped."

"Thank you, Silvia, not for the reminder of my shoddy appearance, but for the tea."

She smiled and teased, "Well, just doing my job, sir."

"Silvia, you are always good at anticipating my needs and most of the time you take the appropriate action. This, my dear, is a rare find in an assistant and I want you to know I truly appreciate you. I do not know what I would do without you."

"Thank you, Mr. Donae', but I think you're getting punchy. So why don't you get out of here and go home to get some sleep before you give me a raise."

Donae' tried to sleep but he kept tossing about the bed. He could not kick this feeling; it was the same awareness he had had earlier. He knew he was overlooking something . . . . something so minute that he continued to do so. *But, what?* he thought. He could not find anything in the files that pointed to any one significant clue. However, he knew his gut feelings were rarely wrong. It had to be there; he was just going to have to go over all the material, one more time.

In the end Donae' gave up his attempt to sleep and got up to shower and dress before he ate his first meal since lunch with Brian the day before. He finished his Denver omelet and burnt toast and left the dishes in the sink for the maid along with a note apologizing for the mess. He knew she would understand since he rarely cooked, so she would not expect the kitchen to be anything but in disarray.

Eventually, he grabbed his coat and headed for the door. As he closed it behind him, he heard the first jingle of the phone. Hurriedly he reentered his key to unlock the door. If it was Mitch, he did not want to miss the call. Donae' grabbed the phone from the receiver and yelled a breathless, "Hello." At once he was surprised by the voice on the other end.

"Hello, Donae', this is Brian Peterson. I hope you don't mind me calling you at home, but your secretary said you were out for the day. So, I took the chance on trying you at home."

"Mr. Peterson, what an unexpected surprise. How did you get my home phone number? And in all honesty, I do mind uninvited calls at my private residence." Donae' intended to sound exactly like he knew he did. He still wanted Brian to be secure in his belief that they did not suspect him of anything, that Eric was the culprit and that he was not significant in anything except as a possible employee. This, he believed, would achieve his goal in letting Brian feel he was still in control.

Donae' immediately heard the tone change in Brian's voice as he began to speak coarsely, "Well, excuse me if I have interrupted your day off. I simply thought you might be interested in some news about my brother, since yesterday you seemed so curious about him and his activities."

"Oh, has something new developed since our lunch, Brian?"

"Yes, last night Eric called and asked me to have dinner. He was in a much more aggressive mood than usual. At one point, he even threatened me. He said he thought he deserved more money then what I had given him. And if I didn't comply with his demands, I would be sorry. He also said that my being adopted gave me a better chance at success than he had. And since our natural father had limited his opportunities by keeping him, I now owed him the same kind of break. I tell you, Donae'. I tried to reason with him, but he was unreasonable and would not listen. In truth, I have never seen him like this before. It seems that Eric has a dark side that I was completely unaware of. And I was positively frightened by the whole situation. Eric is beginning to exhibit extreme jealousy. I fear you may be right about him and what he might be capable of."

"Oh . . . . do you Brian?"

"Yes, I am quite sure, especially after last night that you are absolutely correct in your perception. Eric was acting stranger than I've ever seen or remember from the past. Or then, maybe I just never noticed it before. Either way, I was more than a little frightened by it."

"Calm down, Brian I am sure that your fear was a very normal reaction to Eric's conduct, but you are safe now."

"I know, but still . . . , with Eric's threats and . . . ."

"Thank you for calling, Brian, and I will let Mitch know about this as soon as I see him."

Donae' thought Brian's call was quite ingenious, since he was sure he was aware that someone was following Eric, in which case he knew Mitch and he would have known of their dinner rendezvous. So, in Donae's estimation, this call was nothing more than a mere ploy to cover his own ass. Although, despite the effort, there was a fly in Brian's ointment since he was unaware that Donae' himself had observed him and Eric last night. And from what Donae' had seen, there were no threats whatsoever coming from Eric's meek side of the table. However, more than a few aggressive moves came from Brian's side.

Nonetheless, Donae' thought it best to play along with Brian's act of the guiltless brother. Before he hung up, he added with false sincerity, "Brian, be very careful out there. After all, you never know what a person like Eric might do. He does appear to be somewhat off-balance and with that temper you mentioned, well . . . . . . well, let's simply say, one never knows, so take caution." Donae's face held a self-satisfied grin when he hung up because he could hear Brian's goodbye held a feeling of gratification. He thought he had been successful in pointing a guilty finger at his demented twin.

Donae' thought as he once again rushed out the door: *This will really help our effort this afternoon. I can hardly wait to see Eric's face when he hears all his hypocritical brother has told us thus far.*

Donae' pulled up in front of the Centurion and spotted Mitch outside puffing away on a Lucky Strike. He was vigilantly watching a smoke ring he blew dissipate into thin air, then he kicked a rock into the flower bed next to where he stood. He looked home like in his plaid shirt, jeans and Western boots and resembled a billboard advertisement for cigarettes.

Mitch looked up and saw Donae's car and read his excitement. It covered his face and clearly showed through the broad windshield of the Jag. Mitch knew it had to be something pretty damn good if Donae' was that charged.

When Donae' cavalierly sauntered over to where Mitch stood, his grin revealed a renewed confidence. Other than that, it unveiled little else except a hint of mischief, and this intrigued Mitch immensely. Now he was dying to hear what had transpired since last night. When he had left Donae', he was pretty downhearted and centered on the stack of field notes he had. Did he find something?

"Mitch, I am delighted you could join me. I have so much to tell you and we need to set up a plan before we speak to the acrimonious Eric Van Murck. Mitch, I think we are going to have a little fun with this one."

Donae' and Mitch had their meeting in the cocktail lounge. They sipped at the scotch and water they had ordered while they kept an eye on the front entrance. They didn't want any surprises, like Eric deciding to have an early cocktail before dinner.

Donae' went through every detail he had found, then asked Mitch, "Do you have any suggestions on how to bag our mark?"

Mitch immediately replied, "I'm for the old standby. But, I'm afraid playing bad cop, good cop wouldn't work in this case, especially since Eric so obviously hates everyone and most certainly wouldn't warm up to either good or bad cop."

"Yes, I agree. Right now, I'm afraid Eric believes we are to blame for this complete mess he is in. Yes, I'm fairly sure him warming up to us will be a challenge. I guess our best bet is to play it by ear.

At a quarter to five Mitch motioned to Donae' that Eric had just entered the room. They waited until after he had ordered his cocktail before they stood up and approached his table. When Eric looked up and recognized who they were, Donae' effortlessly read the indecision that instantly covered his face.

Eric started to stand up to leave, then decided against it. He stayed perched halfway between sitting and standing for a second or two. Then his usual smirk crossed his disrespectful lip and he plopped himself back onto the seat and mumbled, "So what the fuck do you two assholes want?"

"Donae's smile was warm and friendly as he quipped, "Oh, we simply wanted to welcome you to the wonderful city of New York. Is this your first visit? I hope you take the time to take in some of the sights; we do have a lot to offer."

Eric didn't reply and Donae' continued, "Thank you. We would love to join you. Right, Mitch?"

"Sure would; thanks for asking. I hope you're having as good of a day as we are, Eric, my friend."

After what seemed was an impasse, Eric answered, "Very funny, Mr. Comedy-man, and I ain't your friend, asshole, so leave me alone."

"Come on, Eric. With all that we've been through together, I would think that the least Donae' and I deserve is your friendship. Don't you?"

"I don't have to talk to you guys. All charges have been dropped and I'm free and you can't do nothing to me, so get the hell out of my face."

Donae' sat down in the booth and Mitch pulled up a chair. Donae' appeared troubled as he looked around the room.

Eric wondered: *Who's he was looking for*?

Then, in a voice so close to a whisper that Eric unconsciously leaned forward to hear what he had to say, Donae' spoke his first words of their deception, "Eric, we are not here to harass you. Mitch and I are here purely to help you. We know you met with Brian last night; you had dinner with him."

"So, is that against the law in New York? And besides, I knew you guys were following me; I wasn't trying to hide nothing. Brian's my brother and we can have dinner without being arrested."

"See, Mitch, I told you Eric was smart enough to figure out you were tailing him."

"Yeah, you were right, but that's not the only way we found out," added Mitch.

"What do ya mean?" asked Eric?

"Your brother. He called me this morning to tell me that you threatened him last night," replied Donae'.

Donae' saw the confusion that flashed across Eric's face. Then instantly it went back to his usual sneer. It was easy to see Eric had questions, but he was afraid to ask in fear of divulging any secrets.

He and Mitch fell silent and waited while Eric fought his emotional dilemma. Soon he determined this was all a ruse and his expression changed back to its familiar sarcastic hostility. Donae' could no longer read his face, but he was absolutely sure Eric was still trying to figure out why Brian might say something like that.

Behind Eric's cynical grin he was arguing with himself. *What is Brian up to? Whatever it is he hasn't filled me in on it. I don't think he mentioned anything last night about calling Donae'. But then, maybe he did, and I forgot. Then, maybe he didn't want me to know. Why would Brian call Donae', unless it was to . . . ?*

Donae' watched Eric's eyes as they darted back and forth and asked himself, "Is he trying to find the answers in mid-air? Then maybe he's hoping to find more than just solutions; maybe he is trying to figure out what the chances are that his brother might betray him.

After some time Donae' saw anger cover Eric's face as he struggled to gather his thoughts; then unconsciously he mumbled. But the only words Mitch or Donae' could make out were, "Oh, dammit, Brian." The rest was a jumble of sounds, even though Donae' guessed that Eric was asking himself how to answer the insinuation. His eyes showed he was fearful that he would botch things up if he spoke a single wrong word. At last Donae' was rewarded with a momentary flicker of doubt.

Once this registered on Eric's face, Donae' added one more douse of fuel to the flame. "Brian said you were trying to get more money from him. Matter of fact, he said that you almost sounded crazed, that you frightened him with all your insane babble. Did you tell him that you were angry that he had more money then you? And that you felt threatened that he was so much more successful and prosperous than you? He said, he never heard you talk that crazy before."

"I'm not crazy and Brian wouldn't say that. I know he wouldn't, and you're a liar."

"No, I am not lying, Eric. Your brother said that and quite a bit more. Here, listen to this tape I recorded yesterday at lunch."

Eric pushed the recorder away, and Donae' added, "Just listen, Eric. Listening is not going to hurt you in any way. But if Brian is setting you up for a fall, that is going to hurt."

Donae' and Mitch waited . . . . and when Eric said nothing, they knew he was thinking about what Donae' had said. After a minute of complete silence Donae' related, "I'm sure once you hear the tape, Eric, you will agree your twin is trying to set you up to take the entire blame."

For an instant Donae' thought Eric was about to grab the recorder and throw it. Then Mitch jumped in and said, "You can't lose anything by just listening, right Eric?"

Donae' could see that Eric's curiosity had grown stronger than the suspicions he held against them. Slowly, Eric shook his head but said, "Okay, but I think this is some kind of fucken trick, so anything I hear isn't gonna make a bit of difference." His right cheek twitched several times before he succumbed, "Come on, dammit; let's get it over with. Then I want ya out of here and to leave me alone. Do ya understand? No more harassment from ya guys."

Mitch nodded and Donae' pushed play. When the words began to pour from the recorder, Mitch saw the anger mount in Eric's eyes and within minutes he was close to the point of hitting something or someone. Betrayal was written all over his face.

Eric did not want to believe what he was hearing, but there was no mistaking Brian's intention. Yet, could he be sure it was Brian? He wondered if it could be a trick because Brian wouldn't do this to him. Eric's mind moved from trust to distrust then back to trust. He wasn't sure what he should believe. He knew he couldn't trust Mitch and Donae'; they were unethical. They would do anything to debase Brian and him. In the end, he decided they had to have done something to the tape, that Brian's conversation wasn't intact. Donae' had to have recorded bits and pieces of conversations. He used to do the same thing in the military when he wanted to set someone up. That had to be it, just words out of context. That's all. He would go tell Brian what they did, and he would tell him the truth; he would explain everything, he reassured himself.

Mitch and Donae' could see that Eric still distrusted them, yet there was a small feeling of doubt that lingered towards Brian. This was all they could ask for. The seed of doubt was planted; and when the tape began to flap as it ended the recorded exchange Eric's face was stolid. Nevertheless, at this point Donae' knew from instinct that they were on their way to solving a murder case. He knew Eric was going to react just as they had hoped he would.

Mitch was the first to speak when he asked, "Eric, do you want to hear it again?"

"No, dammit! Hell, no. I know you guys altered the damn tape. You're just tryin to make me mad at Brian. But it's not going to work so get the fuck out of my face like you promised you would."

"Okay, Eric. But we were just trying to help you by keeping Brian from blaming everything on you."

"There's nothing to blame me for, so get the fuck out of my face, ass-hole.

"Donae' asked calmly in an unobtrusive voice, "Eric, did you kill Jennifer and Patty Jean Peterson, or was it Brian that did the deed?"

At that moment, Eric jumped up and slammed his fist onto the recorder, then turned and walked away.

Donae' and Mitch sat there for several minutes before they faced one another with a smile and Mitch whispered, "Gotcha."

Suddenly, Donae's face grew pensive and he said, "Mitch, stay on him and I will keep an eye on Brian. I don't know why, but I keep getting a feeling that something just does not fit." Donae' shook his head then added, "Hopefully, when the two get together and tear into each other, one will say something that will finally give us a clue to the missing link.

Mitch looked over his shoulder and watched as Eric ordered another drink at the bar. Then he said, "Well, for right now it looks like he's going to be spending some time drinking and thinking about what he's just heard. I guess he needs to figure out who he's going to believe. And if it's not Brian, then what is he going to do about him and his tricks?"

# CHAPTER 18

The next morning Mitch caught up with Eric as he was about to get in his rental car. It was obvious that he had been up all night and was now in a hurry to get somewhere, which Mitch presumed was to find his mutinous brother.

Once they were on the open road Mitch stayed a couple of car lengths behind Eric, although it probably didn't make a bit of difference how close or far behind he was because it wasn't hard to spot the bright red sedan with its rental sticker plastered smack dab in the center of its rear window. Mitch snickered, "A car couldn't be been more conspicuous if it tried."

Mitch also noticed that Eric probably wasn't thinking about being followed. He wasn't bouncing from lane to lane; he was simply driving as fast as traffic allowed. Apparently, the only thing on his mind was Brian and reaching him as fast as possible.

It was about forty-five minutes later when Eric turned into a spherical driveway and abruptly stopped in front of an attendant who stood at attention outside the building. Mitch decided it had to be Brian's office when he saw that Eric had no intention of waiting for the valet. As soon as the car was at a full stop, he swung the open door and jumped out and rushed up the stairs. He didn't even slow down long enough to hand over his keys to the valet, who was now yelling for Eric to stop. Finally, the young man ran after him and caught him at the top of the stairs as he started to enter the building. When the guy touched his arm, Eric swung around and gruffly handed over the car keys with what, Mitch would guess, a curse word or two.

Eric's ruckus gave Mitch the time he needed to park his car and get him back in his range of vision. Once Eric entered the building, he wasted no time creating another disturbance. He went directly to the security guard and loudly demanded directions. Before the guard could finish, Eric took off in the direction of the elevators.

Mitch heard what floor Brian's office was on and headed for the stairs. He took them two at a time, all the way up to the sixth level. When he walked through the doorway that entered the lobby, he saw a confused but adamant receptionist who was trying to explain to Eric that he had no choice; he had to fill out the information card or he was not stepping a foot beyond the lobby.

Mitch felt sorry for the girl. Eric towered over her and bellowed, "I want to see Brian Peterson now."

The girl behind the desk finally realized that she was not going to get anywhere with the irate visitor and picked up the phone to call security. However, before the guard could react to the call, a nice-looking professional woman came out of another doorway and approached Eric. She started to explain in a loud voice to heard over Eric's ruckus, but caught herself as the resemblance registered. But her control was almost immediate, and she voiced, "Mr. Peterson is in a meeting and can not be disturbed, so throwing a tantrum is not going to do anyone any good."

At that point Eric walked over to a bench in the seating area and sat down. Angrily, he shouted, "Fine, then I'll wait, and I intend to wait all damn day if that's what it takes, bitch."

The lady who Mitch assumed was Brian secretary took a deep, frustrated breath and replied, "Okay . . . . fine, I'll see if I can get a note to Mr. Peterson. I'll let him know you are here waiting to speak with him, but I can't promise you that he will have time to see you. He's very busy with *scheduled* appointments and meetings the entire day. Who can I say is waiting?"

"Just tell him his fucken brother's here and I guarantee he'll see me. Now dammit, go tell him I'm here."

The secretary's expression had registered disbelief at the onset of the confrontation and now as she bustled towards the same doorway she had come out of a few minutes earlier, it was clear to read in her movements, as well as her expression; she was still baffled by Eric and his overwhelming resemblance to Brian. *She didn't even know he had a brother. Yet brother or no brother,"* she thought: "*I do not like being treated in such a disrespectful manner and I refuse to be put in such an unpleasant predicament again. And Mr. Peterson is certainly going to hear about it.*

It was only minutes before the secretary returned to the lobby and told Eric coolly to follow her. When she had opened the door to the stairwell, Mitch had caught a quick glimpse of Brian who was rushing down the stairs to meet Eric. His face was red with controlled rage.

Mitch was sure he was embarrassed by the scene his brother had created by showing up unannounced and, more so, by his aggressive behavior to his secretary. Mitch would also guess that Brian's co-workers did not know about his twin; since the lobby began to have a flow of people walking in and glancing at Eric, then scurrying away. Mitch grinned as he visualized Brian's anger when he found out he was the new topic of gossip, throughout the entire building.

Brian closed the door behind Eric and then turned abruptly to face his twin. His rage had continued to grow all the while he led Eric to his office, and now it was to the point of boiling. He could have killed him for the sheer pleasure of it, but instead he bit his lower lip and tried hard to gain control of himself.

It took several minutes for him to calm down. Then he calmly asked in a sharp tone, "What the hell are you doing here, Eric? Have you completely lost your mind? You can't just walk into this building and demand to see me. Dammit, now everyone will be talking about Brian and his retarded twin brother. I'm sure it'll be all over the building in less than an hour. What kind of moron are you, anyway? Why can't you get your shit together?"

"Brian, I told you to stop calling me stupid. And I don't give a damn about you and your fucken building . . . . or your co-workers. All I care about is you trying to set me up, damn you, Brian."

"What! I don't know what the hell you're talking about, Eric."

"Yes, yes, you do, I heard it for myself on the recorder that Donae' had. It's you all right. You telling him how I tried to get money from you, and you're saying that I scared you and how you think I'm crazy. Well, Brian, I'm not crazy enough that I'm gonna take the heat for this rap, and if I do go down, I promise you I won't be going down alone. You have just as much to lose as I do, and if I tell them the whole story, I won't be the only one sent to the electric chair, Brian. You mark my fucken words, Brian; I'm not facing this rap alone."

"Jesus Christ, Eric, listen to me. You let them get to you? How could you do that? You can't panic now; everything will be lost. It'll all have been for nothing. And I'm not trying to set you up; you must know better than that. I've always been there for you and I'm not going to turn on you now. Think, Eric. You know that; I know you do."

"Well, I thought I did, Brian. But then I heard what I heard, and I know that was you on the recorder. I know that was you saying all those mean things."

"That's Donae'. He must have messed with the tape and changed my words around. You know how cops work; they take things out of context and use them for their own advantage. You know that. You only heard what they wanted you to hear."

Eric surrendered for a minute and thought about what his brother had just said, then grunted an agreement. "Yeah, sure, you know, I thought that at first."

Not as certain as he was before, his voice cracked and dropped a pitch and his words came out less threatening than his prior assertions. "But . . . but right now I'm not sure anymore. I don't know if you're trying to make me the fall guy or not." His voice steadily grew louder when he shouted one last threat. "But, if you are, I'm not gonna sit by and let you get away with it!"

"Eric, calm down, and listen to me. Those guys are trying to use you to get to me and you can't let them do that." Brian moved across the floor and put his arm over Eric's shoulder and finished his statement, "Eric, it's me and you, together, as always. No one's going to stop us. We just have to stay one step ahead at all times, and that means no panic. Do you understand? We do not let creeps like Donae' and Hauser get to us."

"Yes, Brian, but I stil . . ."

"No Eric, listen. I'll tell you what we need to do. We need to sit down and go over this step by step. Do you understand me, Eric? Do you? We need to do this the same way we did with Jennifer and Patty Jean, okay? We have to be one hundred percent together. So . . . Eric, why don't you meet me at the house tomorrow evening about seven? Okay?"

Eric's voice started to raise one pitch higher than before as he violently yelled, "I don't want to wait until tomorrow; I want answers now. No more fucken around, Brian. I want some goddamn answers now."

"Eric, lower your damn voice and watch your foul mouth. We can't have the whole building hearing you and your idiot threats."

"Don't call me an idiot. I'm not an idiot. And I'm not a stupid fool, either. I know your u . . . ."

"Stop, Eric. I know you're not stupid but why can't you hear me? I have meetings all day; I can't just walk out of the office anytime I want. People might get suspicious and that we do not need."

Eric said nothing as he crossed his arms in defiance and glared at his twin.

Brian stopped. He finally understood that he was not getting through to Eric and in the end, he agreed, "Okay. All right, you win. If me meeting with you today will make you happy, then we'll meet tonight. Okay? I should be home by nine o'clock and at that time we will make sure everything is straight between us. And I promise, Eric, you won't have to worry anymore about being thrown in jail. Together we will make you feel secure. Okay, Eric, okay. Will tonight be soon enough?"

"It will, if you're going to tell me the damn truth and not try to set me up again."

"I was not trying to set you up. Donae' is just playing with your mind, by making you think I am. Can't you see that?"

Eric didn't answer, so Brian gave up and said, "Just be at my place tonight at nine and we'll straighten everything out. And don't let anyone know about the meeting. We don't need Donae' bursting in on us. Okay, Eric, can you do that?"

"Sure, I can. I'm not stupid, Brian, so stop treating me like I am. And I'll be there. You just make sure you're there and that you have some answers for me. No more screwing around Brian, no more lies."

"Eric, dammit, forget about me lying. I told you that was Donae' and one of his tricks. Just be on time tonight; then everything will be okay. Maybe it's time we talk about putting an end to Donae', once and for all."

Brian waited about ten minutes after Eric left. Then he called his secretary to tell her to cancel all his appointments for the rest of the day. Once that was confirmed he added, "I'm sorry about my brother, Shirley, and how he treated you. He's usually not that bad, but since he left the military and gotten older, he tends to fly off the handle frequently. I should be used to it, but I'm afraid this episode has upset me so much that I don't think I can concentrate enough to be any good to anyone today. I think I'm going to call it a day and go home and rest. If you can, I'd appreciate it if you could please cover for me."

Eric and his tantrums were more than Brian could have hoped for. It couldn't have gone any better if he had planned it himself. "Yes, Eric, my brother, you are an idiot, and this is the last time I'm going to have to deal with you and your hysteria." He grabbed his briefcase and headed for the door, then hesitated. Donae' was sure to have a tail on him and he had so many things to put in order before nine o'clock tonight.

After some speculation, he went back to his desk and picked up the phone. Again, he called his secretary. "Shirley, I'm sorry to bother you, but my car has been acting up lately and this morning I barely made it in. I'm afraid it's overdue for its service. And since I won't be using it, I might as well get it taken care of today. So, if you can call the towing service to pick it up, I would appreciate it. Do you know if there's a company car available in the carpool?"

"I can check and call you right back, Mr. Peterson."

"That'll be fine, and Shirley tell them I'll pick it up at the garage. I can use some fresh air."

"Are you sure you don't want them to drop it off here, sir?"

"No, no, I would rather pick it up there. Like I said, I need a little fresh air. With all that has happened this morning, the walk will do me good."

"I understand, sir."

He smiled to himself as he hung up the phone and mumbled, "I just bet you do, Miss Kelp." He was sure the gossip had already begun, and the gossip mongers were enjoying Shirley Kelp's every word.

A minute later Shirley informed him that a car was in the garage waiting for him. "They said just pick it up whenever you are ready, sir."

Brian picked up his coat and briefcase again and headed out the back entrance of the building. He decided to walk through the alleys. It was two city blocks to the company carpool, and he didn't want to chance being seen or followed. Once he approached the parking garage he leaned against the building and waited several minutes before he moved inside. If someone was tailing him, he didn't want the guy witnessing him entering the facility. He waited, then moved inside.

The garage attendant was busy working on another vehicle across the building. He never took notice that Brian was there, so he used the opportunity to take a few items he felt might come in handy later.

When he drove the car from the garage, he cruised slowly past its exit ramps and out onto the street. Afterward, he drove around the block twice before he felt safe that Eric or someone from Donae's group wasn't following him.

As soon as he felt confident that all was good, he headed for parts unknown. He needed time to think without distractions before he set his plans in to motion.

Brian had concluded that he was not going to be at anyone's mercy any longer. And most of all, he was not about to become accountable to his backwards brother. Eric had now become a liability that he could not afford to have around. He should not have brought him into this in the first place, but he had thought Eric would be more helpful than he had turned out to be. He should have learned a long time ago that the only person he could trust and count on was himself.

Suddenly, Brian felt a strong surge of anger. His entire body wrenched as he relived his hatred for his adoptive father and mother. Just as suddenly a smile spread across his face as he recalled the joy he felt at the sight of their lifeless bodies. They deserved what they got, and he would do it all over again if he could. He had hated them from the minute he had learned about all their lies.

How could they have said they loved him? They had disregarded his feelings for years by hiding the truth. As far as he was concerned, their adoption of him was nothing less than a kidnapping and they deserved to die. They should have answered that letter from his father's lawyer and sent him home where he belonged. Instead, they chose to betray him by never telling him the truth that he was adopted. They never revealed that his real father had tried to find him and wanted him back. And for that he hoped they'd burn in hell . . .

Throughout that morning and afternoon Donae' tried to talk with Brian, but the receptionist said repeatedly, "Mr. Peterson is scheduled to be in meetings all day, sir. After that he will be attending the dinner meeting in the Awards room downstairs, so I don't expect he'll be free to speak with you until tomorrow morning. But if you leave a message, I'm sure he'll return your call if he gets a free moment, Mr. Donae'."

Donae' inquired, "What time will he be out of his dinner meeting?"

"Oh, well, I'm not sure, but I imagine it'd be sometime after eight o'clock, or it may even be later, depending on the agenda."

For this reason, Donae' did not hurry to the office building where Brian worked. Since Brian was tied up and wouldn't be leaving the premises anytime soon, there was no need to stand watch. So, he went about his daily routine of administering the family's business, while he assured himself that he would catch up with Brian around eight o'clock that evening when he left work.

Meanwhile, Brian continued with his plan to rid himself of his burdensome brother. Once he had decided not to deal with Eric and his threats any longer, he felt stimulated, and after a quick lunch he celebrated by making a toast with a glass of champagne. "Here's to you, and to no more threats of you spilling your guts to the half-witted Donae' or, worse, the cops."

Before Eric was to leave the Centurion, he searched for Mitch to see where he had positioned himself. He knew he would be in clear view of the comings and goings of his bungalow. After he spotted him, he went to the lounge and ordered a bottle of vodka and a couple of sandwiches. He swallowed the first glass of vodka as he waited for his order to come, followed by a second slug when he decided to take the bottle and the food back to his room.

He smirked to himself as he determined, "This is going to be like taking candy from a baby."

When the sandwiches were ready to go, Eric, in a loud drunken voice provokingly toyed with the waitress, "Hey, sweet ass, when you get off work, why don't you meet me upstairs and we can party? What do ya say? I'll make it well worth your while." He laughed out loud as she gave him a fully disgusted look when she walked away. He staggered and laughed again when he made a last attempt to grab her and missed.

Mitch followed as Eric stumbled and swayed out of the lounge toward his room. He continued to watch him while he fought for several minutes with his room key, trying to unlock his door. After a few minutes and more cuss words, he finally was successful and shoved the door wide open with a loud bang. He stumbled against the door jamb and cussed it while he angrily slung the bag of sandwiches across the room unto the bed. He entered the room heading for the bed then abruptly returned to close the door with a hard bang. This closed off all range of vision from Mitch and his surveillance.

Once Eric entered the room; he turned on the television and made sure it was close to full volume. Then he staggered to the window and pulled the blinds closed. He assured himself, "If anyone's out there, they'll see nothing but darkness." As he turned off the last of the lights, he moved to sit on the bed to wait.

He waited about a half-hour before he cautiously crawled out the rear window. As soon as he was out, he lay flat on his belly, and scooted his frame along the side of the building. Then he maneuvered his body over the two-foot high hedges. He stayed down until he was safely out of sight of the hotel and Mitch's range of vision.

After he felt safe, he hoisted himself up over the four-foot wall that surrounded the grounds. He ran the last block to where he had parked a car behind a thicket of trees. He had bought the vehicle from a private party the first day he was in town. He had a feeling it would come in handy. That's why he parked it out of sight and used the flashy rental car.

Once he was safely behind the wheel, Eric leaned back and took his first calm breath. Glancing around, he mentally inspected his supplies before he started the car and drove slowly out of the grove. He did so without turning on the headlights and continued this way for at least two miles. Then he threw it in gear and hauled ass for Brian's place and what he assumed would be peace of mind.

Mitch nibbled at the sandwich he'd ordered while he kept an eye on Eric's bungalow. It looked as if Eric was in for the long haul. With the bottle of vodka he had bought and the drinks he had slugged away while he waited for his dinner, Mitch figured the drunken Eric would be out soon and it would probably take him all night to sleep it off.

He took one more mouthful of his sandwich and thought about the conversation he had just had with Donae' when he reported that Eric was inebriated, and he thought he was down for the count.

Donae' told him that he sounded like death warmed over and suggested, "Why don't you get some rest while you can, Mitch? There's no need to watch a closed door if Eric's out for the night."

Mitch agreed and after he finished his dinner he intended to go to his room and do just that. Donae' said he deserved a break, but Mitch knew it was more like a need, for he was extremely groggy with fatigue. And if he didn't get a few hours' sleep he wasn't going to be good for anything.

When Donae' pulled up in front of the office building where Brian worked, it was close to eight o'clock. He waited diligently until about a quarter past nine before he went up to the front entrance and tried the door. It was locked tight.

A guard saw him and walked over to the glass doors and yelled, "We're closed. You'll aft ta come back tomorrow."

Donae' shook his head and said, "No, I . . ."

The guard interrupted him with a loud, "I can't hear ya, ya need to speak louder. What do ya want?"

Donae' spoke up and informed the guard, "I am looking for Brian Peterson. From what I understand he was supposed to be having a dinner meeting in one of the conference rooms. Is that still going on?"

"That meeting was over more than an-hour-and-a-half ago. Everyone has left and won't be back until tomorrow morning. Try again after eight a.m.", he yelled.

Donae' thanked the guard and headed for his Jag. He knew that Brian had not come out of the front entrance. He turned and headed straight for the back of the building to see if there was another exit besides the fire exit. There was not so Brian would have had to slipped out by way of the fire-escape. Donae' was certain most people in Brian's position would not exit via the fire door for any reason other than they did not want to be seen leaving. What was Brian up to that he would go to that extreme?

"Damn," cursed Donae' as he jumped in his car and rushed to the nearest phone to call Mitch.

Mitch answered the phone after the third ring. He was in a sleepy haze when Donae' asked, "Where is Eric?"

"What? What, Donae'? Oh, um, in his room, Why?"

"Hurry go check his room right now. I will wait on the line."

Mitch threw on a pair of pants and ran out the door. He knocked at Eric's door several times. When no one answered he knocked louder several more times. Still there was no answer. Mitch muttered, "Maybe he's passed out." He hurried around the building to check for anything that might be suspicious. Around the back of the bungalow he noticed that a window had been left open. He listened for a second or two, and after hearing no sound other than the blaring of the television coming from inside the room, he hefted himself up and over the windowsill. Once he entered, he tiptoed quietly towards the open bathroom door and peeked around the corner into the bedroom. The lights were off, and the television screen was showing nothing but static. But it did give him enough light to tiptoe safely across the floor to the bed so he could get a better look. It appeared as if someone was fast asleep in the middle of the bed, but when he approached its left side Mitch could see it was nothing more than two pillows shoved together under the comforter. Mitch smacked at the pillows and shouted, "SHIT, goddamn you, Eric." He jerked the door open and rushed back to the phone, "Dammit, Donae', he's gone. He must've slipped out after I went to sleep, damn it!"

"Well, do not beat yourself up too badly for I too have the same problem. Brian has also ditched me."

"What! What could they be up to? You don't think they're going to slip out of town, do you?"

"No, that would not fit Brian's M.O. And at this point, I don't believe they feel that they are in any real jeopardy of being caught, so to flee would not benefit them in any way. There has to be another explanation.

Donae' grew quiet, then suddenly said, "Mitch, meet me at Brian's residence. There we may find some answers.

# CHAPTER 19

B rian parked his car around the corner and up the block from his street. He gathered his booty, then quickly locked his auto and moved onward through the alley. The night was dark with only a sliver of moon for light and he tripped when he mounted the stairs to the back entrance of his house. He had decided to enter from the back in case Donae' or Mitch thought to check his home. By now he was sure they realized he had given them the slip; this is why he didn't park in the garage or the driveway. He also left most of the lights off when he went in; he wanted it to appear that no one was around. Immediately he began to put things in order. *Soon*, he thought, *this will all be in the past and then finally I can get on with my life without the constant irritation of Eric and his tantrums.*

Brian heard a car pull up in front of the house. He swiftly moved to the other side of the room and turned off the only light he had on except for the night light in the corner of the living room. A minute later he heard the same car back up and pull away. Whoever it was didn't get out, because he didn't hear a knock or the doorbell ring. Slowly he moved to peek through the drapes in the hallway; no one was out front. Maybe it was Donae' or Mitch and they had assumed he wasn't home and left. He was sure it wasn't Eric, because if it had been, he would be pounding on the door by now.

After a minute, Brian moved to sit in his favorite armchair in the middle of the living room. This, he decided, was the perfect position to confront Eric. No sooner had he sat down and started to get comfortable than suddenly, he heard a sound from behind him. Startled, he jumped up and turned and unexpectedly came face to face with his brother. Eric was standing next to the fireplace. His stance was arrogant and resembled that of a model in an old-time portrait. Neither said a word for full minute. Finally, Eric sardonically smiled and greeted, "Good evening and welcome home, brother. I've been patiently waiting for you for some time."

At first Brian was caught off guard, though it didn't take long before he regained enough composure and asked, "What the hell . . . how . . . how did . . . how did you get in here, Eric?" Then in a puzzled tone, "Never mind that. Why in the hell are you wearing my clothes? What the hell's going on, Eric?"

Eric's demeanor was completely different than what Brian had ever witnessed before. The tone in his voice was controlled and well-projected when he properly retorted, "Your clothes, Brian? My, my, dear brother, what's mine is yours and what yours is mine, just as it should be. I am sure you would agree that we are a duo through and though."

"NO! Dammit . . . no, no, I do not agree. And I don't appreciate you stalking around my house in the middle of the night . . . co . . . .completely uninvited," stuttered Brian.

"I am invited. Remember, you asked me to meet you here earlier today? And Brian, don't you mean . . . . Jennifer's house?"

"No, I do not. I mean my house and knock off this bullshit game you're playing. I want to know how you got in here and what kind of *stupid* prank you are up to now."

Eric came across as extremely calm, and his speech was the same when he answered, "Brian, dear, Brian, I have asked you more times then I dare count not to call me stupid. Yet that does appear to be a problem for you. However, I anticipate that that will change in the very near future.

You, I might say, will no longer be calling me or anyone else for that matter, stupid."

By this time Brian had started to regain some of his composure and promptly Eric sensed his brother no longer felt threatened by his intrusion. Almost simultaneously, Brian's face grew stern and his renewed strength was evident when he asked in an exasperated tone, "Eric, are you drunk? You don't sound right. Dammit, Eric, what the fuck are you up to. Why are you talking like this and . . . .?"

Eric didn't wait for Brian's momentum to build. He answered before he could finish his barrage of questions. "Thank you, Brian. I believe you have grown extremely perceptive, and of course, you are shrewdly correct. You must recognize that I am speaking exactly like you taught me to. If you remember, you told me a gentleman always speaks slowly and deliberately. Aren't you pleased, Brian, I finally got it? I suppose you would probably say it finally sank into this thick head of mine. Am I right, Brian? Though, I dare say, a lot later than you had wished for. But that is neither here nor there, is it Brian? Especially since the past is something we chose to ignore and hope everyone else forgets."

"Goddammit, Eric, just knock off the bullshit and forget this stupid game. Let's just get down to business. I don't intend for this to take all night."

Brian quickly stepped over to the other side of the room where he had set everything up. Without any indecision he opened the desk drawer and reached in to pull out a small pistol. Instantly, he pivoted and pointed the gun at Eric, and after only a second's hesitation he quickened his steps to move closer to where his twin stood by the fireplace. Eric's casual stance became frozen and his face registered disbelief as he realized what his brother was pointing at him.

At last Brian said, "Yes, Eric, that's right, you are stupid. stupid enough that I can't take any more chances on you screwing things up. All this . . ." he waved his hand around the room, "that I have worked so hard and so long to get, I refuse to let you annihilate it. I deserve to reap the benefits of my fortune and I am not about to lose it because of you or anyone else. Yes, you should have learned that from Jennifer's misfortune . . . . Don't you think if you weren't stupid you would have remembered that?

Brian sucked in a huge gulp of air before he went on . . . . . . "So, see I am right. You are dull-witted, Eric and that, I'm afraid, has always been your ill fortune and my inconvenience." Brian pondered before he once more started to degrade his brother. "You see, we may be physically alike but that is where it ends, Eric. And as I said, you are a risk that I am not willing to have any longer. See, Eric, you are not as strong as I am and I'm afraid you in time will crumble and ruin everything for me."

As soon as Brian had started his onslaught of debasing, Eric was reduced back to his old insecure self and he asked, "Why . . . . Brian? I don't understand. Why would you hurt me? I'm your brother, your identical twin. Are you gonna kill your only family? You know you can count on me; I've always been there when you needed me. Right . . . . ya know that, right. I'm not gonna say nothing to nobody; I promise."

"Laughing, Brian never acknowledged Eric's bemoaning. Instead he unforgivingly replied angrily, "Yes, you are my brother, and what a disappointment you have turned out to be. Eric, you have always been a thorn in my side, and as I told you before I am not going to end up in prison because of you and your moronic stupidity."

"Sooo . . . .so you're just gonna shoot me? Brian, how are you going to explain that to the police . . . and to Donae'?"

"Oh, that will be very easy. You see here, dear brother?" He presented a sheet of paper for Eric to see. "I have this letter I wrote for you; it tells the world how you killed my dear, sweet wife and our darling, innocent child. And now sadly, after all this time, you can't live with yourself any longer. That's why you came to town in the first place, so you could confess your sins to me and then you shot yourself to death, right here in front of me."

Brian sighed, "How sad a day. Can you imagine, Eric, how that is going to make me feel? And I'm sure everyone is going to understand when I tell them I am beside myself with grief. Not only from your unexpected confession, but your suicide as well. Yes, I guess it's quite normal and most would expect a person who witnesses such a scene to go a little haywire. So, you see Eric, you need not worry yourself. Everyone will believe

me. Even when I don't call the police or ambulance for an hour or so after witnessing your traumatic ending. Yes, they will understand, and
there will be little or no question of my integrity. My actions will simply
be labeled trauma."

He smiled and his voice filled with pride as he asked, "Don't you
think that's a great plan, Eric? I mean, it's almost as good as my last one,
with Jennifer and the kid. Wouldn't you say? I think it's simply genius."

Eric stood there with his mouth open and tongue-tied. Then Brian
asked, "Come on, Eric, you have to agree, don't you? You know I'm
right. I'm the genius and you're the idiot." Suddenly Brian burst into
laughter, then as instantly stopped and glared at Eric calmly.

Eric begged, "Brian you can't be serious. They'll know you did it to
hide something. Donae', he's not dumb."

"It won't matter what Donae' thinks; he can't prove anything, not
anything at all. And you'll be dead and out of my hair for good."

Eric walked several steps closer to Brian and pleaded, "Come on. I'm
not gonna say nothing to anyone; we're in this together, just like we always been."

"Yes, that's very true, Eric. You won't be saying anything to anyone.
Because you're not going to be around for me to worry about . . . ." At
this instant, the battery acid he had acquired from the garage earlier that
day went flying through the air. And in a flash the first scream bellowed
into the darkness and echoed throughout the rooms and into the large
hallways of the house. The gun fired once, then suddenly once again, and
his body finally crumbled and hit the floor. At this same time in slow
motion a knife cut a small slit into his throat, barely missing his jugular
vein. Then suddenly there was nothing, not a single sound except the
drone of silence.

He didn't know how long he was out. He tried hard to push himself
up and fell again to the floor and into the puddle of blood. He lay there
panting, trying to gain enough strength to make it to a sitting position.
The pain was excruciatingly as he moved upward. Finally, he stood and
moved slowly around the room so he could do what was necessary before
he fainted from the wretched pain again. Moments later for a second
time he began to feel weak, then listless and suddenly darkness . . . .

Sometime later he felt himself awakening. His mind struggled to become aware. He had no idea what time it was or how much time had passed. From far away he thought he heard the doorbell ringing and then the phone and eventually voices; he concluded he was becoming delirious. Then once again everything became a mixture of pain and faraway sounds . . . then darkness and once more nothing.

When he woke, it was to the constant bleep of "beep, beep, beep." He heard the scuff of shuffling feet and tried to move his head in the direction of the sound, but the throbbing pain in his throat was more than he could bear, and he fell back into a deep, dreamless sleep.

At last he opened his eyes abruptly and stared motionless at the ceiling as he tried to remember and figure out where he was. His eyes darted around the room until he saw a nurse, and he tried to lift his hand to ask her for some water, but his arm fell back onto the bed with a thump. With the fall of his arm she turned to face him and immediately smiled a warm greeting. Then she hurried over and said, "Oh, good morning, Mr. Peterson. It's so good to see you awake. You've been out for several days. It's nice to see that you've come back to us."

He started to speak.

Quickly she shook her head and lifted her hand to halt his words, then patted his hand for comfort as she continued, "Honey, I know you're feeling a lot of pain and you're not going to be able to speak, but this will only be temporary. So, please, don't try to use your voice until the doctor tells you it's okay."

He tried to nod his head to let her know he understood, but he could only get as far as a half-nod before the strangulating pain engulfed him.

The next morning, he awoke to the bustling sounds of the hospital outside his half-opened door. About a minute later the door flew wide open and in entered a different nurse. Humming away contentedly she smiled brightly as she announced, "Good, you're awake. You have a visitor. That lovely fiancée of yours has been worried out of her mind over you. And she's been hanging around here since you were brought in. I'm sure she's going to be ecstatic to see you're finally awake."

After taking his blood pressure she informed him, "Earlier, the doctor told Miss Carter you would be stirring soon. He also tried to cheer her with the news that you will be as good as new in no time. He also urged her to go home and get some rest, but she wouldn't hear of leaving, not until she saw you open your eyes for herself."

He tried to smile but again he fell back into a light slumber, which he continued to fall in and out of the rest of the day. He remembered seeing a sea of faces throughout the day but wasn't coherent enough to speak or let them know he knew they were there. The next day he was feeling stronger, and when the doctor came in, he forced himself to wake fully so he could see he was conscious.

"Good, good, I'm glad you decided to join us today." The doctor messed with the bandage around his throat and said, "Ya, this looks good. Don't look so worried, Mr. Peterson. Everything is going to be just fine, and in a month or two your injuries should be close to completely healed."

With this news he began to feel even stronger. Immediately the doctor added, "I say close to completely healed, because after you're well enough and if you want, a little bit of plastic surgery will be required to fix you up as good as new. But in my opinion a little scar like that makes a great conversation piece. Don't you agree, Mr. Peterson?"

Brian smiled as much of a smile he could muster up and nodded his head.

At this time the nurse came in and announced, "Excuse me doctor, but I have two detectives here to see Mr. Peterson. Should I let them in?"

Dr. Kratz looked over and asked, "Are you up to a visitor, Mr. Peterson?

He nodded yes.

The doctor smiled his consent at the nurse but cautioned, "Okay, go ahead tell them that they can come on in, but only for a few minutes."

The nurse turned to relay the invitation when suddenly the door swung open and in walked Detective Lauwdry with Detective Bronson close behind.

Lauwdry opened his big mouth and bellowed, "How in the hell are ya, Doc?" and slapped Dr. Kratz on the back as if they were old friends.

"I'm fine, boys, but I'm not the patient here and I expect you two to behave and not upset Mr. Peterson. Do you hear me? And remember, he can't speak right now so don't badger him with all kinds of questions that he can't answer."

He turned to face his patient, "Mr. Peterson, no speaking. If you have something to say; do so on paper." Then he turned back to the detectives and warned, "Got it, Lauwdry, no upsetting him? He can scribble a few words on paper, if his wrapped fingers allow."

Lauwdry laughed, "Sure, we know he can't talk. Don't be so uptight, Doc. We're not here to cause any trouble. We're just here to inform Mr. Peterson that everything has been settled. It's all clear now and the case is closed. I'm sure this'll help make him feel a hell of a lot better than those happy shots you so freely give around here. Right, Doc?"

"Give the harassment a rest, Lauwdry. And yes, I'm sure a little good news will probably help Mr. Peterson's condition immensely. Now if you two gentlemen will excuse me, I have other patients that need attending to."

Dr. Kratz touched Brian on the shoulder to reassure him before he left the room, and as he started to close the door behind him, he stopped abruptly and said, "Well, come along. I nurse, I don't have all day. Besides, I doubt I can trust these two to behave in front of a lady." Then he nodded a last goodbye while he added, "I'll see you this afternoon, Mr. Peterson."

Lauwdry gave a lecherous laugh as he slapped Sandy Bronson on the back and smiled broadly at Brian. He took the derogatory remark as a compliment, of which he usually got few.

Once the door closed Lauwdry remarked, "Well, Mr. Peterson, we hear that you're doing a hell of a lot better than they first expected. I guess that brother of yours wasn't as good as he thought, huh?"

Brian nodded and closed his eyes for a second.

Sandy immediately threw Lauwdry a dirty look and added, "We know you're tired, so we won't keep you up any longer than we have to. We just wanted to let ya know that we found a letter your brother wrote. It was stuffed in his pocket. He made a full confession to the murders of your wife and your little girl."

"Yeah," Lauwdry cut in. "I guess the guilt just got too much for him to deal with, so he was just gonna end it all after he confessed to you. But

I guess it looks like he had a change of heart and decided to take you with him, doesn't it? I tell ya, it was a good thing that you were able to fight him off, Mr. Peterson. You did get burned a little from the acid, although it looks like he got the worst of it. What a crazy thing, I just can't guess what he was thinkin."

"Yeah . . . . I agree, added Sandy.

"A nut case," settled Lauwdry, "Even though, I guess it really doesn't matter, the why. I mean, who knows what a person like that thinks or what they'll do next. I'm just sorry you had to find out who killed your wife and child that way. But at least it's all over now and you can move on, no more living with the turmoil of not knowing. And, if ya stop and think, Mr. Peterson, maybe this is better."

Brian gave Sandy and Lauwdry a confused look before Lauwdry pushed on. "Because, as sure as I'm standin here, some crazy lawyer would've gotten him off. You know how they always use that psychological bunk to get these lunatics off. Anyway, like we said, we're really sorry for the pain you suffered. But the doc said you're gonna be fine. Well, we'll get out of your hair for now, Mr. Peterson. Best of luck on your recovery, ooh, and from what I hear, wedding."

Detectives Bronson and Lauwdry headed for the door when Lauwdry suddenly stopped, "Oh, and by the way, if you see that jerk Donae', just do us all a big favor and tell him to fuck off, okay? He's still trying to bring up questions that he says don't fit."

Brian tried to smile and nodded his head in agreement.

When the door closed, he felt his body relax and contemplated, "Yes, this is great news." He lay there for some time weighing his options before he settled. Now that all his problems were in the past, he could once again move on with his life. Eventually he felt himself falling into a restful sleep and he thought, *everything is working out just exactly as I had planned.*

Several hours later the nurse entered his room and opened the drapes. It looked as if the sun was very close to being down and darkness was creeping its way into the room. The short, stocky nurse smiled and fluffed his pillow before she said, "I have one more visitor for you. Your lovely lady can barely wait to see you and she's been waiting for hours. Believe me, Mr. Peterson, she's been tireless throughout this whole crisis. Her devotion to you is heartwarming. Should I send her in? Oh, what a silly question. Anyone can see by your eyes that you're bursting with anticipation."

His smile was as big as he could get it without bringing on further pain when Allison P. Carter walked into the room. Instantly his heart fluttered at her beauty. He wanted to burst at his extreme good fortune.

Allison kissed his forehead and stepped back and studied his appearance. After a few hums and a grin or two, she grew serious and said, "Brian, I decided that we should not wait any longer. We should get married right away. I mean, while you are still in the hospital. There is no reason why you should have to go back to that house; it has far too many painful memories for you to deal with in your condition. Brian, if you agree, I will become Mrs. Brian Scott Peterson in just three days." She waited as she searched his face. Then she recognized his look of surprise, so she hurried on. "Sweetheart, please, this way, when the doctors release you, you will be able to come straight to my estate." She waited, then pleaded, "Please, Brian? I do hope you will agree. And in hopes that you would say yes, I took a chance and scheduled everything. So, see the event itself will not be burdensome for you."

She paused and there was silence for several minutes. Then Brian nodded his head in consent and between his bandaged hands he squeezed her hand to show his love. "Oh, Brian, I love, you and I know it's not what we planned but this is better considering the circumstances. In all honesty I will feel much better having you home with me where I can keep an eye on you." She winked and teased, "I don't want some sexy nurse stealing you away from me."

He smiled to let her know he appreciated her humor. And she continued, "I promise sweetheart, as soon as you are ready, we'll start our honeymoon."

Again, he smiled and nodded as enthusiastically as possible, while at the same time he thought, "And in three days, I'll be even richer than I ever hoped."

# 10 WEEKS LATER

I t was over a month-and-a-half since he had been released from the hospital and about two months since the wedding, and finally they were on their honeymoon in the South of France. It was the perfect place for a honeymoon, and almost immediately after arriving Brian decided it was a perfect place to live indefinitely.

A few days after they arrived, he explained to Allison, "Here, we'll have peace of mind with no reminders of the past. As a matter of fact, I've already looked at a villa that I think we should consider purchasing."

Allison thought only an instant before she had excitedly agreed, "Oh yes, yes. Brian, our life here will be so very perfect. Just you and I and . . . ."

By this time, he was no longer listening to her words and he finished her sentence in silence . . . , *and with all your money we will live happily ever after.*

He slowly sipped the drink he held in his hand for his throat was still healing and often became dry. However, he was told it was very close to being completely well. Even though his voice was no more than a whisper when he spoke and the traces of several scars were slight but evident, he still felt well. And the doctors assured him that he should be remarkably close to the same man he was before the cut. He laughed at the thought, then inspected his hands, they were also healing nicely from the acid burns.

He smiled again and laid his head back against the lounge chair. He was seated under the shade of the cabana and a warm breeze that blew softly in the summer afternoon felt great. Brian glanced over to appreciate the woman that now lay sleeping on the lounge next to him. She was beautiful, his wife, Allison was a trophy he was proud of. He swallowed another sip of the fruity cocktail, and snickered confidently, "The acid was genius."

Silently he engaged in a discourse with his deceased twin. "I want to thank you, brother, for thinking of everything." Suddenly he contemplated, "Jesus, I guess I really never realized how much we were alike, especially in thought. I mean, what's the chances of us both coming up with virtually the same plan. Genius, just like you said."

He pondered the thought then went on, "You know, I should give you a toast, dear brother. Let's see; okay here it goes." He feigned clearing his throat, then continued with his game. "This is for you and for all that you taught me. I also want to thank you, as well, for being such a good student. Because without you becoming an expert at what I taught you, the police might have been tempted to look deeper. Yes, we all both know that Eric was the perfect stooge. Regardless, as you can see, life turned out just the way it should have, with me in the lap of luxury. I guess I should take a minute to bestow homage to a brother that always gave his very best to everything he did."

Laughing as quietly as possible, he glanced over to where Allison still slept before he looked toward the heavens and asked, "Well, before I applaud you further, I have a few questions, dear brother. I mean, now that you are where you are and I . . . , as they say, am here in the lap of luxury. Who do you suppose is the stupidest twin, *you* or *me*? Or . . . . maybe you still need some time to rethink your idiot theory. Well, either way, brother. I guess it really doesn't matter any longer what you think. So, here's to you my twin, bottoms up . . . ." He raised his glass to the heavens, and whispered between chuckles, "Thank you for Jennifer's and

Patty Jean's inheritance, along with the couple of mil insurance. As well, I to thank you for the beautiful and extremely wealthy, but clueless Allison. What can I say my fortune runneth over? But most of all, I want to say thank you, Brian, for the life I've always deserved."

# NEW YORK, NEW YORK

Donae' sat at his office desk going over the Peterson files. Page after page, he studied the words for hidden implications. Since the death of Eric Van Murck he had studied these same pages multiple times. He almost knew them by heart, yet still he could not find the one clue he knew existed and kept overlooking. He had tried several times to talk with Brian Peterson before he left the country, but he continually refused to speak with him. And now that he had quit his job and gone on an extended honeymoon, Donae' did not know when he would see him again. Donae' felt sure there was more to Brian's story then what he had told the police. But, once again, Detective Lauwdry had refused to hear his suspicions and stamped the case closed.

Donae' puckered his lips and blew a tune against his fingers as they kept beat with the tempo. Finally, he thought, *I need to move on. What's done is done, and all the pondering in the world will not change the outcome. However . . . .,*

From what Donae' had been told by Doctor Kratz; Brian's wound from the knife cut Eric had inflicted was healing rather nicely. The damage looked a lot worse than it really was, and the only long-term effect on Brian would be a slight change in his voice. As for the acid Eric had thrown on him, it only burned the surface skin of his hands as he fought off his brother's attack. It seemed Eric got the worst of it with damage to his hands and face.

"So . . . ," Donae' whispered, "right now life should be very close to normal for Brian and his new wife, Allison." Then, on the other hand, he thought: *What if Gerimee and Addison Hobart were right? What if Brian was the culprit who had killed his wife and child? Then that would mean Allison could eventually be in great danger. But Eric did confess to the murders. Even though, I still have my doubts about the hand scribbled confession. Yet it did sound like Eric went on one of his tirades.*

Donae' tapped his pen against the open file. He had always had a sneaky suspicion that Eric was much more intelligent then he let on, but still, he never thought he was capable of masterminding the crime itself. He started to set the file aside, then stopped and looked again at what he had just noted. Brian's throat wound was near a vital organ but had missed doing any major damage other than changing his voice slightly. He searched as he mumbled, "Where, where, where are you. Where is it . . . ? there you are." And he pulled out several sheets of paper from the center of the folder and read. Barbara Baxter, the airline attendant had said that Brian had a bad cold and slept most of the way to Washington. She said, he didn't sound like himself and was more curt than normal.

The hotel clerks, along with the valet at the hotel, confirmed that Brian's cold was so bad he could barely talk. "Damn!" Donae' smacked the pages and muttered, "That is it; now I understand. Brian never went to Washington. It was Eric that everyone saw that dreadful night. It was Eric who flew to Washington and who ordered the desk clerk to make him a late dinner reservation. And all that was for creating an alibi for Brian, when, in fact he had stayed here in town and killed his wife and child. Damn." He cursed himself for not seeing the obvious long ago. Brian would have never trusted his inferior brother to deal with something as crucial as killing Jennifer and Patty Jean. There was no way he would take the chance on him bungling things up. Sending Eric to Washington as himself was a perfect alibi since no one knew Eric existed. All Eric had to do was keep his mouth shut and no one would ever be the wiser. Eric's physical appearance could easily pass for Brian, but not his vernacular and phraseology. *Yes,* thought Donae', *with Brian's ego he would only have trusted himself with something as important as murdering his wife and child.*

Addison was right all along when he guessed that Patty Jean's smile was because she recognized her daddy that night. And in the same sense, Jennifer's look of horror was for the same reason. *She knew it was you, didn't she, Brian? But why kill Eric?*

Was Brian afraid he was going to crack? Did he see the distrust Mitch and I had planted and decided that Eric was an uncertainty he was not going to risk? Is there any love or empathy in Brian's makeup? Anything at all that comes close to kinship?

He asked out loud and his voice echoed against walls, "Is anyone safe with you, Brian?" The Petersons certainly were not, and neither were Jennifer and Patty Jean. Now Eric? Damn, how in the hell am I going to prove this? Worse, how in God's name am I going to stop you before it's too late for Allison?"

Annoyed and frustrated, he pushed the file aside and sat quietly while he evaluated the incidents in his mind.

Suddenly, he took a sharp breath and slowly picked the file up again. Quickly he flipped through the pages until he found the doctor's medical report. He held it for several minutes as he stared at it as if it were an alien being. Finally, he determined, *Simple incision, no major damage, but Eric was an expert with a knife.* Before long he began to read the doctor's report for the hundredth time, yet for the first time everything fell in order and made sense. Throat injury, not life threatening. May have slight pitch variation. *Eric was an expert with a knife. Why would he make a clean incision, especially during a fight? Unless he did it after and to himself....* Donae' stood up and walked over to stand in front of the window. After some time, he looked back at the paper he still clutched between his fingers and asked as if he expected an answer, "**Eric?**"

## Three Years later

**Obituaries:**

The Pierce family from the state of New York regretfully announces the death of their beloved daughter and socialite, Allison P. Carter Peterson. She died in her sleep Sunday night from heart failure; she was forty-seven years old. Allison and her husband Brian Peterson have resided in France for the past three years. Mr. and Mrs. Peterson had no children.

The End

# ELLEN'S BIO

For Ellen the urge to write had started long before her first book, with poems and miscellaneous writings. Her first effort was a short story named Kathleen/Catherine. To prove her dedication to the written word the story was typed out on a small portable Smith Corona typewriter, no computer screen, no spell check, no correction key or save or print key. She had gotten a response from Red Book indicating they liked her story but would preferer something more towards women's rights.

As the years rolled by Ellen authored **Kathleen/Catherine, One for the Money, and Murder by Proxy,** and in a different genre **Cee Cee Shades of Black**. A prominent New York Agent was excited about her work and was eager to guide her through the publishing process when 9/11 happened and the publishing industry and her writing went on hold.

Today once again she is looking forward to marketing her manuscripts to the public.